# THE HAMLYN BOOK OF
# HOUSE PLANTS

# THE HAMLYN BOOK OF HOUSE PLANTS

By Jiří Haager

HAMLYN

LONDON • NEW YORK • SYDNEY • TORONTO

Colour illustrations by Z. Berger (135), J. Kaplická (73),
F. Severa (2), L. Urban (4).
Line drawings by Z. Berger

Translated by O. Kuthanová
Designed and produced by Artia for
The Hamlyn Publishing Group Limited
London · New York · Sydney · Toronto
Astronaut House, Feltham, Middlesex, England



ISBN 0 600 34617X

Printed in Czechoslovakia
3/13/03/51-01

# CONTENTS

# GROWING FLOWERS IS GOOD FOR YOUR HEALTH!

Man has lived in the company of plants since time immemorial. If we were to seek in the annals of history we would find plants playing their roles in man's life from the very beginning. Chronological dates, however, could not serve as the sole guideline, for the evolution of different cultures in the various parts of the world was marked by great diversity. Many civilizations could not even have arisen without plants. It is well known, for instance, how important agaves and cacti, and in particular opuntias, were to the Indians of Central America. No wonder, then, that many of these plants were regarded as gods. At the Museum of Bogotá, capital of Colombia, the many gold, gourd-shaped vessels of pre-Columbian days, which were unearthed at the archeological site at Quimbaya are sure to attract the visitor's notice. One can easily surmise that the fruit played a very important role in the natives' diet. However, it was not regarded merely as a utilitarian object; the shape was also valued, in other words the aesthetic aspect of the fruit. Floral motifs can be found in dozens of primitive cultures, and there they are well established as a matter of pure aesthetics. In the life of mankind flowers have often figured as symbols. The lotus blossom of the Buddhists, for example, is used for offerings and is the traditional companion of birth and death, as well as a simple decoration for the home. Even in our modern world one can find people living simply, close to nature, and it is interesting to note that, as a rule, they have a very sensitive feel for plants and flowers. The author found flowering orchids in the simple huts of Indians in Ecuador's Rio Pastaza region, and also in the pile-dwellings of the Muongu tribe in Vietnam. But let us go back to cultivated flowers in the history of civilized mankind.

The Gardens of Semiramis in Mesopotamia were built by Nebuchadnezzar more than 2,000 years ago. Bills for thousands of floral arrangements for the feasts of Egyptian pharaohs have survived to this day. As for the ancient Greeks and Romans – no feast or ceremony was complete without flowers. Gardening in southern and eastern Asia also has a thousand-year-old tradition, particularly amongst the Japanese and Chinese. One would be hard put to find a single important poet, painter or architect for whom plants and flowers are not objects of prime concern. Further development of this tradition has yielded such aesthetic forms as the landscaped Japanese garden, the art of bonsai and of ikebana.

What, however, do plants have to offer man living in the fast-paced world of today? First of all it is a well-known fact that a plant in the home provides a man who is alienated from nature with the necessary contact with greenery. This psychological effect must not be underestimated. The modern urban interior is above all functional, and without flowers, which add supplementary colour and form, it would be too austere. Besides this, genuine health problems are beginning to play a significant role. Plastics, though hygienic and aesthetically acceptable can have an adverse effect. Coming into contact with them man is 'charged' with static electricity and functions like a condenser. Plants have the opposite electric charge and contact with them causes man to be 'discharged'. The importance of this effect would be corroborated by any physician but sufficient for most of us is the feeling of relaxation, the easing of tension we feel when we go for a walk in the woods, for instance. Many species of plants secrete substances that destroy micro-organisms in their vicinity (this phenomenon is best known in the case of conifers and eucalypts, but occurs elsewhere, too).

Plants also greatly reduce the amount of dust in the atmosphere (a single hectare of forest captures 40 to 70 tonnes of dust a year); they act as humidifiers in a room, in other words moisten the air and make it easier to breathe; plus many other advantageous things. Noteworthy, also, is the educational effect of plants. A child that grows his first beans at the age of five and in the ensuing years regularly tends his own plants in the home is more likely to develop into an adult with a creative bent. Furthermore, it cultivates his sense of aesthetics as well as regard for life. Gardening has always been an art in the true sense of the word and it is a pity that we often lose sight of this fact in the fast-paced, commercially-oriented world we live in.

So in conclusion, let us reiterate what was said in the title of this opening chapter – grow flowers! They will not only improve the look of your interior décor but will also benefit your physical and mental health.

# THE WORLD IS CHANGING – FOR US AND FOR PLANTS

The past few decades have brought marked changes to our standard of housing. Small windows have been replaced by glass walls or picture windows across the width of the room and fireplaces and wood or coal stoves by central heating, governed and regulated by thermostats. The result is more sunlight indoors, higher temperatures kept at a set level in the winter months and a much drier atmosphere, often with a relative humidity of only 20 to 40 per cent. These changes have naturally affected the selection of plants that can be grown in the modern household and therefore the choice offered by nurserymen.

The late 17th and 18th centuries witnessed a great development in horticulture. Hundreds of new species made their way from all parts of the world to newly established botanical gardens as well as to private collections. The loveliest of these were cultivated in the greenhouses of the wealthy as well as in horticultural establishments. Later years were characterized by selection and breeding. Heading the list for popularity were those species that were readily propagated, easy to grow, and flowered freely and reliably – in short, those that thrived indoors.

Changes in housing and people's life-style during the past decades caused a veritable revolution in the florist's trade. The classic selection of azaleas, cyclamen and other plants that need considerable attention have, to some extent, been replaced by more suitable species. People today rarely have enough time (often both husband and wife work) to care for difficult plants. Furthermore, holidays are being increasingly spent in travel, so a potted plant on the window-sill does not have much chance of surviving. Most important of all is the unsuitability from the aesthetic viewpoint of many of the traditional plants. The austere, boldly divided spaces of the modern home require a special arrangement of furnishings and ornaments, including plants. That is why the classic selection of plants must be supplemented by epiphytic species (plants growing on other plants without harming them in any way), climbers and bog plants. New opportunities are also afforded by terrariums, where it is possible to create congenial conditions even for the most demanding plants with comparative ease.

This book takes note of the changes that have taken place in interior design and acquaints the reader with many non-traditional plants such as epiphytes and plants suitable for growing in bottle gardens, keeping in mind, of course, the fact that not everyone has central heating and thus including also the classic standbys.

# DO YOU KNOW YOUR OWN HOME?

Naturally this question is not meant literally, but if we want to grow plants successfully then we must give some thought to providing the conditions that will satisfy their basic needs and keep them happy.

Plants grown indoors require approximately the same conditions as in their native environment. It is important that they be provided with a suitable growing compost, temperature, amount of light, and moisture (both in the compost and the atmosphere). It is comparatively easy to provide the proper compost and regulate its moisture, but it is far more difficult to regulate the other factors which often require fairly complex equipment. Most amateurs who grow house plants are not able or do not wish, for instance, to install special fluorescent lighting or automatic misting equipment. Similar difficulties are posed by the problem of stabilising temperature fluctuations or heating the home to the temperature required for growing plants from lowland tropical regions.

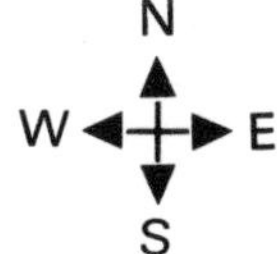


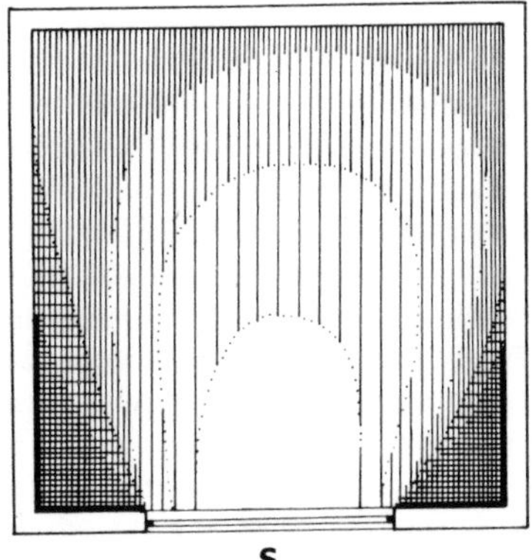


a

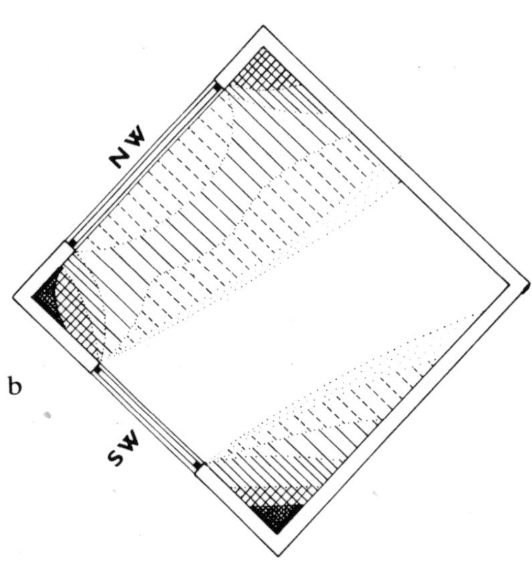


b

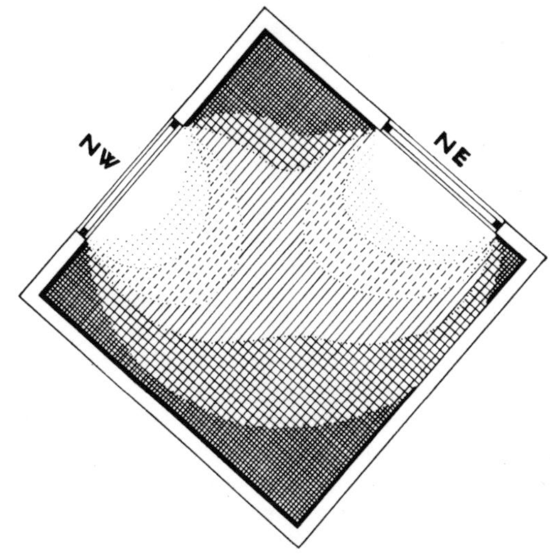


c

One solution is a flower case with its own built-in lighting and heating, where one can grow even the most delicate and tender plants. If there is enough space it is often possible to provide congenial conditions for cold-loving plants by turning off the heating in one of the rooms. Otherwise take things as they are and select plants that will adapt to the given conditions.

One important thing that should not be forgotten, however, is that no factor acts independently of the others; all are interrelated. If, for instance, the light factor changes then it is necessary to adapt the temperature and watering accordingly. In general it may be said that there is a direct correlation between light and heat: if the intensity of light increases most plants require higher temperatures. Atmospheric moisture is often correlated with light indirectly. Here, too, temperature plays an important role. If the thermometer in a room with a temperature of n°C and relative humidity of 100 per cent registers a rise of 10°C (18°F), the relative humidity will decrease to a mere 55 per cent and vice versa, a 10° drop in temperature will cause the relative humidity to increase by approximately 50 per cent. From this it is easy to understand how plants with entirely different requirements can grow in the same locality in the wild. Picture a giant tree in the tropical rainforest: sunning itself at the top of the crown is a bromeliad and nestling at the foot of the trunk is a clump of ferns. In full sun the air at the top of the tree is often overheated and the humidity is very low; such a spot is occupied by bromeliads which are well adapted to dry conditions. The ground at the foot of the forest giant is naturally shaded, the temperature lower, and the relative humidity therefore higher. Thus, ferns can be cultivated in a shaded spot and sprayed over several times a day even at high temperatures whereas bromeliads would soon be destroyed by such conditions. In order to grow house plants successfully it is necessary to know not only their place of origin and the climatic conditions in which they grow in the wild, but also the type of situation they occupy in the wild.

Naturally there are exceptions to every rule and this is true also of plants. For instance, some species which flourish in mangrove swamps bordering river banks and tidal basins in the tropics (members of the genera *Avicennia* and *Rhizophora*) grow in full sun at high temperatures but are also happy in marshes or on flooded banks, in other words in an environment with a high relative humidity.

Let us return to the conditions of our homes. These are generally classed according to temperature into three categories: cool, semi-warm, and warm, characterized roughly by winter temperatures of 10 to 15°C (50 to 59°F), 14 to 20°C (57 to 68°F), and 15 to 25 or 30°C (59 to 77 or 86°F) respectively. Very cold homes are now becoming a thing of the past. Conditions for growing cold-loving plants are to be found only in conservatories, the hallways of some houses and foyers. Here it is possible to put to good use plants such as azalea,

Distribution of light in a room with
a) windows facing south
b) windows facing SW and NW
c) windows facing NW and NE

bouvardia, cissus, clianthus, euonymus, fuchsia, hedera, mikania, pelargonium and of the orchids *Encyclia citrina, Coelogyne cristata* and certain cymbidiums and odontoglossums. Most bulbs and tubers also do well in this sort of situation.

These temperate plants can be grown in warmer conditions as well. In warm homes one can grow practically all species of subtropical and tropical plants as long as their other requirements are met. In very warm conditions when the temperature rises above the desired level the room should be aired more frequently. Most plants, however, tolerate fairly marked temperature fluctuations for a brief period.

Another important factor for growing plants is light. Sunlight is necessary for the process known as photosynthesis to take place. During this process inorganic substances are transformed with the aid of radiant energy into organic substances that form the body of the plant.

The intensity of light is measured in lux, either by means of luxmeters or photographic light meters with a luxmeter scale. Lux is a unit of illumination equal to the illumination of a surface uniformly one meter distant from a point source of one candle. The intensity of sunlight in nature ranges from 0 to 100,000 lux, the first figure representing full darkness and the other full sunlight falling upon the earth at noon on a clear day.

It is difficult to determine exactly how much light is necessary for photosynthesis to begin. Also the amount differs according to whether the given plants are sun-lovers or shade-lovers. Photosynthesis usually takes place at a light intensity of as little as 100 to 1,000 lux. As the light intensity increases so does the rate of photosynthesis, up to approximately 10,000 lux. This data, of course, only serves as a guideline, for photosynthesis, just like any other process in living matter, depends on many other factors, particularly temperature.

Both maximum and minimum light intensity are harmful to plants if they are long-term, though we come across exceptions in both instances. Ferns and selaginellas growing in the continual shade of the tropical rainforests require only minimal radiation for their life processes (often they are very sensitive to marked temperature fluctuations and lowering of the atmospheric moisture). In such forests the solar radiation in the treetops is close to the upper limit but the dense canopy reduces the amount of light that reaches the ground to a mere 1 per cent of full sunlight. Many bromeliads, growing as epiphytes in the uppermost reaches of such a forest, are adapted to these maximum values and need them for good growth the same as cacti, echeverias or sedums growing on sun-drenched rocks. With a little experience one can guess a plant's light requirements by its appearance. Species with delicate, pale green or often blue-tinged foliage generally require shade. Plants whose leaves are thick-skinned and coloured red, violet or silvery can be put in full sun without hesitation. The general rule of thumb is that full sun is needed by most cultivated plants with decorative blossoms, succulents and stiff-leaved bromeliads. Permanently shaded situations are suitable for ferns with soft foliage and most selaginellas, also for certain species of fig, such as *Ficus villosa,* some members of the ginger family and of the genus *Costus* and for almost all species of plants in the seedling and juvenile stages. This again is determined by natural conditions, for most plants germinate and pass their early stages of development in the dense shade of other herbaceous plants, shrubs and trees.

How much light enters your home, and where is the best place to put plants? As an example, let us take a room 4 m (13 ft) long with a large window taking up most of the space in the centre of one wall. Least suitable are the corners on either side of the window which are more deeply shaded than any other part of the room. Through the middle of the window to a distance of about 1.5 m (5 ft) the amount of full sunlight is 40 to 60 per cent. At a distance of about 2.5 m (8 ft) it is 20 to 40 per cent, whereas farther from the window it drops to a mere 15 per cent. The corners that are far from the window are not suitable places for plants because the amount of light penetrating there is only about 5 per cent of full sunlight. Much depends also, of course, on the aspect. Windows facing south, south-east and south-west provide the most light (60 to 80 per cent); where windows face north-west or north-east the amount of light penetrating the room rapidly decreases the farther the distance from the window. Plants requiring direct sunlight, in other words most flowering species, cannot be placed by north or north-west windows.

Almost all plants tolerate diffused light. Such conditions are readily recognized by moving the hand or some other object between the plant and the window; this should cast a distinct shadow on the foliage. However, the plant will call attention to its needs by itself. If it leans towards the light, has smaller, paler leaves and longer internodes (sections of stem between the leaves) then it should be put in a spot with more light.

Last of all, a few words about atmospheric and soil moisture should be added. Soil moisture is regulated by watering. Some plants need to have their roots kept continually damp, the roots do not tolerate drying-out and the soil must be moist all the time. In the case of other plants the soil is allowed to dry out slightly before each thorough watering. A separate case altogether is hydroponics – the soilless cultivation of plants in clear nutrient solutions, anchored in inert material, such as siliceous gravel, sand or granules of various kinds. This book does not deal with the subject but lists special literature where those who are interested can find more information. It should be noted, however, that most house plants do very well in such solutions and even species that are otherwise difficult to grow can be cultivated by this method.

How much and how often a plant should be watered depends on the plant's origin, that is the amount of rainfall in its native habitat during the various months of the year, and on the temperature of the room. Water should be supplied in smaller quantities at lower temperatures and *vice versa.* This, however, is not a standing rule. Even in winter, when most plants need only limited watering, flowers placed on the window-sill above a radiator must be watered daily, otherwise the soil will rapidly dry out and the plant wilt.

The atmospheric moisture in the modern household is usually low. This can be offset by means of various humidifiers, generally suspended on radiators, and sometimes also by syringing the plants directly with water. Many different types of syringes and misting equipment are available to choose from. Misting should be limited in winter and totally withheld in the case of plants from tropical or subtropical regions where the winters are dry. If several house plants are being grown then better moisture conditions will result by grouping them together on a table or in a large container where the evaporation from the soil surface will be greater. In the case of some tropical subjects from moist, humid regions it is impossible to provide the degree of moisture they need in the home and either we must do without them or grow them in closed plant-cases. There are comparatively few such instances; one, however, is the attractive pitcher plant *(Nepenthes),* which will grow but not form pitchers in dry surroundings.

# HOUSE PLANTS IN THE WILD

Even an extensive library cannot serve as a substitute for the knowledge gained by a few weeks' stay in the tropics and subtropics so let us make a brief excursion into these realms; let us take a look at how our green friends live.

Let us start in Ecuador, by the small river Río Negro, tributary of the Pastaza, which in these parts widens and flows slowly towards the Amazon region. The altitude above sea level is no more than 600 m (2,000 ft), the temperature constantly high, and the humidity likewise. Only at night does the temperature drop to a 'mere' 15°C (59°F), which means that the vegetation is drenched with dew in the early morning. The dew, however, does not remain long on the leaves. Many tropical plants have smooth, waxy foliage, off which the water quickly runs. Also, leaves often terminate in a tapering point which enables a quick run-off of water from the leaf blade. The well-known rubber plant *(Ficus elastica)* has leaves such as this, and here on our excursion we find them on *Philodendron verrucosum,* one of the most striking plants of the local undergrowth. It grows on the banks of the river in damp places rich in humus and some older specimens climb like lianas up the trunks of neighbouring trees to weave an impenetrable canopy of green above the stream, together with yams *(Dioscorea polygonoides* and *D. trifida)* and members of the *Vitaceae* and *Leguminosae* families, beneath which permanent twilight reigns. In the undergrowth we will find many plants that we recognize as familiar house plants. At the edge of the forest is *Costus comosus,* a few paces farther the robust *Heliconia wagneriana* and at its base a lovely begonia growing in the deep shade.

The smooth trunks of the trees are not devoid of life. Several bromeliads are found attached to them, their leaves forming funnels which hold water from the morning dew as well as from the previous evening's rainfall, thus not only providing a reserve supply for the plant's use but also serving as 'hanging pools' in which small tree frogs can rear their offspring. The water in the funnels of bromeliads is also inhabited by the larvae of mosquitoes and other insects. This is of advantage to both partners: the animals have an assured supply of water and the remains of the animals' bodies provide the plants with organic matter which they would otherwise find difficult to obtain high up above the ground. Their roots serve only as anchorage, they are stiff and wiry and merely hold the plant to the bark. Food and water are obtained mainly through the leaves.

Other plants that have caught a foothold in the cracked bark of the tree include various members of the genus *Peperomia,* which are compact in habit and far prettier in their natural habitat than when grown in the home, where they generally become tall and spindly. Orchids are to be found here too; one that is easily recognized from afar is *Oncidium varicosum* with its sprays of golden-yellow flowers. The tuft of roots faces upwards, thus catching every falling leaf and every stone dropped by an ant or termite on its way up the tree trunk. Over the years the orchid thus collects a small amount of humus on which to feed. A little nourishment is also obtained from the dust captured by rain. Traces of this humble diet are absorbed through the velamen, the corky outer layer of the aerial roots.

Returning to the river where marantas grow in the damp and shade amidst selaginellas and mosses, let us follow it down to the road. On the steep road bank, about 2 m (6 ft) high, grows a bromeliad of the genus *Pitcairnia.* It grows in the ground and its roots have retained their function. It is also equipped for unexpected periods of drought, not with a rosette of leaves, as are many plants, but with a kind of bulb at the base of the leaf. Its beautiful flowers, not very long lasting, were at one time considered the loveliest of the whole family. Another lovely plant growing by the roadside that attracts our notice is the large-leaved *Anthurium,* its leaves hanging freely down the almost vertical bank. Anthuriums, with their long-bladed leaves, (the blades are often longer than the leaf stalks) are either epiphytic or grow on steep rocks, often covered with moss, down which water continues to run a long time after it has rained. The sodden moss thus supplies the required moisture to the roots. It is definitely a mistake when these plants are grown in open beds in botanical gardens, for the leaves often rot when the leaf tips touch the ground.

We shall now make our way to the border of North and Central America, to a land that has provided horticulture with many magnificent plants – to Mexico. We are in the semi-desert near the city of Tehuacán in the state of Puebla, about 1,670 m (5,500 ft) above sea level. Let us imagine that we have arrived at this spot in October, in other words after the summer rains, and are greeted by fairly lush vegetation. The shrub *Gymnosperma glutinosum* is bright with yellow blossoms, the cacti are in flower too, particularly striking being the giant cushions of *Ferocactus robustus* composed of hundreds of individual specimens. There are many other cacti growing here, such as cylindopuntias and mammillarias. The other vegetation is also xerophilous, in other words, able to withstand long periods of drought.

Creeping along the ground is a short-stemmed plant with only a few leaves – a member of the genus *Cissus.* Plants of the same genus growing in the tropical rainforest are quite different: their leaves are large, thin and brightly coloured, whereas those growing in semi-deserts have small, fleshy leaves covered with a thick grey felt. The greatest surprise, however, is the difference in the root system. That of the

*Yucca periculosa* occupies the semi-deserts of central Mexico

tropical species growing in permanently moist soil is comparatively shallow, whereas in the semi-desert species, which has to make the most of every drop of water that rapidly soaks into the gypsum-rich soil, the roots grow from a huge underground tuber (huge, that is, compared to the size of the aerial parts). The same disproportion between the top and underground parts may be found in many other succulents and cacti.

We may also come across bulbs of the genus *Zephyranthes* which have already had time to die back since the rainy season. They belong to the group known as ephemeral plants which have a brief life cycle – germinating, flowering and producing seeds during the brief growing season and waiting out the unfavourable, usually dry season either in the form of seeds (annuals) or as latent buds or tubers.

In the awesome landscape of the semi-desert, dominated by yuccas, agaves, *Beaucarnea gracilis* and other plants of this type, we will also encounter flowering annuals that are popular garden plants – the ubiquitous tagetes, and on sun-baked rocks zinnias, their red flowers just fading so that they can form seeds in time. Epiphytes are to be found here, too. Growing on an old woody opuntia is the bromeliad *Tillandsia capillaris*. It is one of the least demanding of plants. Protecting it from the sun is a silvery coat of scales that catches every drop of moisture, both from rain and night-time mists, passing it to the cells in the inner leaf tissues. The leaves are long and narrow, and round in cross-section so that evaporation is kept to the minimum. We can even see this plant growing in clumps on telegraph wires. How it must economize with food and water in such conditions! All plants, of course, have to economize with water here. Many mechanisms for trapping water were not discovered until fairly recently. The spines of many cacti, for example, are capable of catching tiny droplets of water from mist, absorbing them and passing them on to the storage tissues inside the plant.

The semi-desert of Mexico that we have been referring to has a low annual rainfall, approximately 48 cm (19 in) with a maximum of 12 cm (4¾ in), a minimum of 0.2 cm (⅛ in) per month, and a comparatively stable temperature – the mean annual temperature is 18.6°C (65°F) with a minimum of 15°C (59°F) and maximum of 21.5°C (71°F); of course the difference between day-time and night-time temperatures is very great. These figures indicate that it will not be difficult to grow the plants of this area in the modern household if they are provided with ample light on a window-sill facing south.

The last place we shall visit is the Vietnamese village of Tam Dao (altitude about 1,000 m [3,300 ft] above sea level), located some 100 kilometres (62 miles) north of Hanoi. The mountains are covered with dense forest, which may be characterized as a transitional form between the lowland tropical areas and the evergreen subtropical regions. The main characteristic is ample moisture in the form of mist and lower temperature throughout the year, but never less than 10°C (50°F). The forest consists of a great variety of trees and shrubs, mostly of the family Dipterocarpaceae, and the genera *Castanopsis, Podocarpus* and *Bucklandia.* Here, too, we will find countless epiphytes on the trees. Not bromeliads, of course, for these are almost totally restricted to the American continent, but ferns of the genera *Pyrrosia* and *Drynaria,* orchids of the genera *Dendrobium, Bulbophyllum* and *Coelogyne* and the typically Asian epiphytic genus, *Aeschynanthus.* Also worthy of note are the banks of the stream where sweet flag *(Acorus gramineus)* forms a thick cover on the damp stones (contrary to the widely held belief that it grows in mud). The trees are not inhabited only by epiphytes but also serve as a support for countless creepers. These include *Rhaphidophora decursiva* and other species of the same genus, numerous members of the genus *Pothos, Ficus pumila* and many members of the vine family such as cissus, ampelopsis, vitis, tetrastigma and cayratia. Impressive and stately are the tree ferns, *Cyathea spinulosa,* reaching a height of almost 3 m (10 ft). In dark places in the forest undergrowth we will find selaginellas and ferns, in lighter spots begonias and in sunlit places the well-known gynura, with its gleaming violet hairs (trichomes). Characteristic of Tam Dao, however, are plants of the Araliaceae family, be they the comparatively large and well-known species of the genus *Schefflera,* or the delicate but sharply-spined *Aralia armata.* Near the village there are also several specimens of the shrub *Tieghemopanax fruticosus;* these have probably escaped from gardens and become naturalized but, as one can see, they have found conditions here to their liking. Some plants strike one as odd that they have not yet been introduced into cultivation. It is hard to understand, for instance, why a magnificent foliage plant such as *Ficus semicordata* has remained unnoticed, though it might do quite well as a house plant. If we stop once again to consider the possibilities such a locality offers to horticulture then we find that many of the local plants could perhaps be grown successfully in the modern home if the leaves were sprayed over every now and then or if the atmospheric moisture was slightly increased.

Let us hope that this excursion into the realm of plants and their native habitats has not tired the reader but, on the contrary, has awakened his desire to go out after them into the wild himself. If so, then it will be useful for him to know how to take plants and their seeds home with him without damaging them on the way or how to bring home a plant that does not have ripe seeds when discovered. This problem is discussed in the following chapter.

# GREEN SOUVENIRS

In the world of today when distances are being continually shortened by modern means of travel, a trip to the tropics no longer represents an adventure of several months' duration accompanied by guides, bearers, horses and supplies. Nowadays we simply board an aeroplane, sleep awhile and disembark at an airport which greets us with a breath of hot humid air. The following day we can already be hundreds of kilometres from the city in a wilderness where we have come by hired car and where we can devote ourselves to our hobby.

First of all, however, while we are still at home, we must find out what regulations the country we are planning to visit has concerning the export of plants. The flora in many countries is protected by law and the export of plants may be either totally, or at least partially, prohibited. We should not be surprised by such restrictions for in this world, with its pollution, fertilizers, pesticides, expanding agriculture and increased felling of forests, some 20,000 species of higher plants are in immediate danger of extinction. If we find that rigid prohibition is the rule then we should equip ourselves with only a camera and a notebook. This should also be our approach if collecting a certain plant is not prohibited, but we ourselves see that it is rare in the given locality and that even collecting its seeds might endanger its future existence. A person who loves plants is also one who loves nature and is concerned about its conservation, and that must apply not only to his immediate home environment. It is likewise necessary to know the regulations concerning the import of plants. Most countries wish to prevent the possibility of any pests or diseases being introduced inside their borders and have various regulations concerning this.

Let us assume that we have met with no obstacles or complications, that we have filled in the necessary forms and that we are setting out on our trip into the wilderness. What should we take with us? The equipment we will need is quite simple. Large plastic bags, a great number of paper envelopes or bags, pencils, rubberbands, a good strong garden trowel, secateurs, a garden knife and a small bottle of water. It is also a good idea to have a spare box or carton in the car and a supply of old newspapers in case cacti or other succulents are collected.

Let us presume that we shall be staying several weeks in the tropical or subtropical country to which we have journeyed and that we shall be collecting plants from the very beginning, which is a wise thing to do, for it may happen that a species which was plentiful when we started out is suddenly not to be seen as its season is over, and then it is too late for reproaches. How, then, should we care for the plants so that they will survive till we return home?

The simplest method is to collect ripe fruits and seeds. If the seeds are ripe the fruit can be crumbled and they can simply be poured into a paper envelope, the same as when collecting the seeds of annuals in the garden. If the fruit is not dry then it must be dried. In the tropics, particularly in a humid and warm environment, there is always the danger that the fruit will rot or go mouldy and that the seeds will thus be destroyed. Such fruits should be put in a cloth or paper bag, hung on the air conditioner in the hotel room and dried by the current of air. Fruits the size of a rose hip will dry in this way in a single night. The dried fruits should then be put in a clean bag on which we should always remember to write all the relevant information about the plant and the locality where it was found. This should include the name of the species, name of the locality, its aspect, altitude above sea level, the soil in which the plant was growing (in the case of an epiphyte, the plant on which it was growing), the moisture conditions and the date. Do not rely on your memory, which will be deluged by impressions after a two-week trip. The spores of ferns are handled in the same way; the spore-bearing fronds, however, will dry well in the open air in partial shade without the aid of air-conditioning equipment, for they generally do not rot.

One more important thing should be remembered: only collect the fruits of plants that you know well, do not touch unknown herbs and shrubs with bare hands, and never taste anything you know nothing about. When blisters appear on the hands after touching a plant or the mouth is filled with an odious taste, then it is too late for regrets. Sometimes a mere trace of a plant poison or irritating substance carried to the mouth by a cigarette handled by unwashed hands is enough to make life very unpleasant.

Preserving cacti, succulent spurges, plants of the genera *Echeveria, Cotyledon, Sedum, Senecio, Stapelia, Caralluma* and other fleshy-leaved plants is fairly simple. After removing them from the ground, always taking care not to damage the roots, let them dry in partial shade for several days. Then wrap them in newspapers and pack them loosely in a carton. They must not get wet for then they would be irretrievably damaged.The period of drying out should be continued for several more weeks after the return home. Then put the dry plants in dry gritty compost and do not water them for one or two weeks.

The procedure is more or less the same for other xerophytes including the popular bromeliads of the genus *Tillandsia.* Spread them out in partial shade in a dry place. Curling of the leaves into balls or dying-down of the leaf rosettes is nothing to worry about, it is quite natural and will not affect the future growth of the plant in any way. It is recommended to gather these plants together with a piece of the bark or branch on which they grow so as not to damage their roots. Replanting can then be put off until after the tillandsia is fully acclimatized.

Bromeliads from moist locations, soft-leaved plants such as the genera *Vriesea, Guzmania* and *Catopsis* and most orchids require somewhat different treatment. They should be kept dry and the water in the leaf funnels should be poured out. The plant should be spread in the coolest possible place in the light, but not in full sun, and syringed with water once every three days. The water must not trickle down and form puddles under the plants, for then they would quickly rot. It you plan to return home within ten to fourteen days then it is better to keep the plants dry (better too dry than too wet). Before shipping let them dry out completely, wrap in newspaper and pack them loosely in a carton. Loose packing goes a long way towards a guarantee of success. Orchids are treated in the same way. The rule that dry conditions will not harm them applies to orchids, too, both to epiphytic species and ones growing on rocks.

Species growing in the ground often have real tubers (genus *Bletia*) or at least fleshy roots (genera *Habenaria, Spiranthes* and *Sobralia*) instead of pseudobulbs at the base of the leaves. The underground parts of these must not be allowed to dry out. When lifting these plants do so very carefully, gently remove any remaining bits of soil from the roots or tubers, shorten broken roots by cutting them straight across with a sharp knife, and then dust the cut surface with charcoal powder or, if you have nothing else, cigarette ash. The entire underground part may be dusted with one of the several preparations available for preventing the growth of moulds. Then put the plants on a layer of moss in a plastic bag and cover them with another layer of moss; this will keep them moderately moist during transportation.

Often, we come across plants which we like, but which would be difficult to move in their entirety, such as philodendrons, monsteras, syngonias, peppers and members of the grape family which reach heights of many metres in the wild. These, however, can be readily propagated from cuttings, as can plants of the genera *Ixora, Jasminum, Ficus, Columnea* and *Aeschynanthus*. If we decide to take cuttings instead of whole plants, how should these be handled so that they will remain in good condition for as long as several weeks?

The first and most important prerequisite is a fairly large plastic bag. Rinse the bag out with water, then pour all the water out, the purpose being merely to moisten the inside. Always take larger cuttings than will be necessary for propagation. In the case of large-leaved species such as monstera and philodendron, remove the leaf blades to help reduce transpiration. If you are out in the field the whole day it is recommended to suck the air out of the bag after putting the cuttings in so that the sides stick together, at least in part, and close the opening tightly with a rubber band. The bag should always be placed in the baggage compartment or on the floor of the car so that it is protected from the sun.

In the evening, when you have returned to your hotel, spread out the cuttings as well as the whole plants (small ferns and begonias) you have gathered during the day and spray them with lukewarm water for at least an hour. This will not only remove all remaining bits of soil from the roots but will allow the plants to absorb water. Then put them in clean plastic bags, which have likewise been rinsed out with water beforehand, place them in a light but shaded spot on a cool surface and smooth the bags lightly with the hand for better retention of moisture. The open ends may be tucked under but should not be closed completely. Ensuing care consists of rinsing out the plastic bags every evening and putting the cuttings and plants back the way they were. Spray them thoroughly once a week and remove any leaves and roots that are showing signs of rotting. In the damp tropics cuttings and small plants can be kept in good condition by this means for a period of four to five weeks. Whereas epiphytic bromeliads and orchids are shipped 'dry', epiphytic ferns of the genera *Platycerium, Drynaria, Pyrrosia,* the rare genus *Utricularia* and epiphytic lycopodiums are shipped in the same way as cuttings, that is in moist packets. Easiest of all to ship are bulbous and tuberous plants. Let them dry, then remove the top parts, clean the bulbs and put them in paper or cloth bags.

When you return home from your trip, wire orchids and bromeliads to a tree branch or log and put them in a light place but out of direct sun. Water them regularly from the start but only by syringing them lightly for the first few weeks until they become adapted to their new environment. Water may be applied more liberally only after orchids start putting out new shoots and bromeliads stand up straight. Cuttings often root directly in the bags. If not, then make a fresh cut and put them, along with those that have rooted, in a warm and moist propagator, shaded to keep out direct sunlight.

# CONTAINERS AND DISPLAY

Most of us start to grow house plants in the same way – by putting a potted plant we have received as a gift on the window-sill. To this we add a second, then a third, and all of a sudden we are faced with the problem of where to put the next. Besides, though flowers in themselves are beautiful, this rather arbitrary grouping on the window-sill has not really added to the interest or attractiveness of the interior décor. What then is the answer? How should we display our house plants to achieve maximum effectiveness?

The simplest and often the most attractive solution is to group carefully selected plants in a ceramic bowl. This may be glazed, so that there is no danger of water condensing on the outside and marking the furniture on which it stands, or unglazed, and with or without a drainage hole (in the latter case, take care not to overwater). Many attractive bowls and dishes are available, but certain principles must be observed when selecting one. First of all the shape and size must be suitable for the assortment of plants. In the case of plants that are of sculptural interest the bowl should be as simple as possible. The same applies to decorative foliage plants. Only in the absence of any distracting elements will the full beauty of the plants be appreciated. Another thing to remember is to leave room around the plants for growth, so do not fill the bowl from the start. Also, remember that plants do not all grow at the same rate, so select ones that have a similar rate of growth, otherwise the slower-growing species will be crowded out by the more vigorous plants or may even die. Most important, however, are the conditions required by the various plants for good growth. Choose only those plants that have the same light, temperature, moisture and soil requirements. Species with decorative foliage are particularly suitable for this will make the arrangement attractive throughout the year, but the choice and how you arrange them depends really on your taste and experience. Remember, however, to try and keep it looking natural. A good arrangement in a large bowl, for instance, is *Dieffenbachia* x *bausei* (as the highest point), *Aglaonema oblongifolium* or *A. modestum* (as 'shrubs') and the rewarding *Maranta leuconeura* cv. Massangeana 'Tricolor' (as 'undergrowth'). It is also possible to use plants of approximately the same height with a large stone added for interest and to break up the uniformity; the stone may also be covered with plants (such as succulents).

The Vietnamese are masters of the flower arrangements generally known as 'landscapes in a bowl'. The dishes they use for the purpose measure up to 1 m (3 ft) in diameter. In these they put pieces of travertine 70 to 80 cm (28 to 32 in) high, sometimes even higher, surrounded by a 'lake'. Miniature copies of these can be made at home. Drill holes in water-absorbent rocks in appropriate spots, fill them with a handful of potting compost and either sow seeds or plant seedlings in the pockets. The compost provides nourishment for the first plant roots. Later roots, however, grow down over the rock into the water that fills the bowl, where other aquatic and bog plants complete the arrangement. Woody plants that can be shaped well, such as ficus, tieghemopanax, aralia, schefflera, adenium and bauhinia are recommended for growing on rocks. Growth of the roots may be promoted by temporarily providing the rock with a light cover of moss which is then gradually removed. The growth of woody plants cultivated in this manner, of course, is not very rapid but patience will reap its rewards.

Example of a 'landscape in a bowl' flower arrangement

Bonsai – shaping
a) removing superfluous branches
b) bending branches to the required shape with the aid of a thick wire

a

b

Moss panel

Hanging arrangements (similar to growing plants in demijohns) show off the beauty of the plants. They can be combined well with lighting fixtures

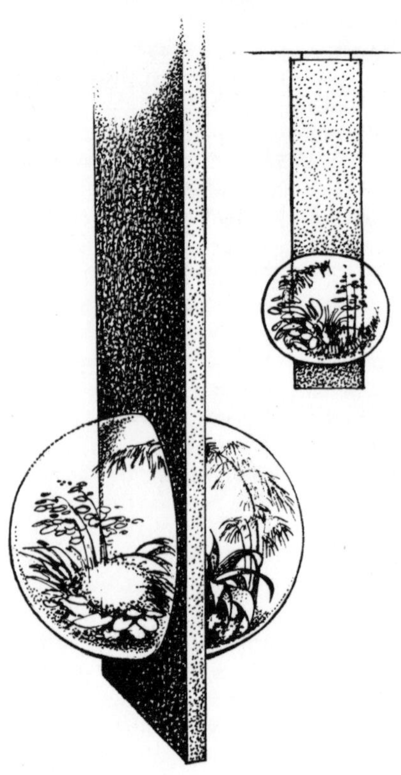

The rock can be supplemented by small species of bamboo, to give a particularly striking effect.

A similar arrangement may be fashioned with a piece of tree trunk or attractively shaped old tree branch placed in a bowl of water. Hard wood that does not rot is the most suitable. Plants that are otherwise difficult to grow can be put on these, such as certain species of the family Melastomataceae, plants of the genera *Bertolonia* and *Sonerila,* and even peperomias or the minute *Anthurium scandens.*

Very similar to this type of arrangement is the art of Japanese bonsai. Here, the aim is to create in miniature, within the confines of a small bowl or dish, what appears to be a landscape with a centuries-old tree stunted by time and weather.

Ceramic bowls and troughs used as containers are not only suitable for use indoors but also outdoors, in gardens, on balconies, or on window-sills. In these situations the containers, which must be well drained, are usually filled with rock garden plants to which a few small woody plants may be added.

Another type of arrangement that is rarely used despite its evident advantage is a moss cone or moss panel. A moss cone is really a supplementary feature of the bowl in which it is placed, and its construction is very simple. Select a round wooden stick of the desired length, singe it so it will not rot (or use a plastic rod instead), and wrap sphagnum moss round its entire length. You can also put a little nourishing soil between the stick and layer of moss. Fasten the moss to the stick with a 2- to 4-cm- (3/4- to 1 1/2- in) -mesh wire or nylon netting. Then place the cone (or pillar) in the dish and anchor it with a few large stones, which will form part of the layer of drainage material (gravel). Top this with a layer of the required growing

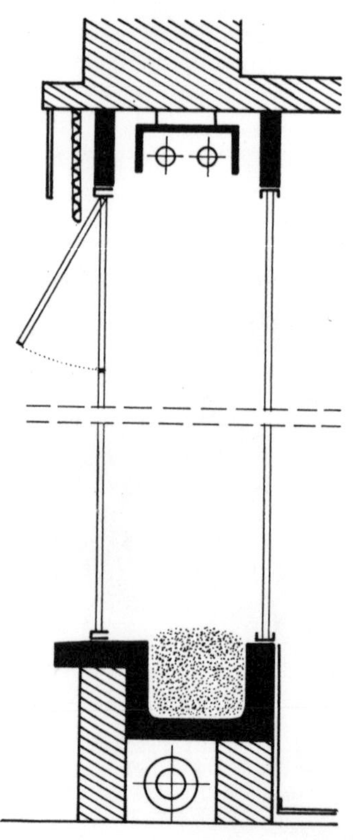

A diagram of a glass plant-case with bottom heating, hinged ventilation, and fluorescent lighting in the cover. Fluorescent lamps may also be placed vertically at the sides of the case

Various types of glass plant-cases: the light framework and see-through construction show off the beauty of the plants and the arrangement. Less traditional materials, such as perspex and plastic, which can be moulded to give more interesting shapes, can also be used. Similar see-through plant-cases can be used instead of doors as room dividers

compost and put in the plant, for example monstera, philodendron or syngonium, tying it in with wire so that it will grow up the moss cone. As the plant starts to grow, it sends its roots into the moss pillar and anchors itself there. The arrangement can be supplemented by plants that will cover the surface of the bowl or ones that will hang over the rim. You can also put various smaller species on the cone where they will be attractively offset by the leaves of the main climber. Ferns, smaller species of the Gesneriaceae family (episcia, hypocyrta, columnea) or small species of pilea are particularly suitable.

A moss panel is in fact a cage filled with sphagnum moss. The walls of the cage are made of wire or nylon netting stretched to a frame of metal or wood. The best way to put plants in the moss is to wrap the roots in sphagnum moss first so they will not be damaged during insertion. A metal or plastic trough should be attached to the bottom of the panel to keep water from dripping on the floor. If you wish to hang the moss panel on a wall put a sheet of polythene behind it. However, it is better to hang it freely in space and put plants on each side of the panel. Both sun-loving and shade-loving species (put on the appropriate sides) can be used for the purpose. Suitable plants to choose from include aeschynanthus, anthurium, begonia, ceropegia, cissus, columnea, dischidia, episcia, small species of ficus, hedera, hatiora, hoya, hypocyrta, lycopodium, mikania, peperomia, pothos, rhipsalis and remusatia.

When growing plants in moss, it must be remembered that the moss itself contains no plant food and thus it is important to provide fertilizer as well as water accordingly. Liquid fertilizer is the easiest to apply, and a weak solution should be used as required, always applying it from the top. The advantage of moss cones and moss panels is that not only do many plants seem to grow better under these conditions, but they also flower more freely, for example hoya. At the same time moss arrangements also act as efficient humidifiers, greatly increasing the amount of moisture in a room.

In recent years the cultivation of plants in demijohns has become particularly popular. Very delicate and rare plants that require constant humidity thrive in demijohns and fishbowls. Once established, such a 'garden' requires the minimum of care. Pour soil into the demijohn with a funnel, tamp it down with a cotton reel on the end of a bamboo cane, insert the plants with the aid of a spoon and fork, also attached to canes. Water them very carefully, and supply feed with subsequent applications of water, which should not be too frequent. The microclimate in a bottle, demijohn, large brandy glass or fishbowl makes it possible to grow plants that are otherwise very demanding, for example, small carnivorous dionaea, cephalotus or heliamphora. This environment is also suitable for small, rare ferns and begonias.

It is only a step from these half-closed containers to indoor plant-cases and glasshouses. Features common to all indoor 'glasshouses' – be they next to a window as the main source of light or plant-cases dependent solely on fluorescent lighting – are bottom heating by resistance wire (located in the double metal bottom of the case); fluorescent lamps in the top; various forms of ventilation (a hinged strip of glass near the top or a battery- or motor-powered ventilator); a deep camouflaged dish (or submerged flowerpots) at the bottom to hold plants, and a sliding front glass panel. Equipment should also include a thermostat to regulate the temperature, a thermometer and a hygrometer. It is recommended to purchase such a glasshouse from a specialist dealer rather than run the risk of being injured by faulty electrical installations in a homemade glasshouse.

Almost ideal growing conditions can be provided in a plant-case, thus making it possible to grow successfully even rare species of orchids, delicate nepenthes and other plants, particularly epiphytes, which otherwise cannot be grown indoors.

Other containers are terrariums and aquaterrariums, which are similar to but smaller than plant-cases. As a rule, these are not described in gardening publications, for they are primarily enclosures for keeping small animals, but they can also be used for house plants. In fact they are aquariums with a glass cover or top with fluorescent lighting. The bottom is covered with a layer of peat or sand and part of it may form a pool (aquaterrarium). The selection of plants depends on the temperature, light and moisture conditions, and also on the animals inhabiting the enclosure. If these are turtles or large snakes then it is better to omit plants. Small lizards, geckos and tree-frogs, however, will do no harm to plants. An ideal plant for the terrarium is *Ficus stipulata,* which quickly covers the walls even under poor light conditions, thus providing numerous places of concealment for its inhabitants. Also very good for terrariums are sansevieria (dry sandy terrariums), *Philodendron surinamense, P. scandens,* aglaonema, syngonium, peperomia and many species of ferns and selaginellas, which should be planted close to water. Recommended aquatic plants include small species of cyperus, cryptocoryne, aponogeton and spathiphyllum.

The plates of cork oak bark that often form the rear wall or sides of a terrarium are good for growing delicate epiphytes, such as small orchids or moisture-loving bromeliads. Best, however, are trailing species, particularly of the genera *Aeschynanthus* and *Columnea,* and climbing plants such as *Hoya.*

Paludarium

A paludarium provides another possibility for growing plants that are not commonly found indoors, namely bog plants. The material of which the container is made is not important. It may be of glass, ceramic ware, metal or plastic. Before making a paludarium, however, go out and get some ideas from nature. Take a look round the shore of a lake and note in particular the diversity of the site. Cover the bottom of the container with a thin layer of well-rotted compost mixed with peat. How much space is covered with water, where to put stones and branches, and where to leave spots of 'dry land' – all that is a matter of personal choice. On top of the compost put a 10-cm (4-in) layer of washed river sand and then add water. Wait a few days to let the substrate settle before planting, the same as in an aquarium. A paludarium can also contain potted plants (particularly larger and more demanding species), the pots being masked with gravel and sand if desired. Water plants may include the water lily *Nymphaea* x *daubenyana,* the lotus *Nelumbo luteum* 'Mikado', cryptocoryne, yallisneria and aponogeton, and floating aquatics that will do well include *Pistia stratiotes* and *Eichhornia crassipes* (water hyacinth). Suitable bog plants for the 'shore' include typhonium, sagittaria, spathiphyllum and pontederia, and recommended for 'dry land' are ferns, selaginellas and many aroids.

A paludarium greatly increases the humidity in a room and plants that require a particularly moist atmosphere for good growth do well in its vicinity. Caring for a paludarium is simple, consisting merely of adding water to replace that which has evaporated. Occasionally a liquid fertilizer is added instead.

The following text deals with epiphytes, which deserve particular attention because of their diversity and the wide variety of arrangements they afford. Epiphytes, as has already been stated, are plants that grow on other plants without doing them any harm. The host plant, usually a tree (the scientific name for such a plant is phytophore, meaning bearer of plants), is merely the habitat of the epiphyte, affording it nothing more than a dwelling place. Similarly, the epiphyte merely holds on the bark, its roots in no way damaging the inner tissues of the tree. That is why some epiphytes, such as orchids of the genera *Anguloa, Clowesia* and *Catasetum,* even grow on dead trees.

Mention has already been made of the adaptations plants have made to the epiphytic form of life, such as the funnel or cupped leaf base formed by the leaves of bromeliads; the absorbent layer of velamen covering the aerial roots of certain orchids; the humus-catching, 'brush-like' root system of other orchids; and the scales on the leaves of bromeliads that serve to absorb moisture from the air and pass it to the tissues inside the leaf. There are, of course, many more. Take, for instance, the ferns of the genus *Platycerium.* Note that these have two kinds of leaves, one fertile (carrying the spores), divided and upright, the other sterile, flat and undivided or differently shaped and pressed close to the ground. Platycerium and drynaria are epiphytic ferns that grow on tree trunks. The base of the sterile leaves is pressed to the bark from an early age and the upper end extends outward, thus catching leaves shed by the tree, dust and mineral particles carried by insects to the crown of the tree, as well as rotting wood. In time this forms a sufficient quantity of humus for the fern's growth.

In bromeliads we can observe a different form of adaptation. The marginal leaves of the rosette often curl and die. These are naturally removed by gardeners, for they add nothing to the plant's attractiveness. In the wild, however, where bromeliads often grow on dry, slender twigs, the layer of dry leaves plays a vital role, for as it slowly decomposes it forms a substrate in which the plant roots, thus feeding itself. Removal of the leaves in collections and botanical gardens prevents thorough acquaintance and understanding of the life of the plant.

Epiphytes are ideal for growing in the modern home. They are both warmth- and light-loving plants which can withstand lengthy periods of drought and which require the minimum of care. A total of about 28,200 species belonging to 850 genera of vascular plants have been described to date; in other words a full ten per cent of all higher plants are epiphytes. Among them are true gems of the plant realm such as bromeliads and orchids, which have become increasingly popular in recent years. The choice of bromeliads offered on the market, how-

Epiphytes growing on a trunk provide one of the loveliest types of plant arrangement in the modern home

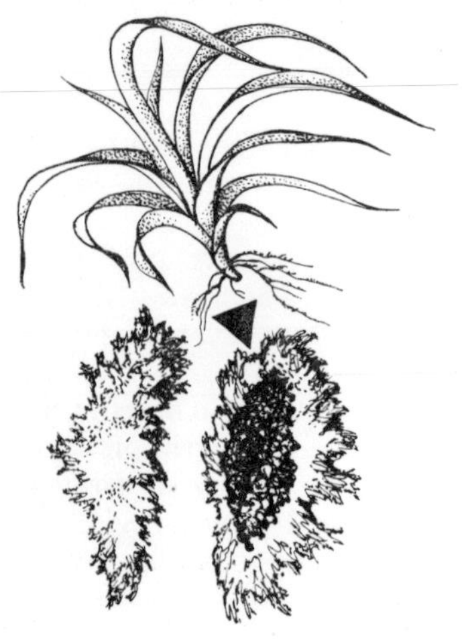

Attaching epiphytes to a trunk

ever, continues to be rather unsuitable. One of the commonest, for example, is *Vriesea splendens* and its hybrids, a plant that is far from being a good subject for growing indoors for it is indigenous to Guyana where it grows in the tropical rainforest by the Kaieteur Falls and requires constant moisture and warmth. It does well in a glasshouse but in the home it will last only a few months, or rather weeks, unless kept in a plant-case.

How should one go about preparing a branch or trunk for growing epiphytes? Depending on the available space it may be anything from a small twig anchored in a flat dish, to a plate of cork oak bark suspended in a terarium, or an actual piece of trunk. Always choose the material with care. Particularly suitable is a branch from an oak or locust tree, or an arborvitae or cypress trunk for they are the least prone to decay. For small-scale arrangements use cork oak bark or the roots and base of the stem of vine. If you come accross a suitable and attractively shaped branch or a nicely branched trunk, shape it as desired by removing unwanted branches and attaching branches with wire if you want to fill in empty spaces. Then decide where to put the plants. You may have read that you should gouge out holes to hold the plants, and sometimes also grooves for drainage, but this is not necessary. If you want to put plants on the smooth part of the trunk hammer three small nails in the desired spot leaving the heads and a short piece projecting for attaching the plant. Then anchor the trunk in the dish in which it is to stand. Keep in mind that water will drip from the plants when they are watered and provide a dish that is large enough to catch all the run off; for safety's sake add a few extra centimetres. Ideal for this purpose are laminated plastic or metal (zinc) trays masked on the outside with wood. The base of the trunk that will be in soil should be singed and may also be coated with a preservative agent. Take care to use one that will not have an adverse affect on the plants. Once the trunk or branch is firmly anchored (stuck on a metal spike, inserted in a metal collar or in a stand such as is used for Christmas trees) you can begin planting.

First of all get your materials ready: a soil mixture for epiphytes, plenty of sphagnum moss, a firm, thin, insulated wire or nylon line, and a waterproof adhesive. Tip the plants out of their pots, remove the soil from the roots and then prepare the ball. Make a 'cushion' of sphagnum moss, sprinkle with the epiphytic soil mixture (equal parts of peat, sand, crushed pine bark, bits of charcoal, crushed polystyrene, and sometimes also roots of ferns such as osmunda or polypodium), insert the plant roots and cover them with a handful of the mixture. A sprinkling of bonemeal or chopped dry beech leaves may be added to the mixture to make it more nourishing. Then wind wire round the moss, compost and roots, forming them into a compact ball and attach it to the branch with wire or nylon line, which may be hidden by a piece of sphagnum. Tiny bromeliads of the genus *Tillandsia* (*T. filifolia, T. ionantha*) that grow without soil may simply be cemented to the branch with a drop of waterproof adhesive. Otherwise tillandsias (except for large species and ones with a well-developed root system such as *Tillandsia complanata, T. cyanea, T. gigantea* and *T. prodigiosa*) are just tied to the bark either with fine wire or a strip of old nylon stocking.

There are naturally many different kinds of epiphytic soil mixtures. The most simple one consists of crushed polystyrene and peat or crushed polystyrene with bits of cut plastic foam and crushed pine bark. Larger plants that require a greater amount of mixture for successful growth may be inserted in small perforated plastic pots filled with the mixture and covered by a layer of moss. These larger plants utilize the mixture only for rapid initial growth and later their roots catch hold of the bark or wood. There is no need to transplant epiphytes or replace the substrate. As for water, this should be supplied regularly (though not liberally) at least in the beginning, for the moss ball will not absorb water if at any stage it is allowed to dry out completely. Epiphytes also appreciate an occasional application of feed. Use an organic fertilizer diluted to one-tenth the concentration used for other plants.

If you add a few trailing plants such as philodendrons or syngoniums to the dish in which the trunk stands, you will have a true illusion of the tropics in your home. Other recommended plants (they must all tolerate permanently moist soil) include ferns, costus, aglaonema, anthurium, alocasia and marantas.

This book has perhaps devoted more space than is usual to the subject of growing epiphytes on a branch or trunk but if you select suitable species and have at least a slight instinct for creative arrangement, you will be well rewarded for your efforts. Furthermore, in the modern home epiphytes have proved extremely hardy besides being some of the loveliest of house plants.

# FLOWERS OUTSIDE THE WINDOW

'... There is not excuse for a window in a city apartment that has no flowers, no life outside. The only explanation is moral poverty ...' These words were written in the thirties by the great Czech author and lover of flowers, Karel Čapek, and though it was almost fifty years ago none could be more valid.

If there are no flowers or plants on balconies and window-sills then a city has a cold, lifeless look. Even the best architecture will not change this fact. On the other hand, towns noted for their flower-bedecked windows and balconies, for example in Spain, southern France, and Mexico's Cordoba, strike even those merely passing through as bright and cheerful.

A window-box is not a natural place for plants and conditions there are far from ideal. The soil dries out readily, roots in a box on a sunny window-sill easily become overheated, and there are sharp fluctuations in temperature. The problem of moisture has been solved to a certain degree by the use of plastic containers in which the soil dries out much more slowly. Such containers have the added advantage of being light and easy to clean. In the case of slanting window-sills, wedges should be put under the containers so the soil surface is level and the containers should be secured in position to prevent their being dislodged by strong winds.

What soil mixture should be used for window-boxes? Annuals are usually grown there and if they are to be fully grown within the shortest possible time the soil must be sufficiently nourishing. It must not compact and cake, neither should it be too light, for then it would dry out too quickly. An ideal growing medium, which is readily available at garden centres or nurseries, is the John Innes potting compost No. 2. However, before this is put in the box, the bottom should be covered by a 2 ½-cm (1-in)-layer of drainage material consisting of fine gravel. If there are large drainage holes in the window-box, these should be covered over with pieces of broken clay flower pot (crock) or stones to facilitate drainage and prevent the compost from being washed away.

The plants to be used for the window-box display may be raised from seed in the home in early spring, or purchased as young seedlings with a root ball from the nurseryman. Seed can also be sown directly into the container, in which case the seedlings must be thinned in time so that each plant has room to grow. The plants should be thoroughly watered as soon as they have been put out and then lightly sprayed over during the next few days. Feed should not start being applied until a month later; liquid fertilizer is the most suitable, and the soil surface should be loosened before each feed. Plants are generally watered and fed in the late afternoon, never at midday in the full heat of the sun. Foliage should be syringed after every feed to wash off any remnants of fertilizer.

Whereas the selection of plants for growing indoors provides the grower with scope for experiment, the choice for the window-box is generally restricted to the tried and tested plants that grow well and flower reliably. In the case of a balcony, plants can also be put out in large earthenware urns and wooden tubs. Suitable plants for such containers are rock plants, bulbs, small trees and shrubs, and even a bonsai. Small conifers are particularly attractive in such arrangements, and can be kept within bounds by wise pruning; of the prostrate forms cotoneaster and euonymus are recommended. Also attractive are dwarf willows such as the twisted, stunted *Salix matsudana* 'Tortuosa' together with ornamental grasses. All depends on the imagination and instinct of the grower. The window, vibrant with life and colour both inside and outside will be his creation.

# THE ROAD TO SUCCESS

Growing plants is not particularly easy, a fact that both beginners and experienced growers will confirm – even specialists, when they remember the time they waited in tense anticipation for a plant to bloom. The most important trait for every lover of house plants is patience. This is particularly true in the case of uncommon species that do not have a rapid rate of growth. Often it is necessary to try out several different places in the home before finding the spot that suits the plant best. Finding the best growing compost, how much and how often to feed and water, all this is a question of trial and error that sometimes requires starting anew. Perhaps it is for this very reason that growing plants is such a popular pastime. A person can give his imagination free rein. Experiments often bring surprising results and the reward is a blossoming plant in all its glory.

Mention has already been made of light requirements and

Orchids and most epiphytic plants require a porous and well-drained soil; drainage is provided by a plastic insert

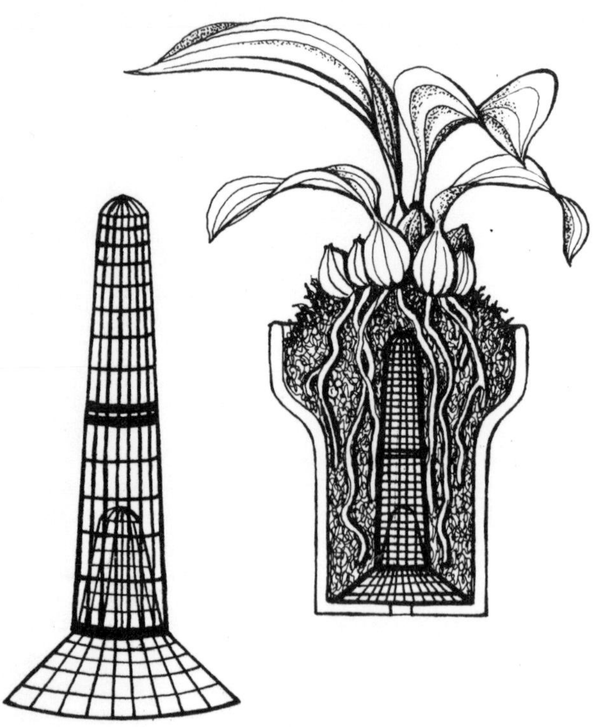

the fact that plants are divided into light-lovers and those that tolerate shade. Growth is promoted chiefly by the red to infra-red range of the spectrum; violet and ultraviolet rays tend to retard growth. If plants are grown in plant-cases with artificial illumination it is recommended to use fluorescent lamps with violet-red light or a combination of these and white fluorescent lamps.

As for temperature requirements, we already know that it is necessary to find out as much as possible about the origin of each species and adapt the temperature according to its native habitat. In many cases flowers will not develop unless the plant is exposed to low temperatures for a period.

This is true of bulbs and tubers, which generally 'die back' and pass the cold period in a dormant state, as well as plants with storage tissue in woody stems, for example brunfelsia, bougainvillea and erythrina. Orchid growers are well acquainted with the requirement of the popular cymbidiums which must be exposed to low temperatures in autumn in order to form flowers. The temperature fluctuations required by the type species, however, need not be observed in the case of many cultivated forms, which can be grown at an even, usually higher temperature.

Water should also be applied according to the climatic conditions of the plant's native habitat, though naturally with an eye to the temperature and amount of light in the home. Soft rainwater is the most suitable and should be used whenever it is readily available. However, in places where the atmosphere contains a large concentration of dust and ashes, for example near industrial conurbations, rainwater may contain many harmful substances which have a toxic effect on plants and should thus be avoided. Only species from dry regions tolerate constant watering with hard water, that is water containing calcium and magnesium salts, without suffering any damage. Such water is also unsuitable for plants that grow in acid forest humus or peat moors. House plants, however, generally tolerate water from the tap. If possible, it should be left standing overnight to allow for the evaporation of the chlorine, which is toxic to plants. The temperature of the water should be the same as that of the room or, preferably, 2 to 3°C (4 to 6°F) higher. Particularly damaging to plants is syringing with exceedingly cold water. In the case of plants with leaves that are felted or covered with long hairs, syringing should be avoided altogether.

Last on the list, but just as important, is the soil mixture. Preparing it can be quite an art. Old gardening books contain instructions for dozens of mixtures and the required portions either by volume or weight. In an effort to standardize and simplify matters, the John Innes potting composts were introduced. These consist basically of loam, peat and sand mixed in the proportion of 7 parts by bulk of loam, 3 parts of peat and 2 of sand. To this mixture John Innes Base Fertilizer is added in varying quantities to give three different strengths of compost: John Innes potting compost No. 1 for slow-growing plants in small pots; No. 2 for medium-sized plants; and No. 3 for vigorous plants in large containers. More recently, soilless composts have become very popular. These may be composed entirely of peat with the addition of fertilizer, or a mixture of peat and sand or peat and vermiculite, again with added fertilizer. Soilless composts are readily available at garden centres and nurseries, as are the John Innes potting composts.

Every plant will at some time fill its pot with roots, leaving no room for further growth. In extreme cases roots will suddenly begin to appear on the soil surface or the pot may even crack. The experienced grower naturally takes care that this does not happen and in the spring of each year he moves rapidly-growing plants to larger pots (older plants every 2 or 3 years). The beginner's chief mistake when re-potting is to select a pot that is too large, with the well-meant intention of providing the plant with plenty of space and nutrients. In such a case the plant is never able to fill the pot with its roots and most of the compost is unused.

When transplating a plant, choose a pot that is only slightly larger than the one used before. Loosen the plant by tapping the pot, tip it out and remove old soil clinging to the roots with a blunt wooden stick. Before putting the plant in the new pot cover the drainage hole with crocks and top them with a layer of new compost. Then put the plant in, add the fresh compost, and firm it down around the root ball. Do not fill the pot up to the rim; leave room for watering.

The new compost will contain ample nutrients so it is unnecessary to apply feed for the first month or two (doing so might even damage the plants). After this time, of course, feed should be applied regularly throughout the growing period. In the autumn, before the onset of the dormant period, feeding should be reduced and then stopped altogether. There are plenty of proprietary feeds on the market and these can be purchased at a nursery, where you will generally be advised as to which kind is best for a given plant and in what concentration. Remember, also, to follow the manufacturer's instructions. Plants with ornamental flowers need fertilizer with ample phosphorus. Nitrogen promotes plant growth, but care must be taken when applying nitrogenous fertilizers to plants with variegated leaves for these turn green if given too much nitrogen.

# PROPAGATION

Quite often one comes across a beautiful plant at a friend's house which is not often seen in the florist's window or at a garden centre. We may visit several nurseries in an attempt to get hold of a similar specimen, but all to no avail. In the end our only recourse is to go back to our friend and ask for a piece or a cutting from the original plant. In fact, this is much the better way, for a plant that we grow ourselves is far more precious than one purchased fully-grown at the florist's, first because of our own involvement (caring for it and watching it develop) and secondly because right from the beginning the plant becomes acclimatized to the surroundings of your home and does not have to adapt itself from the ideal conditions of a greenhouse.

Plants may be multiplied in two ways: either by seed or spores (sexual reproduction) or by parts of the plants (vegetative reproduction). Almost all plants can be increased from seed. The only exceptions are cultivars and selected hybrids which do not come true if propagated from seed, producing instead the original form or a mixture (in the case of hybrids). Growing plants from seed has the drawback that it sometimes takes several years before the plant reaches maturity and starts producing flowers. However, in the case of rare species which are difficult to grow indoors, it is the best way, for of the many seeds that germinate it is usually the hardiest and most adaptable seedlings that survive.

How and where should seed be sown? The most suitable container is a wooden or plastic seed tray, but an earthenware dish may also be used. Seed-sowing composts are readily available at garden centres, either soil-based ones such as John Innes seed compost or soilless ones. If the seed tray has large drainage holes in the bottom, they should be covered over with crocks to help drainage and then the tray should be filled with compost. After firming and levelling the compost, the finished height should be within about 1 cm (½ in) of the top of the seed tray. The seeds can then be sown, sprinkling them evenly and not too thickly.

Some seeds germinate in darkness, others only if exposed to light. If you cannot find the relevant information for your particular seeds in a reference book, leave some uncovered on the surface of the compost, and cover the remainder with a thin layer of soil (about twice the thickness of the seed). However, there are other special methods which must be used for certain plants. For instance, carnivorous plants of the genus *Sarracenia, Drosera* and *Dionaea,* which grow in peat moors in the wild, germinate best in green sphagnum moss covered with water. Ferns may be multiplied from spores, which are sown on the surface of clean, sterile peat kept permanently moist. These should be kept practically in the dark with some light being admitted only after the first seed leaf appears. Bromeliads are sown either on filter paper or on peat; tillandsias, however, should be sown directly on branches, cones or arborvitae twigs tied in clumps. The very delicate, minute seeds of certain members of the Gesneriaceae family are best sown on peat sprinkled with a thin layer of charcoal powder.

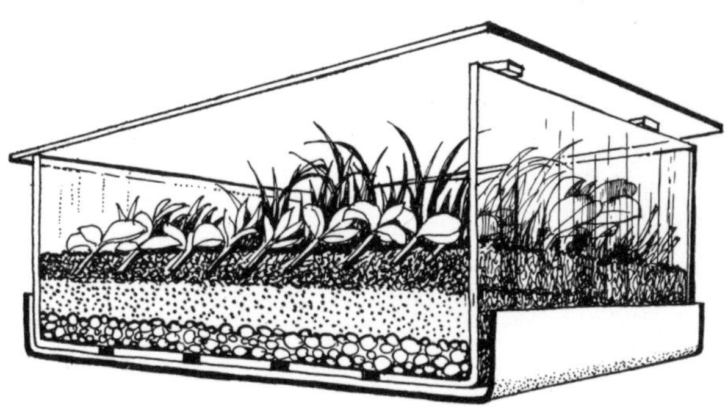

A propagator can be used for growing plants from seed as well as from cuttings. The bottom is covered by a layer of drainage material (pebbles), next is a layer of sand topped by a layer of the rooting medium (peat and sand). A wedge is placed under one edge of the glass cover so that the condensed water does not drip on the seeds or cuttings. An improved version is one with a double bottom in which a heating element is installed

Rooting cuttings in water is the simplest method and is very successful. A dark glass bottle is recommended. The cuttings are held firmly in the neck of the bottle by means of a wad of cotton wool which also keeps out dust

Begonia leaf cuttings should be taken at the point where the veins branch. They may be inserted in the rooting medium or simply placed flat on the surface and pressed in

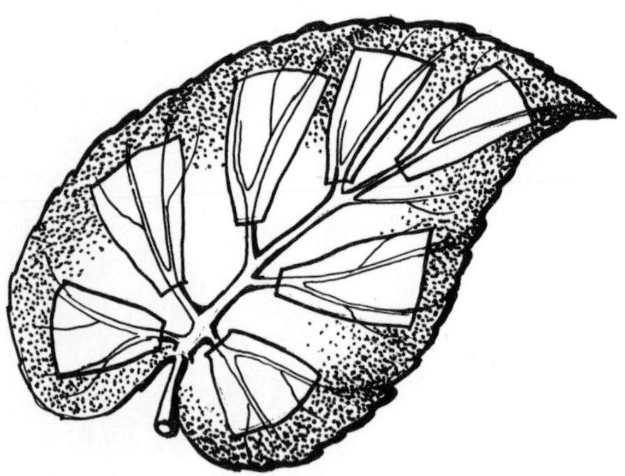

As for the seeds of acacia and the giant sequoiadendron, these will germinate far better if they are scalded with hot water before sowing for in the wild these plants are often exposed to the heat of forest fires and this is one of their forms of adaptation.

After sowing the seeds moisten them from below by standing the seed tray in water and leaving it till moisture appears on the surface of the compost. Then cover the seed tray with a sheet of glass to ensure uniform atmospheric moisture. The glass must be turned over daily so that the drops of water which condense on the underside do not fall on the seeds or young seedlings. As soon as the seedlings are large enough to handle, they should be pricked out.

Vegetative propagation is more widely used to increase plants in the home. The simplest method is division, which can be done when transferring the plants to new pots. Often it is not even necessary to detach a young plant from the parent clump with a knife, for it falls off readily by itself. Offsets of bulbs and tubers are detached in the same way. When using a knife to separate them always dust the cut surfaces, preferably with charcoal powder, though cigarette ash will serve the purpose just as well. The detached plants should be planted immediately, taking care not to damage the roots which are capable of immediate growth.

Taking cuttings is another method of vegetative propagation. These can be rooted in a seed tray or flower pot, or small propagators with heating elements can be bought at garden centres. Moist coarse sand makes a good rooting medium. Alternatively a mixture of peat and sand can be used.

Cuttings are usually made of stems or leaves; only occasionally are plants multiplied by root cuttings (generally only members of the genus *Cordyline*). Stem cuttings should be about 10 cm (4 in) long and the leaves on the section to be inserted in the compost should be removed. To promote more rapid rooting, dust the cut end with hormone rooting powder. Some stem cuttings (dieffenbachia, dracaena and aglaonema) are placed flat on the surface of the compost and about half their length is pressed into the rooting medium. Leaf cuttings are taken either with the stalk (saintpaulia) or without; the leaf

Propagation by leaf cuttings is a reliable method for succulents

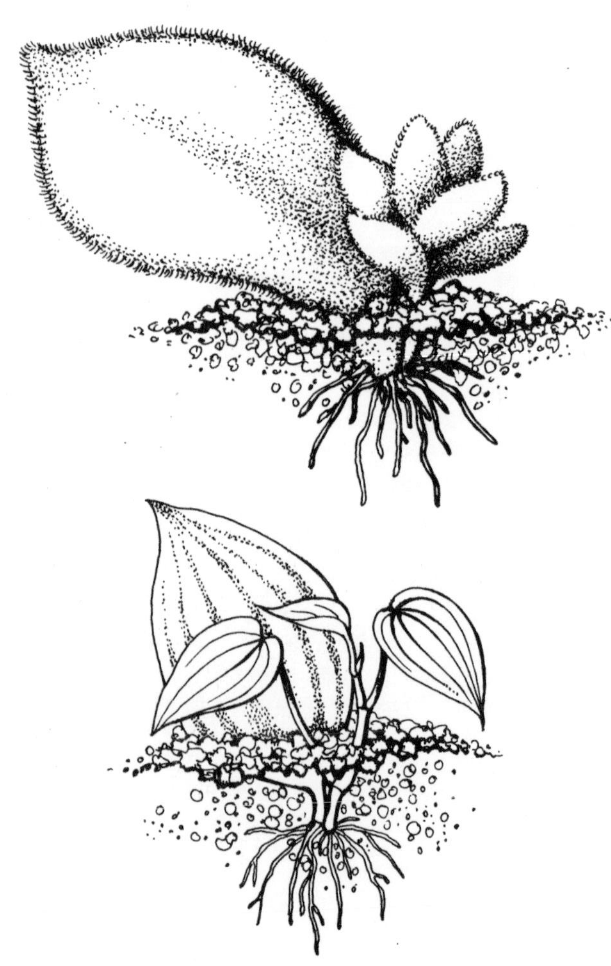

A peperomia leaf cutting should be inserted in the rooting medium together with its stalk

Propagation of orchids:
a) cut off the old leafless pseudo-bulbs and put them with a little peat in a plastic bag in a light place
b) the old pseudo-bulbs begin putting out new shoots within a few weeks

The older pseudo-bulbs of many orchids such as dendrobium and epidendrum produce young plantlets which are detached after they have formed roots

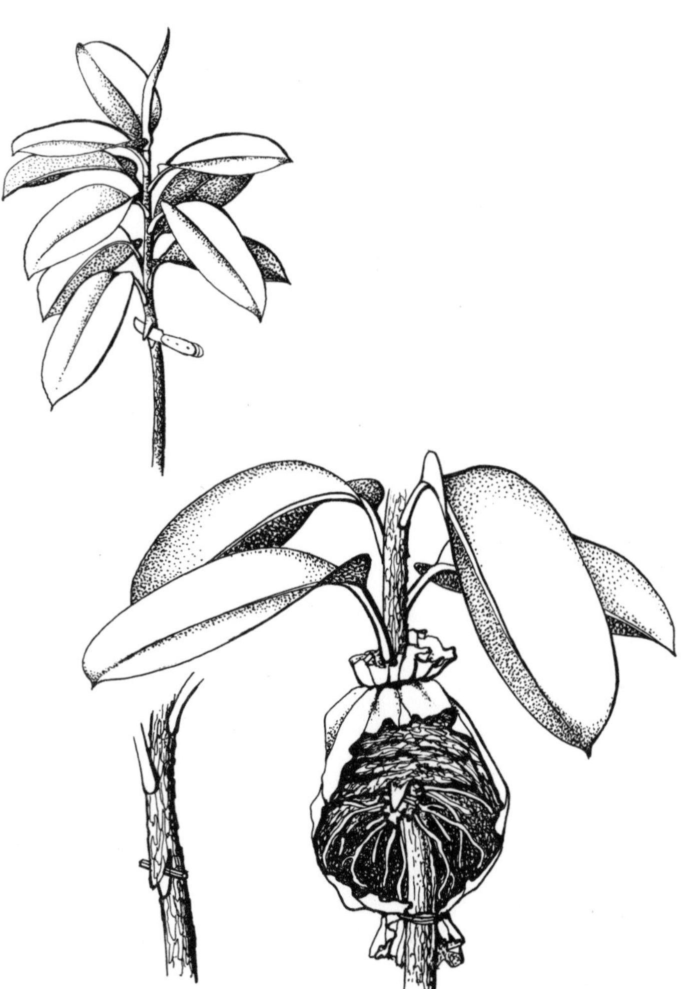

Air-layering is used chiefly for plants that turn woody, drop their lower leaves and become leggy, such as *Ficus elastica*

may also be cut into several sections which are inserted in the soil (sansevieria) or else merely laid on the surface (begonia). In the latter case take care that the section of leaf blade has at least some veining in the shape of a Y.

Cuttings like a warm, moist atmosphere in which to root. This may be achieved by covering them with a sheet of glass, or inverting a jam jar over them, or, if the cuttings are in a flower pot, by placing both pot and cuttings in a polythene bag and sealing the top. The separation of tubers and rhizomes is another method of vegetative propagation and is used for caladiums, aroids, members of the ginger family and marantas. The cut surfaces should be dusted with charcoal powder and left to dry before insertion in the compost.

Some plants, such as ficus and dieffenbachia tend to shed leaves from the base leaving the stem bare and unattractive. Such plants can be propagated by air-layering. At the point on the stem where you want the plant to form new roots, make an upward cut at a strong angle about half-way across the stem, insert a matchstick so the cut will not close, wrap damp green sphagnum moss round the cut and round that, a piece of polythene, binding it at the top and bottom. To prevent the plant top from breaking off tie it to a stake above and below the wad of moss. When well-developed roots appear, which takes several weeks, remove the polythene, cut off the top and pot it up, together with the moss packing. The remaining, lower part of the stem should be kept, as it will often put out new shoots.

Grafting of succulents, particularly cacti, on reliably and readily growing rootstock is another method of vegetative propagation. By this means it is possible to cultivate rare and delicate species that would otherwise grow slowly and would not flower, as well as colour mutations (red and yellow) which lack chlorophyl, and would be totally incapable of growing on their own. The rootstock should be cut at right angles to the axis, likewise the cactus that is to be grafted on. Then the section is placed on the stock so that the vascular bundles coincide with one another as far as possible, and fastened securely by means of rubber bands. The two unite within a week, after which the rubber bands may be removed.

# PESTS AND DISEASES

When a plant that has been a source of pleasure for months suddenly begins to ail, it is not always an easy task for the layman to determine what kind of disorder it is suffering from and what should be done to save it. Plant ailments can be divided into three groups: diseases caused by viruses, bacteria or fungi; insect pests and physiological disorders.

In the case of diseases it is frequently necessary to spray the plants, often several times, with a specific chemical to overcome the problems. Insect pests are generally easily spotted and readily identified and the plants can be treated accordingly. Always remember that a healthy plant is less prone to attack from pests and diseases than a neglected one. As for physiological disorders, these are generally caused by a mistake in the growing conditions and all that needs to be done is to correct it.

The most widespread diseases are those caused by fungi. The following table lists the commonest:

| **Cause** | **Symptoms** | **Cure** |
|---|---|---|
| Damping off | Seedling flop, root necks turn dark and rot, plants disintegrate | captan, Cheshunt compound |
| Greymould (botrytis) | Brown spots on leaves and stems, later a greyish-white coating | benomyl |
| Powdery mildew | Furry coating on leaves and stems, later leaves turn brown, curl and die | dinocap, benomyl |
| Downy mildew | White coating on upperside of leaves, pale yellow blotches on underside turning a darker hue. Plants dry out and die | captan |

Pests can generally be discovered before they cause any visible harm. It is therefore recommended to examine plants thoroughly at least once a week. Only nematodes will escape attention. We usually take notice of them only when they occur in large numbers causing visible signs of damage such as watery spots which later turn black, or thickening and twisting of stems and poor or irregular growth of leaves. Roots, too, are sometimes attacked by nematodes. This disease is easily recognized by the galls that form on roots and tubers. A look through a strong magnifying glass reveals the presence of slender, minute worms in the affected tissues. Because these pests are generally spread via the soil it is recommended that this be disinfected with one of the commercially available soil sterilants. Plants that are heavily affected should be discarded.

Among the commonest plant pests are red spider mites. These generally occur on the underside of leaves in delicate, web-like cases, giving the leaves a mottled, dusty look. They suck the plant sap, causing the foliage to fade and turn yellow and eventually drop off. They multiply rapidly, particularly in a dry and warm environment. They are controlled by spraying with a proprietary house plant insecticide or by inverting the plant into a bucket containing an insecticidal solution made up according to the manufacturer's instructions. However, prevention is better than cure. Ensure plant are kept in a moist, airy atmosphere. In hot dry weather spray the foliage with water frequently and set the pots in moist peat or trays of wet gravel to keep up the humidity level. If this is done red spider mite should not be a problem. Mites of the Tarsonemidae family also attack house plants causing leaves to twist and curl. These are destroyed by spraying with a suitable house plant insecticide.

Plants are also attacked by other sucking insects: white fly, aphids, scale insects, mealy bugs and spring-tails. The tiny white flies are easily detected flying round the foliage; they suck the plant sap on the underside of the leaves. The notorious aphids are found on the underside of the leaves and their presence is also revealed by sticky spots on the foliage which are in turn attacked by moulds. The spots are known as honeydew and are remnants of the plant sap that has passed through the aphids' alimentary canals without change. Both pests may be controlled by any house plant insecticide. An alternative treatment is to hold the plant upside down, plunging the foliage into an insecticidal solution made up according to the manufacturer's instructions.

Scale insects are generally found clinging to stems or the axils of leaves. They are covered by a firm scale and are fairly difficult to combat. If their numbers are few then they can be scraped off with a soft piece of wood or plastic taking care not to damage the plant. Alternatively, they can be washed off with a mild soap and water solution. The same method can be used to control mealy bugs, which look like tiny wads of cotton for they are covered with a white flour- or cotton-like waxy secretion. A more effective method of dealing with mealy bug is to touch each pest with a paint brush that has been dipped in methylated spirits.

Spring-tails live in the soil where they feed on plant roots and sometimes even destroy germinating seedlings. These tiny, wingless insects are generally noticed when plants are watered, at which time they suddenly appear leaping about on the water's surface. They are fairly easy to control by watering the soil with an insecticidal solution.

A word of warning: when using any kind of chemical preparation it is extremely important to follow carefully the manufacturer's instructions. Many insecticides are poisonous to fish and warm-blooded animals (including human beings) and should not be used in the home; so make sure you obtain one of the preparations recommended for use on house plants and keep it out of the reach of children and pets.

Most cultivated plants are tolerant of the preparations mentioned in this book. There are, however, exceptions, i. e. plants that do not tolerate a certain spray or entire group based on a certain compound or element, and use of such preparations may harm or destroy the plant.

**Below is a survey of the so-called physiological diseases generally caused by incorrect care and unsuitable environment**

| Symptoms | Cause | Cure |
|---|---|---|
| Stems are too long, leaves turn pale, new leaves stunted | lack of light, too much nitrogen | move plant to a lighter position, wait awhile before next feed, then apply phosphate fertilizer |
| Stems are too long, lush foliage, soil covered with green coating, plant does not flower | overfeeding, particularly with nitrogen | withhold feed for at least a month, then apply a phosphate fertilizer |
| Stems get mushy, then turn dark and rot, older leaves curl and wilt | over-watering | limit watering, transplanting is recommended |
| Leaves drop (generally in winter) without apparent reason, sometimes turn black | over-watering and draughts – adverse influence of cold air | limit watering, move plant to another spot in the room out of a draught |
| Older leaves turn yellow and drop | | |
| – new leaves are small, growth is slow | under-feeding | increase supply of feed |
| – leaves wilt, leaf tips turn brown | under-watering | increase supply of water |
| Leaves are streaked with yellow or brown mottling | sunscorch | move the plant out of direct sunlight |
| Leaves are spotted with white or yellow (particularly plants with hairy leaves – saintpaulia, sinningia) | spraying with water that is too cold | do not spray foliage or spray with water warmed to room temperature |
| Leaves curl and become frilled | | |
| – new leaves are stunted | too much light | move the plant to a shadier position |
| – leaf edges become frilled and turn brown | not enough atmospheric moisture | spray leaves with water, put plant close to a humidifer or plunge pot into damp peat or gravel |
| – new leaves become stunted, turn yellow and wilt | too high a temperatue in the room | move plant to a cooler spot, air the room |

In conclusion – may the reader have need to consult this chapter as little as possible!

# MORPHOLOGICAL TERMS

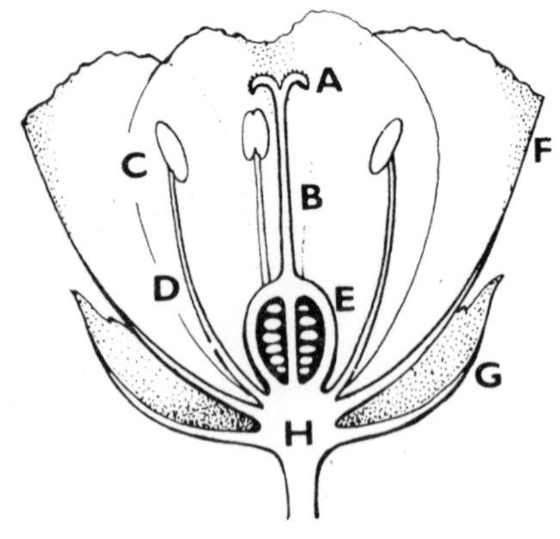


General diagram of a flower: A – stigma, B – style, C – anther, D – filament, E – ovary with ovules, F – petal, G – sepal, H – receptacle

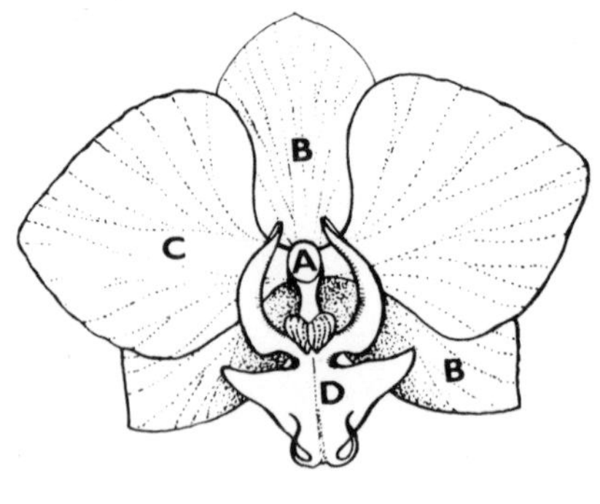


Flower of an orchid: A – gynostemium (column), B – sepals, C – petals, D – lip

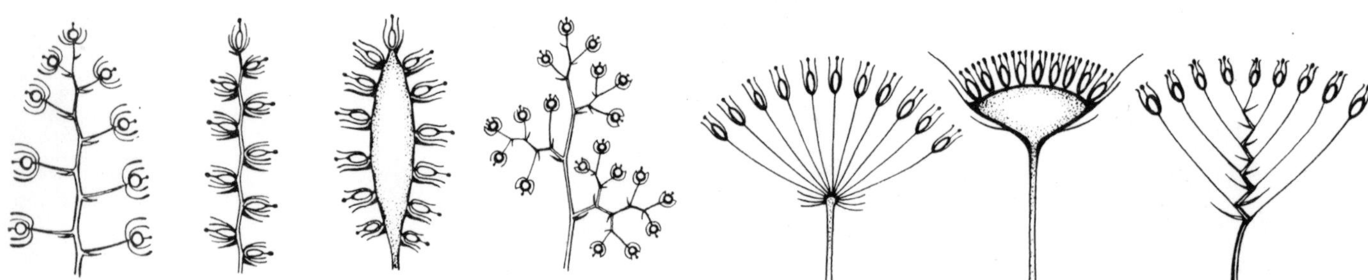

Types of inflorescence (from left to right): raceme, spike, spadix, panicle, umbel, capitulum, corymb

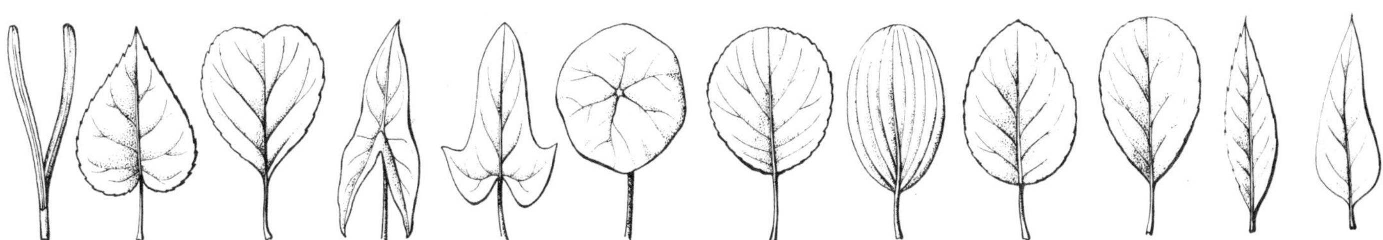

Leaf shapes (from left to right): needle-shaped, cordate, obcordate, sagittate, hastate, shield-shaped, orbicular, elliptical, ovate, obovate, oblong, lanceolate

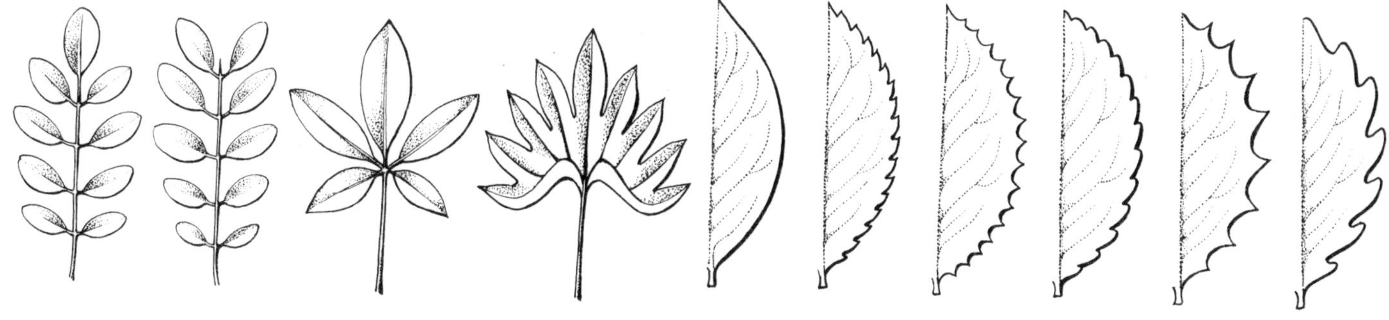

Leaf divisions (from left to right): odd-pinnate, even-pinnate, palmate, pedate

Leaf margins (from left to right): entire, serrate, finely dentate, crenate, coarsely dentate, lobed

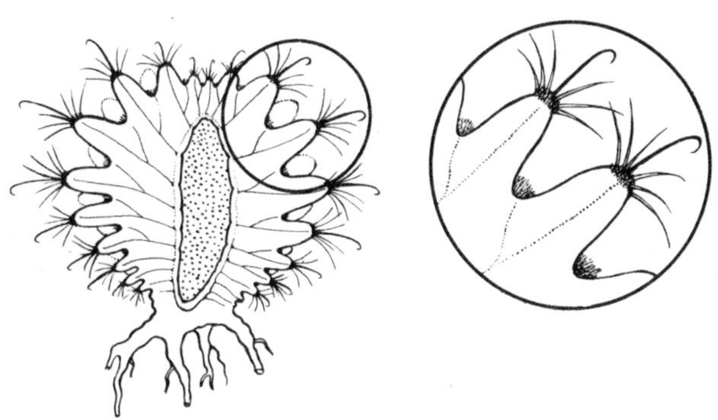

Body of a cactus: the ribs are composed of small projecting tubercles (mamillae) with spine-bearing areoles at the tips that bear flowers. Flowers also arise from the axils of the tubercles.

# GUIDE TO THE ILLUSTRATED SECTION

The plants in the illustrated section are divided into groups according to their use in the home; individual genera are arranged in the alphabetical order of their Latin names within each group. Naturally, it was difficult to make clear-marked distinctions between the groups and prevent them from overlapping. Some foliage plants often have very attractive flowers as well and at the same time may also be epiphytes, so that they could easily be classed in three different groups. Most of the plants listed under 'Orchids' or 'Bromeliads', for example, are epiphytes. In this case we rely not only on the reader's understanding of the difficulty of assigning a given plant to the correct group but also on his reading what the rest of this book has to say on growing and caring for house plants. The index at the back of the book should help him find the plant he wants with the minimum of effort.

An age-old problem for gardeners are the names given to plants. Not only do plants have official scientific names, but they are also known by various traditional names, often old synonyms that are no longer valid. This book observes the new, botanically correct nomenclature. Only in occasional instances is a plant listed under an older synonym, namely in the case of plants where the correct name is not yet commonly used by botanists themselves, or where it has not become an accepted term and the reader might have trouble finding the plant in the index. Of the many synonyms (often a plant has more than twenty) the book lists only the commonest ones, generally those used by nurserymen.



Some of the requirements of the various plants are indicated in this book by the following symbols:

Water

- ▭ – light watering; let the soil dry thoroughly before further watering
- ▭ – moderate watering; let the soil dry, but not completely, before further watering
- ■ – liberal watering; keep the soil evenly moist, the roots may be permanently in water

Light

- ○ – light-loving plant, tolerates direct sunlight
- ◑ – grow in a lightly shaded spot
- ● – tolerates permanent shade

Heat
°C

– only the approximate lower and upper limits necessary for the successful cultivation of the illustrated species are given; if a plant requires radically different temperature during the course of the year the temperature limits for the respective season are given with the following symbols:

**S** – summer
**W** – winter

# PICTORIAL SECTION

# FERNS AND SELAGINELLAS

# *Asplenium nidus*

## Bird's Nest Fern

Because of their inimitable beauty, ferns are favourite house plants. Unfortunately most do not tolerate sun or direct light, both of which are usually plentiful in modern households. For this reason it is necessary to select species that are epiphytes in the wild and thus are accustomed not only to ample light but also to occasional lack of moisture or decreased atmospheric humidity.

*Asplenium nidus* is a member of a genus numbering some 700 species. The illustrated species grows as an epiphyte in the tropics throughout the whole of the eastern hemisphere, from India to Australia, and makes a perfect house plant.

The shape of asplenium indicates that it makes the most of all the available rainwater when growing in the wild. The rosette of fronds captures not only life-giving humus but also directs rainwater straight down to the roots. Since the plant obviously likes water, when asplenium is used as a house plant, the root ball should never be allowed to dry out, be it grown as an epiphyte on a trunk (keep in mind, however, that the fronds may reach a length of 1 m [1 yd]), or in the traditional manner in a flower pot using a potting compost (see p. 22). Aspleniums appreciate a warm atmosphere and frequent misting of the foliage. Feeding is the same as for other epiphytes: organic fertilizers in ten per cent concentration should be applied during the growing period, in other words from spring until early autumn.

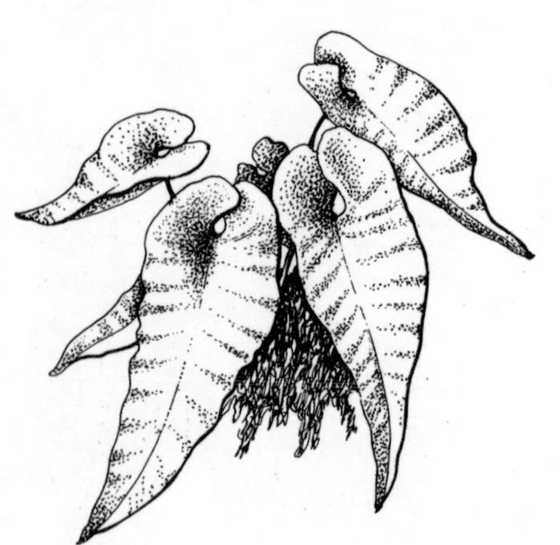

*Asplenium cardiophyllum* is a rare, small fern from Taiwan and Hainan

  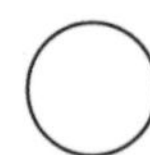 10–30°C

# *Cyrtomium falcatum*

## Fishtail Fern

The illustrated species is native to south-east Asia, its range extending from India to China where it grows at elevations of up to 1,000 m (3,200 ft), in other words on the boundary between tropical and subtropical conditions. It is also frequently found on the slopes of mountains by the sea.

The rather stiff fronds indicate that the fern tolerates a dry atmosphere for brief periods. Every application of water, however, is to the good, and it should thus be sprayed over as frequently as possible. It has no special light requirements and will even tolerate diffused light. The compost should be light and composed of peat, loam, sand, rotted wood dust and beech leaves, or one of the soilless composts. It should never be allowed to dry out. For this reason it is recommended to grow cyrtomium in a plastic pot which allows less water to evaporate than a clay one. Place the pot in a larger dish filled with peat, which should be kept continually damp, thus providing the plant with the moisture it requires. The peat also increases the atmospheric moisture in the room. Feed should be applied only during the growing period. Use organic fertilizers in the concentration recommended by the manufacturer.

This fern need not be transplanted every year. Instead, remove one-third of the compost in the pot and replace it with some fresh mixture, as above.

Although cyrtomium is a typical geophytic fern (one that grows on the ground), it also does well when planted in a peat mixture in a hollow log. This is more attractive than a pot, for a fern always teams up well with natural wood. It thrives also in a 'dry spot' in the paludarium, where it can be plunged in the soil together with the pot.

The related Chinese species *Cyrtomium caryotideum,* which unfortunately is not found amongst cultivated plants, tolerates far more light and a drier atmosphere indoors.

*Doryopteris palmata* from tropical America grows to a height of approximately 25 cm (10 in)

   10–20°C

# *Drynaria fortunei*

Members of the genus *Drynaria* are among the loveliest of the epiphytic ferns. They have the deeply incised fronds that are typical of ferns, an interesting biology, and are furthermore excellent for growing indoors.

The illustrated *Drynaria fortunei* is indigenous to the mountain forests of south-east Asia, where it is found at elevations of 500 to 1,200 m (1,600 to 4,000 ft). It generally grows in the forks of branches but is often found also on entirely smooth trunks. The appressed sterile leaves, which have a beautiful form (they resemble oak leaves but are naturally much larger), capture humus as well as moisture. The fertile leaves, up to 40 cm (16 in) long, are firm and somewhat leathery. In cultivation, where it is provided with much better conditions than in the wild (it is not as affected by temperature fluctuations and periods of drought), the leaves are often up to 75 cm ($2^1/_2$ ft) long.

Like asplenium, drynaria also tolerates more sunlight than most ferns. It benefits from occasional syringing, but the leaves will not dry up without it. However, if the compost (a light mixture of peat, sand, charcoal, crushed pine bark and beech leaves) dries out for a lengthy period then the fern will lose several fronds. Cultivation is the same as for *Asplenium nidus*.

If you have ample room and decide to grow plants on a large epiphyte trunk you can use ferns of the genus *Pseudodrynaria*, generally represented in collections by the species *P. coronans*, which grows to a height of 140 cm (4 ft 8 in). Its thick, dark green leaves are truly magnificent. Pseudodrynaria also grows very well in the ground; for this purpose use a hollow log filled with a rather coarse epiphytic mixture.

The conditions for growing drynarias are achieved in glass plant-cases. However, they also thrive in conservatories, where they have ample fresh air, and excellent results may be obtained in the home.

*Alsophila glauca*, a tree fern, growing to a height of 15 m (50 ft) in southern Asia, is better suited to the larger glasshouse even at the juvenile stage

   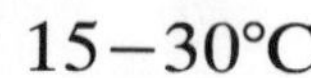

# Platycerium coronarium

*Platycerium* is another genus of epiphytic ferns. It is a well known subject of florist shop windows, which, unfortunately, usually display only the single species *P. bifurcatum,* one that is generally mistaken for the similar *P. alcicorne* 'Hillii'. It is one of the hardiest species of the entire genus, but the requirements of other platyceriums are often greatly exaggerated. All platyceriums do well in the home, but they must be grown as epiphytes. *P. bifurcatum,* however, also does well in pots and that is why it became so popular with nurserymen, who prefer this method of growing plants.

Approximately 17 species of platyceriums are found in the tropics of the Old World. The illustrated species, native to Malaya, is one of the large ones. If grown as a house plant, its leaves normally attain a length of 1.5 m (5 ft). That is why it can be used only in larger epiphytic arrangements, where it forms a magnificent feature. Also commonly cultivated are *P. angolense* from equatorial Africa, and *P. grande* from the warmest parts of Asia and Australia.

Cultivation is the same for all, preferably on large plates of cork oak bark or on epiphyte trunks. Attach them in place together with a ball of light epiphytic compost, which will supply the shortened rhizome with sufficient moisture and facilitate rooting. As for feeding, putting an occasional handful of beech leaves or compost behind the sterile leaves that are pressed to the substrate will suffice. Care consists mainly of spraying the leaves lightly with water; the fern will respond with lush, healthy growth.

Propagation is the same as for other ferns – by means of spores sown on the surface of moist, sterile peat. Spores are formed in sporangia – brown or rust-coloured spots edging the underside of the leaves or else clustered in variously shaped formations. In the illustrated species they form a rusty-brown, kidney-shaped patch at the base of the fertile leaves.

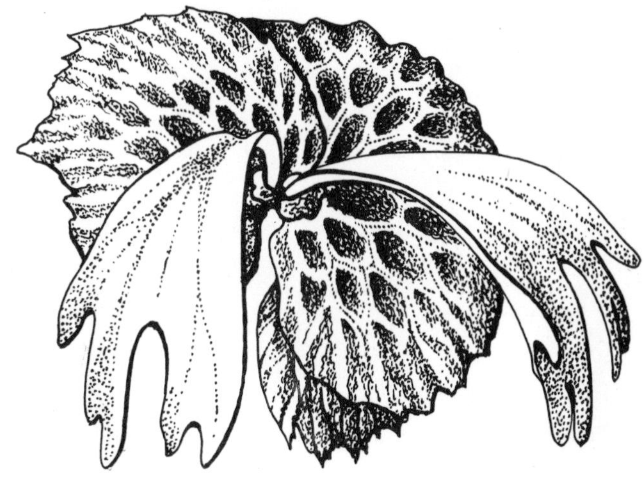

  15–30°C

*Platycerium madagascariense* is a small and very decorative species cultivated, alas, only rarely

# *Polypodium aureum*

## Hare's-foot Fern

Looking at the illustration many will have the feeling they have seen this species before. This may be so, for it is commonly grown by nurserymen and its foliage is often added to bouquets of precious flowers such as orchids. Besides, this striking fern may be found in every botanical garden and is not likely to pass unnoticed.

It is native to tropical America. In the mountain forests where daily mists are the rule it has plenty of moisture. That is also why the stout rhizome, thickly covered with scales, trails over the bare bark of trees without drying out. Indoors, of course, it is difficult to keep atmospheric moisture at the required level and so it is recommended to attach the fern to a ball of moss or epiphytic compost which is kept watered. The fronds tolerate a dry atmosphere; however, they will benefit by occasional syringing. The fern can also be used in a dish arrangement, the rhizome being placed on the surface of the compost with some moss, and perhaps also sand, underneath.

Like other epiphytic ferns this one is also comparatively tolerant of fairly strong light. This, of course, does not mean it should be placed in a southern window, but it does well in partial shade and does not mind morning or late afternoon sun.

*Polypodium aureum* (Syn. *Pleopeltis aureum*) is striking when grouped together with other small epiphytic ferns, such as members of the Asiatic genus *Pyrrosia*.

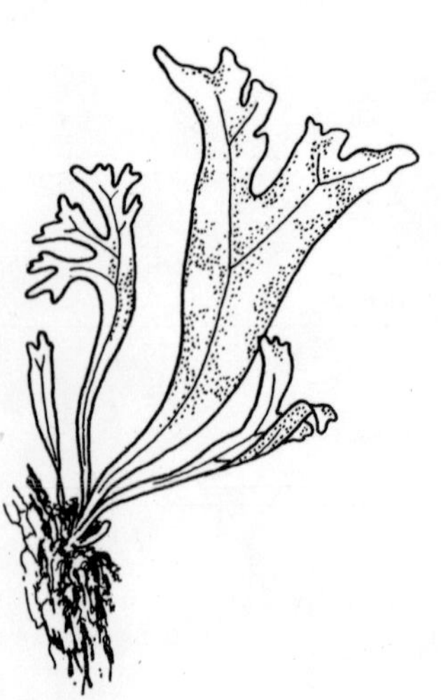

*Polypodium polycarpon* 'Grandiceps' may be used as a small, undemanding fern in epiphytic arrangements in warm surroundings

  10–30°C

# *Pteris cretica* 'Albo-lineata'

## Variegated Table Fern

This fern with pinnate fronds is one of the commonest to be seen in the florist's window, for it is a tried and tested species that thrives in most homes.

The type species, which differs from the illustrated cultivar only by having entirely green leaves, grows in the subtropical and tropical countries of the whole world. It may be found in the forests of south-east Asia in the mist belt approximately 1,000 m (3,300 ft) above sea level, as well as on the southern and eastern slopes of cliffs in the Mediterranean region, where it grows together with xerophilous plants. This in itself is evidence of the great adaptability of the species. At the same time, data on the climate of its original habitats point to the need for cooler overwintering. This, however, is not required by the cultivar 'Albolineata' which likes a winter temperature of about 18 to 22°C (65 to 72°F).

Pteris should be planted in a mixture of humus, peat and sand (or one of the soilless composts), best of all in flat ceramic dishes which permit an arrangement containing several other plants. In such an arrangement the fern's delicate green coloration as well as the interesting shape of its fronds make an attractive display. Keep in mind, however, that it requires partial shade and permanent moisture so that it may be combined only with plants that have similar requirements. It does well in demijohns and fishbowls, which, thanks to its moderate light requirements, may be placed as permanent decoration on a large table or other such place.

Perhaps no other fern can be propagated as easily as pteris. The spores are arranged in clusters edging the underside of the leaves. When ripe they look like dark powder, which may be sown in dishes containing sterilized peat. When the first green leaf-like discs (prothalluses) appear shortly after, the dishes should be moved to a light spot and as soon as the seedlings begin to develop they should be pricked out. This fern has a rapid rate of growth; when fully grown it is approximately 20 cm (8 in) high.

The related species *P. ensiformis* from tropical Asia, and *P. longifolia* and *P. muricata* from tropical America have like requirements, but need somewhat more atmospheric moisture.

*Polypodium ciliatum*

   15–25°C

# *Selaginella tamariscina*

Most of the nearly 700 known species of selaginellas grow in the damp twilight of subtropical and tropical forests. They are also to be found, of course, in the forests of central Europe and some species exhibit quite atypical behaviour: in the southern United States of America and Mexico, for example, at higher elevations (above 1,000 to 1,500 m [3,300 to 5,000 ft]) one may encounter *Selaginella lepidophylla* (resurrection plant), which grows in partly shaded as well as sunny locations where dry periods lasting several months are quite common. The plant effectively counteracts this by curling into a tight ball that 'comes to life' with the first rains (this is known as hydrochasia).

The illustrated *S. tamariscina* is native to the forests of China, where it grows in the damp undergrowth. Only rarely is it encountered in cultivation, even though it is one of the loveliest species and is no more difficult to grow than the others.

It should be planted in dishes containing a mixture of peat, loam and sand. Because of their high humidity requirements, selaginellas are particularly well suited for growing in demijohns, fishbowls, aquaterrariums and glass plant-cases, where they do well even in places with poor light. There is no need to worry that other plants will suffer from their presence for they have a very shallow root system and are low growing. The illustrated species, for example, reaches a height of 5 to 15 cm (2 to 6 in). The nurseryman will doubtless also have other species suitable for growing indoors, such as *S. emmeliana*, *S. martensii* and *S. pallescens*.

At home selaginellas can be propagated only by vegetative means. Many species have branches that rest on the surface of the soil and root along their entire length. All that needs to be done is to cut off such a rooted portion and grow it separately. Another possible method is by cuttings – broken off 'branches' which are inserted in peat.

*Selaginella lepidophylla*

  10–25°C

# FOLIAGE PLANTS

# *Acalypha wilkesiana* 'Musaica'

## Beefsteak Plant

This species is native to the South Sea Islands, where it grows to a height of approximately 2.5 m (8 ft). The leaves are a lovely coppery-green, in the botanical species mottled with red and crimson. The flowers are insignificant. This species is not often cultivated in the home. More widely grown is the related chenille plant – *Acalypha hispida* – an evergreen shrub with long (up to 50 cm [20 in]), drooping, red (occasionally creamy), tassel-like spikes of flowers.

Also grown indoors are several lovely cultivars, most commonly 'Musaica' shown in the illustration. Others include 'Marginata' with large, olive-brown leaves edged with pink; 'Miltoniana' with drooping green leaves edged with white; 'Obovata' with obovate leaves coloured olive edged with orange in the juvenile stage, later copper edged with crimson; and 'Godseffiana' with green leaves edged with cream.

It is hard to understand why this species tends to be bypassed by European nurseries. Anyone who has been to the tropics has seen *Acalypha wilkesiana* planted in public parks as well as being used as a potted plant; there it belongs to the basic assortment. If a home is sufficiently warm and light then there is no need to fear failure. The plant does not need a winter rest period and will do well if its basic requirements are satisfied.

The compost should be as nourishing as possible, a mixture of loam, compost, rotted turves, sand and peat would be ideal. Feed should be applied weekly during the entire growth period, for the plant needs a rich diet. It will also benefit from frequent syringing. It stands up well to pruning so there is no need to fear that it will get out of hand. Acalypha is often attacked by white fly and so it is recommended to take the proper preventive measures.

Propagation is by tip cuttings inserted in a mixture of peat and sand in a warm propagator.

*Breynia nivosa*

  10–30°C

# *Aglaonema commutatum* 'Treubii'

## Ribbon Aglaonema

Aglaonemas are not only some of the loveliest but also the hardiest of house plants. More than forty species grow wild in south-east Asia and the Malay Archipelago, mostly in the undergrowth of the evergreen tropical forests on a thick layer of humus formed by decaying leaves. They often form part of the vegetation bordering forest streams and are also found at the edge of the forest, but mostly they are plants that do extremely well in the permanent shade of taller vegetation.

Aglaonemas are considered extraordinarily beautiful plants even in their native south Asian home, and not just the variegated species. *Aglaonema simplex,* for example, is grown for decoration even in the most primitive of homes and *Aglaonema costatum* may be seen in practically every city and airport in south-east Asia.

The most generally available at garden centres are the variegated species, such as the one shown in the illustration or the old cultivar 'White Rajah', incorrectly designated *A. pseudobracteatum.* Magnificent is the small *A. costatum* which is dark green with a white midrib and white blotches. Those with plenty of room can grow *A. crispum,* up to one metre high with large greyish zones alongside the midrib. The illustrated species from Java generally grows to a height of 50 cm (20 in) indoors (up to 1 m [3 ft]) in the wild and the leaves are 25 to 30 cm (10 to 12 in) long.

Cultivation is simple. A mixture of peat and sand, with a possible addition of leaf mould, is sufficient. Bowls are preferable to taller containers. The plants are readily propagated by tip or stem cuttings.

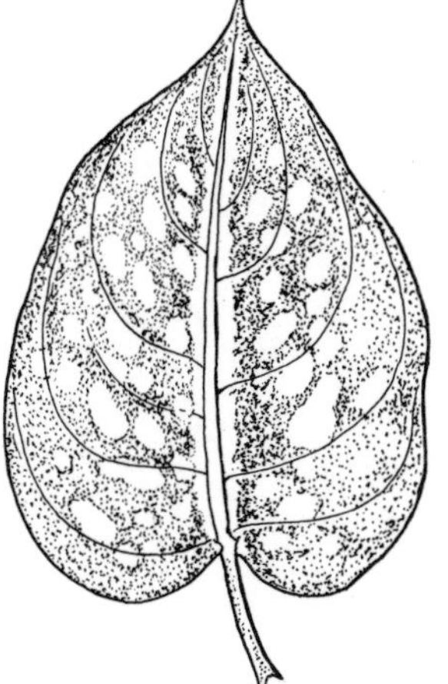

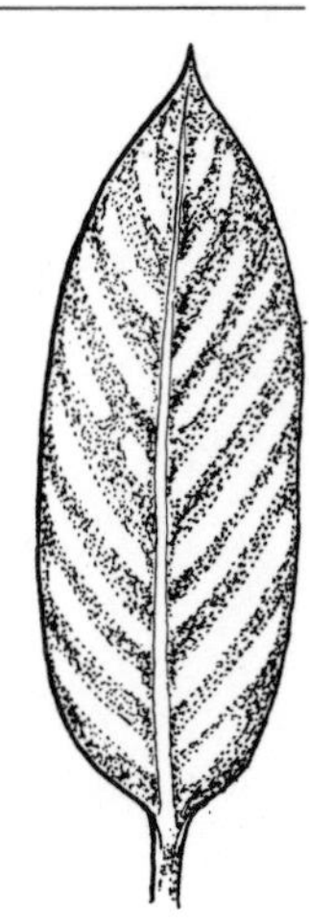

  15–30°C

*Aglaonema costatum* is one of the smallest and prettiest variegated species of this large genus

*Aglaonema oblongifolium* 'Curtisii' grows extremely well in terrariums

# Alocasia korthalsii

It is hard to say why some attractive plants have not become popular or widely cultivated by growers. Perhaps because it is thought their cultivation is difficult and yet often a single try leads to unexpected success.

Alocasias belong to this group. Most are rather robust but there are also some quite small and attractive species that can be used in any household.

The illustrated *A. korthalsii* (syn. *A. thibautiana*) is indigenous to Borneo. It grows to a height of about 50 cm (20 in). The leaf blades, which are about 30 cm (1 ft) long, are patterned greyish-white on a glossy, olive-green background. The well-known *A. micholitziana* from the Philippines attains about the same height. The leaves are approximately 40 to 50 cm (16 to 20 in) long, with a dentate sinuate margin, the midrib and other principal veins being coloured white. It is very similar to the cultivar 'Amazonica', for which it is often mistaken. Perhaps the most beautifully coloured of the alocasias is *A. cuprea* which has oval shield-shaped leaves about 35 cm (14 in) long with a pronounced metallic sheen; the basic colour is coppery-green, the underside being deep purplish-violet (in the juvenile form a coppery deep-pink).

For those who are looking for robust plants for the conservatory, to put beside a pool in the greenhouse, or for a large indoor paludarium or dish arrangement there is also a wide choice, for example *Alocasia odora, A. macrorhiza* (green), *A. indica* 'Metallica' (leaves have a metallic reddish-violet tinge). These all grow to a height of 1 to 2 m (3 to 6 ft), *A. macrorhiza* even 4 m (13 ft).

Alocasias are particularly well suited to the warmth of modern homes. They should be put in a good rich compost such as John Innes potting compost No. 2 and fed regularly during the growth period. Some species have a dormant stage in winter when they drop some of their leaves, but they do not demand dry conditions. Propagation is simple – either by means of seeds or by cutting up the stem and rooting it in a warm propagator.

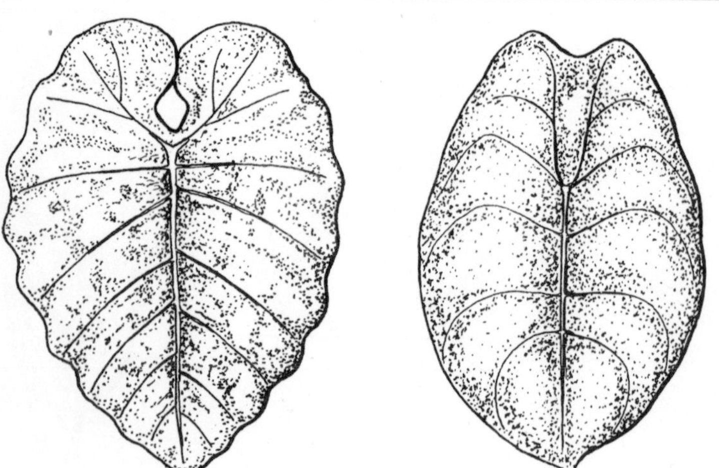

*Alocasia macrorhiza* is a hardy house plant; however, older specimens reach a height of 2 m (6 ft)

*Alocasia cuprea* with its glossy, coppery leaves is one of the most attractive members of this genus. However, it does not tolerate a dry atmosphere

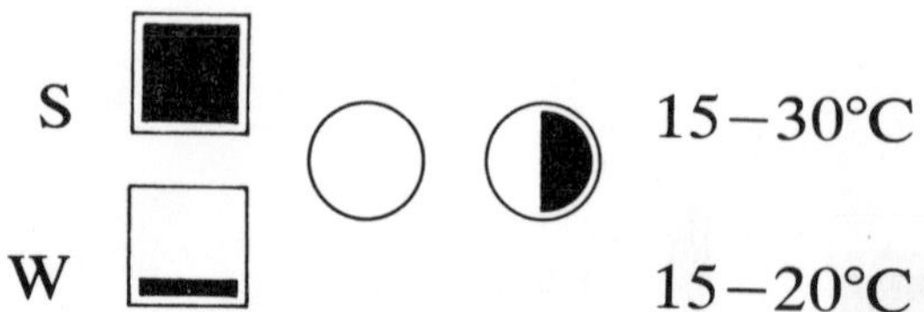

# *Anthurium magnificum*

One would be hard put to find a plant that is more attractive, exotic and at the same time simply ideal for the modern home than *Anthurium magnificum*. The fears of growers acquainted with this species in botanical gardens that they could not possibly satisfy the plant's high requirements have proved to be groundless. Modern, light, centrally heated homes meet the needs of this plant far better than a greenhouse and it will readily attain its fullest beauty.

There are approximately 550 species of anthurium and they are found chiefly in Central and South America. The illustrated species from Colombia grows on steep rock faces. The leaf blades, which may be more than 60 cm (2 ft) long, would often touch the substrate on level ground and thus be exposed to the danger of rotting. That is why if this, or another large-leaved anthurium, is used in a larger arrangement, dish or paludarium it should be put in an elevated spot, such as on a hollow stump, where, as an added bonus, it makes a striking feature.

Very like the illustrated species is *Anthurium crystallinum*, with only slightly smaller leaves, oval leaf stalk, and different, but not particularly attractive, flowers. Several other species, for example *A. forgetii*, *A. leuconeurum* and *A. regale*, also have veins of a contrasting colour and heart-shaped or shield-shaped leaves. The beautiful *A. warocqueanum* has leaves more than a metre (a yard) long but only about 25 cm (10 in) across at the widest point, terminated by a long, tapering point and coloured dark velvety green with silvery veins. *A. veitchii* has equally long leaves, which, though they are entirely green, are marked crosswise with prominent corrugations. These are only a few of the many anthuriums with ornamental foliage. Except for the first two, however, they are rather delicate and better suited to large indoor plant-cases.

Anthuriums should be grown in a compost consisting of peat, sand, and loam with bits of rotting wood or rotted wood dust. Alternatively, use one of the soilless composts. The simplest method of propagation is by sowing the seeds on the surface of a peat and sand mixture in a warm and moist propagator.

*Anthurium tetragonum* is an epiphyte, like most of the rosette-forming members of this genus

*Anthurium veitchii*

15–25°C

# *Aphelandra squarrosa* 'Louisae'

## Zebra Plant

If plants are divided according to their attractive features, such as foliage, flowers, stems, there are bound to be certain anomalies. Even foliage plants produce flowers and sometimes, as in this case, very pretty ones. Nevertheless, the chief value of aphelandra lies in the variegated leaves which make an attractive display throughout the year.

Some 150 species of aphelandra, which grow wild in the subtropical and tropical regions, have been described to date. Most are subshrubs or robust herbaceous plants growing in rich humus at the edge of tropical forests in the shade of shrubs. The flowers, coloured yellow, orange or red, are usually covered with large, often attractively coloured bracts.

The flower spikes of the illustrated species are up to 15 cm (6 in) long; the flowers, coloured pale yellow, are barely half as long as the bracts, which are also pale yellow with a green centre. The related variety *leopoldii* has deep yellow bracts with toothed margins, much paler flowers and broader leaves. Often cultivated as well is the hybrid of the two subspecies 'Fritz Prinsler', which is smaller and flowers more reliably than the parent plants.

A similar species, *Aphelandra liboniana* has leaves with a single white median line, bracts coloured deep orange and arranged in four rows, and small yellow flowers. *A. aurantiaca roezlii* from Mexico has pale green leaves with silvery markings and deep orange-red flowers. Most species flower in late summer and autumn.

Aphelandras are fairly sensitive to a dry atmosphere and so if they are to be grown successfully over a long period they do best in an indoor plant-case or glasshouse. Even then, they should not only be watered liberally but the foliage should be syringed frequently. The growing medium should be a mixture of peat, loam and sand. In spring older plants should be cut back so that they will put out numerous new shoots and will continue to have leaves from the base. This is a good time also for propagating the plants, either by tip cuttings or by means of leaves with one eye, but in the latter case it takes longer for them to develop. They are also readily multiplied from seed.

*Ruttya scholsei*

  15–25°C

# *Asparagus falcatus*

## Sickle Thorn

The name asparagus generally brings to mind a sprig of the delicate, green *A. plumosus* or *A. sprengeri* added to a bouquet of flowers purchased at the florist's. This, of course, is a very limited view and if it were to be observed by the grower then the selection of attractive plants for indoor cultivation would also be greatly narrowed. The reader may be unaware of the fact but the genus *Asparagus* contains some 300 species, some of which are extraordinarily lovely and far from mere 'supplementary greenery'. The 'leaves' of asparagus are not true leaves, for these are atrophied and generally form only membranous scales from the axils of which rise phylloclades resembling leaves.

The illustrated species is native to tropical Asia and Africa, where it grows in thin, open forests. It is a climber, reaching a length of 15 m (50 ft) and in the wild it climbs over the surrounding vegetation. The phylloclades are up to 10 cm (4 in) long, the leaf scale is furnished with a thick spine. The stem branches greatly so that the plant soon fills the space around it. There is no need, however, to be taken aback by the data of the length to which the plant grows; that applies to adult specimens many years old that were not kept in check by pruning. Nevertheless, it is recommended to grow this asparagus in a conservatory or a large room because its beauty shows off to best advantage if the plant has ample space.

Many other, mostly smaller species are cultivated which the grower can choose from. Particularly lovely is *A. sprengeri* 'Meyerii', bushy like a fox tail, and only recently introduced to the market. Only the well-known *A. plumosus,* a fine asparagus from South Africa with branches that are arranged to give a layered appearance, is not very well suited for indoor cultivation because it does not tolerate a dry atmosphere.

Asparagus may be propagated by division or by seed, which should never be fully covered nor unduly shaded.

Cultivation is relatively easy. The potting compost should be relatively heavy, rich in humus and well fertilized. John Innes potting compost No. 2 or No. 3, depending on the size of the pot, would be ideal. Feed should be applied frequently during the growth period. Many species require at least a partial resting period with limited watering in winter.

*Asparagus sprengeri* 'Meyerii'

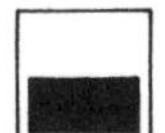  10–25°C

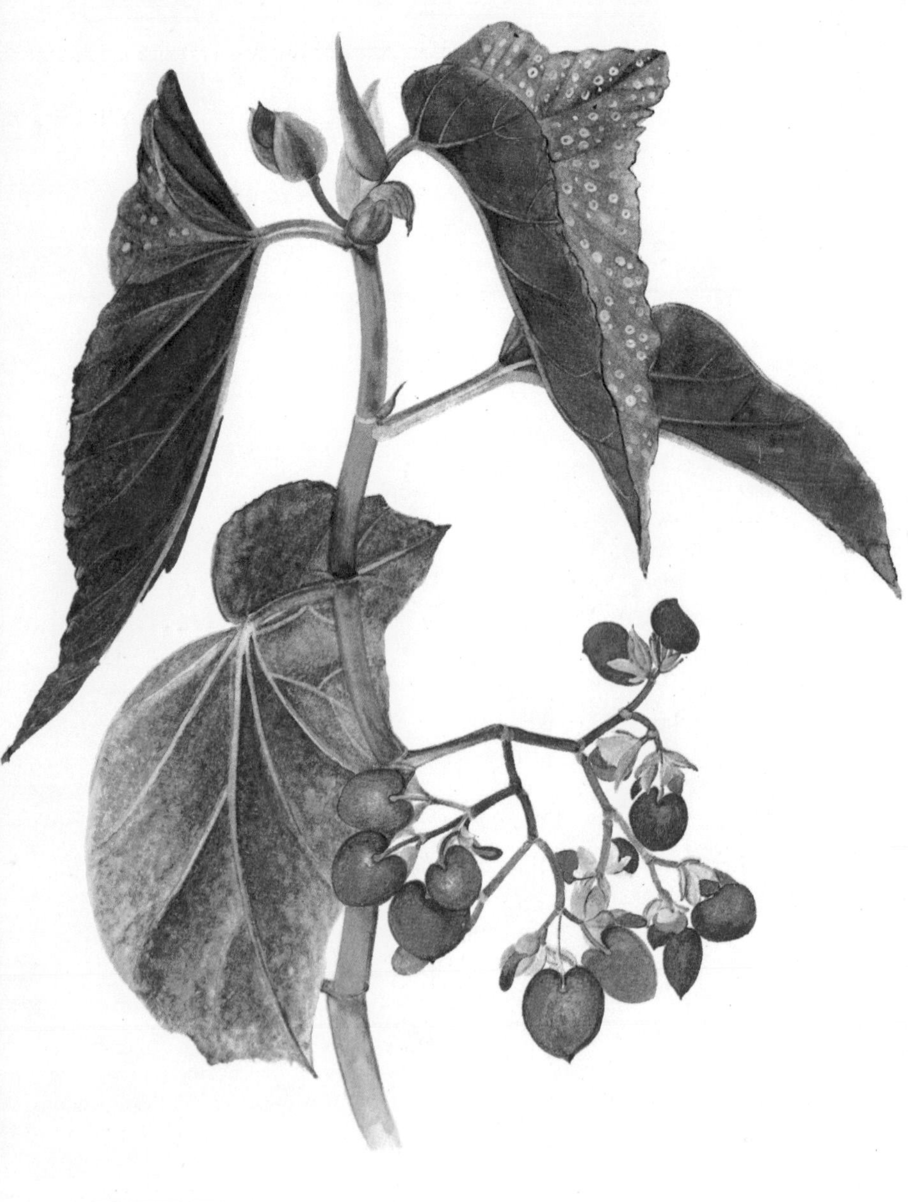

# *Begonia × corallina* 'Lucerna'

The subtropical and tropical regions of Africa, America and Asia are the home of some 1,000 species of begonias, which grow at sea level in lowlands up to elevations of 4,000 m (13,500 ft). The large majority grow in deep shade, in the undergrowth of the tropical rain forests or on shaded wet rocks. This, of course, does not rule out exceptions. *Begonia veitchii* grows in Peru at elevations of more than 3,000 (10,000 ft) in crevices on sunny rocks the same as *B. michoacanensis* from Mexico; the latter furthermore requires heavy, compacted laterite soil. In general it may be said that begonias, particularly the cultivated forms, are shade-loving plants and require an acidic compost that is permanently and adequately moist.

*Begonia* x *corallina* 'Lucerna' is living proof that the old tried and tested hybrids should not be forgotten. It was raised in the early 19th century by crossing either *B. corallina* and *B.* 'Madame Charrat' or *B. corallina* and *B. teuscheri.* It reaches a height of 2 m (6 ft), is nicely branched, and in ideal conditions the leaf blade may be up to 35 cm (14 in) long. The large, drooping, coral-red male flowers which last for a long time, make a magnificent display.

Begonia is suitable for indoor plant-cases and also for demijohns. Particularly good are the small and rare species such as *Begonia paulensis, B. rajah, B. imperialis* 'Smaragdina', *B. acida,* and *B. masoniana* 'Iron Cross'.

Cultivation is not difficult. The growing medium should consist of peat with an addition of sand, enriched by a little compost, or John Innes potting compost No. 1.

Propagation is also simple – by stem cuttings or leaves. Insert the leaf stalks in a peat and sand mixture where they will root rapidly; even a piece of leaf blade containing some of the main veins can be used – place it on the surface of the same mixture in a warm and moist environment.

*Begonia heracleifolia*

*Begonia herbacea*

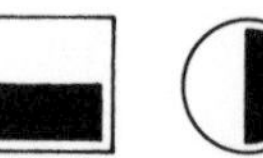

10–25°C

# *Bertolonia maculata*

Many plants, even though truly magnificent, have not yet been 'discovered' by home growers and continue to be only permanent fixtures in botanical gardens. This is true of the illustrated species and, in fact, the whole genus *Bertolonia.* To date nine species have been noted growing in the wild in South America, chiefly Brazil and Ecuador, where they are to be found on the forest floor, in the shade of undergrowth, as well as beside streams both in the humus layer of soil and on the rotting trunks of fallen forest giants, together with selaginellas and mosses.

The two species generally found in botanical gardens as well as private collections are the illustrated *B. maculata* and *B. marmorata,* which is also small, barely 10 to 15 cm (4 to 6 in) high, but has a less hairy stem, leaves that are shortly-elliptical rather than shortly-oval and hairy only on the margins. The flowers are coloured purple. More commonly encountered, however, are the hybrids of the two (for bertolonias interbreed readily), and these exhibit marked diversity. An extremely handsome but rare species is *B. pubescens,* which has leaves covered with long white hairs and marked with a brown stripe between the midrib and adjoining vein.

Frequently cultivated are hybrids between the genera *Bertolonia* and *Sonerila* designated as x *Bertonerila.* Commonest of these is x *Bertonerila houtteana,* about 30 cm (1 ft) high with dark green leaves veined purple and coloured purple on the underside.

Bertolonias should be grown in a mixture of peat, sand, rotted wood dust and crushed charcoal or one of the soilless composts. They also do well on rotting pieces of wood covered with sphagnum moss. High atmospheric moisture is a must and for this reason the plant is ideal for growing in demijohns. Propagation is by seeds sown on the surface of the compost.

*Sonerila margaritacea* is good for demijohns and smaller plant-cases; it can be grown successfully in a light compost containing rotted wood dust and crushed charcoal

   15–30°C

# *Caladium* (Bicolor-Hybrids)

Caladiums have belonged to the basic assortment of foliage plants for years. They have only one drawback, namely that the magnificent leaves appear in spring and die back in late autumn for a period of winter rest. Inasmuch as in the wild they inhabit the banks of tropical rivers that dry out in winter the tubers should be put in a warm and dry place for the winter. However, they must not dry out altogether and thus should be stored in dry sand or peat in a warm room until spring. In late February the tubers should be put in a mixture of peat, loam and sand and watered thoroughly. When growth has started the compost must never be allowed to dry out. In summer the plants should be fed regularly. Nitrogen fertilizers should be limited in the case of cultivars that have large white patches on the leaves for otherwise these turn green.

Caladiums grown as house plants are generally hybrids obtained by crossing *Caladium bicolor* from the Amazon region with other species such as *C. schomburgkii* and *C. picturatum*. *C. bicolor* has dark blue-green leaves patterned with randomly scattered white and reddish spots between the veins. Gardening literature lists hundreds of hybrids – all of them beautiful.

The inflorescence, like that of other aroids, consists of a spadix enclosed in a spathe. The female flowers (which are separate from the male flowers) open about a week earlier than the male flowers thus preventing self-pollination. If several plants happen to flower at the same time you can try crossing them at home, simply by transferring the pollen to the female flowers of another specimen. This must be done between 11 a.m. and 4 p.m., otherwise the plant will not be fertilized. The fruit is a many-seeded berry. The seeds germinate on the surface of a peat and sand mixture in a moist and warm propagator within 14 days. Caladiums are more commonly propagated by cutting up tubers when planting them out in late winter. The cut surfaces should be dusted with charcoal.

Because they are warmth- and moisture-loving plants, caladiums are suited for growing in a paludarium or indoor plant-case, but they will also do reasonably well if placed freely in a room.

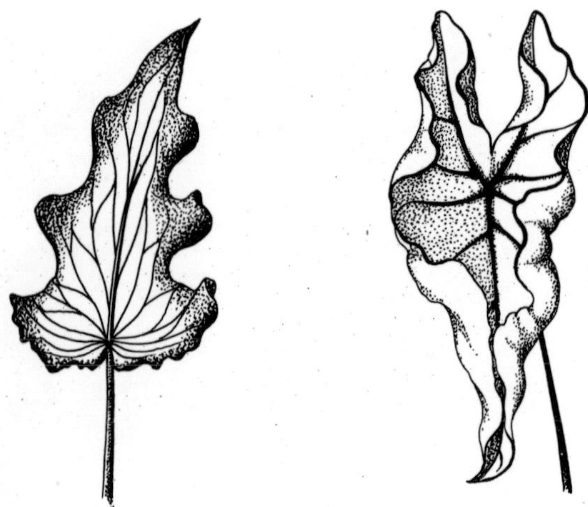

*Caladium sagittifolium*

*Caladium* 'Lord Derby'

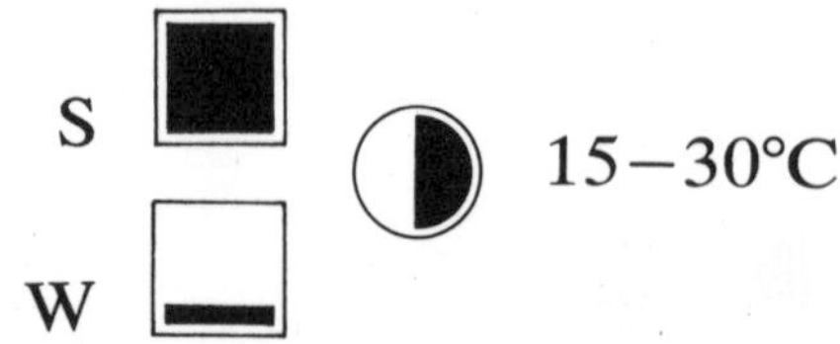

# Calathea × insignis

## (syn.: *C. lancifolia*)
## Rattlesnake Plant

Often the origin of certain cultivated species is not clear or else the parents that gave rise to the hybrids are not definitely known. Such is the case with the illustrated plant which is probably a hybrid. At some time it appeared in collections under an incorrect name and from there found its way into cultivation. The true *Calathea insignis* is not cultivated at all and besides it is a plant that is almost 2 m (6 ft) high with leaves coloured green on both sides. The illustrated calathea barely reaches a height of 60 cm (2 ft) and has beautifully coloured foliage.

Most of the loveliest *Calathea* species appeared in botanical collections in the middle or no later than the end of the 19th century. Despite this they are not often found in shops, in the same way that the related and equally lovely genus *Ctenanthe* is not often seen. The reason is that they are relatively difficult to grow, both as regards cultivation and speed of growth. It takes a very long time for the roots of these plants to fill the pot and to form adequate stores of reserve food in the underground rhizomes. Until then they produce comparatively few and small leaves and not till after do they form nice attractive clumps and become gems of a collection. Furthermore, since they are typical plants of the undergrowth of hot and permanently humid tropical rain forests, mostly in Brazil, they are not always successful indoors, where they find the dry atmosphere uncongenial. Often even frequent spraying does not satisfy their needs and they must be placed in a closed plant-case or glasshouse. Small species also do well in demijohns. Even though they are demanding plants we should not give up when growing them, but try over and over again to achieve success, with which we will usually be rewarded in the end. Often the plant becomes acclimatized and after several years will begin to do well even in a dish arrangement, though it previously showed only slight signs of life. In such cases the grower's patience will truly have been well rewarded.

Use John Innes potting compost No. 1 or a peat-based compost as the growing medium.

*Calathea vittata* *Calathea setosa*

  15–30°C

# *Calathea makoyana*

## Peacock Plant

We have already said that calatheas do best in a glasshouse or plant-case. The growing medium should be a mixture of peat, coarse beech leaf mould that is not fully decomposed, sand, and coarsely crushed charcoal; an addition of rotted wood dust will further improve the compost. Alternatively, one of the peat-based composts would be ideal. The plants do not require a dormant period in winter so that the compost must be kept permanently moist throughout the year. The result of this somewhat laborious care, however, is truly splendid for these plants are living symbols of the lush tropical wilderness. Though not large, reaching a height of only about 50 cm (20 in), the beauty of their coloured markings is truly exceptional.

Your assortment of calatheas may naturally also include species that, for lack of space, are not illustrated here. Very hardy is *Calathea picturata* 'Argentea' with leaves roughly the same shape but coloured silvery-grey in the centre and edged with green, which will last a long time even if placed freely in the room and not in a plant-case. More tender *C. bachemiana* is about 40 cm (16 in) high, with ovate-lanceolate leaves coloured silvery-grey above with dark green bands running forward at an angle from the midrib; also *C. leopardina* with ovate, pointed leaves marked with blackish-green triangular patches placed at right angles to the midrib, and with an attractively sinuate margin. Suitable for large rooms is *C. zebrina,* up to 1 m (3 ft) high, with leaf blades the same length as the leaf stalks, that is about 50 cm (20 in). The leaves are velvety, striped in two shades of green with a deep purple underside.

Calatheas are generally propagated by division, but only after several years so that the roots have plenty of time to fill the pot. If you wish to transplant them, this should also be done only after several years. The plants produce flowers fairly readily and can also be pollinated without difficulty, even at home. Plants grown from seed are generally better adapted to fluctuations in temperature as well as atmospheric moisture.

*Calathea leopardina* *Calathea veitchiana*

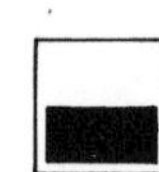  15–30°C

# *Chlorophytum comosum* 'Variegatum'

## Spider Plant

*Chlorophytum comosum* is a plant of our parents' and grand-parents'day but that is no reason why we should not continue to cultivate it, and besides, there are few other such reliable growers. The more than 100 species of this genus are native to the tropics of the Old and New World, where they grow chiefly in the shade of forests alongside water courses in a light soil, rich in humus.

*Chlorophytum comosum* was introduced into cultivation from South Africa in 1850. In the gardening catalogues of that time it is listed also as *Anthericum comosum, Phalangium comosum* and *Cordyline vivipara,* the last name indicating an important characteristic of this species, viviparity, that is producing plantlets at the ends of long runners or rather flower scapes. The plantlets form roots in the air and can be easily separated and grown on in pots.

The type species has green foliage and is about 40 to 50 cm (16 to 20 in) high. Generally cultivated, however, is the cultivar 'Variegatum' striped green and white. Like the type species, it is one of the hardiest of house plants, growing well both in cool as well as warm rooms. It is most attractive planted in a hanging container but may also be put in a dish arrangement. It should be grown in John Innes potting compost No. 1 or 2, depending on its size.

Much more attractive, but at the same time more tender, is *Chlorophytum amaniense* from east Africa with leaf stalks about 10 cm (4 in) long and leaves up to 30 cm (1 ft) long and 8 cm (3 in) across, rather leathery and coloured a beautiful bronze-green. Young leaves are coppery-gold with dark green veins. More commonly grown is *C. capense,* native, as the name indicates, to the Cape Province region of South Africa. The leaves are up to 60 cm (2 ft) long and 4 cm ($1^1/_2$ in) across, with prominent veins; there are also variegated forms that are listed under separate names or collectively as 'Variegata'. These species require much more heat in summer than the illustrated species, otherwise their requirements are similar.

*Dracaena phrynoides*

 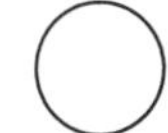  5–20°C

# *Codiaeum* × *variegatum*

## Croton

One of the first things to surprise and impress a visitor to the tropics is the fact that just outside the airport there is practically always a magnificent park and the ornamental shrubs there are almost always crotons – lovely, shrubby plants up to 2 m (6 ft) high with brightly coloured foliage.

These plants, native to the Sunda Islands, southeast Indies, and Malay Archipelago, are great favourites throughout the whole world; and no wonder, for few plants are so variable in shape and colour of the leaves.

All modern cultivars are derived from a single variety of the type species *Codiaeum variegatum pictum.* They are the result of multiple crossing of the frequently occurring form and colour deviations. Cultivars are divided into several groups according to the shape of the leaves. Recommended are 'Imperialis' and 'Clipper' from the oval-leaved group; 'Arthur Howe' from the group with leaves having two side lobes and an elongate middle section; 'Tortilis' and 'Corkscrew' from the group with spirally coiled leaves; and 'Punctatum Aureum' of compact habit with small, narrow leaflets spotted with yellow.

Though gardening books often state that crotons are excellent plants for the modern home and do well in warm rooms, the author's experience, unfortunately, does not back this up. They are ideal plants for a large plant-case, where the necessary humidity can be maintained, but if placed freely in a room they generally do not survive undamaged for more than six months. Naturally there are exceptions and the author himself has seen several nice large crotons in various homes; practically all, however, are solitary specimens that are exceptionally hardy. Crotons should be grown in a peaty substrate with the addition of leaf mould and sand. Propagation is relatively easy by means of tip cuttings in propagators with bottom heat.

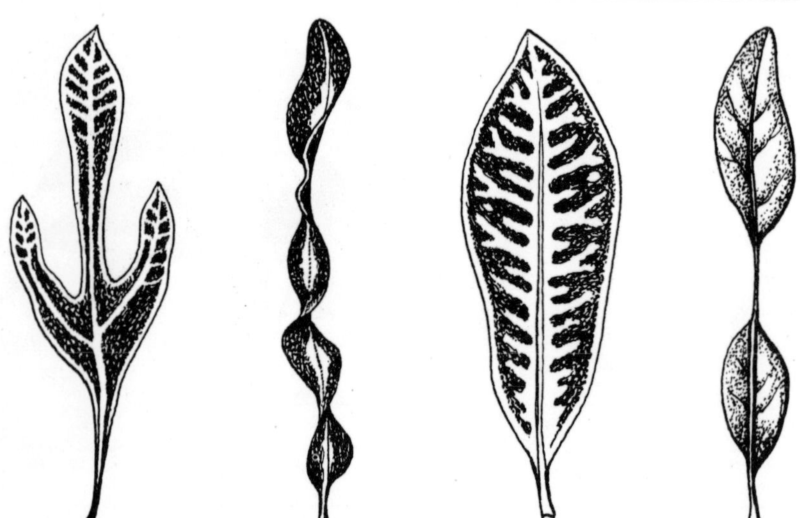

The leaves of various cultivars of *Codiaeum* x *variegatum* (from left to right): 'Disraeli', 'Tortilis', 'L. Staffinger', 'Appendiculatum'

   15–30°C

# *Coleus* (Blumei-Hybrids)

Unlike the preceding genus, hybrids of the genus *Coleus* are models of easy and reliable cultivation and at the same time extremely ornamental plants. If they are provided with full sunlight then success is assured.

The more than 120 species of this genus are native to tropical Africa and Asia where they grow in places exposed to full sun, from sea level to mountain elevations in excess of 1,000 m (3,300 ft). The originally described species *Coleus blumei,* growing in gardens in Java, was probably already a hybrid and not a true botanical species. It was introduced into cultivation around 1850 and about 15 years later in England breeders raised the first cultivars, partly by crossing with other species, partly by selection of seedlings and their back crossing.

The plants are 30 to 80 cm (12 to 32 in) high with angular stems (becoming woody at the base) and leaves extremely variable in both shape and colour, generally softly hairy, often lobed or toothed on the margin. The flowers, which appear in late summer and autumn, have a white upper lip and usually a blue lower lip.

It is very difficult to recommend a particular cultivar for almost all are lovely. Two examples are 'Otto Mann' with brownish-red leaves edged with yellow and 'Bien Venue' with variegated red-yellow foliage, but you can choose what appeals to you most from the wide range offered by your nurseryman or from a catalogue.

In Europe mature plants generally do not overwinter well. It is best to take cuttings in summer and overwinter the young rooted plants at lower temperatures or else overwinter the cuttings in water. The soil should be acidic, best of all a mixture of peat, loam and sand. Feed, however, must be supplied liberally. Coleus also does extemely well in soilless cultivation (hydroponics).

*Coleus* 'Majesty'

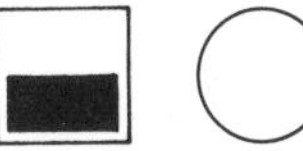  10–25°C

# *Colocasia affinis jenningsii*

## Elephant Ears, Taro

Those who are interested in useful tropical and subtropical plants will doubtless know at least the name of this genus for *Colocasia esculenta* (syn. *C. antiquorum*), or taro, is one of the most important edible plants of Asia and Africa. The tubers contain a large amount of starch and are the source of poi. Particularly well-known for this are the colocasias from Java, Fiji and Hawaii.

The illustrated species grows wild in the East Indies by the edge of lowland swamps. The stems are up to 30 cm (1 ft) long, the leaves usually 15 cm (6 in) long and about 10 cm (4 in) across. The root is a small underground tuber which serves as a storage organ.

Of all the colocasias the illustrated one is perhaps the most delicate but at the same time also the most beautiful. It is well suited to growing in a paludarium in a warm and light room that is not often aired. The ideal place for it is a well-lit aquaterrarium or a glass plant-case, where it must be put in a shallow dish kept permanently filled with water. It is important that it is provided not only with a constant and fairly high temperature but also with constantly high atmospheric moisture, for the leaf margins quickly dry out if the humidity decreases for even a few days.

Much hardier is the previously mentioned *C. esculenta,* which can grow to a height of as much as 1 m (3 ft). The leaves are shield-shaped, up to 70 cm (28 in) long, with a sinuate margin. Similar, and equally large is *C. indica,* which differs by having pronounced veins. Only somewhat larger than the illustrated species is *C. fallax* with velvety leaves that have a metallic blue sheen.

All colocasias should be grown in warm, moist conditions in a peaty compost with a small addition of sand and loam. They must be fed frequently throughout the growing period. Some species drop some of their leaves in winter, the same as alocasias. They are readily propagated by cutting up the tuberous roots or by seeds, which germinate rapidly.

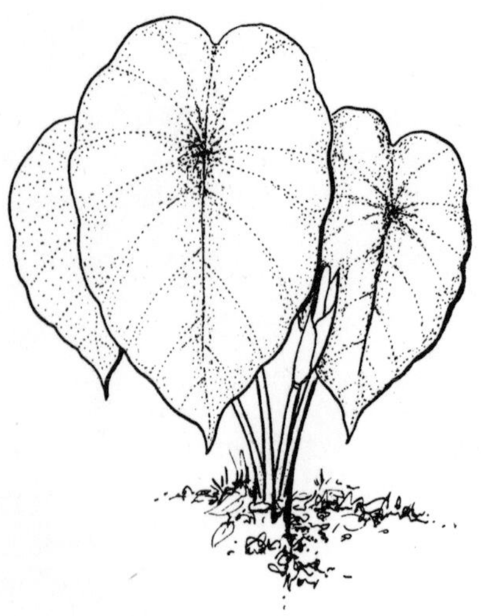

*Homalomena peltata*

    15–30°C

# *Cordyline terminalis* 'Tricolor'

## Tricolored Dracaena

These are well known and commonly cultivated plants, though most, or rather all species excepting *Cordyline terminalis* and its cultivars, are plants for growing in cool rooms, requiring a winter temperature of about 2 to 12°C (36 to 54°F).

There are some 15 to 20 described species distributed in the tropics and subtropics of Asia, Australia and Africa. Only one – *C. dracaenoides* – is found in the tropics of the New World; it grows in Brazil. In the wild cordylines are found either in forest undergrowth (in thin, open forests or more dense, taller thickets), or else growing on steep rock faces, often on cliffs rising from the sea or on rocky ledges by the seaside (*C. australis* grows thus in New Zealand).

The illustrated species is native to the large area extending from India and Pakistan through the Malay Archipelago to north-east Australia and New Zealand. It is one of the smaller members of this genus, for it grows to a maximum height of 2 to 3 m (6 to 10 ft) in the wild. The stem of this subshrub is slender, only about 15 mm (5/8 in) in diameter. The leaves are deep green, lanceolate, up to 50 cm (20 in) long and circa 10 cm (4 in) wide, with prominent midrib. More commonly grown, however, are the cultivated variegated forms, most popular being the illustrated cultivar 'Tricolor'; the small cultivar 'Red edge', which has dark green-bronze leaves edged a bright crimson, is also gaining popularity in recent years.

Cordyline can be used to good effect in dish arrangements as a vertical feature and for its strikingly coloured foliage. It is particularly attractive in large arrangements planted in a group of 3 to 5 specimens.

Cultivars may naturally be propagated only by vegetative means, in this case by root cuttings (a rarely used method). They may also be readily multiplied by tip cuttings or by placing pieces of stem flat on the surface of the compost.

The potting compost must be very nourishing; John Innes No. 3 is particularly suitable.

   10–30°C

*Cordyline australis* grows to a height of 12 m (40 ft) in its native New Zealand

# *Cyanastrum cordifolium*

The Cyanastraceae family is a small and practically unknown group that is most closely related to the spiderwort and lily families. The single genus comprises several African species of herbaceous plants, their common characteristic being a shortened rhizomatous tuber.

The illustrated *Cyanastrum cordifolium* from tropical west Africa is cultivated only occasionally. In the wild it is found in the undergrowth of tropical rain forests, where it grows on a thick layer of humus formed by decayed leaves. Nurseries do not offer this species yet and so it may be obtained only from a botanical garden or private collection. Cultivation, however, is not difficult and we would thus acquire for a centrally-heated home a plant that likes deep shade, and furthermore, tolerates a dry atmosphere very well. In general cyanastrum may be used in very dark corners where usually only *Cissus antarctica* or aspidistra could be grown successfully. Cyanastrum is also very suitable for dish arrangements where its decorative foliage soon forms a lovely, dense, dark green undergrowth which is an excellent foil for the brightness of variegated or attractively coloured cultivars of tropical plants.

The foliage is decorative both by its dark green colour and its striking deep veins. The inflorescence is relatively scant, the individual small pale blue flowers insignificant; despite this the plant is very attractive when in flower.

Cyanastrum should be grown in a mixture of peat and humusy loam and propagated by division.

*Costus igneus*

10–30°C

# *Dieffenbachia* hybr. 'Amoena'

## Dumb Cane

Some hundred years ago a new genus was introduced into cultivation which was to play an important role, but not until much later. It was a native of tropical America and so could be used only in a glasshouse; homes at that time were too dark and cold and the plants did not thrive there. Besides, dieffenbachia was also waiting for 'its time' to come in fashion. And sure enough, the imposing, large, spotted leaves came into their own much later, together with modern architecture, central heating and interior decoration.

The genus *Dieffenbachia* includes some 30 species distributed from the Antilles and Mexico to Peru. The two most important in cultivation are *Dieffenbachia picta* from Brazil and *D. seguina* from the West Indies. The two are very similar and both exhibit marked variability. They are robust plants with a stout stem; the leaves, 3 to 4 times as long as the stalks, which may be up to 20 cm (8 in) long, are coloured green with numerous white or yellow blotches. A reliable identifying characteristic that makes it possible to distinguish between the two species are the leaf stalks: in *D. picta* they are grooved, in *D. seguina* they are flat. Several other species, however, have also been used in hybridization, for example *D. imperialis* from Peru, which has nearly 60-cm-(2-ft)-long stalks and equally long leaves with yellow-green blotches. Another important species used in the first hybridizations was *D. weirii* from Brazil, which is only about 60 cm (2 ft) high with a quantity of white or yellow blotches on the leaves.

Cultivation is easy and almost always successful in the modern home. The compost should be an acid, peaty one. Feed should be applied frequently but in the case of variegated cultivars nitrogen fertilizers should be limited in order to preserve the pale markings (too much nitrogen causes the leaves to turn green). Propagation is also simple. Cut up the stem into pieces about 10 cm (4 in) long, place them flat on the surface in a peat-sand mixture and press them in lightly. The propagator must be kept warm and permanently moist.

*Costus sanguineus* likes a fair amount of light. Other species, such as *C. igneus*, will also tolerate heavy shade if given warm conditions

  15–30°C

# *Dizygotheca elegantissima*

## Spider Aralia, Splitleaf Maple

Members of the Araliaceae family are among the loveliest of foliage plants. Many have yet to find their way into cultivation, for instance the lovely plants of the genus *Trevesia*.

*Dizygotheca elegantissima* (syn. *Aralia elegantissima*) was introduced into cultivation in the late 19th century. The scientific name *'elegantissima'* is fully merited for few plants can boast such airy and 'architecturally' perfect foliage. Its cultivation is not one of the easiest and thus there is never an over-abundance of these plants on the market. It is generally propagated by seed, or by stem cuttings in a warm propagator in summer, or root cuttings in similar conditions in spring.

The illustrated species is from New Caledonia, the same as the other fifteen or so species of this genus, distributed throughout the South Sea Islands. In its native habitat it grows to the size of a small tree but this is far from being the case in Europe, where the largest specimens are only slightly more than 3 m (10 ft) high. The stem is upright and fairly stout, the leaves long-stalked, compound, composed of 7 to 11 leaflets, which are coloured olive-green with a red midrib, the tip and lateral teeth being likewise red. Also cultivated, but only rarely, are other species such as *D. kerchoveana* with broader leaflets, glossy green above and reddish below; *D. veitchii*, with leaflets that have a white midrib and sinuate margin; and its variety *gracillima*, which is only slightly smaller than the type species.

The requirements of *D. elegantissima* are often overestimated. It does very well in a warm and light room. Only very juvenile plants are delicate; these do better in a plant-case but after a time they may be placed freely in a room. The right choice of compost is important; it must be nourishing but light. A mixture of loam, compost, rotted turves, sand and peat is ideal. Alternatively, use John Innes potting compost No. 1. The plant appreciates frequent syringing of the foliage.

*Oreopanax peltatus* (syn. *O. salvinii*)

  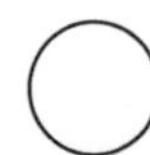 15–25°C

# *Dracaena × deremensis* 'Bausei'

## Corn Plant

Dracaenas are so like cordylines that they are often mistaken for them. One of the several characteristics that distinguish them clearly from the latter are the roots which are not thickened (they are not suitable for propagation) and are either a bright yellow or deep orange inside, whereas the roots of cordylines are white.

Many more species of this genus have been described than is the case with *Cordyline;* as many as 80 have been recorded, distributed in the tropics and subtropics of Asia and Africa. It is also from there that they were introduced into cultivation between the mid-18th and early 19th centuries, with the loveliest shape and colour deviations naturally being selected for further cultivation.

The illustrated cultivar has leaves about 40 cm (16 in) long and 6 cm (2¼ in) wide. Characteristic are the arching leaves; in older plants these are sometimes almost pendant. Also frequently grown is the cultivar 'Warnecki', in which the creamy-white centre is often patterned with longitudinal green stripes of varying width and narrower pale zones at the leaf edges on either side of the main stripe. The type species, up to 5 m (16 ft) high, with green foliage, is very rarely found in cultivation.

The related *D. fragrans,* likewise from tropical Africa, has yielded several attractive forms, for instance 'Massangeana' with green margins to the leaf and a centre striped yellow-green and creamy-white; and 'Lindenii' with leaves that are nearly white with narrow green margins. There are naturally many more.

Also lovely are dracaenas with smaller, long-stalked, oval leaves such as *D. godseffiana* from the Congo with leaves patterned with white, blurred spots; and *D. goldieana* with leaves spotted crosswise.

Dracaenas are among the hardiest of house plants, tolerating the conditions of modern centrally-heated homes as well as colder situations. Cultivation is the same as for cordyline. Propagation is by tip and stem cuttings laid on a peaty-sand compost in a warm and moist propagator.

*Dracaena godseffiana* *Dracaena goldieana*

  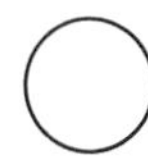 10–30°C

# *Episcia cupreata* 'Silver Sheen'

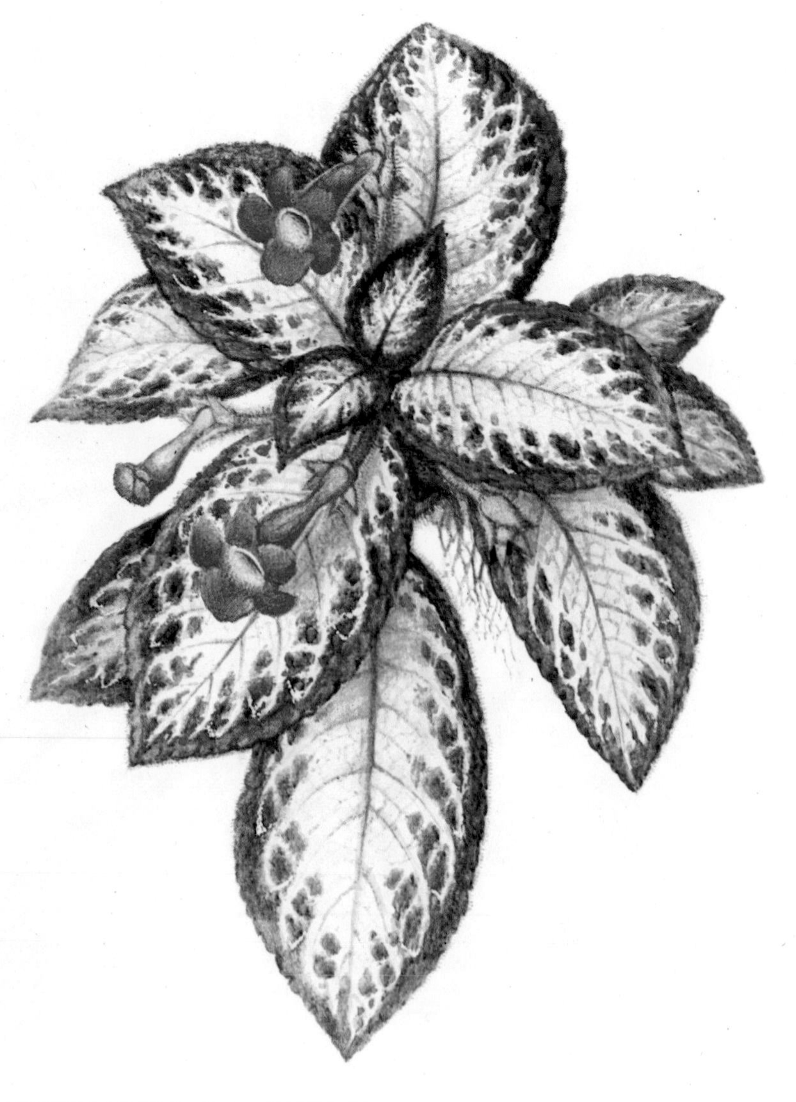

The Gesneriaceae family includes a great many lovely plants such as the popular saintpaulia, sinningia and streptocarpus. Most have attractive foliage, but are grown particularly for their lovely flowers. In the case of episcia it is generally the leaves that are the plant's chief attraction.

The ten or so species that make up the genus grow wild in the Antilles, in Central and in South America. Of these at least half deserve to be included in every collection of decorative plants for they are the prettiest of the small foliage plants.

*Episcia cupreata* is native to Colombia, where it grows on the banks of forest rivers. The leaves are approximately 12 cm (4½ in) long, coppery brownish-green, with a whitish-pink stripe alongside the midrib. The illustrated cultivar was obtained solely by selection from the various forms of the species. *E. reptans* from Colombia and Brazil is a similar species that has olive brownish-green leaves with a pale zone round the midrib and principal veins; the flowers are bright red. Only one species – *E. dianthiflora* from Mexico (now *Alsobia dianthiflora*) – is grown mainly for its flowers, not for its foliage. The leaves are small, only about 4 by 3 cm (1½ by 1 in). The fairly large white flowers (up to 3 cm [1 in] long) have fringed petals the same as some pinks.

It is usually recommended that episcias be grown in hanging containers but they are put to better use in shallow dishes as part of the undergrowth in epiphytic plant-cases, where they can also be put at the base of larger branches. They are also lovely in a demijohn and do well in a terrarium and by the waterside in an aquaterrarium, for which their small size makes them eminently suitable.

Propagation is very simple, either by sowing the tiny seeds on the surface of fibrous peat in a closed propagator, or by detaching the young plantlets produced on the numerous runners. Cultivation is not difficult either. All that is required is a compost such as John Innes potting compost No. 2 and a constantly high atmospheric moisture. The compost must not be allowed to dry out, but spraying the foliage does not really benefit the plants.

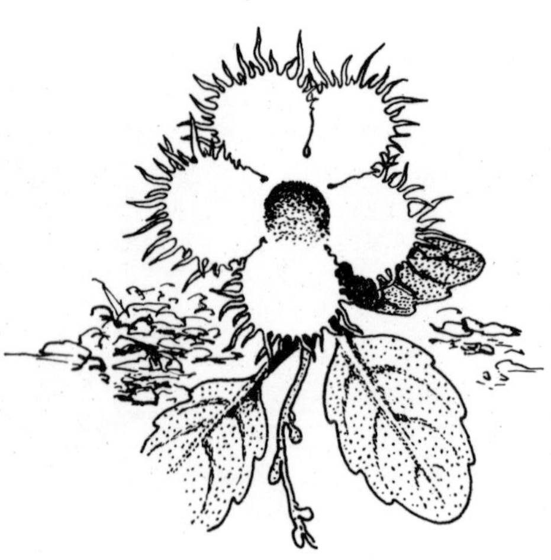

*Episcia dianthiflora* (now *Alsobia dianthiflora*)

  15–25°C

# × *Fatshedera lizei*

## Ivy Tree

If one has a conservatory or other large room that is unheated in winter then the ideal plant to grow successfully is fatshedera. Its heat requirements, in other words cold conditions in winter, are a characteristic inherited from the parent plants – *Hedera helix* and *Fatsia japonica*.

The hybrid was cultivated by Frères Lizé in Nantes in 1912, but it did not become more widely cultivated until some 15 years later. In habit, it is a combination of both parents: the stem is upright, up to 5 m (16 ft) high and covered with rust-coloured powder in the juvenile stage. The leaves are palmate, 3- to 5-lobed, up to 20 cm (8 in) long and nearly 30 cm (1 ft) wide, in other words smaller than those of fatsia. Less common is the cultivar 'Variegata' with partly white leaves.

Cultivation is very simple. It should be grown in John Innes potting compost No. 2 or 3 and should be watered and fed liberally during the growth period. Though the leaves are slightly leathery the plant is much more beautiful if it is syringed regularly.

The only problem is providing it with cold conditions in winter, but even in modern centrally-heated homes one can generally find a cool place with good air circulation, such as a corridor or glassed-in foyer. There is one form that can be recommended for permanent room decoration in a warm, centrally-heated flat, and that is the variegated cultivar 'Variegata', which, on the contrary, requires a higher temperature in winter.

Propagation is easy, either by tip or stem cuttings in a propagator. The stems from which the cuttings are taken must not be entirely woody.

*Hedera helix* 'Digitata'

  5–25°C

# *Ficus elastica* 'Variegata'

## Rubber Plant

One would be hard put to find a more typical house plant than the rubber plant, and yet it is not the most suitable for indoor cultivation since if the growing conditions are not correct it generally drops its leaves, and so one very often comes across specimens with long stout trunks and only a cluster of leaves at the top. Moreover, if conditions are favourable it fairly rapidly grows too tall. Furthermore, it requires relatively cool conditions (about 15°C [59°F]) in winter and this may be difficult to provide for in the modern home. The latter problem is done away with by the variegated cultivars, for example the illustrated 'Variegata', which generally requires warmer conditions.

The type species is native to the East Indies and Malaysia, where it commonly grows to a height of 25 m (80 ft) and is used in avenues, the crowns being pruned to a round shape. There is no need to describe it for it is well known to all. More important are the cultivars, be it the illustrated and other variegated forms or 'Decora', a larger type with thicker, broader and shorter leaves, discovered amongst seedlings in the 1940s.

The growing medium should be a blend of loam, rotted turves, leaf mould and peat, or John Innes potting compost No. 1 or 2, depending on the size. Water should be applied fairly liberally but only when the surface dries. Ficus does not tolerate watering concurrently with a stream of cold air in winter when the room is being aired, its reaction to this being browning or immediate dropping of the leaves.

The genus *Ficus* embraces some 650 species from climbers through twiners and shrubs to huge trees. A great many are already in cultivation and many more will surely be introduced in future years. Some of the loveliest and most suitable for growing as house plants are *F. lyrata, F. retusa, F. benjamina,* and *F. benghalensis.* Excellent for very warm and humid places is *F. parcellii,* a shrubby plant with large green leaves marbled with dark green, white and grey, which are hairy. The reliable *F. diversifolia,* which can also be grown as an epiphyte, is recommended for small spaces.

*Ficus lyrata (F. pandurata)*

*Ficus krishnae*

  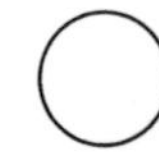 15–25°C

# *Fittonia verschaffeltii*

## Mosaic Plant

Sometimes botanists are hard put to decide – particularly in the case of plants raised by nurserymen – whether two plants are extreme forms of a single species (which may exhibit marked diversity) or two closely related but separate species, or even hybrids that have occurred spontaneously in cultivation without any intervention on the part of the grower. Well-known, for example, is the controversy on *Eranthis hyemalis* and *E. cilicica,* two very different forms at first glance, which thorough investigation of their habitats proved to be extreme forms of one and the same species.

In the case of the Peruvian genus *Fittonia* there is similar confusion. Various authorities cite varying numbers of species (1 to 3) for many consider aberrations to be either varieties or even mere cultivars arising in cultivation. However, let us not concern ourselves with these matters. For us it is enough that these foliage plants can be used for room decoration. They are upright or prostrate herbaceous plants growing to a maximum height of 60 cm (2 ft) *(Fittonia gigantea);* most, however, are barely half that size. The leaves are broadly oval to ovate with variously coloured veins. *Fittonia gigantea* has glossy green leaves with crimson veins; *F. verschaffeltii* dark green leaves tinged crimson and with crimson veins; *F. verschaffeltii argyroneura* bright green leaves with white veins; and 'Pearcei', similar to the illustrated species, differs only by having the leaves a paler, more vivid green with veins a deeper crimson.

Since they are plants of tropical forests (chiefly in Peru but also in Brazil, Ecuador and Colombia), fittonias tolerate deep shade but require high atmospheric moisture. The compost should be light, porous and acid, composed, for example, of peat and sand with an addition of loam and leaf mould. These plants are particularly suitable for glass plant-cases, where they fill the poorly lit bottom, and for demijohns and fishbowls.

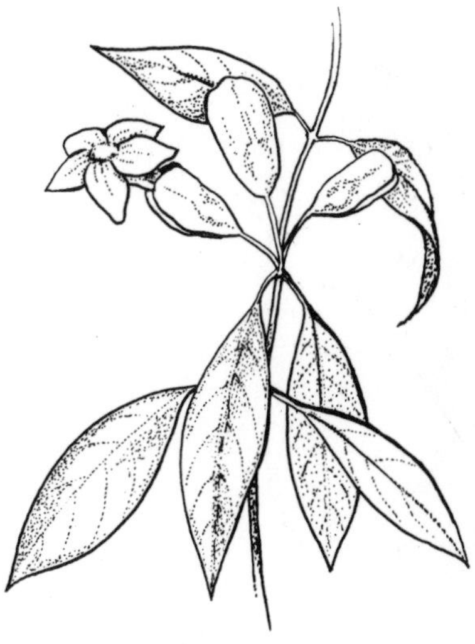

*Mendoncia retusa*

  15–30°C

# Geogenanthus undatus

Many people like to visit botanical gardens where they find inspiration galore. It is truly worthwhile to try and grow many of the attractive species one sees in such a place, even if they do look delicate. *Geogenanthus undatus* (syn. *Dichorisandra undata*) is listed in garden catalogues and yet it is also very tender, being particularly sensitive to drops in temperature below 16°C (61°F) and to low atmospheric moisture. Its introduction into cultivation, however, is to be welcomed for it is a plant of truly exceptional beauty which might be likened, perhaps, only to certain foliage orchids.

The illustrated species, one of the three members of the genus, is native to the Amazon region where it grows only in lightly shaded places on the forest floor, generally together with mosses. Because it is so delicate it cannot be grown openly in a room but must be put in a closed plant-case, demijohn or terrarium, where it does very well and where growth is surprisingly rapid. The best compost is a heavy loam mixed in equal proportion with peat and some sand is added. A full-grown plant is approximately 25 cm (10 in) high, the leaves about 10 cm (4 in) long and 7 cm ($2^3/_4$ in) wide. The combination of the longitudinal stripes and cross ridges on the leaves is truly magnificent. The pale blue flowers are carried on a fairly short stem covered with rusty hairs.

The synonym indicates that this genus is closely related to the genus *Dichorisandra,* comprising some 30 species found in the same type of environment as *Geogenanthus,* chiefly in Brazil. They are beautiful plants. Generally cultivated are the hybrids, which have deep violet leaves with silver markings. Cultivation is the same.

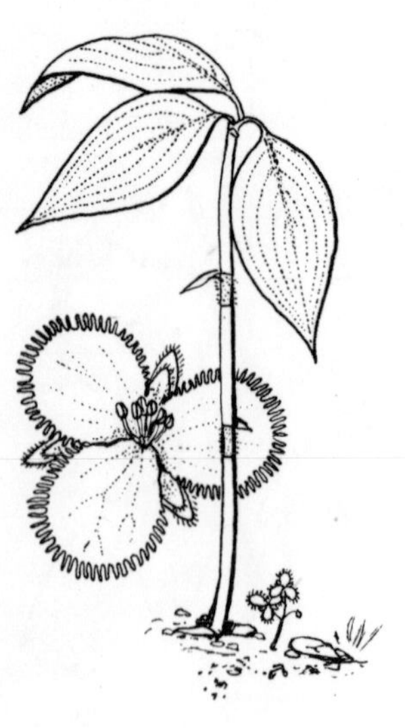

*Geogenanthus rhizanthus*

  18–30°C

# *Hedera × helix* 'Goldheart'

## Ivy

Ivy is well known to everyone. Formerly it was cultivated as a plant requiring cool conditions in winter but nowadays it can also be used for modern room decoration because certain variegated cultivars need warmer conditions and tolerate a warm winter.

According to some authorities there are 7, according to others up to 15 species of ivy found chiefly in Europe and Asia, but they also occur in North Africa. All are shrubby plants that become woody and that climb with the aid of clinging rootlets; only very few forms are not climbers. The leaves, placed alternately on the stem, are leathery, rigid and generally deeply lobed. An interesting feature is the fact that the flowering branches of mature plants bear leaves of an entirely different shape, usually much larger and with an entire margin.

Most cultivated forms are derived from *Hedera helix,* the common ivy, found in every European park as well as growing wild in the forest. It is naturally also found in the Caucasus, the Balkans and Asia Minor. Its range of distribution is truly vast and affords a wide choice of shape as well as colour.

There are dozens of cultivars that either have interesting foliage (generally very thick with remarkably twisted leaves or with leaves arranged in an unusual pattern) or else variously variegated leaves. Best for centrally-heated homes are the dwarf forms with small, greatly variegated leaves that can not only be used to best advantage for room decoration but are generally also the most tender.

Ivy should be grown in loamy compost, rich in humus. It is readily propagated by cuttings inserted in peat and sand in a warm propagator.

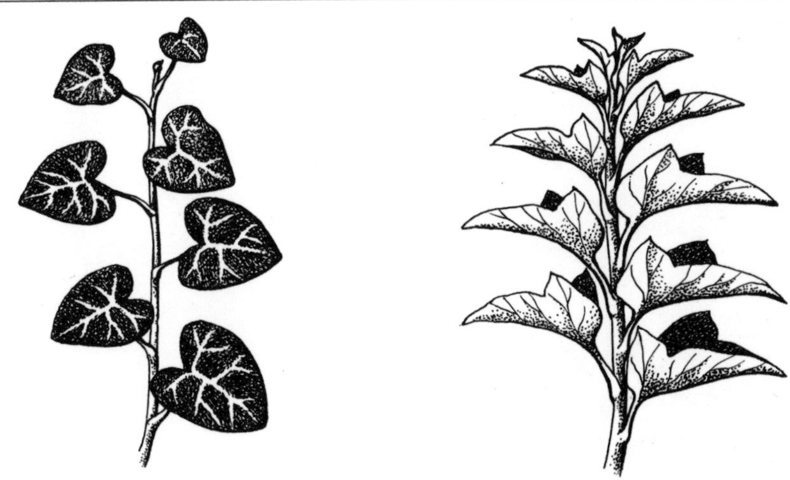

   5–15(20)°C

*Hedera* x *helix* 'Erecta'

*Hedera* x *helix* 'Scutifolia'

# *Hoffmannia roezlii*

## Quiltec Taffeta Plant

The shaded undergrowth of tropical rain forests, where the temperature constantly remains more or less the same and the humidity is high, conceals an immense quantity of various forms of life. Thanks to flower collectors of old as well as present-day botanists many plants from there have become permanent guests in our homes. Often, however, it is necessary to provide them with special conditions in which they can exist permanently. *Hoffmannia roezlii* (syn. *Higginsia refulgens roezlii*) is a plant that is very sensitive to changes in atmospheric moisture and should therefore be grown solely in a glasshouse, terrarium, or demijohn. Attempts to grow it anywhere else rapidly meet with failure.

The genus *Hoffmannia* includes some 50 shrubby, semi-shrubby and herbaceous plants native to Central and South America. Most have handsome leaves, often with a metallic sheen or tinged various colours. The illustrated species is indigenous to Mexico and is named after Benedikt Roezl, the noted Czech orchid collector who spent many years in that country. It is a low herbaceous plant, only about 7 to 10 cm (2 3/4 to 4 in) high, with leaves arranged in a rosette. They are some 10 to 20 cm (4 to 8 in) long and 6 to 14 cm (2 1/4 to 5 1/2 in) across with a silky sheen and coloured purple on the underside. The shapely, pale-red flowers are either short-stalked or sessile. More commonly cultivated is *H. refulgens*, also native to Mexico, which is much taller – up to 60 cm (2 ft) high. The sessile leaves, borne on a stout, upright, red stem, are up to 12 cm (4 1/2 in) long and resemble those of the illustrated species. Mexico and Guatemala are the home of another frequently cultivated species – *H. ghiesbreghtii*, a subshrub reaching a height of 1.5 m (5 ft), with longish, lanceolate, velvety leaves up to 30 cm (1 ft) long, coloured olive-green above and purple below. There is also a white-variegated form 'Variegata'.

The best growing medium is a mixture of peat, pine leaf mould and beech leaf mould with added sand. Plants are readily propagated by soft stem cuttings inserted in a warm and moist propagator, where they root after about 3 weeks; they are also multiplied fairly readily from seed.

*Bouvardia ternifolia*

  15(10)–30°C

# *Iresine* × *herbstii*

## Bloodleaf

The genus *Iresine* embraces some 70 species distributed in tropical and subtropical America, the Antilles, Galapagos Islands and Australia. They include annuals, perennials as well as subshrubs.

The illustrated cultivar is derived from an annual species native to Brazil, which also grows wild, however, throughout all of Central America. In the wild it reaches a height of 80 cm (32 in) whereas in cultivation it is barely half as large. Because it is derived from an annual it is maintained by taking cuttings in late summer, overwintering the rooted plants in a light room and the following summer either leaving them where they are or using them in outdoor arrangements in pots and window-boxes. Often, however, merely pinching the flowers, which are insignificant anyway, will prolong the life of the plant for another year. The type species has purple leaves with crimson veins, but there are many cultivars of different coloration, for example 'Aureoreticulata', which has green leaves with golden-yellow veins. Others are distinguished by small size and thick foliage, such as 'Biemuelleri' with crimson leaves. Other species are also cultivated, for example *I. lindenii* from Ecuador, about 60 cm (2 ft) high, much-branched, with oval, elongate, pointed leaves coloured dark red with lighter veins.

All species do well in John Innes potting compost.

*Iresine* × *lindenii*

   15–25°C

# *Maranta leuconeura* cv. Massangeana 'Tricolor'

## Prayer Plant

Marantas and calatheas are both members of the same family. The only difference between them is that the flowers of marantas have two staminodes instead of one and these are shaped like petals. Marantas, the same as calatheas, are plants of the bottom layer of hot, humid, tropical rainforests. All the 25 or so known species are native to tropical America.

Marantas are distinguished by thickened, tuberous roots in which the plants store starch. That is the reason why one species – *Maranta arundinacea* – became an important article of commerce grown for its starchy roots in many tropical countries of the world. Some 30 years ago, it was classed as an ornamental plant. It grows to a height of 1 m (3 ft) and has long ovate-lanceolate leaves reaching 30 cm (1 ft) in length. Nowadays, only the diverse colour forms are cultivated, particularly the yellow-variegated 'Variegata'.

*M. leuconeura,* the type species from which the illustrated cultivar is derived, is native to Brazil. It reaches a height of 30 cm (1 ft), the leaves, about 15 by 8.5 cm (6 by $3\frac{1}{4}$ in), are pale green above with white spots in the centre surrounded by dark green spots and pale green, (very occasionally reddish) on the underside. From this species were selected two types of aberrations, sometimes described as varieties, namely 'Kerchoveana', which has larger, emerald-green leaves with blackish-green blotches, and 'Massangeana', with leaves spotted brown and coloured purple on the underside. Both cultivars are shorter than the type species, barely 15 cm (6 in) high, and prostrate. Besides the illustrated cultivar, which is one of the loveliest of foliage plants, 'Manda's Emerald' is also recommended. Unlike calatheas, all marantas flourish indoors, even if put out openly in the room. Otherwise, cultivation is the same as for calathea.

*Stromanthe sanguinea* does not tolerate a dry atmosphere and is therefore better suited for cultivation in a plant-case

15–25°C

# *Monstera deliciosa*

## Swiss Cheese Plant

Monstera, like ficus, is a favourite house plant; its large incised leaves up to 1 m (3 ft) long are a veritable symbol of the tropics. And yet this is a very adaptable plant and one that stands up extremely well to a dry atmosphere indoors, requiring little in the way of care.

Some 50 species of the genus *Monstera* have been described to date. All are distributed in tropical America, both on the continent and islands, such as the Antilles. All are climbing plants which in the wild climb up trees to great heights, though often one may come across specimens growing without a support. Characteristic are the numerous aerial roots that trail to the ground where they become anchored in the soil. It is naturally quite wrong to remove these aerial roots. Some smaller species grow as epiphytes, rooting in the small amounts of humus formed in the forks of branches; more about these will be mentioned in the section on climbers.

The illustrated species is native to Mexico, where it may often be seen, for instance in Veracruz, climbing up palms of the genus *Sabal*. The stem is stout and woody, the leaves, with rough stalks about 50 cm (20 in) long, are entire and heart-shaped in the juvenile stage, palmate and perforated when fully grown. The fruits – berries – are edible and truly delicious, hence the Latin name of the species. The variety *borsigniana* is often cultivated, which is similar, only smaller in all respects and with smooth leaf stalks. The leaves of juvenile and mature plants are very different in shape. The commonly grown *Philodendron leichtlinii* is merely a juvenile form of *Monstera obliqua*, a species with leaves that remain entire but are regularly perforated on either side of the midrib. Some authorities believe, however, (wrongly so in the author's opinion), that these are juvenile specimens of *Monstera pertusa;* but the leaf margins of this species do not remain entire in aged specimens.

All monsteras should be grown in a mixture of peat and loam. They are propagated by tip or stem cuttings inserted in a propagator or just in water.

*Monstera dubia*

  15–30°C

# *Musa × sapientum*

If assigning cultivated plants to groups in a valid system is difficult then in the case of food plants grown and improved since time immemorial this is doubly so.

Bananas are robust herbaceous plants with a 'trunk' composed of closed leaf sheaths. Up the middle grows a stem with symmetrical flowers covered with variegated bracts. To date some 80 species of banana have been recorded, distributed in the tropics and subtropics of the Old World. The well-known fruits are many-seeded berries; cultivated varieties, however, are often seedless (sterile) and may be propagated only by vegetative means.

When mature, the plants (even small species) attain dimensions that allow them only to be grown in a greenhouse.

*Musa* x *sapientum,* also known as *M. paradisiaca sapientum,* is probably derived from the crossing of *Musa acuminata* and *M. balbisiana.* Likewise derived from *M. acuminata* in all probability are a number of cultivars sometimes listed under the name *M. cavendishii,* grown chiefly in the Canary Islands.

Though interested persons will probably only find some of the cultivated banana plants in the botanical garden it is also possible to grow the true species, of which the most suitable would be *Musa lasiocarpa* from China, only 60 cm (2 ft) high, with the leaf blade making up half of this length. In this species the bracts are yellow, the fruit inedible and dry. Also comparatively small are *M. nana* (2 m [6 ft]) from China, *M. sanguinea* (1.5 m [5 ft]) from Assam and *M. uranoscopus* (2.5 m [8 ft]) from Vietnam.

All banana plants should be grown in open ground or large containers of nourishing compost such as John Innes potting compost No. 3. Feed, chiefly organic fertilizers, should be applied liberally during the growing period. Propagation is not difficult; usually only by division, but botanical species also by means of seed. Germination is unreliable and slow if old seed is used.

*Heliconia psittacorum*

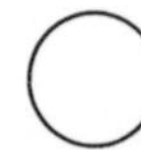
10–25°C

# *Pandanus tectorius*

## Screw Pine

The Pandanus family can be traced as far back as the late Cretaceous period from fossilized remains of plants that have been discovered. The genus *Pandanus* includes some 300 species distributed in the tropics of Asia and Africa, the Malay Archipelago and the Pacific Islands. They are mostly robust plants with numerous prop roots; some are climbers. The leaves are arranged in rows of three or in a spiral; often they form a tuft at the top of the stem or at the tips of separate branches.

The illustrated species is indigenous to south Asia, its range extending to Polynesia and Australia. In its native land it often grows on the banks of canals which it strengthens with its numerous prop roots. This, of course, is not its only useful aspect. The firm leaves provide fibres for primitive fabrics and the plants also yield volatile oils. In its native land *P. tectorius* (syn. *P. odoratissimus*) is a tree-like shrub reaching a height of 5 m (16 ft). The leaves have sharp white spines on the margins and on the keel formed by the midrib. The entire leaf measures about 2 m (6 ft).

More often encountered in cultivation are the variegated species or variegated cultivars of green-leaved species. Most widely grown are *Pandanus veitchii* with leaves 5 to 6 cm (2 to 2¼ in) across, and with whitish-yellow longitudinal stripes; *P. sanderi,* which is very similar but is much more spiny; and occasionally also *P. variegatus,* which has linear leaves with fine, pale-coloured stripes and white or purple spines. A green-leaved pandanus worthy of note is the magnificent *P. pacificus,* which forms a ground rosette of dark-green leaves up to 80 cm (32 in) long and about 12 cm (4¾ in) across. The correctness of the naming of individual 'species' of pandanus is very doubtful; often it is a case of 'florist's names' given to plants that are, in fact, cultivars.

Pandanus is propagated by detaching the shoots that form at the base of the stem and inserting them in a peat and sand compost. Mature plants need a more nourishing substrate with peat, sand and loam. Pandanus is a very decorative plant which is much suited to modern homes where the temperature does not drop below 15°C (59°F).

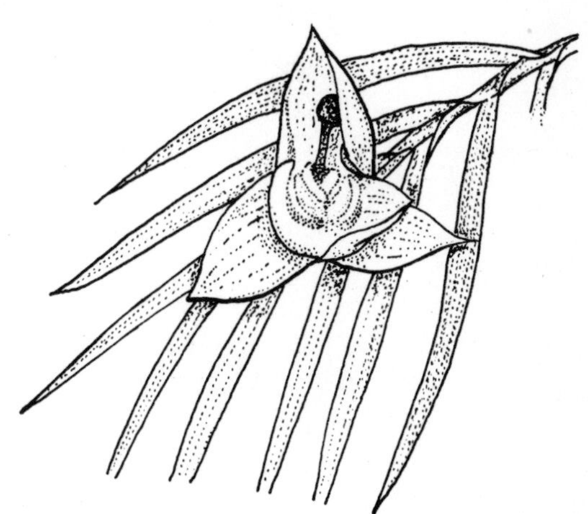

*Freycinetia multiflora* from the Philippines, also known as the climbing pandanus, is an attractive climber which can be put to good use in larger epiphytic arrangements. Flowers are a deep pink

10–30°C

# *Pedilanthus tithymaloides* 'Tricolor'

To date, European horticulture has not given many foliage plants the attention they deserve. The genus *Pedilanthus* has not yet become as common as it is in Japan and the United States, for instance.

The genus *Pedilanthus* comprises some 30 species distributed in tropical and subtropical America. The characteristic they all have in common is the zigzag growth of the stem and the alternate leaves, which only at the upper end of the stem are sometimes opposite.

The illustrated species is the only one commonly found in cultivation in Europe. It grows wild in a large area extending from Florida through Central America and the Antilles to South America – to Venezuela and Colombia. In the wild it is a robust plant, commonly reaching a height of 2 m (6 ft), with dark-green leaves and the midrib forming a prominent keel on the underside. The succulent stems and foliage indicate that it grows in places subject to lengthy periods of drought during the dry seasons. As in all plants of the spurge family, the flowers of pedilanthus are cyathiums. This means they are inconspicuous and soberly coloured but surrounded by bright red bracts more than a centimetre (half an inch) long. A flowering specimen is thus truly handsome and the pride of any collection. Commonly grown is the cultivar 'Variegatus' with white-edged or variegated leaves. From this were selected plants which developed another, third colour – red.

Pedilanthus grows reliably indoors in a mixture of loam, sand and peat in a sunny spot. It is readily propagated by cuttings inserted in a propagator where they root reliably within several weeks. To prevent the tissues being clogged by the milky sap that oozes from the cut, the cuttings should be immersed briefly in warm water to wash the milk away.

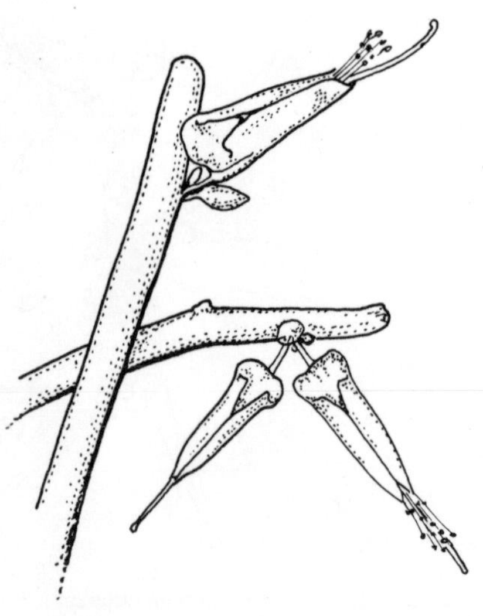

Inflorescence of *Pedilanthus tithymaloides*

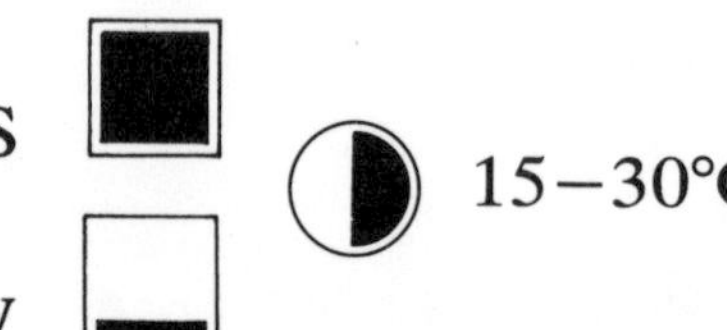

# *Peperomia*

## Pepper Elder

Though this book depicts only individual species and cultivars, peperomias are such a large group that there was no choice but to depict several, for there are some 600 found in the wild, mostly in South and Central America as well as in Africa and Asia. Almost all are suitable for growing indoors, which makes selecting an assortment rather difficult. Better, perhaps, to take note of the exceptions. Only a single species is grown both for its foliage and for its fragrant, but otherwise nondescript white flowers, namely *Peperomia fraseri,* more commonly known as *P. resedaeflora.* Exceptions are also the species with foliage coated with white 'wool', which serves as protection, for the plants grow in dry and very sunny or even sunbaked places on rocks, often together with cacti. A representative example of this group is *P. incana* from Brazil. These species require entirely different conditions from the others and should be grown in full sun in a porous medium consisting of humus, sand and stone rubble.

Most peperomias, however, grow in damp lowland and mountain forests either on moss-covered rocks or as epiphytes on the trunks and branches of trees. Only if grown thus are they of the typical compact habit which is truly lovely. They will grow even on bare cork oak bark without any substrate but will do better and grow faster if inserted in a ball of moss and light soil (just a handful) before being attached to the trunk. Naturally, even plants that are grown thus must be provided with feed – mainly organic fertilizers in liquid form (in concentrations 10 times less than those given in the manufacturer's instructions) sprayed on the leaves. Peperomias, of course, can also be grown in the more traditional manner, with the roots covered in compost in a demijohn, fishbowl or terrarium.

Propagation is very easy, either by means of cuttings inserted in a mixture of peat and sand, or by means of entire leaves with stalk inserted in the rooting medium.

**1 – P. rubella**
**2 – P. sandersii (= P. argyreia)**
**3 – P. caperata**

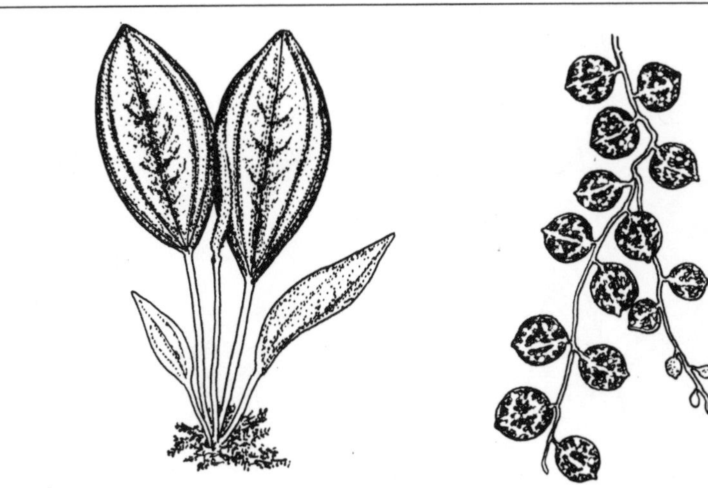

*Peperomia ornata*

*Peperomia prostrata* has minute leaves, about 0.5 cm (1/4 in) across; it does extremely well when grown as an epiphyte and tolerates the conditions of cultivation indoors

10–30°C

# *Philodendron sodiroi* – juvenile form

## Silver-leaf Philodendron

Philodendrons often pose difficulties with the nomenclature of species if the traditional florist's names are to be avoided, for the genus comprises more than 220 species which have been cultivated for a very long time and therefore one often encounters selected natural variations as well as hybrids and at the same time vast differences in habit between juvenile and adult specimens of the same species. Added to this is the fact that cultivated philodendrons are incapable of attaining the adult form and many old specimens develop a 'transitional' habit.

The illustrated species is cultivated under many different names in the home and in botanical gardens. Generally it is found under the name *Philodendron imperiale* or the synonym *P. asperatum.* Most accurate, probably, is its classification as. *P. sodiroi,* for the said philodendron has velvety green leaves and leaf stalks covered with a thick fringe of wart-like growths. The plant is native to Colombia. In adult specimens the leaf blade is up to 40 cm (16 in) long; in cultivated subjects, however, it is barely half that length.

What species should be recommended for room decoration? For larger rooms *P. sanguineum* from Mexico, with stem and undersides of the leaves coloured red, the upper surface of the leaves dark green, and their length 30 cm (1 ft) (in adult specimens up to 70 cm [28 in]), or the similar *P. erubescens* from Colombia. For smaller rooms *P. scandens* with long, heart-shaped, glossy, dark green leaves about 15 cm (6 in) long; *P. surinamense,* similar but smaller, the leaves velvety olive above and light purple on the underside; or the beautifully shaped *P. laciniatum* with symmetrically deeply lobed leaves.

All philodendrons should be grown in a mixture of peat, loam and sand. They are readily propagated by cuttings which will root in water or a warm propagating frame.

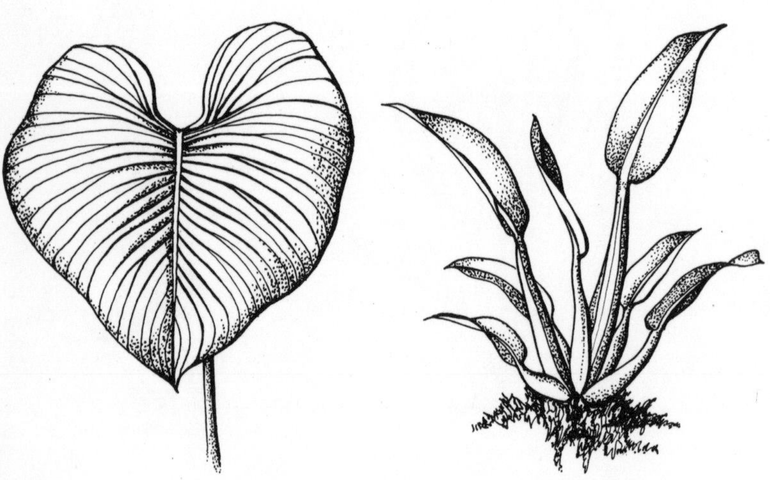

*Philodendron fragrantissimum* *Philodendron ventricosum*

  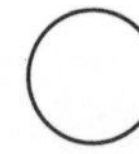 15–30°C

# *Pilea cadierei*

## Aluminium Plant, Friendship Plant

The nettle family includes many attractive genera that can be used for gardening purposes. In all botanical gardens (often also in rock gardens) one will find *Helxine soleirolii,* a pretty prostrate plant with small, dense leaves that is sometimes used as a substitute for turf. Also frequently cultivated are the ornamental species of the genera *Boehmeria, Debregeasia, Laportea* and *Pellionia.* Most widely used in homes, however, is the genus *Pilea,* comprising some 200 species distributed in the tropics on all continents excepting Australia.

*Pilea cadierei* is native to the tropical rain forests of Indochina (reference books often say Africa, more specifically the Congo, but this is probably a mistake). It grows to a maximum height of 40 cm (16 in), but is usually shorter. The leaves, marked with large silvery patches (hence the name aluminium plant) are almost 10 cm (4 in) long.

Another commonly cultivated species is *P. microphylla* from the South American Andes, where it grows up to elevations of 2,000 m (6,600 ft). It is a small herbaceous plant with tiny leaves up to 0.5 cm (1/4 in) long at the most, which often grows on stone walls and rocks and is the only member of the genus that tolerates direct sun. *P. spruceana* from the region between Venezuela and Peru has brownish-red leaves covered with blister-like growths. More often grown are its cultivars, 'Norfolk' and 'Silver Tree', both lovely, small, variegated plants.

Most species grow in the bottom layer of rain forests and even though they prefer places with more light, such as stones in stream beds and the banks of streams, they will tolerate only diffused light. They are very good subjects for a demijohn or a plant-case. The compost should be a mixture of peat, sand and loam. Propagation is easy; cuttings root readily even in water.

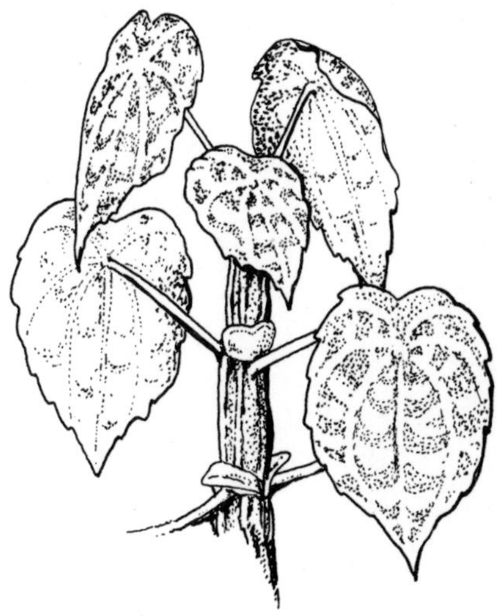

*Pilea selbyanorum*

  10–25°C

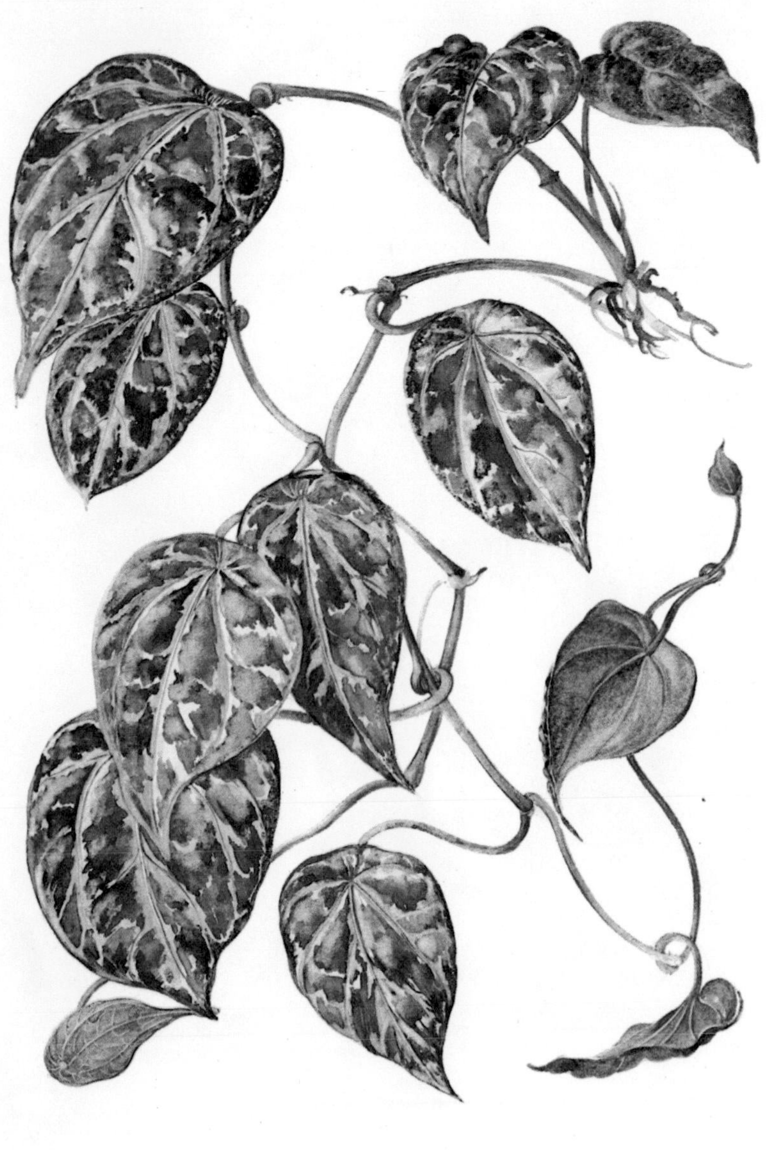

# *Piper ornatum*

## Pepper

It is difficult to select from the 700 or so species of peppers the one most suitable for one's home, for these woody climbers or shrubs are among the loveliest of foliage plants, be they variegated species, ones with glossy green leaves or ones with a lovely habit of growth.

The illustrated pepper is from Celebes and is one of the best-known of foliage plants. It is a climber with a weak stem and clinging rootlets that grow from some of the nodes. The leaves have crimson markings in the juvenile form; these later fade and the patches turn an ashy greyish-pink. The similar *P. porphyrophyllum* from Indonesia has leaves that are velvety olive green with fine rosy-crimson markings on the upper surface and a deep purple on the underside.

Green-leaved species are equally popular, be it the common *Piper nigrum* from which black pepper commonly used in cooking is obtained, or the well-known *P. betle* whose leaf is chewed along with lime and betel nut (the fruit of a palm of the genus *Areca*) by some south-east Asian peoples. Unlike the variegated species, these are less demanding, both as to heat and moisture requirements.

Many species, of course, are not climbers but upright shrubs, for example *P. bicolor* (syn. *P. magnificum*) with large elliptical leaves up to 25 cm (10 in) long coloured dark green with a marked metallic sheen on the upper side; and *P. auritum* from Mexico, an erect, thickly branched shrub with heart-shaped leaves about 20 cm (8 in) long and erect whitish-green flower spikes up to 15 cm (6 in) long.

Variegated peppers are generally used in plant-cases or in other places where the temperature and humidity can be kept more or less constant. Green-leaved species may also be used for room decoration in centrally-heated homes. A suitable growing medium is a mixture of peat, sand and loam.

Propagation is by tip cuttings inserted in a peat and sand compost in a propagator under glass.

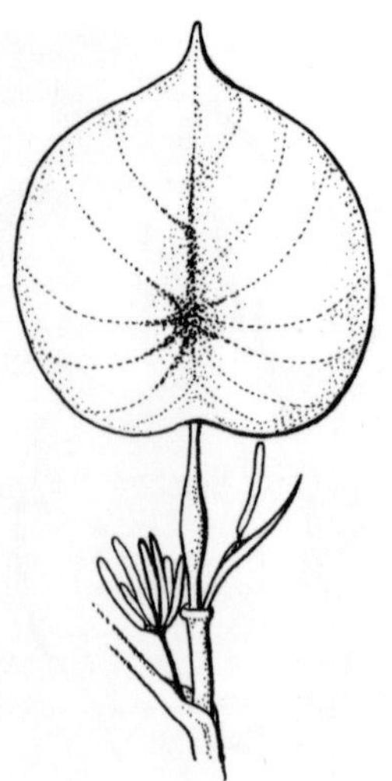

*Pothomorphe peltata*

  18–25(30)°C

# Remusatia vivipara

Sometimes, to our great surprise and delight, we come upon plants in the wild that previously we have only admired in the botanical garden. Some readers may have seen, at least in a picture, that many trees, for instance in southern India, are attacked by stranglers of the genus *Ficus,* for example *F. beddomei.* This plant grows as an epiphyte at first, later anchoring in the ground when its roots reach down to the soil. The roots then begin to thicken, and after a time become joined to form an impermeable mantle round the trunk of the tree, which eventually dies. The roots are not joined completely, leaving spaces where fallen leaves and the rotted wood of the original tree trunk collect, in other words a substrate that provides nourishment for a number of epiphytes. And it is in such places that we often find *Remusatia vivipara.*

Nourishing humusy compost, shade and frequent feeding are recommended for its cultivation in the home; in the wild, however, it is improbable that one will come across these plants growing in any way other than in the described manner (even though there is plenty of room in the humus at the base of the trees).

*Remusatia vivipara* is a tuberous plant. Growing from the tuber, which is nearly spherical, are several stalks about 30 cm (1 ft) long, bearing shield-shaped, cordate-ovate leaves about the same length as the stalks. They are vivid green in colour with prominent veins. Very attractive, but unfortunately not long-lived, is the flower, or rather the inflorescence, with its vivid yellow spathe. Stolons which produce small tubers also grow from the base. It is this method of vegetative reproduction that has earned the plant its name 'vivipara'.

Probably the best method of growing this plant is as a partial epiphyte in a light mixture of peat, rotted wood dust and charcoal. Additional feeding promotes rapid growth, particularly in young plants, the same as syringing the foliage. It can also be grown in the traditional way as a pot plant. Propagation is very simple – by means of the tiny tubers.

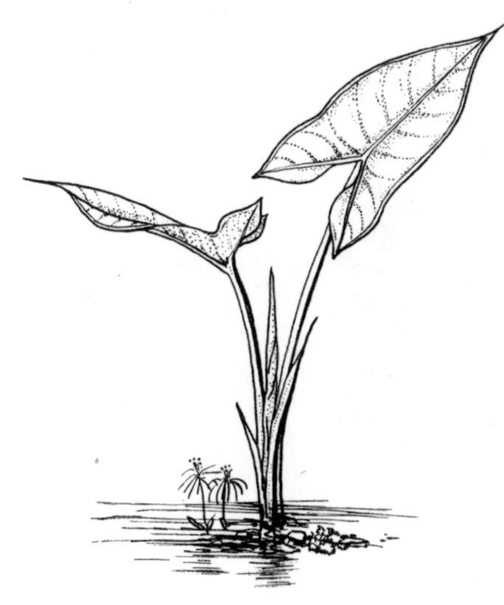

*Caladiopsis atropurpurea*

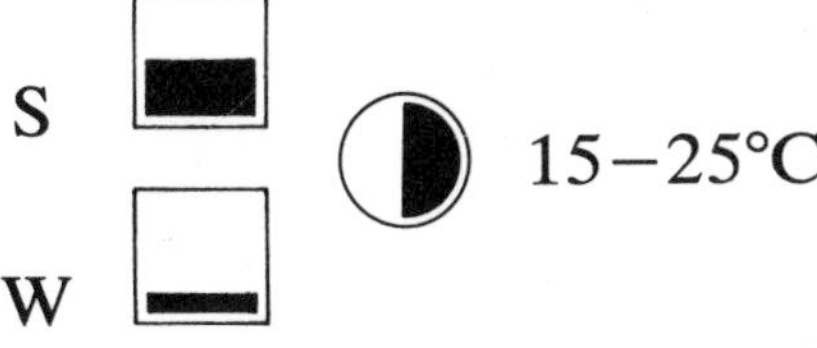


15–25°C

# *Rhoeo spathacea* 'Vittata'

## Boat Lily

This plant, like the previous one, may provide cause for surprise when we encounter it in the wild. In Mexico, for instance, rhoeo may be found growing as an epiphyte on an old rotting stump on a sunny bank. The leaves are arranged in a rosette, so that the plant greatly resembles the funnel of cistern bromeliads. This morphological adaptation of plants due to similar modes of life is known as convergence. As a result of it, two totally unrelated plants may come to resemble one another. In the given case, the arrangement of the leaves has an evident purpose – to bring rainwater directly to the roots or to store it in the funnel as a reserve supply.

*Rhoeo spathacea* (syn. *R. discolor*) is the only member of the genus. It is native to tropical Central America but often grows wild elsewhere in the tropics. The leaves of the type species are linear lanceolate, about 40 cm (16 in) long, dark green on the upperside and purplish-violet below. The white flowers are clustered between leathery, shell-shaped bracts in the axils of the leaves. More widely grown than the type species is the illustrated cultivar 'Vittata', longitudinally striped yellow on the upperside of the leaves.

This plant is one of the easiest to grow and will succeed well in a modern home with central heating even in the hands of a beginner. The most suitable compost is a light mixture of peat, rotted wood dust and sand with only a small addition of more nourishing loam. They can be used in many ways but visitors to botanical gardens, where rhoeo is grown as an epiphyte, will surely support the view that plants grown in this way make a striking display and at the same time look natural.

Propagation is easy, either by means of seeds or by side-shoots that are produced in large numbers, particularly after the original leaf rosette has been cut back.

*Rhoeo spathacea* often grows as an epiphyte in the wild and can be grown as such indoors

   15–30°C

# *Sansevieria trifasciata* 'Golden Hahnii'

## Mother-in-law's Tongue

The illustrated plant needs no introduction for it is grown practically everywhere. One of the hardiest of all plants, it tolerates both full sunshine as well as deeper shade and temperatures ranging from the highest greenhouse temperatures to 12°C (54°F) (and even less). What is more, nothing will happen if the grower forgets to water it for even a whole month.

Altogether, there are some 70 known species. In the wild sansevieria generally grows in dry places sparsely covered with shrubs or on stony grass banks and in many tropical countries it grows as an escape on rubbish dumps. Most species are found in equatorial Africa, several in South Africa and the remainder in tropical Asia. In cultivation there are a vast number of species and cultivars, notably the several outstanding hybrids introduced by growers in the United States during the past years.

Most widely cultivated is *Sansevieria trifasciata* from equatorial west Africa. It is a robust, herbaceous plant up to 160 cm (5½ ft) high with a creeping rhizome and leaves circa 7 cm (2¾ in) across, banded light and dark green. Though the type species is still cultivated, more widely grown are the various cultivars: 'Laurentii' – tall with leaves edged golden-yellow; 'Craigii' – with leaves striped longitudinally with whitish-yellow; and 'Hahnii' – a low plant forming a dense rosette and coloured like the type species. The last-named cultivar has given rise to two further forms: 'Golden Hahnii' ('Aureomarginata') and the silver-striped 'Silver Hahnii'. *S. grandis* is a lovely large sansevieria with leaves up to 60 cm (2 ft) long and about 15 cm (6 in) wide, coloured dark blue-green and banded with silver. Of interest also are species with leaves that are circular in cross section, such as *S. cylindrica* from west Africa with rush-like leaves about 75 cm (30 in) long and 2.5 cm (1 in) across, horizontally streaked in two shades of green.

Sansevierias should be grown in rather heavy, nourishing soil, such as John Innes potting compost. They are readily propagated by leaf cuttings, but variegated cultivars should only be increased by division of the rhizome, for plants grown from cuttings produce green instead of variegated leaves.

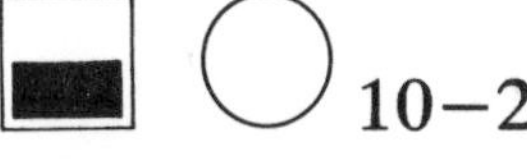 10–25°C

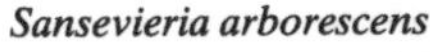

*Sansevieria arborescens* *Sansevieria stuckyi* has leaves that are round in cross-section

# *Saxifraga sarmentosa*

## Aaron's Beard, Mother-of-Thousands

Saxifraga is a name generally associated with rock garden plants, but the illustrated species, the only one of the genus, is a classic and favourite house plant.

*Saxifraga sarmentosa* is native to China and Japan, where it grows on the subtropical mountain slopes amidst stones. Characteristic of this species are the thread-like runners bearing a series of baby plants that readily root in the ground. Within a few years' time these form a lovely spreading carpet which, when in flower, attracts attention from afar.

The genus *Saxifraga,* comprising some 300 species, is systematically divided into several sections. The illustrated species belongs to the Diptera section, which includes species with petals of unequal size. Diptera is also the zoological term for two-winged insects and it is impossible not to take note of this coincidence when one sees the flowering plant, for the blossoms are extraordinarily light and airy and from a distance reminiscent of a swarm of lovely small butterflies. They are fairly large, white and sometimes lightly spotted with yellow; only the shorter petals are tipped with red.

*Saxifraga sarmentosa* is one of the traditional house plants that were ideally suited to homes without central heating. Nowadays, with higher winter temperatures, it is less happy. Breeders have developed an attractive cultivar named 'Tricolor' with large whitish-yellow and pale-pink patches on the leaves, which, like most variegated cultivars, has greater heat requirements. It succeeds well even with central heating and winter temperatures of 16 to 20°C (61 to 68°F).

If you have an unheated conservatory or sun lounge you can try to grow the type species. It may also survive outdoors in warm districts if it is protected from frost in the winter by a covering of evergreen boughs or something similar.

The potting compost should be a mixture of leaf mould and loam with some sand. Propagation is easy – by means of the baby plants formed on the runners.

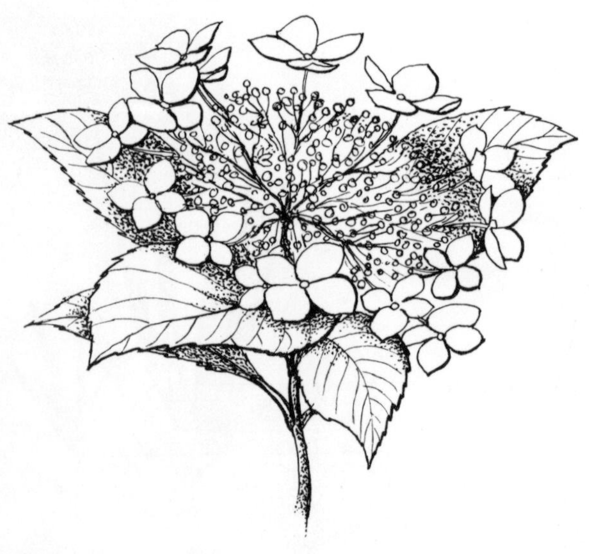

*Hydrangea* x *macrophylla*

 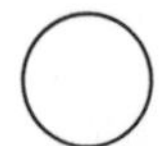  5–15(20)°C

# *Schefflera actinophylla*

## Queensland Umbrella Tree

In the tropics one often sees beautiful plants whose dimensions, however, far exceed the bounds of house plants. This, of course, may not be true, for conditions in the wild and in cultivation are markedly different. Proof of this is *Schefflera,* which in its native Australia grows into a huge tree up to 40 m (135 ft) high, but specimens grown indoors rarely exceed 2 m (6 ft) in height.

More than 200 species, most of them quite similar, have been described to date. They are distributed in the tropics the world over but most are found in south-east Asia, the Australian region and northern South America. In the juvenile stage they often grow as epiphytes.

The leaves of the illustrated species are palmately compound, composed in the juvenile form of three, later five and in adult specimens of seven to sixteen leaflets, which are leathery, glossy, smooth, narrowly-ovate and pointed. In juvenile plants, the ones usually found in cultivation, they are rarely more than 15 cm (6 in) long; in adult specimens, however, the leaflets are up to twice that length.

In cultivation one sometimes comes across the species *S. digitata* (syn. *S. cunninghamii, Aralia scheffleri*). This is a small tree, sometimes only 5 m (16 ft) high, from New Zealand. The leaves are composed of seven to ten narrow, elongate leaflets about 15 cm (6 in) long. Young leaflets are often irregularly lobed.

Cultivation is comparatively simple, and schefflera, particularly in the juvenile stage, is excellent for room decoration in modern homes. For the first few years it requires higher temperatures, which even in winter should not drop below 16–18°C (61 to 65°F) for long periods. Older plants require less heat and for these the winter temperature should not be more than 18°C (65°F) or less than 12°C (54°F). Large specimens are more suitable for well-lit foyers or conservatories.

The growing medium should be moderately heavy, best of all a mixture of compost, peat, leaf mould, loam and sand. Propagation is by seeds obtained from a specialist supplier.

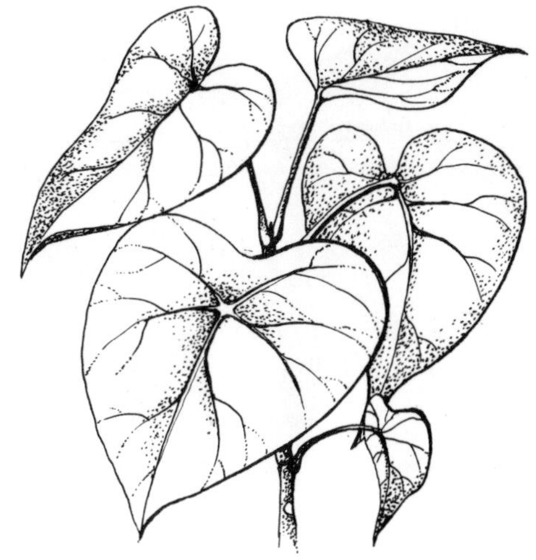

*Oreopanax capitatus*

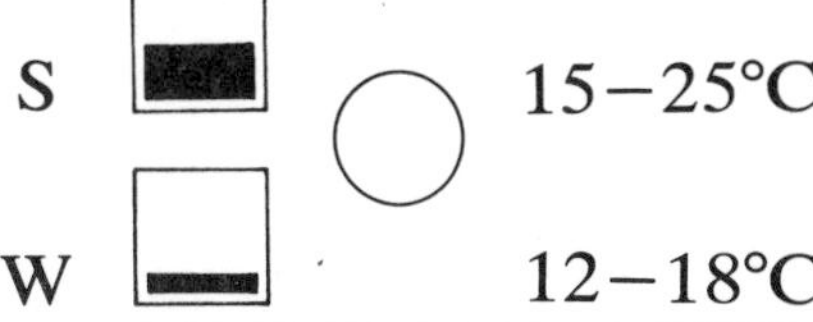


15–25°C

12–18°C

# *Zebrina pendula* 'Quadricolor'

## Wandering Jew

Zebrina, though native to Central America, has been an extremely popular house plant for many years.

*Zebrina pendula (Tradescantia zebrina)* is distributed throughout the whole of Central America, where it grows in damp forests alongside streams and rivers as well as on rocky mountain slopes up to elevations of 2,000 m (6,600 ft). It is a creeping plant with reddish stem and leaves that are more or less smooth, coloured purple on the underside and with two silvery stripes above. The flowers are small, whitish, the petals deep pink on the reverse. This species has been cultivated since 1840. More widely grown, however, is the illustrated cultivar 'Quadricolor' with leaves that are even more decorative although the silvery stripes are often not noticeable.

Because this genus comprises only three species we can get to know them all, for the other two are also often encountered in cultivation.

*Zebrina flocculosa* has a very apt name for the plant is covered with soft white wool-like tufts (floccose). The leaves are entirely green. Sometimes it goes under the name of *Tradescantia commeliniifolia* among florists. *Z. purpusii* greatly resembles the illustrated species but is more robust and without the silvery stripes on the underside of the leaves. The foliage is more reddish. Also occasionally encountered in cultivation is *Z. purpusii minor* with shortly ovate leaves, densely covered with raised hairs, but smaller than in the species.

Zebrinas are grown chiefly in hanging containers but they also do well in water. Propagation is by cuttings.

*Cyanotis somaliensis* (left) and *Tradescantia sillamontana* (right)

  10–30°C

# PLANTS WITH DECORATIVE FLOWERS

# *Abutilon* × *hybridum*

## Flowering Maple, Parlour Maple

In the introductory section of this book we promised that it would also include some of the so-called 'classic' house plants, even though most require cool conditions in winter. This requirement may, in fact, be met even in modern homes by putting the plants in a cool basement, between the panes of double glazing, in a corridor or in a glass-covered patio or conservatory. Many people prefer sleeping in a cool bedroom and so they limit the amount of heat there or shut it off altogether; such a bedroom may also serve the needs of the cold-loving plants. Often such plants will not flower but will only produce lush growth if they are not provided with cool conditions in winter.

*Abutilon* x *hybridum* is a tried and tested plant grown by many generations of flower-lovers. The many beautiful cultivars are descended chiefly from two species: *A. darwinii* from Brazil and *A. striatum* from Guatemala. The first has deep reddish-orange bell-like flowers, the other is light red. The colour of hybrids ranges from yellow through many red and salmon hues to dark brownish-red. The shrubs grow to a height of about 1.5 m (5 ft). Particularly lovely are the variegated forms.

Also popular are cultivars of *A. megapotamicum* from the state of Rio Grande in Brazil. These are also 1 to 1.5 m (3 to 5 ft) high with long, pointed leaves coarsely toothed on the margin. The calyx is inflated, five-edged, dark purple; the corolla pale yellow, not fully opened. The prominent anthers are deep violet.

All type species as well as cultivars require a rather heavy nourishing soil mixture, best of all a blend of compost, loam, leafmould and sand. Feed should be applied regularly at least once a month. The plants are readily propagated from seed but are unlikely to come true in the case of cultivars so that it is better to multiply them by cuttings in late winter or early spring.

*Abutilon megapotamicum* 'Variegatum'

 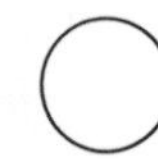 5–25°C

# *Achimenes × hybridum*

## Cupid's Bower

The mid-nineteenth century or thereabouts brought the discovery of beautiful plants of the genus *Achimenes,* most of them indigenous to Mexico. Only one species – *A. coccinea* – had been known since the late eighteenth century but it had not won any great popularity. The discovery of new species and the hybrids derived from them, however, made these plants, which flower throughout the summer and die back to pass the winter as scaly rhizomes, the fashion of the day for a time.

In the wild they are generally found growing in a small amount of humus on large moss-covered boulders or shaded stone walls as well as steep rock faces. Some species, however, also grow on grassy banks. *A. ehrenbergii* may even be found high up in the mountains, and is adapted for life there with a thick coat of long silvery hairs.

Nurseries offer both 'pure' botanical species such as *A. candida,* corolla white with mouth spotted yellow and red; *A. coccinea,* corolla only about 1 cm (1/2 in) across, bright scarlet; and *A. grandiflora,* corolla reddish-violet; and hybrids, noteworthy being 'Little Beauty', small, compact, with large pink flowers borne in profusion over a long period. There are also intergeneric hybrids, chiefly from crossings with *Smithiantha zebrina,* listed in catalogues under the name x *Eucodonopsis,* for example x *Eucodonopsis naegelioides,* a cross between *Achimenes ehrenbergii* and *Smithiantha zebrina;* and x *E. roezlii,* a cross between *A. mexicana* and *S. zebrina.*

Cultivation is not difficult. As has already been said the plants pass the winter in the form of scaly rhizomes which are very fragile. They should be put in peat and kept dry in a warm room for the winter. Some time around March put several rhizomes in flat dishes on a mixture of peat, compost, loam and sand and cover them lightly with a 1- to 2-cm- (1/2-to 3/4- in)-layer of similar compost. During the first few months of the growing period keep adding compost to cover the plants so that they will root thoroughly. For this reason, the dish should be filled only half full at the start.

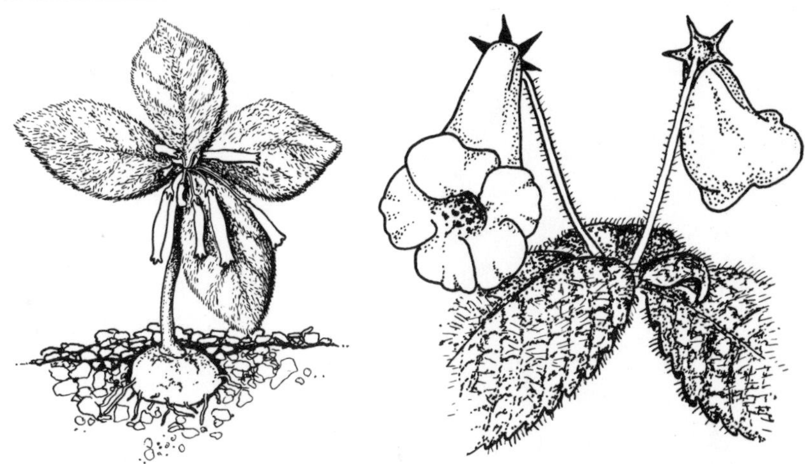

*Rechsteineria leucotricha* grows from a tuber; cultivation is the same as for gloxinias

*Achimenes ehrenbergii* is indigenous to the mountains of Mexico. In cool conditions it is of more compact habit and has a thicker coat of white hairs

S   10–25°C

# Alpinia coccinea

Plants of the ginger family are a group that have been greatly underrated by nuserymen to date. Only a few species are grown in gardens, such as members of the genus *Roscoea.* In collections of thermophilous plants (thriving in hot conditions) one is quite likely to come across members of the genus *Kaempferia* or *Costus,* always represented, however, by only one or two species. And yet these plants generally do well even in conditions that are far from optimal; they produce attractive flowers (which are often fragrant) and have very decorative foliage.

The illustrated species from south-east Asia is a large plant suitable for a large conservatory or sun lounge, for it grows to a height of about 120 cm (3³/₄ ft). The flowers are inconspicuous, concealed in the axils of large, bright red bracts. The leaves, up to 50 cm (20 in) long, are a vivid deep green. Unfortunately, this magnificent plant is not found in European nurseries to date; it is more likely to be encountered in tropical and subtropical parks. More frequently found in European collections are *A. calcarata,* generally less than 1 m (3 ft) high with large white flowers marked pink and violet; and *A.* x *sanderae,* 80 cm (32 in) at the most, with white variegated leaves.

The genus *Costus* includes some splendid species. Most, however, flower only briefly, but they are plants of tropical forest undergrowth and tolerate deep shade. Particularly noteworthy in this respect is *C. igneus* from Brazil, an attractive plant about 50 cm (20 in) high which grows in shade that other species would hardly tolerate. At the same time it is tolerant of a dry, smoky and dusty atmosphere which makes it ideal for providing a bit of greenery even in the least suitable of places. Well-known representatives of the ginger family are members of the genus *Hedychium,* which likewise are found in cultivation only very occasionally – generally *H. gardnerianum.* Much prettier, however, is *H. coronarium* from the Himalayas with large, snow-white and very fragrant flowers. This species requires a permanently moist medium and ample light; it is excellent for a large indoor paludarium.

Plants of the ginger family should be grown in a mixture of compost, leaf mould and peat; most species require a definite dormant period in winter. Propagation is by cutting up the stout rhizomes or, quite readily, by means of seed.

*Costus malortieanus*

 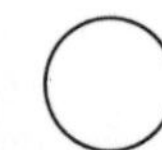 12–25°C

# *Anthurium* (Andreanum-Hybrids)

## Flamingo Plant

In the preceding section on foliage plants mention was made of several members of the large genus *Anthurium,* native to tropical America. It should be noted that foliage anthuriums are more suitable for room decoration than species with handsome flowers, for these have high temperature as well as high humidity requirements and thus often do not flower or else their blooms are not as lovely as those of greenhouse specimens.

Two groups of hybrids are grown for their beautiful and striking blooms, one derived from *A. andreanum,* native to Colombia, the other, designated as *Anthurium* x *hortulanum,* from *A. scherzerianum,* native to Costa Rica and Guatemala.

*Anthurium andreanum* and its hybrids are distinguished by long-stalked, elongate heart-shaped leaves borne on a relatively short stem. *A. scherzerianum* has a shorter stem so that the longish lanceolate, rather short-stalked leaves form a ground clump.

The flowers, like those of all aroids, are composed of a spadix enclosed in a spathe. Whereas the spadix is soberly coloured, the spathe of hybrids is large and flat and coloured briliant scarlet, salmon-pink, pale pink or white, depending on the cultivar. The flowers are extraordinarily long-lived; even cut flowers last more than a month in a vase. For this reason, anthuriums are among the most valuable flowers grown by florists for cutting.

In the home, both groups of cultivars should be grown in a light, only slightly shaded spot in a room that is aired only occasionally and kept at a relatively high temperature. The potting compost must be adequately porous but at the same time water-retentive. Ideal is a mixture of peat and beech leaf mould, plus loam, sand and a little crushed charcoal. The stems of anthuriums should be wrapped in sphagnum moss kept permanently moist; the surface of the soil in the pot or dish may also be covered with sphagnum. Plants are readily propagated from seed, the cultivars, however, only by vegetative means – generally by dividing up the roots when re-potting.

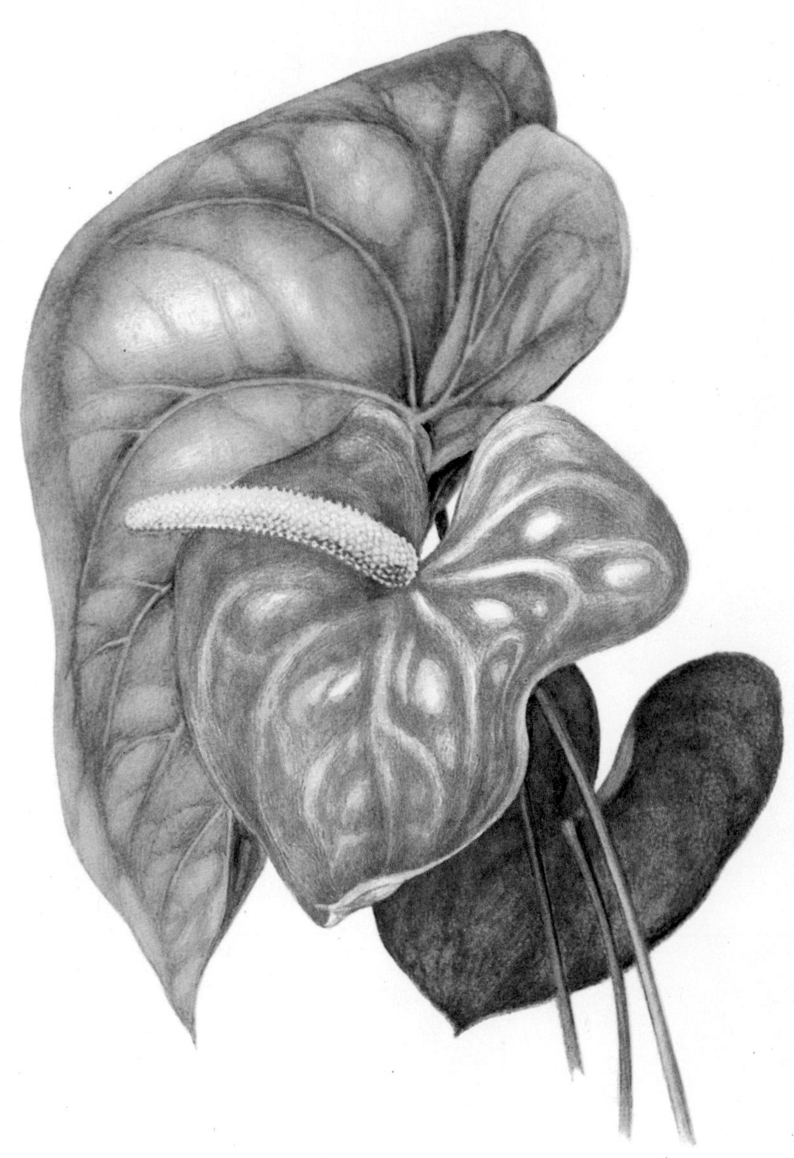

  18–30°C

*Anthurium gladifolium* from Venezuela; older specimens can make a striking feature on an epiphyte trunk

# *Brunfelsia calycina*

## Franciscan Nightshade, Kiss-me-Quick

*Brunfelsia calycina* (syn. *Franciscea calycina*) has been cultivated since the mid-nineteenth century and at one time was a popular plant of palace greenhouses. In recent years it has been 'rediscovered' by European florists. It is a native of Brazil, where it grows in forests in thick humusy layers, particularly in wet places.

*Brunfelsia calycina* is a moderately large shrub branching profusely from the base, with shining, dark green foliage. The flowers, produced in late winter and early spring, are flat, about 5 cm (2 in) across. They are truly lovely and thus this shrub is found in practically every park in Central and South America.

It is a pity that other species of this genus, embracing a total of 30 altogether, are not cultivated more often. *Brunfelsia hopeana,* a thickly branched shrub up to 2 m (6 ft) high, bears flowers which, though smaller than those of the illustrated species, are very plentiful and coloured pale violet-blue, turning white as they fade (the same is true of the flowers of *B. calycina eximia,* which are purplish-violet at first). There are, however, also species of different colours: *B. americana* from the Antilles has fragrant flowers that are white, later changing to yellow, and *B. undulata* has wavy flowers that are snow white.

All brunfelsias have storage tissues in the woody parts of the stems and in the wild they undergo a short dormant period in winter. Because of this they should be provided with at least a three-month period of rest at a lower temperature and with only the minimum of watering to ensure abundant flowering.

Cultivation is not difficult. The compost should be a well-drained mixture of nourishing loam, compost and peat mixed with sand, enriched every spring by an addition of hornmeal. The plants should be cut back hard after the flowers have faded to promote branching; the prunings may be used as cuttings which should be inserted in a peat and sand mixture in a warm propagator. They are slow to root – the pace is not the same for all and the process may take as long as two months.

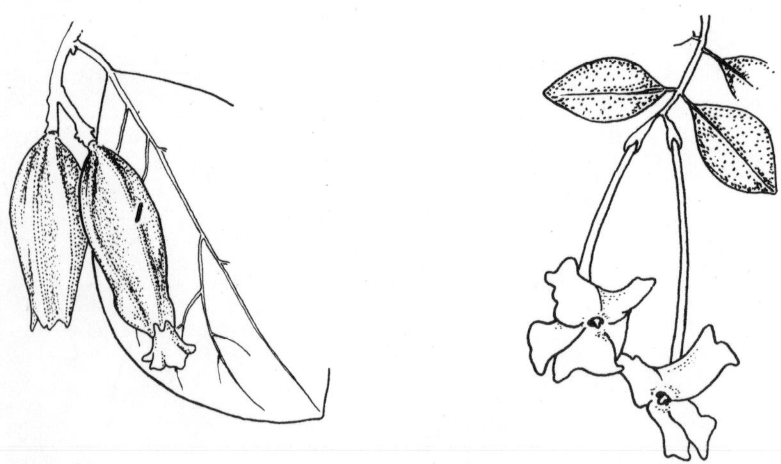

*Juanulloa aurantiaca* is a nice small shrub of the nightshade family. In its native land, Peru, it grows only as an epiphyte, the same as the other species of this genus

*Brunfelsia undulata* from the Antilles has white blossoms

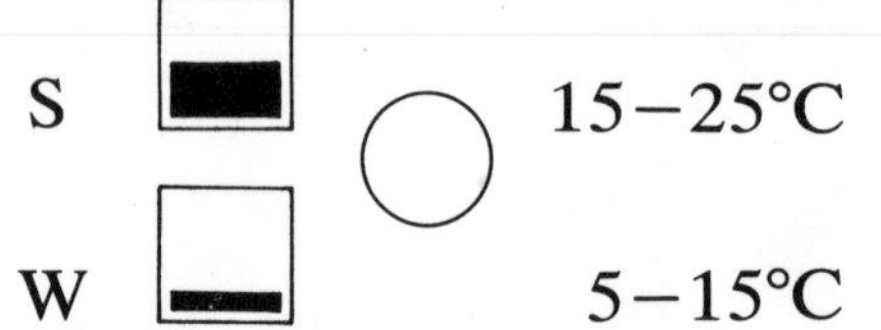

# *Camellia japonica* 'Chandleri Elegans'

Camellias are flowers that, though past the peak of their popularity, remain standard items for the nurseryman, even though they cannot be grown in modern homes with central heating. The reason for this entrenched position is no doubt their beauty as well as the wealth of shape and colour of their blooms. The cultivars raised to date run into the thousands! If we were to leaf through camellia club journals or Japanese gardeners' journals we would surely be tempted, at least momentarily, to try growing camellias ourselves.

Unless you have a conservatory or greenhouse for growing cool-loving species in winter without heat, or, at the most, only with slight heat, then you must truly give up hope of permanent success, for camellias must have a winter temperature of 3 to 5°C (38 to 41°F). In a warm flat, which furthermore has a dry atmosphere, they rapidly fade and finally die. That is why they tend nowadays to be grown only as temporary decoration and the whole plant discarded after the flowers are spent.

The type species, *Camellia japonica,* grows wild in the subtropical forests of Korea, northern China and Japan (the islands of Okinawa and Kyushu), where it reaches a height of 15 m (50 ft). The colour variability of its blooms (in the wild one will encounter white, pink as well as red and a mixture of colours) makes it ideal for hybridization. The illustrated cultivar, most commonly grown in Europe because of the absolute certainty of its flowering, has blossoms about 10 cm (4 in) across. It was raised by Chandler in 1824. There is no point in listing the names of the countless forms; interested readers who are able to provide the necessary conditions for overwintering camellias can select the one they like best by consulting the special journals on the subject.

Camellias need an acid soil with a pH of between 4.5 and 5.5, which can be provided by mixing dark pine leaf mould with peat and adding some sand. They can be propagated readily by means of cuttings, which should be inserted in February or March in a mixture of peat and sand in a slightly warm, humid propagator. When watering, use only soft water or water that has been slightly acidified.

  5–15°C

# *Catharanthus roseus*

## Madagascar Periwinkle

If you were to encounter the illustrated plant, *Catharanthus roseus* (syn. *Vinca rosea*), in the wild for the first time you would hardly believe it was not a house plant. Even its name, derived from the Greek words *katharos,* meaning flawless, pure, and *anthos,* meaning flower, is extremely apt. The low, compact 'shrublets' with dense, glossy foliage and fairly large pink flowers, 3.5 cm (1¼ in) across, reach a height of 30 to 70 cm (12 to 28 in), depending on the site and available nourishment.

Members of this species are to be found in all tropical countries, always in warm, sunny situations, often on sand flats or sand banks. The colour of the flowers, however, is not always pink, but varies from pure white, through white with a pink 'eye' in the centre, to dark crimson – colours which are found also in cultivation.

Though it is a perennial, catharanthus is often grown as an annual in Europe. If sown very early in spring it flowers from as early as midsummer continuously until the frost, so that it can be used, for instance, as a window-box plant. It overwinters well in a cool room and will produce flowers the following year in late spring.

Some years ago this plant became the focus of attention of medical science concerned with cancer research, for it was found to contain alkaloids (vegetable poisons) that have a significant effect on certain types of cancer. This, of course, is not meant as a recommendation but on the contrary as a warning to the reader, for the plant is extremely poisonous!

The best method of cultivation is to sow seeds in February, grow the plant until it flowers, then hard prune it in autumn, using the prunings as cuttings and trying to preserve the parent plant. The cuttings root rapidly and survive the winter better than older plants, often without damage even in a warm room. The substrate should be moderately heavy, relatively nourishing and porous, such as John Innes potting compost.

*Thevetia peruviana*

 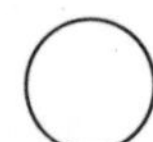  10–25°C

# *Clerodendrum thomsonae*

## Glory Bower, Bleeding Heart Vine

It is not usual for a species that has extremely attractive flowers to be undemanding as regards cultivation. Generally, growing plants with decorative flowers is coupled with the necessity of providing them with cool conditions in winter and many species are better suited for the conservatory or plant-case than for room decoration.

All that is needed for success in growing the illustrated plant, however, is a warm room and plenty of space by a sunny window. It will even be quite content with a cooler room if provided with enough light.

*Clerodendrum thomsonae* is a twining shrub which in its native home – west Africa – grows in warm forests. It generally flowers in spring, but if it is hard pruned after flowering it will flower a second time the same year. The dense clusters of flowers with inflated white calyx and bright red corolla are truly lovely. The decorative effect is heightened by the attractive foliage. Some of the leaves are shed in winter. The calyxes, often a crimson hue, remain on the plant long after flowering has finished.

Though clerodendrum reaches a height of 4 m (13 ft), there is no need to fear it will crowd us out of the room. Not only is hard pruning possible, it is a must for keeping the plant shapely and thus for proper cultivation; 60 cm (2 ft) is the height at which it should be maintained. When pruned, the plant quickly puts out numerous side shoots that produce flowers. Pruning should be carried out in late winter as soon as the light conditions improve and the plant begins growth.

Another very attractive species of the same genus is *C. speciosissimum,* an upright shrub with large leaves covered thickly with soft hairs and large terminal clusters of scarlet flowers.

Clerodendrum should be grown in a heavy, nourishing soil composed of compost, loam and sand, to which some peat may be added. Propagation is easy, for the spring prunings root quite readily in a peat and sand mixture in a warm propagator. In summer the plant requires regular and liberal feeding which helps to turn the new growth woody.

*Petrea volubilis*

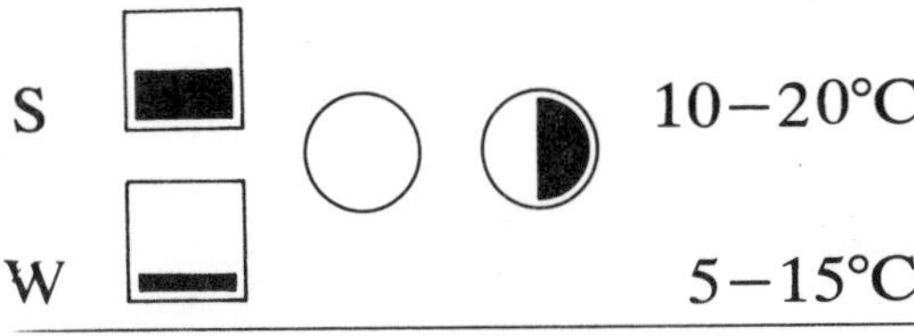


10–20°C

5–15°C

# *Clivia miniata*

## Kafir Lily

Clivia is a typical representative of a 'classic' decorative plant. This, of course, does not mean we should turn our backs on it – on the contrary – whole generations of flower-lovers speak in favour of its cultivation. All that is necessary is a cool spot in winter and we shall be rewarded with nice specimens that will flower every year.

The type species is native to Natal, South Africa, where it always grows amidst taller vegetation, in other words shaded from direct sunlight. Failure to flower may be caused by mistakes growers often make, such as leaving the plant in a warm room in winter (the correct temperature should be between 8 and 15°C (47 and 59°F), putting the flowerpot in a window that is sunny all day, or, putting it in full shade. Growth will be good, even vigorous in such conditions, but the plants will not flower.

Clivia does best in a window facing north or north-east. If it is sunny then the pot should be placed on the floor beneath the window so the plant 'reaches for the light'. In winter the plant should be put in a cool spot and water should be withheld almost entirely; light conditions during this period are not important, a minimum of light suffices.

There are many types of clivias in cultivation, differing in the intensity of the coloration as well as in the habit of growth. Attractive is the cultivar 'Striata' with leaves longitudinally striped white or yellowish.

Other species occasionally cultivated include *Clivia gardenii* and *C. nobilis,* with flowers coloured deep red, almost scarlet.

If you succeed in pollinating the flowers and obtaining seeds, these should be sown as soon as they are gathered in January and the seedlings grown in continually warm conditions for at least $1^1/_2$ years.

The growing medium must be heavy and nourishing, best of all loamy soil enriched with humus and with an addition of sand. Feed and water should be supplied in ample amounts during the growth period. Clivias should not be transplanted until after two or three years when they are thoroughly pot-bound. Before this, merely replace part of the compost in the container with some fresh, nourishing compost.

*Clivia nobilis*

 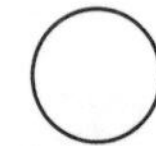  10–30°C

# *Cyclamen × persicum*

## Sow Bread

Like clivias, cyclamen is also one of the 'classic' house plants better suited to cool conditions. It does not do well in modern centrally-heated homes and thus is grown only as a temporary house plant which is discarded after it has finished flowering. This is a pity, for the flowers are comparable to the loveliest of nature's creations as regards shape and colour and a nice tabletop arrangement rivals that of orchids in beauty.

*Cyclamen persicum,* despite its name, is not a native of Persia, but of central Palestine and the area extending from Sicily to Cyprus, the south-east Aegean islands, Crete and Rhodes. It also occurs in one isolated site in Tunisia, but there is justified reason to suspect that it was planted out there intentionally as an ornamental. It grows generally on limestone rocks in the undergrowth of low, open woodlands where the fallen leaves of the trees provide a nourishing layer of humus. Rising from the tuber are long-stalked, obcordate leaves; the flowers of the type species are white or pink and usually very fragrant.

Cyclamen was introduced into cultivation as early as the 17th century and growers soon began raising hybrids. Nowadays there are countless lovely cultivars in single colours as well as mixed colours, with waved or variously twisted petals, and there is no point in recommending any special one. The best thing is to visit the florist and take your pick from his selection.

Growers often have a cool place where they can store the tubers for the winter after watering has been stopped and the plants have died back in autumn. In spring these should be re-potted in a mixture of peat, leaf mould and loam and watered carefully.

If conditions are congenial the grower can brighten his assortment with other species of cyclamen, such as *C. africanum* from Algeria, which is very similar to *C. neapolitanum* grown in gardens. The tuber of this species is up to 20 cm (8 in) in diameter, the flowers relatively large and coloured pink.

*Ardisiandra sibthorpoides*

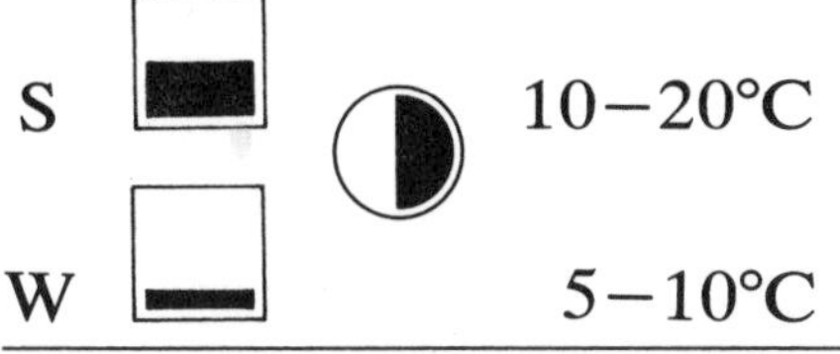


10–20°C

5–10°C

# *Dalechampia spathulata*

Those who often visit botanical gardens are doubtless familiar with the plant in the illustration. Unfortunately, however, it is still not seen at the florist's.

Dalechampia is one of the members of the spurge family that is, quite unjustly, still neglected by growers. The changed conditions in modern homes, of which mention is being continually made in this book as a 'turning point' in the selection of house plants, created a favourable environment for this genus.

Of the more than 100 species found mostly in tropical America, as well as in Africa, Asia and Madagascar, the one chosen for this book is truly lovely. It is a small, upright shrub native to the warm forests of Mexico, where it reaches a height of 1 m (3 ft). In cultivation, however, it is much lower – usually 25 to 30, or 50 cm (10 to 12 or 20 in). The leaves remain the same length – up to 20 cm (8 in) and are attractive even when the plant is not in flower, which is practically never for dalechampia flowers the entire year almost without let-up. The flowers themselves are not exceptionaly pretty but they are enclosed by lovely pink bracts.

From its native land dalechampia inherited relatively high heat requirements but these can be easily met in the modern home. The temperature should remain above 15°C (59°F) throughout the year; only in autumn, before the central heating has been turned on, is there a temporary drop in temperature and the plants undergo a brief dormant period.

This plant is most effective in combined arrangements, in the 'undergrowth' in a larger dish, or on 'dry land' in a paludarium, a terrarium or a plant-case. The soil does not need to be a precise blend – a mixture of leaf mould, peat and sand will do. Propagation is by means of cuttings or readily from seed.

*Dalechampia scandens*

   15–30°C

# *Dorstenia contrajerva*

If the preceding species was little known but did not escape the notice of the keen observer in the botanical garden, the genus *Dorstenia* is even less known. However, it is to be found in probably every botanical garden, for the shape and arrangement of its flowers make it an extremely interesting plant.

The genus *Dorstenia* includes some 120 species distributed in tropical America and Africa (one species, perhaps, in the East Indies). Most are herbaceous plants or low subshrubs, often with decorative foliage. Flowers of both sexes grow from a flat spreading receptacle of widely diverse shape. The male flowers are numerous, markedly simplified, usually with two anthers; the female flowers are far fewer, nearly closed, with a prominent style. The whole cluster is often enclosed by bracts that are fringed, thread-like or of some other unusual shape. Very attractive are the succulents Dorstenias with the thick stem.

*Dorstenia contrajerva* is found in Central America and the Antilles, its range extending into South America as far as Venezuela and Colombia, where it generally grows in damp tropical forests alongside waterfalls and rivers, sometimes also on moss-covered rocks at elevations of 300 to 1,000 m (960 to 3,300 ft). It always seeks deeply shaded places, which is a very important character from the viewpoint of cultivation, for plants with similar requirements are relatively few. It needs a relatively high temperature and moist substrate as well as a moist atmosphere throughout the year and is thus suitable for growing on 'dry land' in a paludarium or in the 'undergrowth' in a larger combined arrangement.

Dorstenias may be propagated from seed and also, fairly readily, by cuttings in a warm, closed propagator.

   15–30°C

*Dorstenia nervosa* from Brazil has leaves with greyish-silver blotches

# *Euphorbia fulgens*

## Scarlet Plume

It sometimes happens that plants, and not only those with decorative flowers, fall into oblivion, even though they have been regularly cultivated for decades, only to be suddenly 'rediscovered' – a single exhibition and an enterprising nursery are all that is necessary to make such a plant a 'hit' overnight.

*Euphorbia fulgens* (syn. *E. jacquiniaeflora*), a spurge from Mexico, was the subject of such a rebirth of interest several years ago, even though it had been introduced into cultivation as far back as 1836. Previously, it was grown more for cutting and thus only now is it becoming a plant for room decoration in the modern home.

This small shrub has one drawback in that it is not much branched and the cyathiums are borne at the tips of the branches. Flowers are borne more profusely only by older, regularly pruned plants. The leaves are about 7 to 13 cm (2¾ to 5 in) long (including the stalk). The flowers generally appear in autumn and early winter, for flowering is closely tied to a decrease in light intensity, in other words it occurs only when the period of daylight is 12 to 13 hours. Such plants are called short-day flowers.

Cultivation is relatively simple. The compost should be light and porous but relatively nourishing; a loam-peat mixture, lightened by adding a little sand is ideal, or a chrysanthemum mixture may be used. In late March the plants should be given a period of rest (about 6 weeks) during which time the heat should be lowered and watering greatly limited, but not altogether withheld.

Propagation is not difficult. Cuttings should be soaked in tepid water, to release the milky sap which otherwise blocks the conductive passages in the tissues when it congeals, and then inserted in a mixture of sand and peat in a warm, moist propagator.

Another species of spurge with decorative flowers, the poinsettia, *Euphorbia pulcherrima,* is grown in the same manner, only the dormant period in spring is longer and more thorough, water being withheld completely during the entire time.

*Jatropha podagrica*

  18–25(30)°C

# *Euphorbia milii*

## Crown of Thorns

Of the nearly 2,000 species of spurge approximately 500 are succulents (see the section on succulents). Many may be seen in botanical gardens but only one has become a house plant grown for its decorative flowers.

*Euphorbia milii* (syn. *E. splendens*) is native to Madagascar, but nowadays may be found growing wild in practically all the subtropical and tropical countries of the world. The stem is the only succulent part of this small shrub, furnished as a defence against possible enemies not only with a poisonous milk sap, but also with long, rigid spines. The leaves are flat, oval to elongate-ovate, depending on the variety or cultivar, and only 1.5 to 7 cm (³/₄ to 2 ³/₄ in) long. The whole plant is usually about 1 m (3 ft) high, but occasionally one may also encounter robust specimens up to 180 cm (6 ft) high. The flowers, like those of all spurges, are small, nondescript and borne in so-called cyathiums enclosed by two bright red bracts.

This species is definitely the easiest to grow. All that it needs is a warm sunny spot on the windowsill, the right growing medium, John Innes potting compost with extra sand added and watering in summer (any excess water that collects in the saucer should be poured off so that the roots do not rot). It is recommended to lower the heat and limit watering in winter but this is not a must as the plants successfully survive warm conditions in winter. During the growing period the plants require an occasional application of feed.

Propagation is likewise easy – by means of tip cuttings which should be immersed in tepid water to wash off the exuding milk, then left to dry for a day or two in the sun and inserted in sand. When they have put out roots they should be moved to more nourishing compost, such as the mixture already referred to.

*Jatropha multifida* of the spurge family is a rewarding succulent for growing indoors

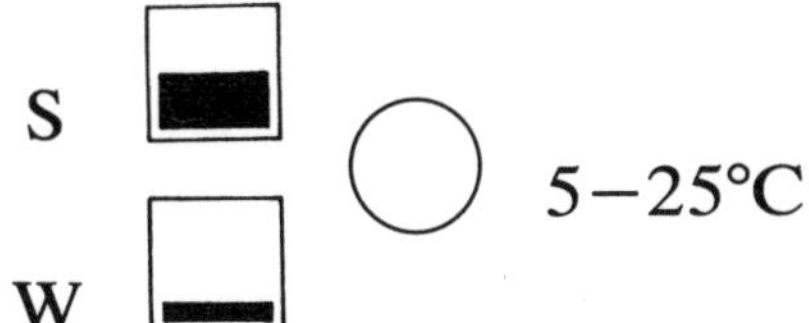

# *Fuchsia magellanica*

Fuchsias were and still are great favourites with house-plant growers. Their lovely flowers, composed of a tube with spreading sepals subtending a four-petalled corolla, come in various bright colour combinations, particularly the cultivars. It is interesting to note that flower-lovers also prize the 'botanical' fuchsias, and so even in homes one encounters fairly small-flowered but very handsome type species.

This does not mean that type species do not include among their number ones with large flowers. *Fuchsia macrantha* from Peru has blossoms (unusual in that they lack a corolla) which are up to 12 cm (4³/₄ in) long. On the other hand, there are also miniature forms. Anyone encountering, for example, *F. minimiflora,* which is a common shrub in the fir forest at the foot of Popocatépetl in Mexico, would certainly be hard put to identify this plant, with reddish flowers less than 0.5 cm (¹/₄ in) long, as a fuchsia.

Unfortunately, members of this genus, embracing some 100 species found mostly in the mountains of Central and South America with several reaching as far as New Zealand and Tahiti, require cold conditions in winter with temperatures close to freezing point. Many species tolerate light frosts, and even in central Europe it is possible to try and grow them permanently in the garden with only a light protective cover of evergreen twigs in winter. This applies also to the illustrated species, native to the Chilean coast of the Strait of Magellan and to Argentina. This shrub, reaching a height of 5 m (16 ft) in the wild, overwinters well, for example, in England and in Germany's wine-growing region.

The first prerequisite for growing fuchsias successfully is overwintering them in a suitable cold place (even a cellar will do). During the growth period they should be put in a sunny or lightly shaded spot with plenty of fresh air; they will welcome being put out on the balcony or patio. The soil should be rather heavy and nourishing, for example a mixture of loam, rotted turves, leaf mould, sand and peat. The plants should be pruned fairly hard every spring. The prunings may be used as cuttings which will root readily in a propagator at a temperature of about 18°C (65°F).

*Fuchsia excorticata* from New Zealand may attain the size of a tree when full-grown

   5–15°C

# *Heliconia imbricata*

Whereas the preceding genus took us to the cold mountain heights, we now descend again to sea level or slightly above it, to the tropical rainforests and steaming swamps — the home of magnificent plants which have only recently begun to find their way into cultivation as house plants.

At first glance most species of *Heliconia* resemble a several-storeyed *Strelitzia*. The resemblance is not a chance one, for the two genera are closely related. *Strelitzia*, however, consists of only five South African species, whereas *Heliconia* is a genus of tropical America embracing some 150 species.

Botanical gardens generally contain other species than the illustrated one from Costa Rica. The one mainly found there is *Heliconia bihai*, distributed from Mexico to southern Brazil, which reaches a height of 6 m (20 ft) in the wild (in cultivation, barely half that as a rule). The flower spikes are about 60 cm (2 ft) high; the bracts bright scarlet tipped with yellow, the flowers yellow. Noted for its beautiful coloration is the species *H. metallica*, about 2 m (6 ft) high. The leaves have red stalks and are coloured violet-purple on the underside and glossy, velvety green above. The flower stem is red, the bracts green, the flowers green-red. Readers will surely agree that the illustration and descriptions suffice to support the statement that these are not only exotic but also spectacular plants that merit the attention of growers. Not all species, however, are nearly so robust and vigorous. For example, in the mountains round Machu Picchu in Peru the author once collected *H. affinis*, a plant barely 1.5 m (5 ft) high, with a full half of that taken up by the bright yellow-pink-orange-red flower spikes. Cross-breeding, particularly of the miniature species, offers interesting and far-reaching prospects.

Heliconias should be grown in a peaty compost enriched with loam at a permanently high temperature and with high humidity, in other words in a glasshouse, large plant-case or paludarium.

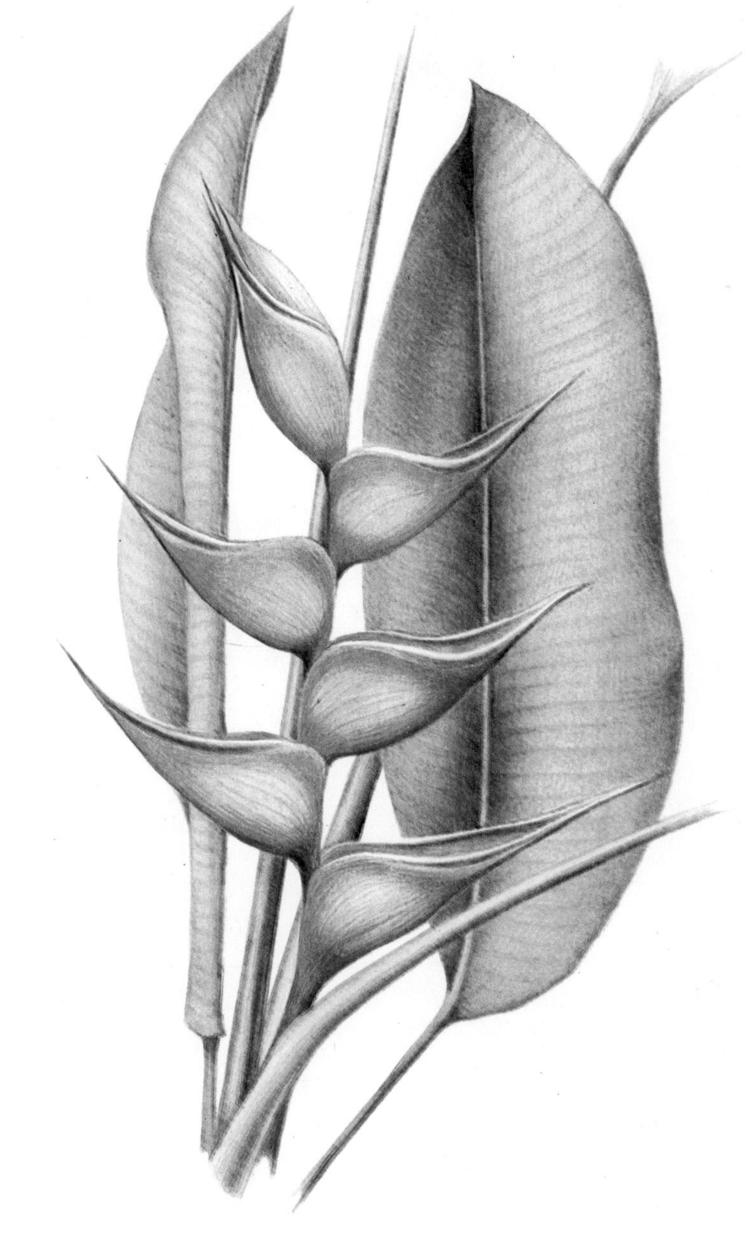

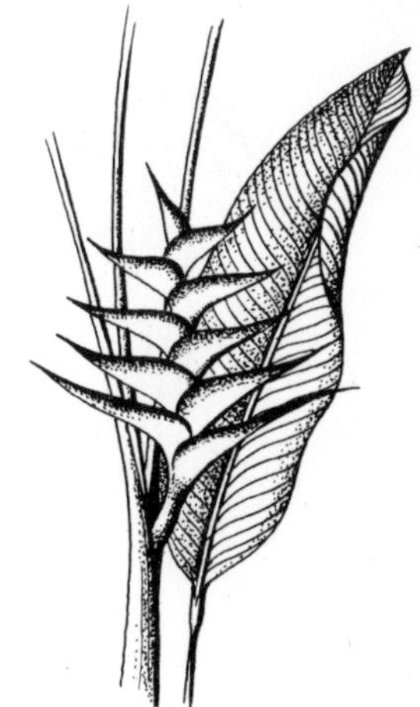

*Heliconia caribaea* is a robust herb with leaves measuring up to 1 m (3 ft). The bracts are waxy, red-yellow patterned with vivid green.

    18–30°C

# *Hibiscus rosa-sinensis*

Few exotic plants have won such popularity as the hibiscus; rarely will one find such magnificent, large, colourful flowers in the plant realm. There is one drawback, however – hibiscus takes up too much space. Growers can therefore thank the growth regulating chemicals commonly used by nurseries nowadays for the plant's comeback in recent years.

Hibiscus is probably truly a native of China, as its name *sinensis* indicates. But its beauty has been prized for many years and thus it spread to the subtropical and tropical countries of the whole world – hence the author's use of the word 'probably'.

If left unchecked the shrub grows to a height of 6 m (20 ft). Its growth, however, need not be kept within bounds by chemical means; this can also be done by a good pair of secateurs. The principal requirements of the hibiscus are heat, light and good nourishment. Overwintering in a cool room, though recommended, is not a must. However, if you can put the shrub in a cool spot and limit watering, then profuse flowering the following year is assured.

Besides many cultivars differing in shape and colour the variegated *H. rosa-sinensis* 'Cooperi', with leaves edged white and spotted crimson and pink, is also frequently encountered. The flower, however, is not as nice – the petals are narrow and coloured an unattractive pink. Gorgeous, on the other hand, is the African species *H. schizopetalus,* which has pendant, turban-like flowers with blood-red, fringed petals. It requires ample heat even in winter and is thus very suitable for modern centrally-heated homes.

All hibiscuses can be readily multiplied by spring prunings used as cuttings and inserted in a warm propagator. Hard pruning is a must, particularly in the case of *H. schizopetalus,* which otherwise readily grows too big.

The soil should be a nourishing mixture composed of rotted turves, leaf mould and a smaller portion of peat and sand. Feed should be applied liberally throughout the entire growing season.

*Hibiscus schizopetalus,* an African species very well suited to growing indoors; it must be kept a reasonable size by pruning

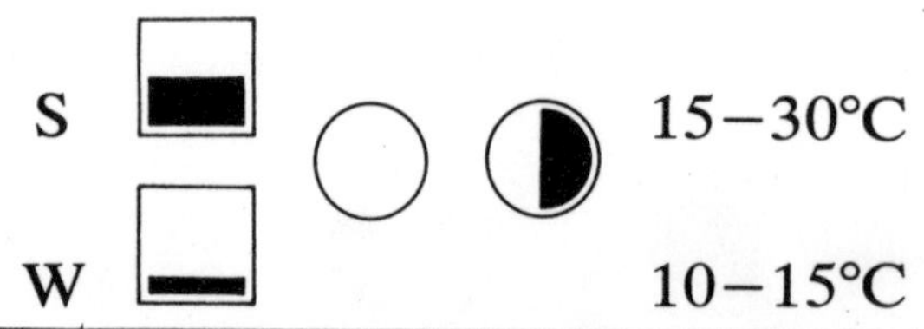

# *Jacobinia pohliana*

Tropical America provided horticulture with truly vast opportunities and there is still much to be discovered in that territory. Many plants that were described and introduced into cultivation have since disappeared from the scene and await their come-back and it is practically certain that vast areas of this continent have yet to reveal countless treasures.

Members of the genus *Jacobinia* (often listed under the name *Justicia*) are, perhaps, likewise waiting to be rediscovered. More than 50 species with pretty flowers and attractive foliage have been described to date. Most were at one time cultivated and yet they gradually disappeared so that nowadays only the following two are generally found in nurseries and botanical gardens: *Jacobinia carnea* and the illustrated *J. pohliana*. Of the other species, occasionally one comes across a few with scant or nondescript flower clusters, such as *J. pauciflora* and *J. ghiesbreghtiana*.

*Jacobinia pohliana* (syn. *Cyrtanthera pohliana*) native to Brazil, is very similar to *J. carnea* but is much larger in all its parts and also has denser foliage. In the wild the shrub grows to a height of more than 2 m (6 ft), but in cultivation it hardly reaches half that height. The leaves measure more than 20 cm (8 in) in length, the individual flowers are about 5 cm (2 in) long and slightly sticky. Unfortunately, they are not very long-lived and so jacobinia is used for decoration where the flowers are not a decisive element, such as in a combined dish arrangement.

Cultivation is not difficult. If the plants are grown in heavy, nourishing soil, watered regularly and in summer provided with fresh air and protection against sunscorch by light shading, then there is no need to fear failure. In winter they appreciate some rest but this is not a must; they will flower from May till October even without it. Propagation is easy by means of cuttings.

*Chamaeranthemum gaudichaudii*

  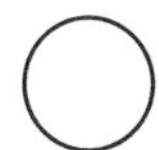 5–25°C

# *Kaempferia rotunda*

It is interesting that the popularity of plants that die back for the winter is greater in tropical countries than in Europe. Homes in the tropics look quite different before plant growth starts in spring and after it has started, when some appear to be filled with twice as many plants. This is probably due to the fact that the natural environment is so bright and colourful that people do not feel the same longing for greenery as do those living in Europe, and do not make an effort to have it constantly about them. It is, of course, a pity to eliminate certain truly beautiful species that are easy to grow, but which die down for the winter. All that is needed to avoid having a seemingly empty flower pot around during the dormant period is to put them in a dish together with some other plant. For example, the illustrated species, which overwinters in the form of a thickened rhizome, can be combined with some evergreen, shallow-rooting species such as maranta.

The genus *Kaempferia* includes some 45 species distributed in tropical and subtropical Asia, and found occasionally also in Africa. The illustrated *K. rotunda* is from the Indo-Malaysian region where it is a great favourite for home decoration.

When its 'winter rest period' (actually the dry season between the monsoon rains) is over, the flowers are first to appear above the ground. These are relatively large (some 6 to 7 cm [2¼ to 2¾ in]) in diameter and very fragrant. They are followed by the leaves, which are silvery on the upper surface, violet-purple below and often more than ½ m (20 in) long. The storage organ is a thick rhizome which yields a yellow oil scented like camphor at first and later like tarragon. Also widely grown is *K. galanga,* whose range extends from India to Vietnam and from Malaysia to New Guinea. It is a small species with prostrate, basal leaves that are broadly oval and only about 10 cm (4 in) long. The flowers, approximately 12 to a plant, are attractive even though they measure only about 2 cm (¾ in) across. The rhizome contains oils and volatile oils, also poisonous substances used by the Papuans of New Guinea as a dangerous narcotic in their ceremonials.

Cultivation is truly easy. The plants should be grown in a mixture of peat, leaf mould and sand in flat dishes rather than pots. In winter they should be watered only very lightly and occasionally after they have died back.

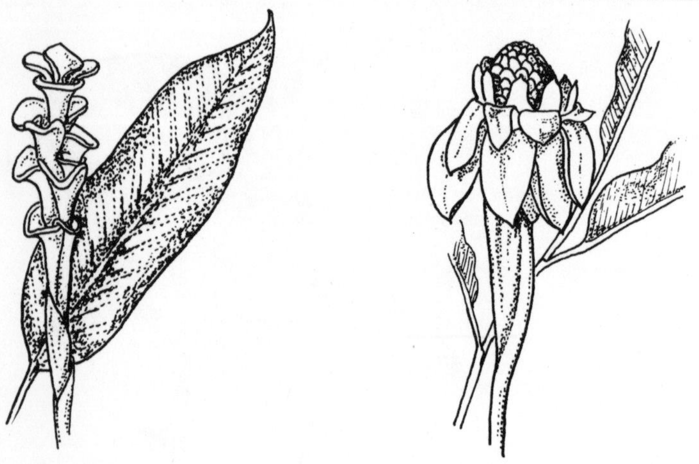

*Curcuma roscoeana* – the green bracts turn red during flowering

*Phaeomeria magnifica* of the ginger family is often known by the name *Nicolaia elatior;* it is a magnificent plant suitable only for a large glasshouse

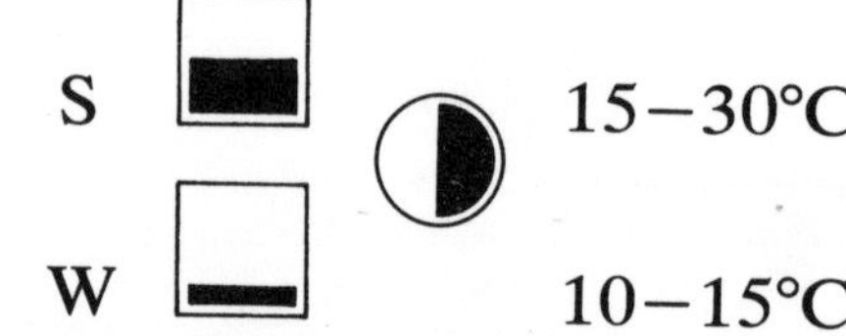

# *Lantana* (Camara-Hybrids)

## Shrub Verbena, Yellow Sage

Plants introduced into cultivation and grown for their beauty are often troublesome weeds in the tropics. Such is the case with the many species of *Lantana,* which in their native land may be commonly found growing on walls and in hedgerows. Because they are rather tall shrubs, they fill the same function as the blackthorn in Europe.

The approximately 160 species described to date are mostly native to tropical America as well as east Asia. The type species are practically unknown in cultivation. Instead, a hybrid produced by crossing *Lantana camara* with *L. montevidensis* and *L. urticaefolia* is grown. Other species may also have been involved in the crossing and the whole group is named *Lantana* (Camara-Hybrids) and contains many cultivars.

The flower clusters develop from the margin inward and the individual florets often change colour during flowering. Thus, for example, a plant in full bloom may have dark pink flowers on the margin and pale yellow ones in the centre ('Arlequin'), or they may be a combination of scarlet and orange ('Professor Raoux'). The range of colour combinations is wide and so growers are sure to find a plant to their liking.

Lantanas are generally woody shrubs that can readily be kept within reasonable bounds. They are suitable for both relatively cool or warm flats, the one prerequisite for successful growth being ample light, best of all full sunshine. In summer they may be moved outdoors and used for decoration on a balcony or in a window-box where they are plunged together with the pot. They are readily propagated by cuttings that root rapidly even in water. Thus, shoots removed from a single plant during late-winter pruning will provide a goodly number of young specimens that will flower profusely the same year in the window-box. The soil should be a heavy mixture composed of leaf mould, compost, rotted turves and loam with a little peat which helps keep the substrate evenly moist in summer.

*Duranta repens*

  5–25°C

# *Medinilla magnifica*

## Rose Grape

Surely the best known, loveliest and also most widely cultivated member of this family is the Medinilla from the Philippines. Though by no means a novelty on the market (it has been a popular plant since the mid-19th century), it did not begin to be grown more widely until the 1960s.

*Medinilla magnifica* is a relatively robust shrub reaching a height of 1.5 m (5 ft). The thick angular stems, turning woody at the base, bear up to 30-cm-(1-ft-) long leaves with pronounced veins. The plant's chief ornament is the inflorescence, and not only the flowers but also the bracts by which they are enclosed. The flowers are borne over a very long period and in robust specimens they are up to 70 cm (28 in) long.

Somewhat less decorative but also suitable for cultivation are the related species *M. curtisii* (Sumatra), *M. javanensis* (Java), *M. sieboldiana* (the Moluccas), and *M. venosa* (Malaysia).

The illustrated species is not particularly demanding and is well suited for home decoration. It does not tolerate temperatures below 15°C (59°F) for a lengthy period and needs a period of rest with greatly limited watering in autumn and winter, which is when it forms the flowers for the next display.

The soil should be the lightest possible and slightly acid. A mixture of beech leaf mould, pine leaf litter, peat and sand with a small addition of loam is ideal. An application of hornmeal should be provided in spring, and during the growing season a weekly application of feed is recommended.

The easiest method of propagation is from seed, but seedlings are slow to develop and little inclined to flower. For this reason propagation by cuttings is preferred. These should be partly woody and inserted in a mixture of sand and peat in a warm propagator. They are slow to root and frequently not all of them do so.

*Miconia magnifica*

  10–30°C

# *Pachystachys lutea*

## Lollipop Plant

It is not very often, in recent years, that nurserymen have been able to offer us a striking new genus but *Pachystachys* is definitely such a plant and a valuable addition to the available assortment.

*Pachystachys lutea* is a small shrub, which turns woody at the base and reaches a height of about 1 m (3 ft) in cultivation. It is native to the South American tropics, more accurately to Peru, the same as the other six species of this genus. It is grown chiefly for its showy flowers, 10- to 12-cm-(4-to $4^{3}/_{4}$-in-) long spikes of deep yellow bracts from the axils of which the snow white blossoms grow. The flowers greatly resemble those of beloperone and aphelandra. That is why, at least at the beginning, this genus was often listed in catalogues under the wrong name or else was mistaken for the cultivar *Beloperone guttata* 'Yellow Queen'. They are readily distinguished, however, for the flowers of pachystachys are erect whereas those of beloperone are pendant.

The plants are loveliest if pruned hard each year. They are then thick, compact, reliably flowering specimens with dense foliage. Unpruned plants drop the lower leaves and become leggy, which certainly does not add to their attractiveness.

Plants should be pruned in spring and the prunings may be used as cuttings. These should be shortened to three buds, the base cut at a slant, and inserted in a mixture of peat and sand in a warm propagator, where they will root well and rapidly even without the use of hormone rooting powder. When they have developed 2 to 3 pairs of new leaves the rooted cuttings should be transferred to a standard peat potting compost or to a mixture of peat, leaf mould and sand.

Plants should be watered liberally throughout the growing period and feed, either organic or organo-mineral fertilizers, should be applied frequently. In winter watering should be limited, and, if possible, the plants moved to a well-lit but cooler place.

   18–30°C

*Crossandra* x *infundibuliformis* is a favourite house plant. Many species of this genus, for example *C. nilotica,* tolerate deep shade

# Pavonia multiflora

The mallow family has provided horticulture with several lovely and valuable species – take *Hibiscus* or *Abutilon,* for example. However, it remains a rich, untapped source. There still exist lovely and easily grown plants that, for incomprehensible reasons, have not yet found their place in botanical gardens.

One such example is *Pavonia,* a relatively large genus comprising some 70 species native to tropical America and Africa. Most frequently encountered in collections is the illustrated species, even though generally under the wrong name of *Pavonia intermedia.* It is a shrub about 1 m (3 ft) high with a stem that is often prostrate, in which case it must be tied to a support. The leaves are approximately 20 cm (8 in) long, deep green, and persistent, remaining on the plant the entire year. The flowers, in terminal racemes, are produced throughout the year. The combination of rosy crimson petals and deep dark blue anthers is truly spectacular, comparable, perhaps, only to the blossoms of certain passion flowers. Many other species are also grown with flowers that are equally striking and beautiful in deep purple, violet, pink as well as yellow, which provide possibilities for obtaining large-flowered and interestingly-coloured hybrids. The fruit is a nutlet often furnished with hooks and spines. In the wild the fruits are dispersed by animals in whose fur they catch. The seeds germinate readily and remain viable for a number of years.

Pavonias should be grown in a warm room without any distinct period of rest. They tolerate full sun as well as light shade, but must be provided with a compost that is kept quite moist and if possible also with fresh air. That is why they are particularly suitable for growing in a larger mixed arrangement as well as on 'dry land' in a paludarium. Propagation is by means of cuttings, obtained from prunings when the plant is trimmed in spring, or by seeds. A suitable compost consists of a mixture of peat, leaf mould, rotted turves and sand. Alternatively, use John Innes potting compost.

*Malvaviscus penduliflorus*

  15–25°C

# *Pelargonium* (Peltatum-Hybrids) 'Crocodile'

## Ivy-leaved Pelargonium

Pelargoniums have been popular plants for room and above all window-box decoration since as far back as the mid-18th century. The approximately 250 species, found mostly in South Africa (a few also occur in Asia), provided a solid foundation and numerous opportunities for cross-breeding so that nowadays the selection includes hundreds of cultivars that have become permanent items in nursery catalogues.

The illustrated cultivar 'Crocodile' (named thus because the leaves are veined like a crocodile's skin) belongs to the large group of hybrids derived from the type species *Pelargonium peltatum,* which is native to South Africa and also occurs in the wild in the Mediterranean region. It has pink flowers and typical shield-shaped leaves that are either five-edged or five-lobed. Peltatum-Hybrids were obtained by crossing *P. peltatum* with *P. lateripes*. Later hybrids were also obtained from crossings with other large groups of pelargoniums – namely Grandiflorum-Hybrids and Zonale-Hybrids. A characteristic trait is the habit of growth; the stems are generally prostrate or even pendant and thus this group includes many types that are good for window-box cultivation.

Pelargoniums cannot be grown in a warm room the whole year. Neither can those grown in window-boxes remain outside during the winter. Before the first frost they should be moved, together with the box, to a cool but frost-free room or cellar. Young plants grown from cuttings taken in August should likewise be overwintered in a cool room (cuttings may also be taken in March) but must be provided with sufficient light. In spring the plants should be put in new compost (John Innes potting compost No. 1 or 2 is ideal) and supplied liberally with water as well as feed throughout the late spring and summer. Since Peltatum-Hybrids are generally grown as pendant plants they should be combined with upright cultivars from the other groups. Another pelargonium that is very attractive and does well in like conditions is the 'botanical' species *P. endlicherianum* from Syria and Asia Minor, which is practically entirely hardy. Its flowers are very interesting in that only the upper two petals are large and crimson-pink, whereas the bottom three are atrophied. It is also very good for a window-box rock garden if it can be protected against too much damp in winter.

*Pelargonium havlasae* from West Australia is a very rare species with soft pink flowers

 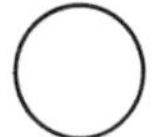  5–20°C

# *Saintpaulia × ionantha*

## African Violet

This plant is a standard item for just about every nursery, it may be seen in every florist's window and its leaves are posted throughout the world in an exchange of breeding material between specialist growers. There are countless clubs, societies and journals devoted to a single species, or rather hybrids derived from crossings between two basic species: *Saintpaulia ionantha* and *S. confusa.*

The 19 known species are native to Tanzania, where they grow at elevations ranging from sea level to 2,000 m (6,600 ft), generally in the undergrowth of rainforests. All have blue or violet flowers and leaves that are often tomentose.

*Saintpaulia confusa* differs from *S. ionantha* by having slightly darker flowers and leaves that, besides being thickly and uniformly tomentose, also have longer, stiffer hairs.

In the 1950s there were already 800 hybrids registered in the USA and, what with the continued popularity of these plants, it may be estimated that their number has doubled since then so that the grower has no problem choosing one to his liking. The range includes white, pale pink, crimson-pink, violet as well as bicolored forms; forms with single, semi-double or double blossoms, with leaves that are variegated, attractively waved, or variously tomentose.

Naturally the plants' popularity is also due to the ease of cultivation. All they need for good results is a warm room, slight shade, a small pot (they do poorly in a large one) and an ever-moist compost composed of leaf mould, peat and sand or one of the proprietary peat-based composts. For assured success the leaves must never be sprayed or splashed with water, particularly at lower temperatures, for then they become spotted and rot. Propagation is easy by means of leaf cuttings; the leaf stalk should be inserted either in sand or a mixture of peat and sand. They root rapidly and reliably.

*Saintpaulia grotei*

   15–25°C

# *Sinningia regina*

## Gloxinia

Sinningias are popular, showy house plants. Known to many (possibly under the incorrect name of gloxinia) is the complex hybrid which is descended from the species *Sinningia speciosa* (syn. *Gloxinia regina*) and has large, velvety flowers.

Both hybrids and type species, of which there are altogether 15 growing in Brazil, have similar requirements: a well-lit spot, shaded from direct sunlight and during the growth period constant warmth and plenty of moisture. Sinningia tubers should be pressed lightly into a nourishing compost composed of a mixture of loam, leaf mould, peat, sand and charcoal. Alternatively, use John Innes potting compost No. 2. Because they are plants that need a very rich diet they must be given regular applications of feed, best of all organic fertilizers, throughout the growth period. If dry cow manure is available, feed the plants the liquid extract obtained by steeping it in water.

Sinningias are readily propagated either by means of the minute seeds, which should be sown on the surface of sterile peat, or else by means of leaf cuttings in the same way as for begonias, that is by laying leaf cuttings on the surface of the rooting medium, or by taking whole leaves and inserting the stalks in a mixture of sand and chopped peat. In all instances, however, the one prerequisite is a warm and moist propagator.

A very important factor in growing sinningias successfully is watering. Water must not come in contact with the leaves, otherwise they rot quickly. Therefore water should be supplied to the roots or else poured into the dish in which the pot is standing.

The illustrated species is not commonly seen in cultivation. Nevertheless, it has already been used for breeding purposes and some 20 years ago gave rise to a new line of hybrids. Somewhat more tender than this readily cultivated species is the miniature *S. pusilla*. The whole plant is only about 2.5 cm (1 in) high and the corolla, coloured white outside and lilac inside, is almost 2 cm (3/4 in) long. *S. barbata* is a truly beautiful species with leaves that have a metallic sheen and are coloured purple on the underside. The white flowers are spotted with red inside.

All sinningias pass through a period of complete rest in winter. At its onset the tubers should be lifted and stored in dry and cool conditions until it is again time for spring planting.

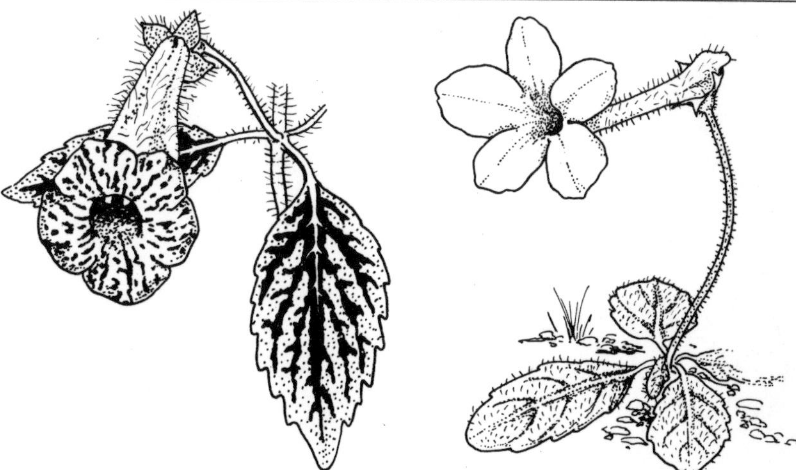

*Kohleria amabilis* from Central and South America is a popular house plant that does well in the modern home

*Sinningia pusilla* is a miniature plant, barely reaching a height of 2.5 cm (1 in). The flower is lilac-blue

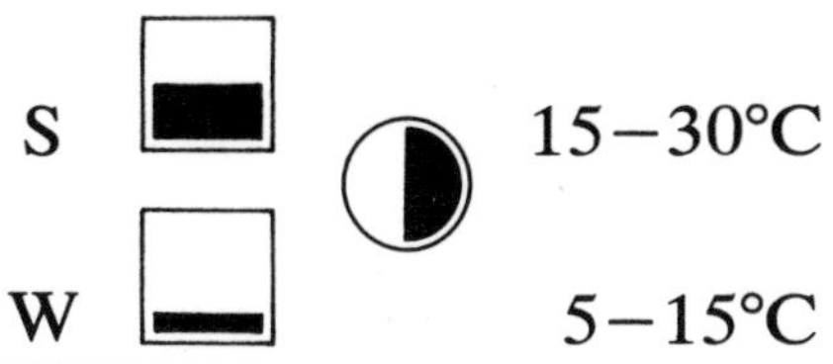


15–30°C

5–15°C

# *Spathiphyllum wallisii*

## White Sails, Lily of Peace

Only a few genera and species of aroids are grown for their attractive flowers. Many are cool-loving garden plants (arum, lysichitum, symplocarpus, calla, arisaema), others are suitable only for cool homes (zantedeschia, with the exception of species with coloured flowers such as *Z. elliotiana*). The selection of aroids with decorative flowers which can be used as house plants in modern centrally-heated homes is very limited; it includes anthurium, typhonium, steudnera and spathiphyllum.

All 36 known species of *Spathiphyllum* are native to South America. The illustrated species has a rather unusual history. It was once picked up 'in the swamps of Colombia' and sent to the botanical garden in St Petersburg, whence it was introduced to botanical gardens throughout the world as well as into cultivation, but was never found in the wild again. The plant is approximately 30 to 40 cm (12 to 16 in) high with dark green, distinctly-veined leaves and a short, thick underground rhizome. Also a fairly common house plant is the similar species *S. blandum,* whose area of distribution embraces a large territory extending from Mexico to Brazil, where it grows in the warm tropical forests alongside water or in depressions in savannas where water is retained a long time after rains.

Spathiphyllums are ideal plants for the paludarium, for most are bog plants or else require a high water table or regular flooding. They need ample heat, even in winter, when the temperature should not drop below 18°C (65°F) for more than a short period.

They should be grown in a peaty compost with an addition of sand and leaf mould. It must never dry out completely, for the roots of these plants constantly reach into water in the wild. One great advantage of spathiphyllums is that they tolerate continual shade, even deeper shade in summer.

They are readily propagated by division of the clumps or by seed sown in peat.

*Spathicarpa sagittifolia*

  18–30°C

# *Strelitzia* × *reginae*

## Bird of Paradise Flower, Crane Plant

It is not too long ago that the selection at the florist's included greater quantities of cut flowers resembling exotic birds in flight – strelitzias. Though they are not particularly difficult to grow, it is only recently that nuserymen have succeeded in raising lower-growing forms (less than 1 m [3 ft] high). Otherwise they are plants almost twice that height and thus too large for home cultivation.

*Strelitzia reginae* from South Africa does not develop a stem, but forms clumps of greyish-blue leaves approximately 80 cm (32 in) long, with thick stalks about 120 cm (4 ft) long. The blades are long, oval and curved like a spoon at the tip. The flowers, protruding from spathes borne on stems the same length as the leaves, are coloured brilliant orange and blue. Shorter forms were not obtained by cross-breeding but by selection from sowings; they are thus clones and hybrids from these clones, which may be multiplied only by vegetative means.

The other species of *Strelitzia* are not suitable for home decoration because of their great size (the only exception being the one in the line-drawing which is not generally cultivated). Their stems, which become woody, may reach up to 5 m (16 ft) in height, such as *S. nicolai.* The only one with possible prospects is *S. parvifolia,* likewise stemless, with short leaf blades and only slightly less striking flowers of the same colour as *S. reginae*. Its growth, however, is slow and it is rarely found in cultivation.

Strelitzias are generally grown from seed but may also be propagated by division of larger clumps. Seedlings reach flower-bearing size in their third year.

Cultivation is not difficult but the grower must have a conservatory or other well-lit but cool (about 10°C [50°F]) place for overwintering the plants. The container should be relatively large, the compost very rich – a mixture of loam, rotted turves, cow manure and sand. To this, coarse stone rubble should be added for rapid drainage of excess water. John Innes potting compost No. 3 would be a suitable alternative. Liberal watering and regular feeding throughout the growing period are a must. When dividing clumps the cuts should be dusted with charcoal powder and left to dry; care should also be taken not to damage the roots for otherwise they are liable to rot.

 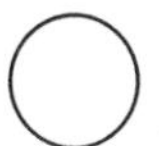  10–30°C

*Strelitzia parvifolia juncea* is unfortunately not cultivated, though it deserves to be

# *Streptocarpus × hybridus*

## Cape Primrose

Streptocarpuses are the best known members of the Gesneriaceae family and also the most widely grown. They number some 90 species; most are native to South Africa, some grow in Madagascar, and their range extends even as far as south Asia. The majority are found in light humus and litter from broad-leaf trees, many species on rocks, and some are even epiphytes (such as *S. caulescens, S. rexii* and *S. saxorum*).

Generally encountered in cultivation are hybrids which are descended from *Streptocarpus rexii* from Cape Province. It is a species with fresh green, wrinkled leaves approximately 20 cm (8 in) long and pale blue flowers with petals of unequal size. The stem is very short, as is the case with most species. *S. kirkii* has a stem of approximately 20 cm (8 in) in height, and is the only exception among cultivated species.

Very attractive and interesting are species with a single leaf which, however, is sometimes extremely large. Examples are: *S. dunnii* with leaves up to 80 cm (32 in) long and brick-red flowers; *S. galpinii* from Transvaal with 20-cm-(8-in-) long leaves and violet flowers; the large *S. grandis* with leaves 1 m (3 ft) long and up to 70 cm (28 in) across and pale blue flowers measuring only about 2.5 cm (1 in); and the well-known *S. wendlandii* with leaves 90 cm (35 in) long and about 60 cm (2 ft) across and flowers of the same colour but somewhat larger.

Cultivation is not difficult – the same as for sinningias. Streptocarpus, however, does not form tubers and thus may be wintered in cool or warm conditions, but in the latter case atmospheric moisture must be kept up. Unlike gloxinias, streptocarpus requires less shaded conditions and more ample ventilation. Propagation is easy – by means of seeds sown on the surface of sterile peat or by leaf cuttings, with stalks inserted in a peat and sand mixture or clean fresh sphagnum moss. The plants are very attractive in small dish arrangements.

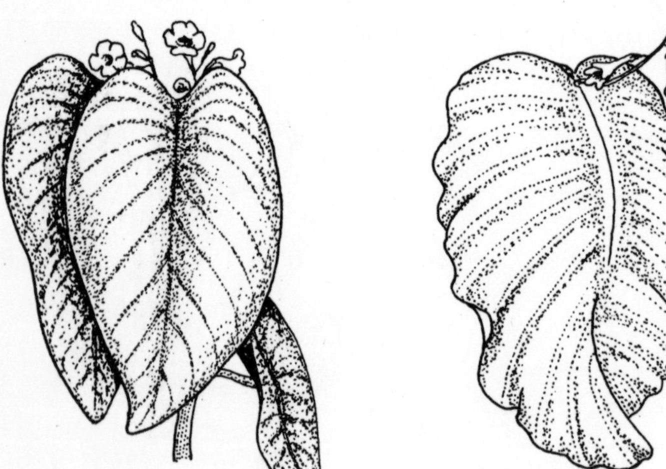

*Chirita micromusa* from the same family looks like a miniature banana

*Streptocarpus wendlandii*

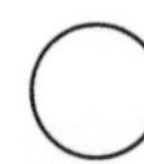

# *Tetranema mexicanum*

One would often like to have some decoration on one's desk or a similar spot where there is not much room. A small dish arrangement is generally chosen for the purpose, containing mostly foliage plants. These, of course, must not be too vigorous, not only so that they do not crowd each other but also that they do not take up more space than necessary. If, however, we should like to have flowering plants then we are generally faced with the problem of size. There are not many species small enough for the purpose and besides, not all tolerate light and heat the whole year round.

What might fill the bill in such a case is *Tetranema mexicanum* – a plant needlessly neglected by nurserymen to date. It is a small herb with 15-to 20-cm- (6-to 8-in-) long leaves forming a ground rosette, from the centre of which rise stems about 20 cm (8 in) high bearing, almost permanently, a large number of pretty pinkish-violet flowers.

As its name indicates, the plant is native to Mexico where it grows at the edges of thickets, alongside streams and at the margins of forests. This suggests also what its requirements in cultivation would be like. Though it tolerates full sunlight, a lightly shaded position is better. The growing medium must be an acid mixture (best of all peat with leaf mould and sand, but peat alone will do) and must never dry out completely. Because the plant has no special food requirements, an occasional application of feed during the growing season will suffice. The temperature should never drop below 15°C (59°F) and the plant finds the conditions of modern, centrally heated homes congenial. Its need of greater atmospheric moisture may be met by an occasional syringe with cool water.

Propagation is easy by means of seeds sown in peat which will produce plants that will flower the same year. Tetranema often seeds itself even when grown as a house plant.

*Ourisia coccinea*

  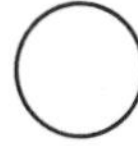 15–30°C

# *Tibouchina semidecandra*

## Glory Bush

This attractive shrub is, alas, still little seen in cultivation. Perhaps now that wider use is being made of window glasshouses and glass plant-cases – in other words of equipment ensuring both sufficient light and, more important, the high humidity required by many members of the Melastomataceae family – the situation will improve. Genera such as *Osbeckia, Heterocentron, Bertolonia, Sonerila, Miconia* and many more would definitely deserve it, for their numbers include both foliage plants and ones with interesting and often large flowers.

Anyone who has been to one of the larger parks in Central or South America has surely admired the large tibouchina shrubs with their huge gentian blue flowers up to 12 cm (4¾ in) across. *Tibouchina semidecandra,* native to southern Brazil, where it grows at higher elevations, has become widespread in cultivation wherever conditions are congenial – chiefly in subtropical regions.

In cultivation it generally does not exceed 1 m (3 ft) in height, whereas in the wild, according to reference books, one will come across specimens up to six times as tall. Because the shrub has unruly growth it should be hard pruned in spring to keep it shapely and compact and thus it is unnecessary to worry about it getting too big.

In summer, these plants tolerate conditions indoors as well as being moved out to the garden or balcony. In winter, it is recommended to keep the temperature between 8 and 10°C (47 and 50°F) but they can also be grown in a warmer room without damage. However, in this case they require frequent and ample ventilation. The compost must be light, acid and lime-free, best being a mixture of peat, leaf mould and sand with bits of charcoal added. One of the peat-based soilless composts would also be ideal.

Propagation is not difficult. Slightly woody cuttings inserted in a peat and sand compost in a warm propagator (22 to 25°C [72 to 77°F]) in spring will root fairly readily.

There are many other species besides this one that are worthy of note for the genus *Tibouchina* embraces 250 all told.

*Osbeckia cinerea*

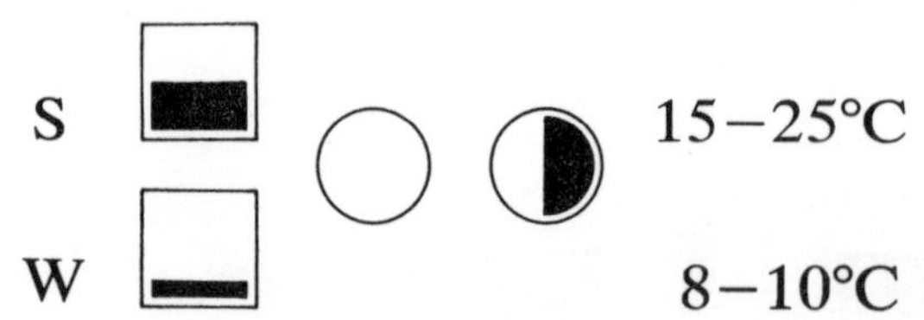

# PLANTS WITH ORNAMENTAL FRUITS

# *Anthurium scandens violaceum*

## Pearl Anthurium

*Anthurium scandens* is perhaps the loveliest of this group of plants not only because of the colour of its fruits but also because of its small size and ease of cultivation in a centrally-heated home.

The illustrated variety is native to the whole of tropical America according to some authorities, but according to others only to the Antilles. It is a relatively small plant that grows as an epiphyte in the juvenile stage. Attachment to the bark of trees is facilitated by the sticky pulp of the berry, as in mistletoe, and growth is very slow. The strong roots penetrate the cracks in the bark where they obtain moisture as well as nourishment from the humus deposited there. Not until later does the plant begin to grow in length to become a typical climbing, or rather creeping plant as indicated by its Latin name (*scandens* meaning ascending). The leaves, together with the stalk, do not exceed 15 cm (2 in) in length, but are often shorter. Flowers are produced by very young plants. The inflorescence, a spadix, grows from the axil of each new leaf and measures about 5 cm (2 in) in length. Whereas in other anthuriums pollination is generally rather complicated, in this case self-pollination occurs very frequently, if not to say regularly, so that the appearance of decorative fruits is almost always assured. They are waxy and coloured white or faintly tinged with blue in the type species, violet in the illustrated variety.

*A. scandens* is most effective when grown as an epiphyte on bare cork oak bark without any compost. It remains small and compact, and at the same time bears a profusion of flowers. It tolerates full sun but prefers partial shade. It may also be grown in a small pot in a light peaty mixture, in which case growth is more rapid. It is readily propagated by sowing the berries on or just below the surface of a sterile peat and sand mixture.

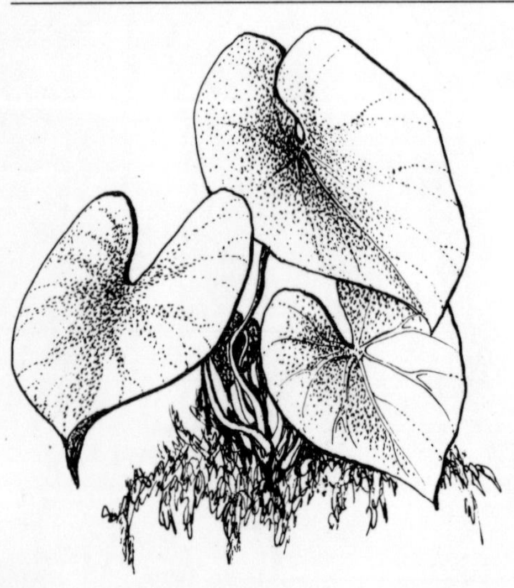

*Anthurium gymnopus*

   18–30°C

# Ardisia crispa

## Coral Berry

Unlike the preceding plant, the one in this illustration belongs to the traditional group of house plants which indicates that it needs fairly cool conditions in winter. However, since the required temperature is approximately 15°C (59°F), which is more or less the average temperature of house corridors and other circulation areas such as glassed-in foyers, it would surely be a pity to bypass this delightful little shrub.

*Ardisia crispa* is native to China where it grows at the edge of subtropical forests that dry out periodically or in similar open situations. According to some authorities its range extends as far as Indo-Malaysia. *Ardisia* is a fairly large genus; its 250 or so species are distributed in the tropics and subtropics.

*Ardisia crispa* is a small shrub with persistent, deep green leaves and lovely scarlet berries which hold for almost six months and add a bright touch the whole winter.

This, as well as other species, for example the very similar *A. crenata* from south-east Asia and Japan, has one biological peculiarity: the edges of the leaves are crinkled and thickened. These thickened edges are inhabited by colonies of bacteria *(Bacillus foliicola)* which live in a symbiotic relationship with the leaf. This association is apparently justified for in experiments where the leaf margins were systematically removed the plants did poorly, even in conditions that were otherwise optimal.

Particularly good for the indoor glasshouse is *Ardisia malouiana* from Borneo. It is a low shrub with large, lanceolate leaves up to 25 cm (10 in) long, coloured dark velvety green on the upper surface with a long whitish-grey blotch by the midrib. In the juvenile stage they are deep red on the underside.

*Ardisia crispa* and like species should be grown in a humusy soil enriched with peat or John Innes potting compost. They are propagated quite readily by means of cuttings or seeds sown in winter in a warm propagator (best of all 25°C [77°F]). Before sowing they should be cleaned of all bits of pulp which might easily cause them to become mouldy.

*Ardisia malouiana* is grown chiefly as a foliage plant

  10–20°C

# *Capsicum × hybridum*

## Red Pepper

In this book a separate section is assigned to annuals, otherwise it deals only with perennials. However, it is sometimes very difficult to determine the borderline between annuals and perennials for many annuals will last a number of years if provided with warm conditions in winter, and thus this division varies in different parts of the world. The pepper, *Capsicum annuum,* whose Latin name suggests that it is an annual, is also long-lived and grows into a large 2-m (6-ft) shrub if given congenial conditions. Furthermore, in the hybridization that yielded the decorative forms perennial species were used, chiefly *Capsicum frutescens* and *C. baccatum,* as well as many species of the genus *Solanum* (nightshade), such as *S. capsicastrum.* Anyone trying to determine the parentage of the modern hybrid peppers would not find the task easy for many of the plants selected for crossing were themselves hybrids, often the result of chance, self-hybridization in a greenhouse where several species were grown side by side.

The most attractive forms have been raised by the Japanese, past masters of horticulture. They succeeded in breeding fruits of widely varied shape and size, ranging in colour from white through green and yellow, and the standard red and orange to black and blackish-violet. A very good selection of ornamental peppers is also to be found in the United States.

Ornamental peppers are usually sold in the autumn covered with brightly coloured fruit and care is focused on keeping them thus as long as possible. They should be put in a well-lit spot in a cool room, best of all with a temperature of about 10°C (50°F). In a room that is too warm the plant soon drops its leaves and sometimes even dies. In spring sow several seeds from the dry fruits and grow new plants in a sunny window. Hard-prune the old plant and transfer it to fresh, fairly heavy, nourishing compost, such as John Innes potting compost. Place the pot in a warm position in full sun where the plant will usually put out new shoots. A word of warning, however; because ornamental peppers are generally also descended from the genus *Solanum,* the fruits are poisonous!

*Datura arborea*

 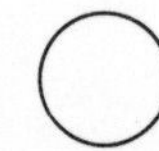 10–25°C

# *Cyphomandra betacea*

The preceding species was a typical example of a food plant that later became a plant used for decoration. The use of poisonous nightshades in breeding resulted in the complete elimination of the original purpose or trait for which the species was cultivated and its function became solely decorative.

*Cyphomandra betacea* is also a food plant that was introduced into cultivation for its edible fruits. Though native to south-eastern Brazil it is nowadays grown for its fruits throughout tropical America. In some places, chiefly Peru, its fruits are among the most popular in village markets even though, to a European, they are nothing exceptional. The freshly picked berries taste somewhat like poor-grade tomatoes and are prepared in the same way; later the taste is reminiscent of gooseberries though never quite like it. Probably more important is the fact that the berries are rich in Vitamin C, which is rare in the Peruvian Andes.

*Cyphomandra* is a subtropical genus found fairly high up in the mountains in its native land, and thus it cannot be grown indoors in a warm room in winter (it would soon die there). It is not particularly suitable for room decoration even in summer for it grows to a height of more than 2 m (6 ft) even in cultivation. That is why after it has passed the winter in a corridor or hall and all danger of frost is past it is better moved to a balcony or patio where it will serve as decoration with its pale green foliage. The tubular flowers, borne in a raceme, are white with a bluish tinge.

The soil for growing cyphomandra must be a fairly heavy, nourishing mixture composed, for example, of leaf mould, loam, sand and peat. John Innes potting compost No. 2 or 3 would be ideal. During the growth period it should be watered liberally and supplied regularly with feed.

It is readily propagated from seeds, which remain viable for a number of years, as well as by cuttings in spring.

*Browallia speciosa*

 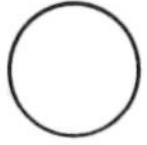  10–20°C

# *Fortunella japonica*

Citrus plants are the most popular plants of the group with ornamental fruits and today there are dozens of citrus clubs and associations throughout the world which perform further cross-breeding, try growing the plants outdoors in the open and publish a number of specialized journals. In truth, these are very attractive plants that have decorative foliage, pretty flowers and furthermore, a lovely fragrance. The fruits are brightly coloured, fragrant, persistent and, what is more, also edible.

Citrus plants (the genera *Fortunella, Citrus* and *Poncirus*) are an extremely difficult group to classify for they have been grown and crossed for thousands of years. Opinions as to the classification of the individual species differ and thus, for example, the number assigned to the genus *Citrus* ranges from 16 to 60 according to different authorities. The genus *Fortunella* has not been fully worked-out yet, either, and at the moment comprises from 6 to 10 species.

All citrus plants are native to south-east Asia and most (including the illustrated species) require cool conditions in winter (about 10°C [50°F].) Indoors they will thrive only if they are put in a room where the heat can be turned off or else in an unheated conservatory.

*Fortunella japonica* (syn. *Citrus japonica*), despite its name, is a native of China and was introduced to Japan, where it was described, as a decorative plant. It is a small shrub with fragrant, pink flowers and numerous small fruits (only about 3 cm [1¼ in] across). It is a favourite house plant which tolerates even very cold conditions in winter, particularly if it is grafted on *Poncirus trifoliata*.

Recommended for home decoration are the mandarin 'Unshiu' and the lemon 'Meyeri', both of which tolerate conditions in a centrally-heated home and reliably bear a profusion of flowers and fruits. The soil should be a heavy, nourishing mixture such as John Innes potting compost No. 2 or 3, depending on the size of the pot.

*Skimmia japonica*

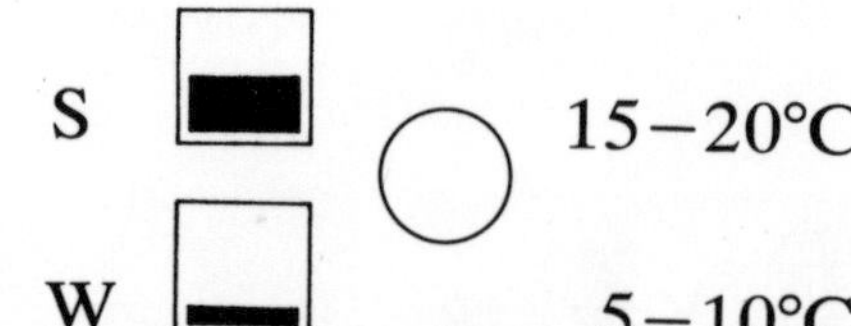

# *Nephthytis afzelii*

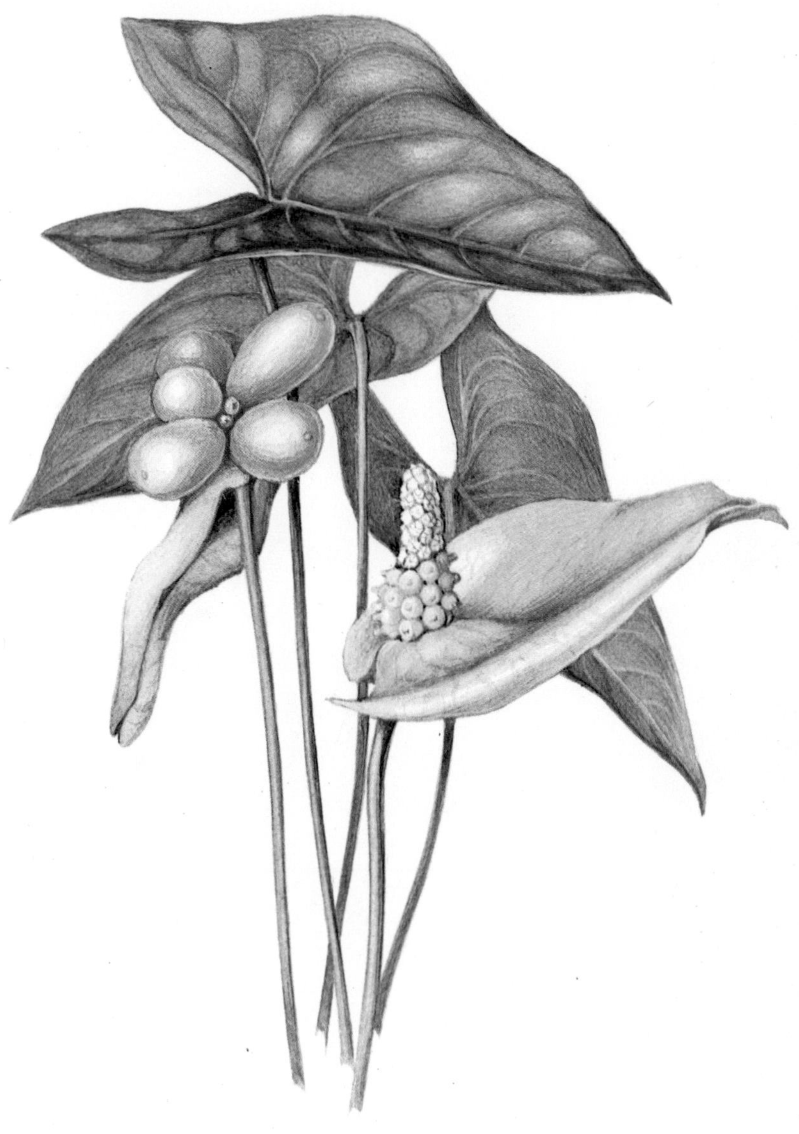

Whereas all the preceding species with ornamental fruits are fairly well known, at least from visits to the botanical gardens, nephthytis is practically unknown and may be encountered only in larger collections. It is a great pity that no one has yet tried to introduce it to market for its fruit, as well as foliage, are exceedingly beautiful and it is furthermore very suitable for warm, centrally-heated homes.

The four species that make up the genus are native to west Africa. They all have an underground rhizome which is horizontal, shortened and tuberous, erect leaf stalks and leathery, sagittate to hastate leaves. The inflorescence is a short, erect spadix composed of female flowers below, male flowers above, enclosed by a rigid, horizontal spathe.

The illustrated species has emerald-green spathes, rigid, leathery leaf blades almost 20 cm (8 in) long, and erect leaf stalks reaching 30 to 50 cm (12 to 20 in) in length. The plant usually bears fruit even without artificial pollination. The bright orange berries, 4 as a rule, measuring about 2.5 to 3 cm (1 to $1^{1}/_{4}$ in) in length, are borne in the axils of the spathes, which are persistent. One advantage of the fruit is that it colours rapidly and then ripens on the plant for a period of almost six months. Each berry contains only a single seed which is very slow to germinate (taking up to 4 months) and must be inserted in a peat and sand mixture together with the casing, in other words the whole berry.

Most frequently grown is *Nephthytis afzelii* (syn. *N. liberica*), though another similar but smaller species – *N. gravenreuthii* – may sometimes be encountered in large, specialized collections. They are both very hardy and rewarding house plants and can be used to good effect in dish arrangements. They are attractive when placed in a dry spot in the paludarium and also very suitable for a terrarium for the rigid leaves are not damaged by animals. They tolerate light as well as heavy shade, temperatures from 10 to 35°C (50 to 95°F), the dust and smoke of cities as well as a dry atmosphere.

The compost should be acid, a mixture of peat and sand and some loam, or John Innes potting compost with additional peat added.

*Rhodospatha latifolia*

  10–35°C

# *Nertera granadensis*

## Coral-bead Plant

The pine forests of the southern hemisphere are the home of the genus *Nertera* comprising only 8 species. What they are like is evident from their name, for the Greek word *nerteros* means low. They are truly prostrate, cushion plants with delicate foliage and inconspicuous flowers but beautiful small fruits.

*Nertera granadensis* (syn. *N. depressa*) grows in the Andes in Central and South America but may also be encountered in the mountains of New Zealand and Tasmania. It makes small cushions of appressed stems with tiny round leaflets resembling those of the well-known *Helxine soleirolii,* or mind-your-own-business. The tiny greenish flowers, which generally escape notice, appear in May and June and are followed by striking orange-red fruits up to 6 mm (1/4 in) across. These attain their bright coloration in mid-August and remain on the plant until well into winter, in other words for more than half a year.

As a mountain plant of the southern hemisphere nertera has two basic requirements: ample air and cool conditions in winter. It is not long-lived in a warm home, sometimes surviving only the first winter but often not even that. It must therefore be grown where the premises may be aired frequently and where the temperature in winter can be kept at 10°C (50°F), in other words best of all in a conservatory, corridor, or in a slightly heated greenhouse, the kind erected for certain cacti.

Nertera has a relatively shallow root system and may thus be used for dish arrangements together with any other plants, particularly if they are shrubs that form stems and it is necessary to cover the surface of the compost. A slightly acid and quite rich compost is required. This can be achieved by mixing loam with an equal amount of peat.

Propagation is easy, either by detaching the prostrate stems that form roots or by cuttings (both in August) or else by means of seed. Neither cuttings nor seeds need much heat for rooting or germinating and should therefore be put in a cool, moist spot.

*Coprosma baueri*

 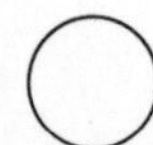  5–15°C

# HOUSE PLANTS OF A WOODY NATURE

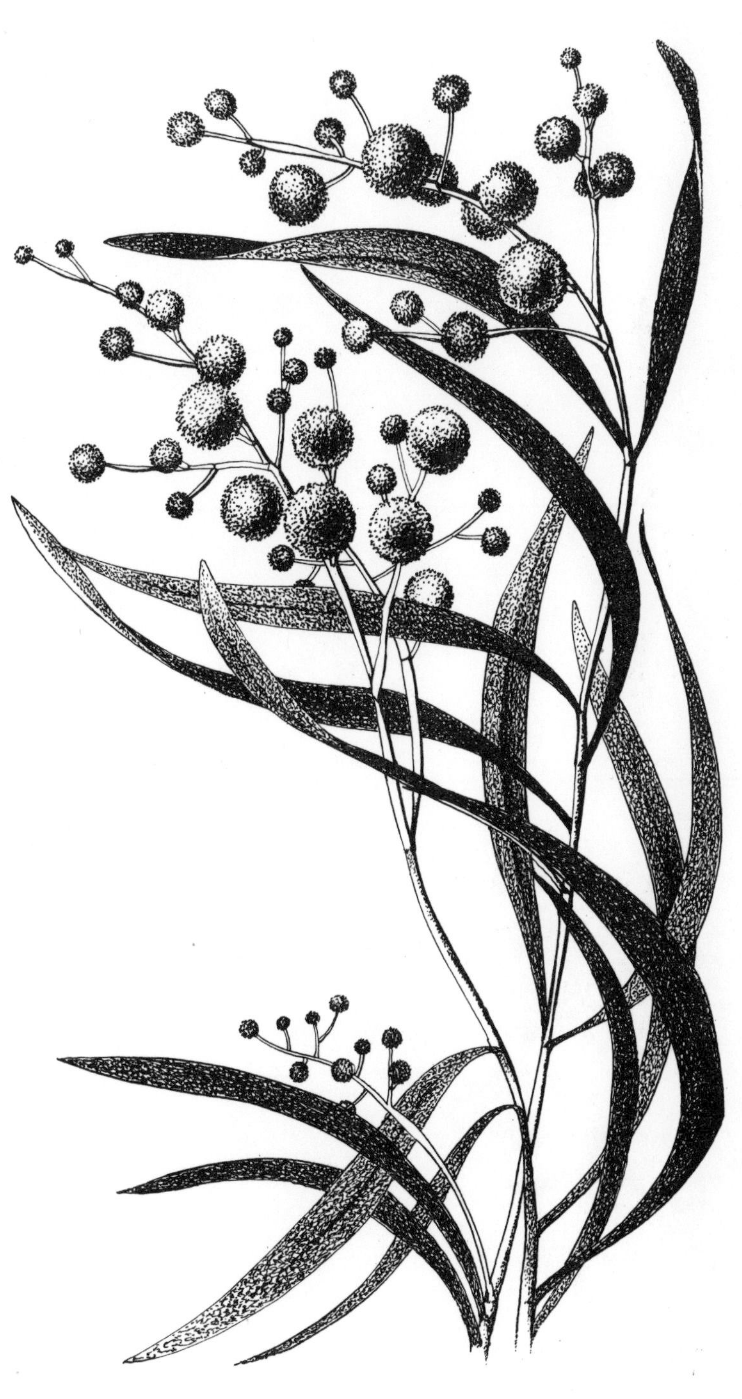

# *Acacia armata*

## Kangaroo Thorn, Hedge Wattle

Before beginning this section on house plants of a woody nature note should be taken of the fact that it could also include certain plants of this kind with decorative flowers (such as hibiscus, fuchsia) or with decorative foliage (such as ficus). Likewise, certain species included here might just as easily be described in other chapters (for example bougainvillea in the section on climbers). Such inaccuracies always occur whenever a book is arbitrarily divided in such a manner and there is nothing the author can do but beg the reader's tolerance.

Acacias are known to practically everyone for come spring they are on display in every florist's window. They are either shrubs or small trees with flowers, coloured yellow as a rule, arranged in ball-like clusters or cylindrical spikes. The foliage is composed of bipinnate leaves or phyllodes, that is leaf stalks of an expanded and flattened form resembling and having the functions of leaves. In most species the leaflets are changed into spines.

*Acacia armata* (syn. *A. paradoxa*) is a native of Australia where it grows as a tree up to 5 m (16 ft) high. In cultivation, however, it is a much smaller, thickly-branched shrub. The foliage is made up of phyllodes about 2 cm (3/4 in) long with a single vein. The leaflets have been modified into paired persistent spines. In March or April the plant bears a great profusion of yellow flower clusters.

Of the species with pinnate leaves most often encountered in cultivation are: *A. drummondii,* with short flower-spikes about 3 to 4 cm (1 1/4 to 1 1/2 in) long, and *A. pulchella* with ball-like flower clusters. Both are indigenous to Australia.

Of particular interest are acacias that live in a symbiotic relationship with ants, for example *A. sphaerocephala* from Mexico. Its hollow, inflated, reddish-brown spines are inhabited by ants that feed on small yellowish, protein-rich particles formed at the tips of the leaflets.

Acacias may be grown indoors only if they can be provided with cool conditions in winter (about 5 to 10°C [41 to 50°F]). The biologically interesting ant acacias can withstand higher temperatures. The growing medium should be a nourishing, peaty compost, such as one of the proprietary soilless composts. In summer the plants should be watered and fed liberally. Propagation is by cuttings or by seed.

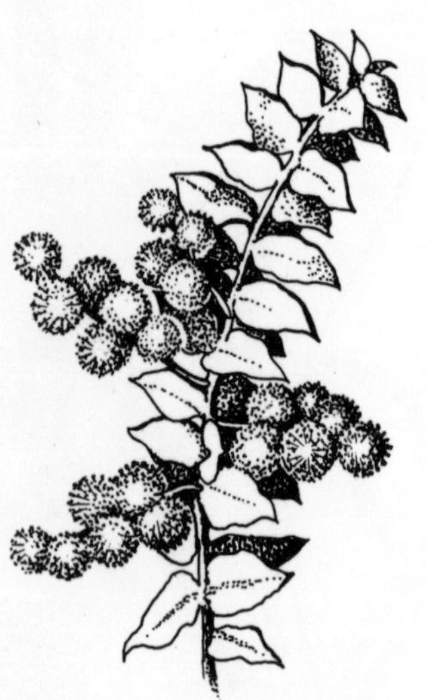

*Acacia podaliriaefolia* from Queensland flowers in winter

   5–15(20)°C

# *Araucaria bidwillii*

## Bunya-Bunya

The Araucariaceae family includes only two genera – *Araucaria* and *Agathis* – whose distribution is confined to the southern hemisphere. They are very ancient conifers from the evolutionary aspect and mostly large trees with branches arranged in whorls. The strikingly straight trunks together with the regular arrangement of the branches give the trees a rather stiff look. The leaves of araucarias are persistent, alternate, needle-like, with a single vein (the leaves of agathis are wider, with many parallel veins). The male and female cones usually grow on different trees (the trees are dioecious). At one time araucaria forests were widespread in Europe and it was not until the late Tertiary period that they were forced back to the southern hemisphere.

The illustrated species is from the coast of Queensland. In its native habitat it is a large tree with a straight trunk and regular horizontal branches. The leaves are needle-like, about 1 to 2 cm (1/2 to 3/4 in) long, and furnished with a keel on the underside, this being the principal characteristic distinguishing this species from *A. angustifolia.* In cultivation, even in good conditions, it reaches a height of only 2 to 3 m (6 to 10 ft). The best-known species of the genus – *A. excelsa,* the Norfolk Island pine – is native to Norfolk Island where it grows to a large tree up to 60 m (200 ft) high with a pyramidal crown and needle-like leaves.

These trees are popular plants for the cold greenhouse as well as for home decoration. However, they require cool conditions in winter and therefore must be moved to a conservatory or other position where a temperature of 3 to 10°C (38 to 50°F) can be maintained. They must have ample air even in summer and should thus be placed by an open window. Unfortunately, cool homes are on the decline and besides, these plants do not tolerate the air pollution of cities so that, despite their beauty, they will probably soon stop being grown as house plants. The compost should be a mixture of leaf mould, loam, peat and sand, or John Innes potting compost. Propagation is by tip cuttings.

*A. araucana,* the hardy monkey puzzle from southern Chile, may be planted outdoors in a sheltered spot in the garden in warmer parts of Europe.

*Agathis robusta*

   5–15°C

# *Aucuba japonica* 'Variegata'

## Spotted Laurel

The evergreen plants of the subtropical forests of south-east Asia have provided horticulture with many fine specimens, mostly with decorative foliage, and aucubas are among those included. In cultivation it is necessary to satisfy their natural requirements. Most need ample amounts of fresh air, a rather moist atmosphere and cool conditions in winter. That is why they are generally used for decoration in a foyer or conservatory, being moved in summer to the garden, patio or balcony. The genus *Aucuba* comprises only three species from the Himalayas and east Asia.

*Aucuba japonica* is a shrub native to Japan and southern Korea, where it forms part of the evergreen vegetation at elevations of about 600 m (1,900 ft) above sea level. In the wild it reaches a height of 5 m (16 ft) and is always found in the shade of larger trees.

The species is plain green, but many cultivars were raised over the years, one of which is shown in the illustration. Others that are worthy of note include: 'Crassifolia' (leaves exceptionally thick, leathery); 'Hillieri' (leaves green, narrowly-lanceolate, about 12 cm [4½ in] long); and 'Luteocarpa' (leaves dentate, spotted with yellow, berries yellow).

Because *A. japonica* is a unisexual shrub and the cultivars are multiplied by vegetative means, many comprise either only male or female specimens. Cultivation is very easy. Aucubas should by grown in nourishing, humusy loam with an addition of peat and during the growing season provided with liberal applications of water and feed. When trimming the shrub the prunings may be used as cuttings which will root rapidly in a warm propagator (about 20°C [68°F]).

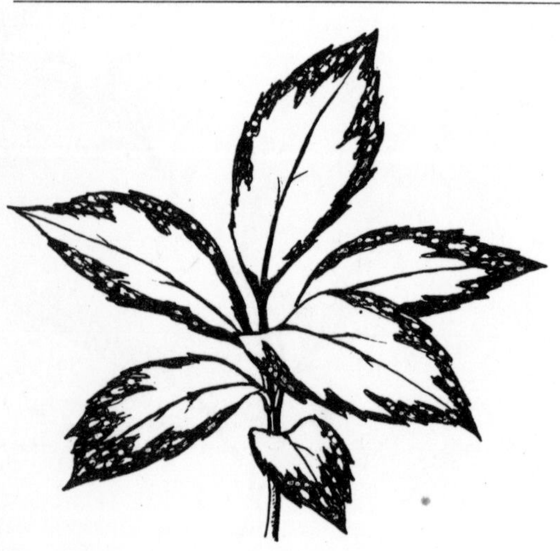

*Aucuba japonica* 'Goldiana'

 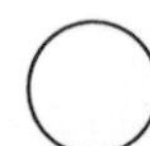 5–15(20)°C

# *Bauhinia variegata*

## Orchid Tree, Mountain Ebony

The genus *Bauhinia* embraces some 200 species of shrubs and trees distributed in the subtropical and tropical regions of Asia, Africa and America. Because many of them have beautiful flowers they spread far beyond the borders of their native land.

The illustrated species is from India and China. It also occurs as a common shrub in city parks throughout North Africa. It produces a profusion of strikingly large and beautifully coloured flowers so that it is prized as an ornamental even in its native land. For example in India, in the Kangra region, it is planted out in abundance in practically every village. The flowers generally appear in early spring, February-March. The fruits are long pods containing 10 to 25 seeds.

In botanical gardens one often comes across other similar species belonging to the genus *Bauhinia.* They are mostly grown as botanical curiosities, as their deeply lobed leaves are equipped with several 'joints': these occur in the place of attachment of the leaf stalk to the branch and also where the leaf stalk and the leaf blades are joined. Furthermore, the leaf blades can also 'fold' along the midrib. Bauhinias are thus able to make the best possible use of light. The leaves of most cultivated species are about 15 cm (6 in) long.

*Bauhinia galpinii* is an attractive, twining, thermophilous shrub from Mozambique and Rhodesia which often bears fruit even in botanical gardens. Also encountered there is the south Asian species *B. purpurea* with violet-red flowers.

The most suitable species for warm, centrally-heated flats is *B. acuminata* from India, Burma and China. Not only is it small, about 1 to 2 m (3 to 6 ft) high, it also flowers readily. The flowers are white and relatively large.

Like all *Bauhinia* species it is grown from seeds, which germinate within about a week of sowing. When the third leaf appears the seedlings should be put in pots in a loose mixture of leaf mould, loam, sand, peat and some small stones added to improve drainage. (Alternatively, use John Innes potting compost.) The growing point should be pinched out after about a month. Bauhinias stand up well to pruning. From spring until autumn they should be watered and fed regularly and placed in full sun. In winter the temperature should be slightly lowered and watering greatly limited. It is quite normal for some species to drop their leaves in winter.

*Bauhinia picta* is noted for its handsome flowers

 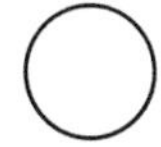 15(10)–30°C

# *Bougainvillea × buttiana* 'Mistress Butt'

Subtropical and tropical America is the home of some 14 species of *Bougainvillea,* named after the famous French navigator de Bougainville. Only two, however, are of importance in cultivation: *B. spectabilis* and *B. glabra,* both from Brazil. The first is a robust, twining shrub with thick curved spines. The bracts of the type species are coloured lilac. The second is somewhat smaller, the foliage slightly tomentose; it is also less spiny. The flowers are the same colour.

Both type species are extremely variable in the colour of the bracts. Cross-breeding has thus yielded many hybrids with bracts coloured white, pink, yellow-orange or yellow, and all shades of red and purplish-violet.

The illustrated cultivar (in older literature it is listed under the synonyms 'Presas' or 'Crimson Lake') is the product of the self-hybridization of *B. glabra* and *B. peruviana* and was named *B.* x *buttiana.* It was found in 1910 in the city of Cartagena, Colombia, and remains one of the most widely cultivated to this day. The principal hybridizations took place on the Riviera, in India and in Brazil, and it is there that one will find the largest assortment of these lovely plants.

Bougainvilleas may be said to be subtropical rather than tropical plants, for like most other plants of a woody nature, they require cool conditions in winter. During the rest period they drop most of their leaves and watering must be limited accordingly; they should be hard-pruned in spring. The prunings may be used as cuttings, which should be inserted in a peat and sand mixture in a warm propagator where they will quickly form roots. They must be moved with great care for the roots are very fragile. When rooted, pot up using John Innes potting compost.

*Mirabilis jalapa*

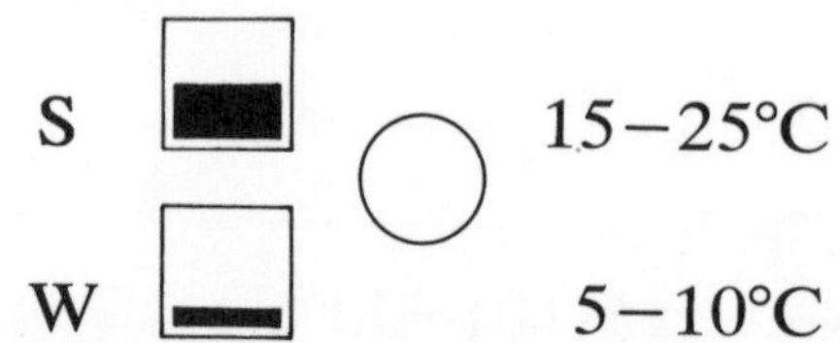

# *Caesalpinia pulcherrima*

## Barbados Pride

*Caesalpinia* is a genus that includes truly magnificent plants. Most are shrubs or small trees, up to about 3 m (10 ft) in height, with pinnate leaves and yellow, orange or red flowers. They are distributed primarily in tropical America and Asia but because most are very decorative they may be encountered practically everywhere and it is not always easy to determine the origin of the given species.

The origin of *C. pulcherrima* is not quite clear either. Though many authorities argue that it is native to the Antilles or Central America, others believe it to be indigenous to tropical Asia. The first is the more probable for it has been proved that the Aztecs and Mayans used this species as a medicinal drug (to treat fever, skin diseases and venereal diseases). Another, though as yet purely theoretical possibility, is that there existed contact between the ancient civilizations of Central America and east or south-east Asia and that these drug plants may have been prized articles of commerce or gifts.

This decorative shrub is fairly easy to grow and it is difficult to understand why it is not commonly found in cultivation. In summer it requires ample sun and liberal watering and feeding, in autumn, after the flowers have faded, water should be limited to the minimum, but the temperature should not be lowered too much. From the foregoing it is evident that it is very well suited to modern centrally-heated homes where its requirements can readily be met if it is placed in a sunny window. It tolerates pruning relatively well. The prunings, however, cannot be used as cuttings and so the plants are propagated from seed. The soil should be a heavy, nourishing mixture, such as John Innes potting compost No. 3.

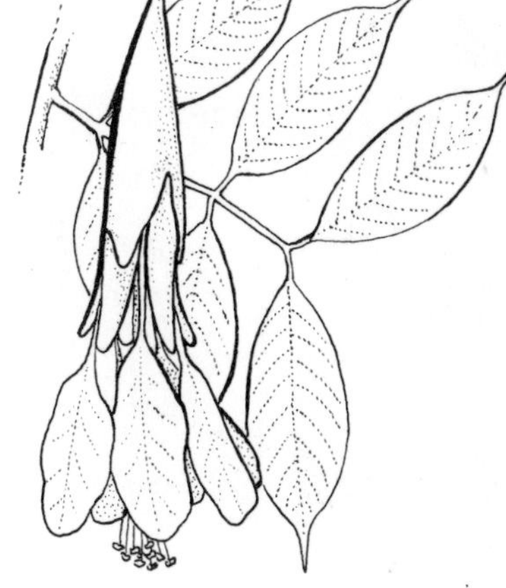

*Brownea angustiflora*

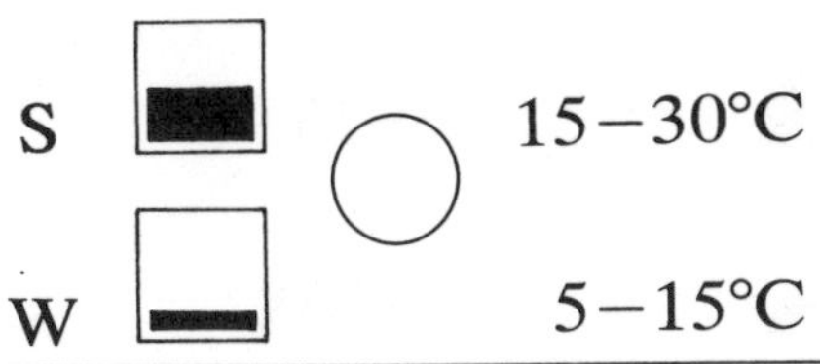


15–30°C

5–15°C

# Callistemon citrinus

## Bottle Brush Plant

The illustrated plant needs no special description for it is found in every botanical garden and in many a florist's window.

Like all the other 11 species (15 according to some authorities) of this genus, *Callistemon citrinus* (syn. *C. lanceolatus*) is native to south-eastern Australia. In the wild it is a tree reaching a height of 5 m (16 ft), but in cultivation it is much smaller – barely half that height. Besides, it can be readily shaped by pruning so there is no need to fear that it will get out of bounds. The rigid, lanceolate, unusually dark leaves are very decorative, but the shrubs do not attain their full glory until spring or early summer, when clusters of flowers with prominent bright-red stamens appear at the tips of the branches.

Although growers are accustomed to presuming that Australian plants are drought-resistant (in this case further evidence being the rigid, narrow leaves) if we look up the habitat of this genus we will find that most species, on the contrary, grow either beside rivers or in moist, sandy places, in other words in places where they have ample water.

This fact must be taken into account when growing these plants at home and they must be given plenty of water and nourishment. *Callistemon teretifolius,* which, however, is rarely found in cultivation, is perhaps the only species that grows on dry stony banks in eastern Australia.

In winter they require really cold conditions; in an absolutely dry spot they will tolerate temperatures near freezing point, but best of all is a temperature between 8 and 10°C (47 and 50°F).

Propagation is not difficult – either by cuttings obtained from early-spring prunings, which should be rooted by the usual method in a warm propagator, or by means of the tiny seeds, which should be sown on moist, sterile peat with sand. If properly cared for the cuttings will develop into flower-bearing specimens within 1½ years. The soil should be acid, best of all a mixture of one part leaf mould, loam and sand and one part peat.

*Eucalyptus polyanthemos* *Eucalyptus cinerea*

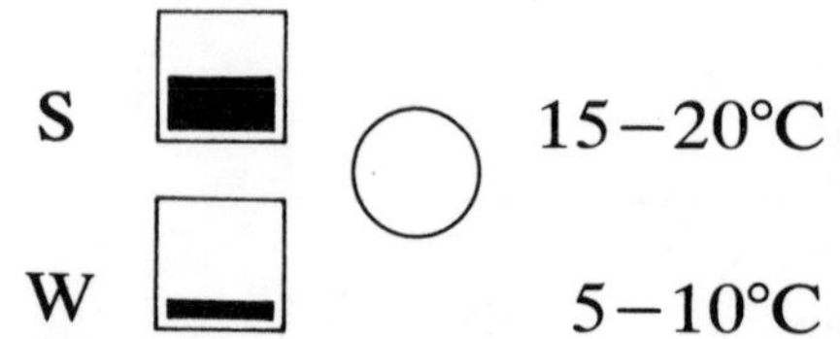

# *Cycas revoluta*

## Sago Palm

This stately plant resembling a thick-stemmed palm is one of the loveliest evergreen species grown for ornament. It has no special requirement and is suitable for a large room, conservatory or glassed-in entranceway.

Cycads are ancient plants from the evolutionary aspect, which is reflected mainly in the structure of the sexual organs. These are arranged in cones or in clusters of woody carpels bearing naked ovules. The leaves of the juvenile form are coiled in a spiral like those of ferns. Altogether, 15 species of cycads (genus *Cycas*) have been described to date. These are found in the tropics and subtropics of the Old World from Madagascar to southern Japan. All have an erect trunk covered with woody leaf scars. The leaves are pinnate, relatively large and their structure adapted to dry conditions. A point of interest is that cycads were found to have the least amount of chlorophyll of all hitherto investigated plants.

The illustrated species is native to south-east Asia, its range extending from the East Indies through China to southern Japan. Adult plants reach a height of 3 m (10 ft), but they have a very slow rate of growth. The leaves are a lovely deep green, up to 2 m (6 ft) long, and last many years.

The compost should be a mixture of loam, peat and sand. Feed should be supplied regularly during the growing season. In the spring it is best to carefully scrape away the surface compost in the container and replace it with fresh compost rather than move the plants. Propagation is relatively easy: either by means of seeds, which are approximately 3 cm (1¼ in) long, or by sideshoots which grow at the base of older trunks. They will root readily with bottom heat and moist compost, however the atmosphere should be on the dry side.

Other related genera, such as *Encephalartos*, *Ceratozamia* and *Dioon*, are just as handsome and, at the same time, very hardy. Some have an underground stem, for example *Stangeria*, probably an adaptation to the regular fires that occur in the savanna areas where they grow.

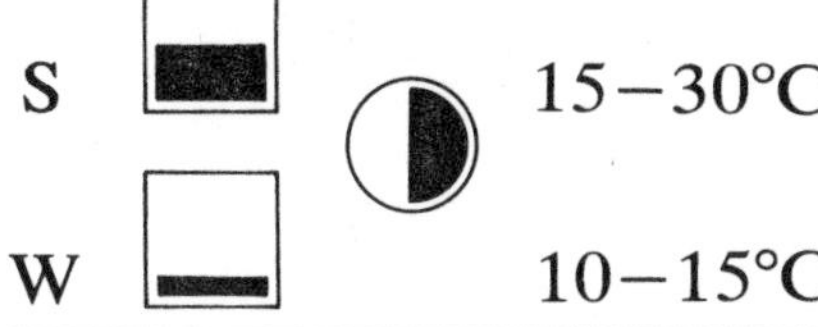


15–30°C

10–15°C

*Stangeria eriopus* from South Africa has an underground stem; this is an adaptation to the many bush fires in its native habitat

# *Erythrina crista-galli*

## Coral Tree

Cool conditions are definitely a must for growing the illustrated species successfully. This popular shrub, so admired in botanical gardens when it is in flower, goes through a period of complete rest in winter at temperatures only a few degrees above freezing point and in absolutely dry conditions. The reason for this is obvious, for it is native to the campos (savanna woodlands) of Brazil where it grows on sandy and stony soils.

Erythrina is a fairly large shrub, generally about 2 m (6 ft) high. In autumn it should be moved to a spot where it can be provided with the cool conditions already mentioned, such as a cool conservatory. When growth starts in spring the plant should be hardened off by ventilating its growing area and around mid-May it should be moved outdoors and the pot plunged in the ground. Once the leaves appear the plant should be watered regularly, allowing the soil to dry out only partially between waterings – the roots must not be continually in water.

During the summer the plant produces long, thick shoots which, like the stalks of the odd-pinnate leaves, are furnished with long spines. If given the proper care, come September it will bear flowers which are truly worth the effort required for its cultivation. Each cluster, of which there are several, contains some 50 large pea-shaped flowers coloured a beautiful cherry-red.

The fruit is a pod. The seeds have good powers of germination but it takes a number of years (4 to 5) before even well-cared-for seedlings develop into flower-bearing specimens. It is better to propagate the plant by cuttings, taken in spring together with a piece of old wood and rooted at a moderate temperature in a sand and peat mixture. They will reach flower-bearing size within two years.

*Calliandra emarginata*

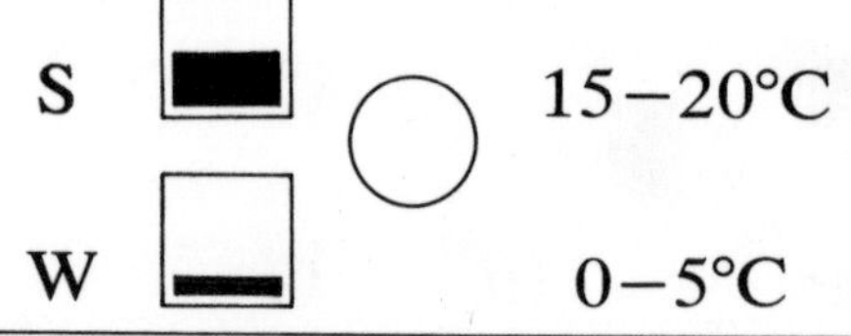

# *Ixora × coccinea*

## Flame-of-the-woods

Though this shrub is no novelty to nurserymen, who have been acquainted with it for many years, it is only in the past few decades that it has become more widespread in cultivation. This is undoubtedly due, among other things, to the fact that it is a plant with good prospects for it can be grown successfully even in centrally-heated homes.

The main area of distribution of this genus, which contains 150 species according to some authorities and as many as 400 according to others, is tropical Asia, but it is also found in the tropical regions of the other continents.

*Ixora coccinea,* the only one grown as a 'pure' species (not crossed) and one which has yielded many valuable hybrids, is native to India. The flower clusters are almost 10 cm (4 in) across and coloured a glowing red. In the wild ixoras often grow at the edges of forests where they are only lightly shaded by trees, or they may also grow singly, in full sun. They require a deep soil rich in humus formed by decaying leaves on a laterite substrate. In the places where they grow the conditions are relatively moist and warm the whole year; the dry season begins late in the autumn and lasts barely 3 or 4 months.

More often found in cultivation, however, are the hybrids such as 'Fraseri', scarlet; 'Savoi', salmon-orange; 'Shawi', with huge flowers, likewise salmon-orange; and 'Bier's Glory', deep orange.

The cultivars have more or less the same requirements as *I. coccinea.* In the home they should be put in a warm, well-lit spot only slightly sheltered against the sun and older shrubs should be given a brief period of rest after the flowers have faded, with limited watering and slightly cooler conditions (airing the room will suffice). The soil should be humusy – John Innes potting compost with extra peat added would be suitable. Propagation, by means of cuttings in a warm propagator at any time of the year, is easy.

*Plumeria rubra* 'Acutifolia' is often cultivated in the tropics. It is readily propagated by cuttings and grows successfully on a sunny window-sill in a warm room

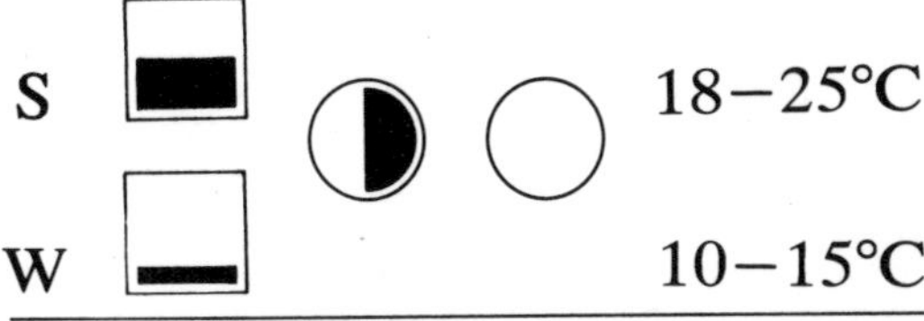


18–25°C

10–15°C

# *Malpighia coccigera*

## Miniature Holly

The Malpighiaceae family, comprising about 800 species native to Central and South America, is not very well known even to connoisseurs. Most are lianas, one of which – ayahuasca *(Banisteriopsis caapi),* dubbed the 'liana of death' – is doubtless not unknown to those who are interested in 'herbal medicine'.

Malpighia is a low, barely 1-m- (3-ft-) high shrub from the Antilles, where it grows in mountain forests as well as in sandy soil round the mouth of water courses.

The leaves are odd-pinnate, the leaflets deeply incised, with tiny, extremely sharp spines on the edge. The foliage is decorative in itself but the chief reason for the plant's popularity are the small flowers (about 1 cm [1/2] in) and the attractive, colourful fruits – bright red drupes.

Malpighia has slender, flexible branches that are easily bent and shaped and can be pruned without harm. This is an ideal plant for the contoured shrubs of east Asia's parks and gardens (a somewhat unaccustomed sight for the European). The way plants and flowers are used naturally depends on many factors, such as the national culture and tradition, the general atmosphere and the architecture. In Vietnam, for instance, one may see shrubs trimmed to look like vases, birds and animals.

Botanical gardens also contain other very similar species, such as *M. glabra* with slightly sour, edible fruits, and *M. urens* with sharp spines.

All malpighias can be grown with ease in a warm room. The substrate should be a mixture of sand and peat (either in equal parts or with sand predominating); older plants should be provided with slightly richer soil containing leaf mould or loam. Propagation is very easy – by means of cuttings inserted in a warm and moist propagator at any time of the year. Plants start producing flowers when they are quite small – barely 25 cm (10 in) high.

*Malpighia glabra*

 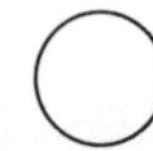 10–25°C

# *Podocarpus macrophyllus*

## Buddhist Pine, Japanese Yew

These plants are conifers even though one would not believe it at first glance. The leaves are flat, longish-lanceolate to linear, with very simple parallel veins, and the inflorescence is a cone. Female cones have a single ovule and several scales.

The genus *Podocarpus* is found chiefly in the southern hemisphere; several species of horticultural value grow in south-east Asia, and some are to be found even at subalpine elevations on Kilimanjaro. They are mostly trees, only occasionally small shrubs, but in cultivation their size is a far cry from that attained in the wild. The trunk is strikingly erect, the branches regular and densely leaved.

The illustrated *P. macrophyllus* (syn. *P. chinensis*) is native to China and Japan. It is a tall shrub with dense foliage composed of approximately 10-cm- (4-in-) long leaves. It is generally described as a plant for the cool greenhouse, but experiments at planting it outdoors in gardens in the warmest parts of Germany have met with success. Its adaptability must be very great indeed for some specimens may do well for years even in very warm, centrally-heated homes. Particularly suitable for such conditions is the cultivar 'Aureus' which, like all variegated plants, is somewhat more delicate than the type species.

In many species the leaves are much wider. The rare *P. fleuryi* from Vietnam, for instance, has broadly lanceolate leaves. *P. acutifolius* from New Zealand, on the other hand, has extremely narrow, pointed leaves; this species stands up exceptionally well to pruning and can be kept the size of a small shrub.

Propagation is by cuttings taken from only slightly woody stem tips and inserted in a peat and sand mixture in a warm, moist propagator, where they will root reliably, though slowly. Rooted cuttings should be transferred to John Innes potting compost No. 1. Liberal watering is a must in summer; plants put in a warm spot will not stop growth even in winter and so watering should only be somewhat limited at this time. Plants will benefit by frequent ventilation and syringing of the leaves.

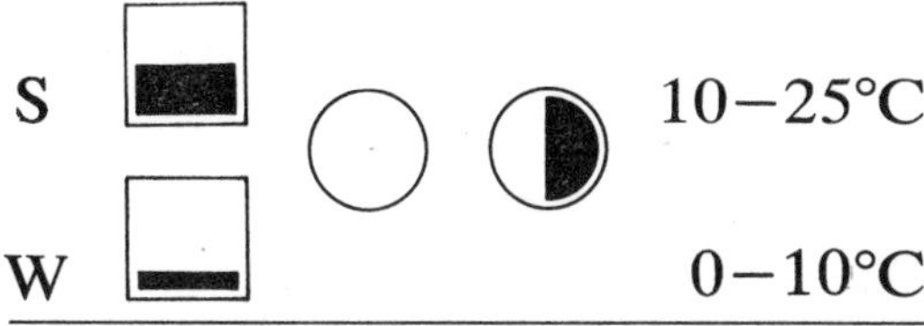


*Podocarpus nagi*

# *Polyscias balfouriana* 'Marginata'

## Variegated Balfour Aralia

Only on occasion does one see the illustrated shrub displayed in the florist's window. This is a great pity for it is a true gem with its delicate, fern-like habit, which has won it a place not only in tropical parks but also in cultivation in some countries, such as Japan, where several lovely colour forms are grown, and the United States.

*P. balfouriana* (syn. *Aralia balfouriana*) is native to New Caledonia where it grows to a height of almost 10 m (33 ft). However, it remains quite small in cultivation and older specimens are generally only 1 m (3 ft) high. The leaves are odd-pinnate, the leaflets about 10 cm (4 in) across. In the type species the margins are spotted whitish yellow. Also relatively common in collections is the species *P. guilfoylei* with pinnate leaves; the leaflets are ovate to orbicular, the terminal leaflet larger (up to 15 cm [6 in]) and elongate. The leaves are likewise edged with white. This is an extremely variable species; an attractive form is 'Laciniata' with finely fringed leaves.

*Polyscias balfouriana* is suitable for very warm, centrally-heated homes, but it must have ample atmospheric moisture, which may by provided by a humidifer or else by putting it together with other plants in a large dish arrangement or on 'dry land' in a paludarium. Ideal conditions are also provided by a large glass plant-case.

The compost should be humusy but not too light and should be kept well drained by the addition of coarse stone rubble and sand. John Innes potting compost with extra sand added would be an ideal mixture.

Propagation is very easy by means of cuttings, which need not, but may be woody. These should be cut at a slant and inserted in a peat and sand mixture in a warm and moist propagator.

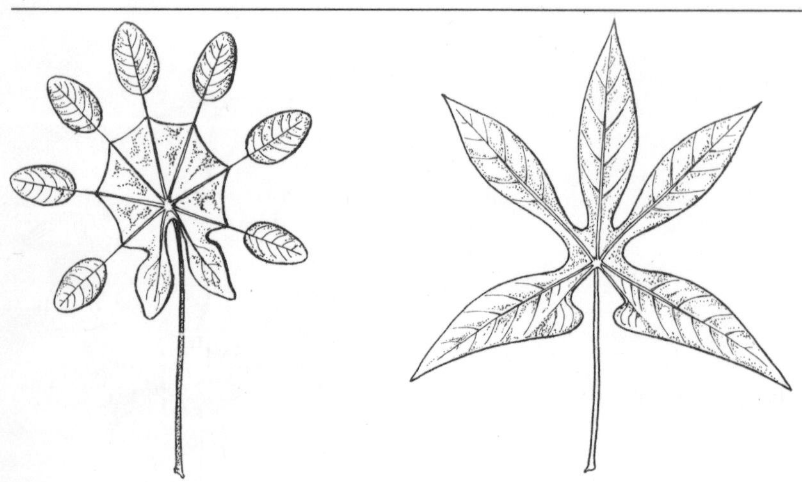

*Trevesia palmata,* found from India to China, attains a height of 5 m (16 ft) in the wild
*Trevesia sundaica* is a small, handsome tree from Java

  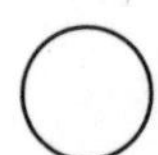 15–25°C

# *Polyscias fruticosa*

In the case of many of the genera illustrated in this book it has been noted that horticulture has unfortunately passed them by. Those were only genera, but here we have a whole family that has been largely neglected, for apart from Schefflera, Fatsia, Hedera and their hybrid x Fatshedera, the Araliaceae are only very occasionally encountered in cultivation. And yet it would surely not be difficult to select from the more than 700 species the smaller, decorative forms that could be used for permanent, evergreen room decoration.

*Polyscias fruticosa* (syn. *Tieghemopanax fruticosus)* is native to south-east Asia, where it was also introduced into cultivation and is among the most popular of plants. Growers have even succeeded in raising more decorative garden forms, for example in Vietnam a variegated form with large creamy-white areas on the leaves, and a form with twisted leaves that give the shrub a very compact look.

The shrub is approximately 80 cm (32 in) high; only old specimens may grow to a height of 1.5 m (5 ft). The compound leaves are about 40 cm (16 in) long, the leaflets 3 to 10 cm (1¼ to 4 in) long. The entire plant is fragrant. The flowers are insignificant and have no ornamental value. The fruits are berries.

These plants are most attractive in a bonsai arrangement or grown in flat dishes on tufa. The shrub does well, of course, even if grown in more traditional containers. The compost should be porous, composed of peat, loam and sand, John Innes potting compost being ideal.

Propagation is simple, either by seeds (these, however, are slow to germinate and do not do so at the same time) or by tip cuttings which rapidly form roots in a peat and sand mixture. The shrub stands up very well to pruning so that it can be trimmed to the desired shape.

In its native land polyscias is widely distributed in both tropical and subtropical regions. A period of winter rest is therefore recommended but it will do very well even without it. If it has ample light and heat in winter, watering should not be limited and the shrub will continue growth even during this season. Feed, of course, should be supplied mainly during the growth period, in other words in summer.

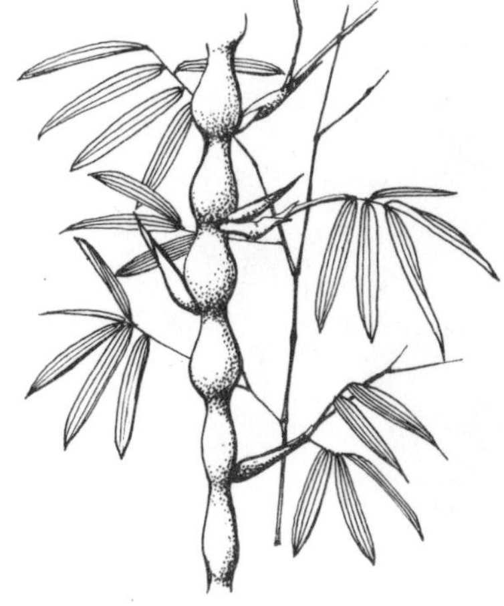

*Bambusa ventricosa* from China is very striking but, like most bamboos, is unfortunately not a common house plant

15–25°C

# *Protea barbigera*

## Queen Protea

If there were to be a contest to choose the queen of shrubs protea would win hands down. In the opinion of many botanists as well as amateurs it is the most beautiful plant of all.

This genus comprises approximately 100 species distributed chiefly in South Africa, though some reach as far as tropical Africa. They are the species growing closest to the equator though remaining in the southern hemisphere.

*Protea barbigera,* called queen protea, is one of the loveliest members of the genus. A shrub up to 2 m (6 ft) high, it is indigenous to the high mountains of South Africa, but also tolerates the moderate conditions of lowland country and is thus widely grown in the gardens of its native land. The flowers are borne in heads surrounded by woody bracts. It is apparently quite variable for near Franschboek specimens were found with melon-pink bracts, and near Du Toit's Kloof (likewise in South Africa) specimens with yellow bracts and deep orange hairs on the margins.

Most commonly imported to Europe are the flowers of *Protea cynaroides* which are covered with white hairs and surrounded by deep pink bracts. The inflorescence is the largest of the whole genus; it measures up to 30 cm (1 ft) in diameter and is extremely long-lived, often lasting as long as two months in a vase without any change. It is lovely even when dried and is excellent for dried flower arrangements.

The high-mountain species with an underground stem and sessile flowers are also noteworthy. These may have thin, needle-like leaves *(P. lorea, P. tenuifolia, P. restionifolia);* twigs reminiscent of heathers *(P. acerosa);* or large, cabbage-like leaves *(P. acaulis, P. amplexicaulis, P. convexa).*

Only the tall shrubby species with spectacular flowers are suitable for cultivation, but it is necessary to satisfy their requirements, namely a relatively cool location such as a conservatory, ventilation, a moist atmosphere and rather heavy soil, composed, for example, of leaf mould, loam and sand, and preferably without peat. Propagation is by means of seeds.

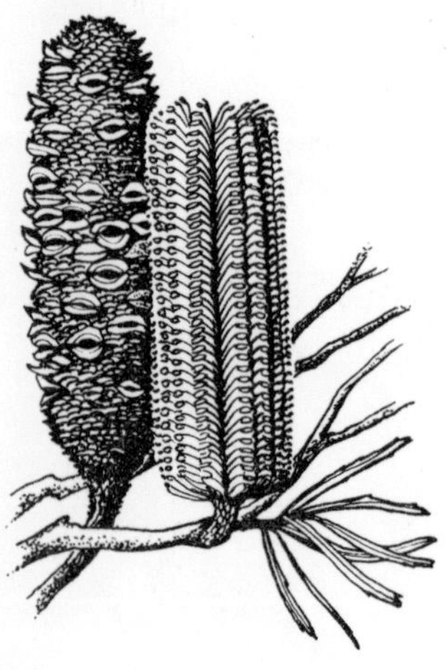

*Banksia littoralis* is a native of West Australia

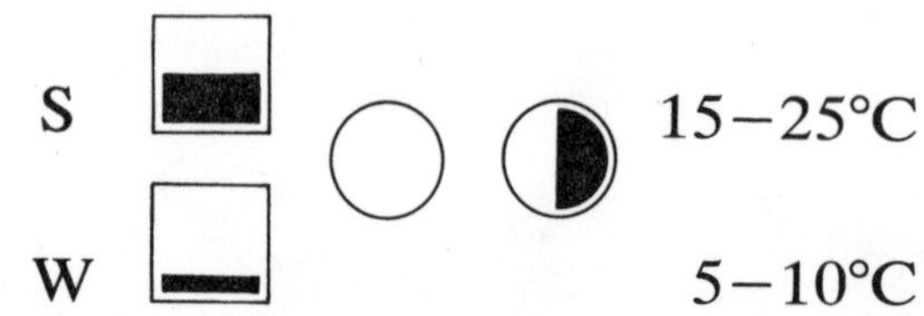

# PALMS

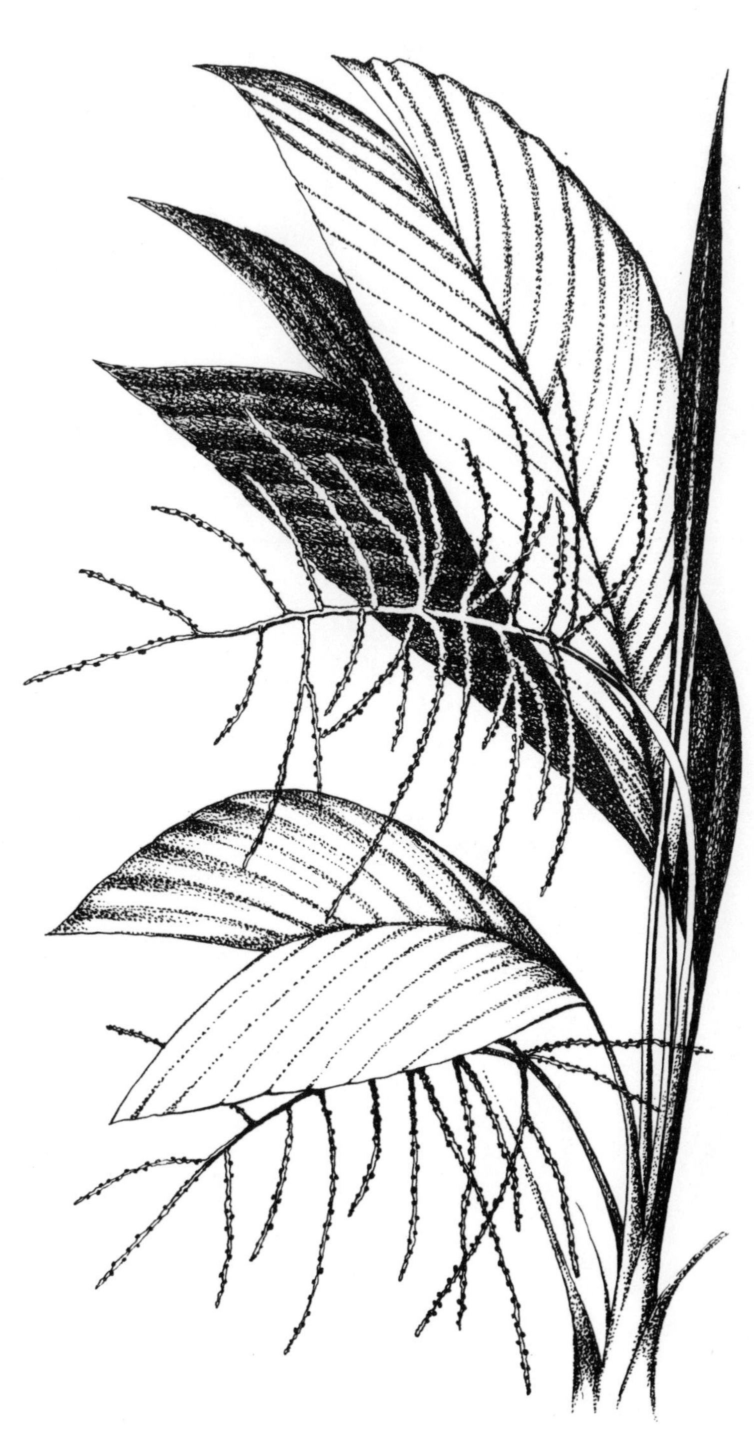

# *Licuala grandis*

## Ruffed Fan Palm

This and the following two illustrations show *Licuala grandis* from New Britain (an island north of New Guinea); *Microcoelum martianum,* often found in shops under the name of *Cocos weddelliana,* from tropical Brazil; and *Phoenix loureirii* (syn. *P. roebelenii*) whose range extends from Assam to Vietnam.

All three are members of the palm family which includes seven subfamilies, some 220 genera, and approximately 1,300 species. What are the common characteristics of the family as a whole? Palms are generally tall trees with a slender, flexible trunk that may reach a height of 60 m (200 ft). However, they also include tufted forms, such as chamaerops, as well as climbing palms with elongated segments and alternate leaves, such as calamus, the rattan palm and daemonorops, some of which have the longest stems in the plant realm – up to 300 m (960 ft). The tree-like species have trunks composed of short segments and leaves growing in a bunch at the top. The trunks are unbranched, the only exception being the African genus *Hyphaene* with dichotomously branched trunks.

The characteristic rings on the trunks of palms are leaf scars. In some species these marks are practically invisible and the trunk is almost entirely covered by leaf sheaths or adventitious roots transformed into thick spines. Spines on the trunks, leaf stalks and even flower spathes are not at all uncommon; a striking example is *Acrocomia mexicana* from the damp lowlands of the Pacific coast. Spines need not serve merely as a form of defence or protection. The thick recurved spines on the leaf stalks of climbing palms help them keep a hold on the trees up which they climb. Sometimes a thorny leaf stalk is elongated and extends far beyond the leaf itself.

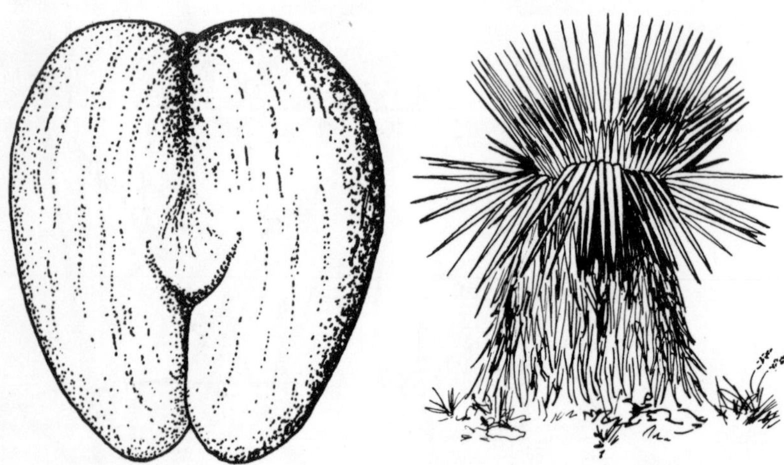

*Lodoicea seychellarum* has the largest seeds in the plant realm, measuring about 40 cm (16 in) in length and weighing up to 10 kg (22 lb)

*Copernicia pauciflora*

  15–30°C

# *Microcoelum martianum*

Palm leaves are large, stalked and furnished with a sheath at the base. In the juvenile stage the leaf is whole but during growth it breaks up into sections along the veins and thus in maturity it is either pinnate (cocos – coconut-palm) or fan-shaped (corypha – talipot-palm). Often it is palmate (washingtonia) or two-lobed (chamaedorea), and in rare instances bipinnate (caryota – fishtail-palm).

The inflorescence of a palm consists of a cluster of trimerous, usually unisexual flowers arranged in a spike (spadix) enclosed by a spathe, or several spathes. Most palms have axillary flowers, produced a number of times during the tree's lifetime. Some species, however, have terminal flowers and these are then extremely large: in the genus *Corypha* it is estimated that a single cluster contains as many as 100,000 flowers. The genera *Corypha, Metroxylon* – sago-palms, and *Caryota* die after the flowers have faded and the seeds have ripened – a phenomenon known as hypaxanthy. Though inconspicuous, the flowers are very fragrant and secrete nectar, a fact well known to entomologists working in the tropics who never pass up the opportunity of examining such a flower which attracts scores of insects. Insects are also the chief pollinators of palm trees, other agents being the wind and in rare instances even humming-birds and other birds that catch insects on the flowers.

The fruits of palm trees are not nuts, as is commonly but mistakenly believed, but berries or drupes, called armoured berries when they are ripe and the outer covers have dried. The seeds have a well-developed endosperm, which is either hard and horny such as in the genus *Phytelephas* (sometimes classed as a separate family) and can be used as plant-ivory for carvings, or soft and oily. In the course of germination the ovary becomes elongated, with part of it remaining in the seed, and serves to carry food from the endosperm to the embryo which develops outside the seed. This form of nourishment from the endosperm may last for several years, as with the coconut.

Palms are typical plants of the tropics and subtropics, represented in Europe by the well-known *Chamaerops humilis* and *C. macrocarpa* from the Mediterranean region. In 1967 a third European palm, *Phoenix theophrasti,* the date palm, was discovered on Crete in the province of Sitía.

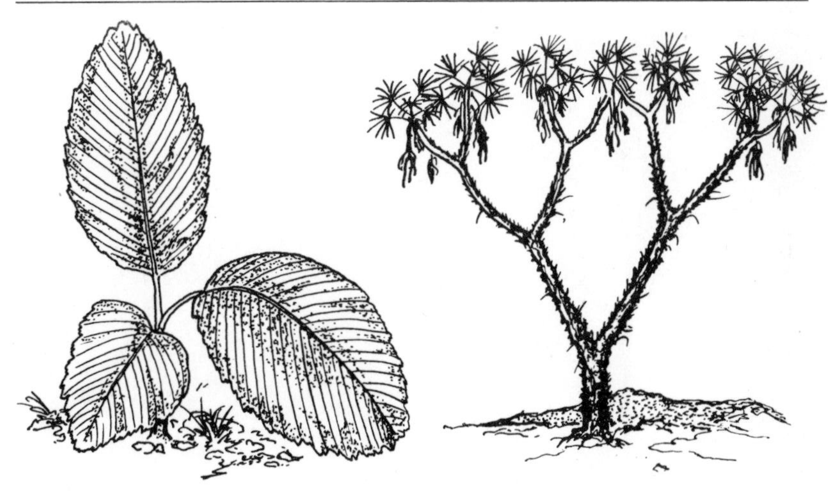

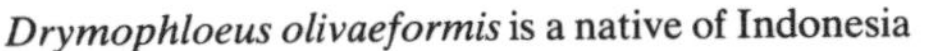

*Drymophloeus olivaeformis* is a native of Indonesia

*Hyphaene thebaica* is the only palm with a dichotomously branched trunk

 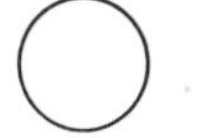 10–30°C

# *Phoenix loureirii*

## Dwarf Date Palm

The illustrated palms are tropical species and enjoy very hot conditions except for the last one, which requires a rather moderate climate. All do very well in modern homes with central heating if provided with ample light, best of all direct sunlight. Licuala requires the least amount of light, for in its native land it generally grows in the shade of luxuriant vegetation, but still it needs a well-lit spot.

All palms should be grown in fertile heavy compost. John Innes potting compost No. 3 would be ideal for mature plants. The compost must never be allowed to dry out completely. Palms need lots of water and this should therefore be supplied liberally, particularly during the growing season. Feed, best of all liquid manure or an organic fertilizer, should likewise be supplied in summer.

Palms are generally propagated from seeds, either brought home from a holiday or else purchased together with the fruit in a package of dates. First of all they should be soaked in tepid water for two days or else carefully grooved with a file and then put in a mixture of peat and sand in a small pot, which should be watered and covered with a piece of glass to keep the compost adequately moist. The seeds will germinate in 1 to 3 months, depending on the species. When the seedlings have two leaves they should be potted up individually in small pots of John Innes potting compost No. 1.

There is no disputing the many uses to which palms have been put by man. Their leaves are used as roofing by natives, the trunks often serve as building material, and some have edible fruits such as dates and coconut. *Copernicia cerifera* from South America has leaves which are covered with wax which is collected; *Arenga saccharifera* yields palm sugar, and *Elaeis guineensis* has oily fruits that yield a good-quality palm oil. These are only the better known examples.

*Licuala spinosa*

*Caryota urens* has oddly-shaped leaves which have earned it the name of fishtail palm

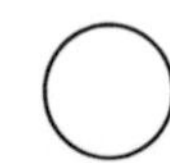

10–20°C

# BROMELIADS

# *Aechmea fasciata*

## Urn Plant

The species selected as the first in this section on the pineapple family is one that will soon celebrate the hundredth anniversary of its introduction into cultivation. *Aechmea fasciata* is native to Brazil, where it grows as an epiphyte. It is adapted against drying out by having the leaves covered with absorbent scales that obtain life-giving water for the plant from the moisture in the atmosphere. These scales are arranged in horizontal bands, chiefly on the underside but also on the upper surface of the leaves. All parts of the plant, including the striking bluish flowers with pink bracts that retain their colour for months, are hard, a form of adaptation to drought. No wonder, then, that this plant became so popular as an exceptionally hardy species for room decoration in modern centrally-heated homes. It also tolerates the air pollution (gases, dust and smoke) of cities, so that it is an ideal modern-day house plant. Though it is not damaged by full sun, light shading is preferred. As with all cistern bromeliads, that is those with leaves forming a funnel to catch rainwater, the water stored in the 'vase' in the centre of the rosette should never dry out for long.

This species can be grown successfully both as an epiphyte and in the more traditional way, in a pot in a mixture of beech leaf mould, peat, and sand plus some orchid-chips or bits of charcoal added to make the mix lighter.

Since the genus *Aechmea* includes more than 150 species it is difficult to say which are the loveliest. As already mentioned, *A. fasciata* is probably the most popular. Another lovely species is *Aechmea chantinii,* whose coloration is extremely decorative. The leaves are stiff, wide and horizontally striped with deep green and silvery white; the flowers are erect with bright red bracts. Unfortunately, it is very difficult to propagate and so is not only rare in cultivation but also expensive.

Most aechmeas are readily propagated from seed, sown either on the surface of sterile peat or directly on the bark where the plants are to be grown as epiphytes.

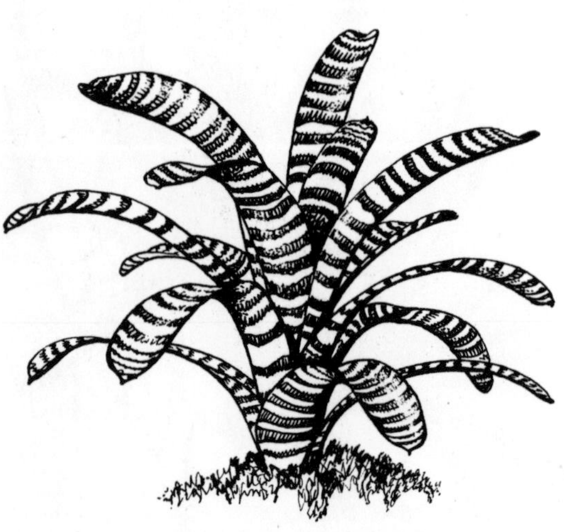

*Aechmea chantinii* is undoubtedly the loveliest member of the genus

   15–30°C

# *Ananas comosus* 'Variegatus'

## Pineapple

Brazil is the home of the pineapple, which gave its name to the whole family. It is likewise probably the best known of all bromeliads, not necessarily as a plant for decoration, but for its edible fruit. One would be hard put to find a locality where pineapple grows wild – none such is known. All one encounters are plants that have become established in the wild as escapes. There is no doubt, however, that originally this species grew on sunny, sandy soils well supplied with humus, perhaps also on alluvial soils. Anyone who has ever seen large pineapple plantations has surely noticed both the good quality soil and the excellent irrigation system. Pineapple, unlike other bromeliads, must have a constant supply of adequate soil moisture. The beautiful reddish-pink inflorescence develops into a collective fruit. In the tropics, where great attention is paid to quality, young fruits are wrapped in newspaper. For several months the fruit ripens protected from the sun in this manner, thus acquiring a better and mellower flavour. The taste, of course, also depends on the type of pineapple, for those grown on plantations include various tried and tested cultivars.

If you would like to grow a pineapple yourself you can do so by cutting off the terminal tuft of leaves crowning the collective fruit, along with a slice of the fruit and inserting it in a mixture of peat and sand. In time this will yield a number of flowering as well as fruiting plants but (according to plantation owners) the fruits will be of poorer quality than those produced by plants grown from side-rosettes. Added to this, plants grown in Europe always have a poorer flavour.

The illustrated cultivar, given optimal conditions (that is a summer temperature of up to 30°C (86°F) and winter temperature of about 20°C (68°F), high atmospheric moisture, an adequate amount of direct sunlight and rich feeding), will develop a rosette up to 1.5 m (5 ft) in diameter. The blood-red inflorescence as well as the leaves, which are reddish in the centre, are extremely decorative. It is generally impossible to provide ideal conditions in the home but even there one can be rewarded with handsome specimens after several years.

*Acanthostachys strobilacea*

   15–30°C

# *Billbergia × saundersii*

## Rainbow Plant

Many bromeliads are plants that can really stand up to 'tough' conditions and take a good deal of neglect without harm. Billbergia is one such genus that tolerates practically everything. The well-known queen's tears *(Billbergia nutans)*, may be put in full sun or deep shade and will flower regularly every year even in the smokiest amosphere and even if the leaves are not cleaned and it is not watered for months. No wonder that it is the most widely cultivated bromeliad.

Equally hardy is *B.* x *saundersii* (sometimes classed as a cultivar, at other times as a 'good species' from Brazil), which is encountered in culture almost as often as *B. nutans*. It, too, tolerates everything, practically any location, even temperatures near freezing point in dry conditions, but also temperatures of more than 30°C (86°F) though it is a cool-loving species. It flowers readily and puts out numerous sideshoots so that it is propagated easily and quickly. Plants attain their full beauty if grown in partial shade and a slightly heated or, better still, a cool room. The leaves turn a deep wine red or purplish violet on the underside while the upper surface is a glossy deep green. They furthermore have translucent, milky-white 'windows' that are characteristic of this species. The illustration shows a specimen grown in poor light conditions (which proves that billbergia flowers well even if neglected); that is why the underside of the leaves is not as brightly coloured as it might be.

Hybrids, obtained by crossings with other species or with *Billbergia* hybrids, also exist. Loveliest is *Billbergia* 'Fascinator' (*B.* x *windii* × *B.* x *saundersii*), raised by the German grower Walter Richter. It forms a closed rosette of leaves coloured reddish green and covered almost entirely with large yellowish-white spots. The flowers, produced in winter, are more compact than those of the illustrated species, the bracts large and purplish red.

Though most of the approximately 60 known species of Billbergia grow as epiphytes in the wild they also do well if grown in flower pots. Use John Innes potting compost with extra peat added.

*Billbergia* 'Fantasia' is one of the loveliest cultivars developed by W. Richter

*Billbergia* 'Muriel Watermann'

 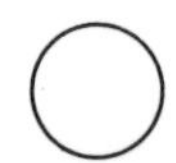 10–30°C

# *Cryptanthus*

Bromeliads, with their vast number of species (nearly 2,000), offer almost limitless selection. They include giants several metres (yards) high (*Puya gigas* has flowers up to 10 m [33 ft] high), as well as dwarfs measuring only a few centimetres (inches); flowers for a damp, shaded spot as well as for bright sunlight; species that are soberly coloured, a uniform green or grey, as well as those which come in brilliant hues – in short, one has a vast choice from which to find something suitable for the conditions of one's own home. One plant, however, that should be in every household is a member of the genus *Cryptanthus*. These mostly stemless plants with attractive rosettes of leaves can be used to make lovely dish arrangements because they can be combined excellently with countless other plants (to provide a harmonious colour supplement or a foil for their shape). Besides, most will survive even gross mistakes in care without marked damage and are thus good plants for those who are amateurs at growing tropical plants.

Unlike most bromeliads, cryptanthuses are geophytes, in other words they grow in the ground. In the wild, in eastern Brazil, they inhabit the undergrowth of rather dry forests. That is why in the home they should be grown in a light, slightly acid soil mixture, best of all a blend such as used for orchids. If a ball of the compost is attached to the plants (see the chapter on Containers and Display, p. 14), they may also be grown in epiphytic arrangements, but not permanently; they will remain in good condition for one year at the most when grown this way.

Most type species have no special heat requirements and will be satisfied with a temperature of about 18°C (65°F) in winter; the optimum for variegated cultivars, such as *Cryptanthus lacerdae, C. zonatus* and *C.* x *fosterianus,* is about 5°C (9°F) higher. Light requirements also differ. Most species need shade or partial shade, but *C. bromelioides* 'Tricolor' and *C. acaulis* and its cultivars require full sun. *C. acaulis,* for example, should be put in a frame exposed to direct sun in summer. During the growth period the plants should be watered and fed fairly often. The ideal fertilizer is dry cow manure added to the potting compost. If this is not available, use liquid fertilizer. Propagation is very easy by means of the sideshoots produced in large numbers from the base of mature plants.

**1 – C. bivittatus**
**2 – C. lacerdae**
**3 – C. x fosterianus**

*Cryptanthus beuckeri* is the only member of the genus with stalked leaves

  15–25°C

# *Guzmania minor* 'Red'

The illustrated bromeliad has been one of the commonest fixtures in the florist's window for years. Often the bracts are coloured orange-yellow instead of bright red, in which case it is the equally common cultivar 'Orange'. Both cultivars often produce flowers when the leaf rosette measures only 25 cm (10 in) across, whereas in the type species they appear later, when the rosette is at least 10 cm (4 in) larger. This is because, for one thing, both cultivars are smaller, and secondly, in today's conditions of culture the flowering of bromeliads is generally provoked artificially by the use of chemicals. These preparations generally release acetylene as they decompose, to which the plant reacts by flowering within a few months. However, after the bromeliad has flowered once, further flowering may be expected only in the plants that develop from the sideshoots produced at the base of the mature rosette, for a plant does not flower a second time.

*Guzmania minor,* the same as most guzmanias, requires high temperatures, shade and permanently high atmospheric moisture. This applies to cultivars as well as specimens of the type species grown in Europe. In the wild, however, one may encounter populations adapted even to quite cool conditions. For example, in Colombia *G. minor* grows high up in the mountains where the night temperature during the winter months drops to near freezing point. Many foliage guzmanias, such as *G. musaica,* are best kept in closed plant-cases. Only one species can be grown successfully in a rather dry, warm room in full sun, namely *G. sanguinea* with leaves longitudinally striped purple and with large yellow flowers. All guzmanias are particularly good for epiphytic arrangements, but they may also be grown as potted plants in a light, slightly acid soil – John Innes potting compost with extra peat added would be suitable.

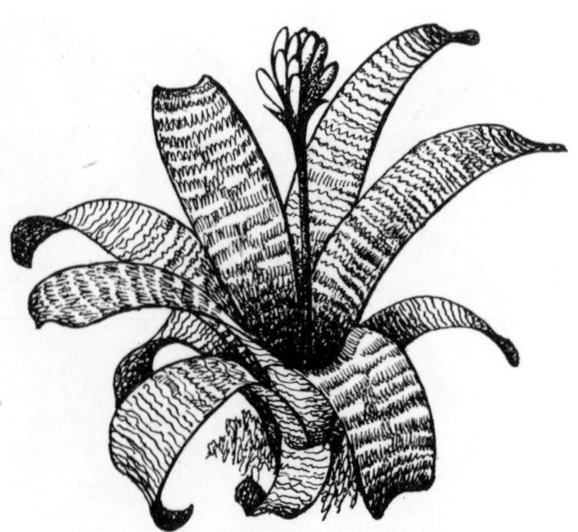

*Guzmania musaica* is one of the most attractive bromeliads but does not tolerate the dry atmosphere of a room. For healthy specimens, a plant-case is needed

  15–25°C

# *Neoregelia carolinae* 'Tricolor'

## Fingernail Plant

It is a commonly known fact that bromeliads are among the loveliest of plants for room decoration in the modern home, both for their decorative foliage and flowers. To date, however, minimum use has been made of this family by nurserymen and many species wait to be 'rediscovered' – this time for those who appreciate plants of exceptional beauty.

The illustrated cultivar is descended from the type species *Neoregelia carolinae,* sometimes found in nurseries under the wrong name of *Nidularium meyendorffii. Neoregelia carolinae* is a relatively large, green-leaved bromeliad (the rosettes are as much as 50 to 60 cm [20 to 24 in] across). The sessile, bluish flowers develop from the margin of the cluster inwards (a good identifying character – in the similar genus *Nidularium* they develop in the opposite direction) and are enclosed by brilliant red bracts. In the illustrated cultivar the whole centre of the leaf rosette turns a brilliant red during the flowering period.

Neoregelias include a great many attractive and rewarding house plants, for example *N. spectabilis,* the painted fingernail plant, with deep green leaves coloured glowing pinkish violet at the tips and violet variegated with brownish red on the underside. This plant really tolerates any conditions and is even hardier than the illustrated species. Particularly lovely for those who are fond of the special beauty of epiphytes is *N. ampullacea,* a small, only about 10- to 12-cm-(4- to 4¾in-) high species with leaves forming a 'vase' at the base and opening out into a rosette between one- and two-thirds of the way up; they are spotted brownish red on the underside. This species can be grown successfully in an indoor plant-case on bare bark without compost, where it will soon form decorative clumps because it puts out numerous sideshoots from the base.

Practically all members of this genus, including cultivars, can be grown on bark, for all the approximately 35 species (34 of which are native to Brazil) are epiphytes. Plants attain their greatest beauty in warm conditions, in full sun, and if supplied with ample atmospheric moisture – a window glasshouse is ideal for this purpose. Cultivation is easy. All that is necessary is to keep the central 'vase' formed by the foliage filled with water. Cultivars of different coloration may be propagated only by means of off-shoots; species are readily multiplied from seed.

*Neoregelia mooreana* from the Amazon region of Peru is better known as *N. ossifragi*

   15–30°C

*Vriesea hieroglyphica* 'Marginata' needs a particularly moist atmosphere

# *Nidularium innocentii*

Though most bromeliads require ample light this large family also includes plants that tolerate or need permanent shade, among them being most members of the genus *Nidularium*. For these, full sunlight is definitely detrimental.

Some 23 species grow as epiphytes or petrophytes (on stones or rocks) in southern and eastern Brazil. They are all much alike: the leaves form a dense ground rosette with sessile flowers appearing in the centre of the 'vase'. The chief decorative feature of this genus are the central leaves which often turn bright crimson during the flowering period. In some species the central leaves do not change colour, for example in *N. burchellii*. Nevertheless, this plant is commonly found in cultivation for its hardiness and lovely orange fruits.

*Nidularium innocentii,* native to Brazil, makes flat rosettes of leaves approximately 25 cm (10 in) long, 5 cm (2 in) across, and edged thickly with delicate spines. They are green on the upper side, purple or reddish violet on the underside; in the variety *wittmackianum* they are entirely green. The central leaves are various shades of red, the flowers white. Very lovely are the cultivars 'Lineatum' and 'Striatum'; the first has the leaves longitudinally striped with white, the second with yellow.

Most often found in cultivation, besides the illustrated species, is *N. fulgens* – somewhat larger, with pale green leaves irregularly spotted with dark green, central leaves coloured brilliant red, and flowers a mixture of white, red, and violet.

Though nidulariums are basically epiphytes, their root system is not well developed and they may also be grown successfully as potted plants in a mixture composed mainly of peat and sand. They must be syringed frequently and the compost kept permanently slightly moist. The fruit, a berry, contains a large number of tiny, dark seeds that should be sown on the surface of sterile peat. The seedlings will reach flower-bearing size in two years; variegated cultivars, of course, can be propagated only by detaching the side rosettes.

   15–25°C

# Tillandsia

These veritable 'gems' of the plant realm could be the subject of a whole book, and not an uninteresting one at that. Nor is it surprising that there are already numerous tillandsia clubs throughout the world, for the requirements and bizarre appearance of many species must captivate every nature lover.

No other plants exhibit such great diversity within a single genus. Many tillandsias are 'typical' bromeliads in that their leaves form the characteristic funnel-shaped rosette to catch and hold rainwater. In others the thickened bases of the leaves form a kind of bulb serving to store water inside the tissues, covered with a thick skin. *Tillandsia usneoides,* one of the best-known, looks like a lichen of the genus *Usnea;* it has no roots and the stems with narrow leaflets trail freely in space like tufts of grey hairs. The varied environment in which these plants grow was naturally responsible for these morphological adaptations. That is why it is also relatively easy to guess from its shape what the requirements of a given plant are. The broad, green leaves of *Tillandsia imperialis* arranged in the form of a regular funnel indicate that this plant comes from an environment with frequent rains and only brief periods of drought, and so it does – in its native land, Mexico, it grows at elevations of 1,700 m (5,650 ft) where the marked fluctuations between day-time and night-time temperatures assure an adequate daily supply of dew.

The leaves of *T. dasylirifolia* likewise form a funnel, but different from that of the preceding species. The leaves are stiff, or rather hard, and fairly narrow, widening only at the base, where the plant stores water. The leaves are also covered with absorbent scales that enable the plant to utilize even water from mist by absorbing it and passing it on to the inner leaf tissues which are protected by a rigid epidermis. The surface of the leaves is a striking colour – green coated by a blend of copper, red, violet and grey. Such colouring usually serves as protection against too much sun – and from this we can deduce the plant's requirements: full sun, heat and drought. Often it grows on columnar cacti, to which it holds fast by means of several wiry roots that have long lost their original function. Water and food are obtained only through the leaves. Many tillandsias growing in localities subject to drought are spherical in shape (the smallest surface area and hence the smallest amount of evaporation), with leaves that are narrow to thread-like and thickly covered with absorbent scales. Examples of such tillandsias are *T. tectorum* (syn. *T. argentea*) and *T. filifolia.* Elsewhere we will find clumps of plants that collectively form a spherical shape; this habit is characteristic, for example, of *T. ionantha* (syn. *T. erubescens*) and *T. recurvata;* the latter is often found growing on telegraph wires.

**1 – T. tectorum**
**2 – T. ionantha**
**3 – T. streptophylla**

*Tillandsia cyanea* grows well as a potted plant

*Tillandsia juncea* – practically indestructible in modern centrally-heated homes

 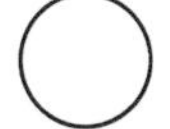 15–30°C

**T. imperialis**
(Continued)

However, it is not only the shape and interesting adaptations that attract the interest of growers. Tillandsias also have lovely flowers, be it the large gentian-blue flowers of *T. cyanea* arranged in a flat spike or the simple dark blue flowers of *T. brachycaulos* emerging from the centre of the rosette and forming a striking contrast with the brilliant red leaves of the rosette. This is not the only species whose leaves turn red during the flowering period; the same is true, for example, of the already mentioned *T. ionantha.*

To be grown successfully, these magnificent bromeliads must be put in a warm spot in full sun, best of all in a southern or eastern window. They should be put on branches or on pieces of cork oak bark (the roots of grape vine are also excellent), to which they should be tied with a thin, coated wire or strip of nylon stocking; small species and seedlings may be attached to the bark with waterproof glue. *Tillandsia cyanea, T. brachycaulos* and large rosette-forming species may also be grown as potted plants in a light soil mixture, such as one of the soilless composts. Water and feed are best supplied by syringing the leaves, but it must be remembered that purely epiphytic forms tolerate only very low concentrations of fertilizer. Propagation is easy – by detaching young plantlets growing from the side or by means of seeds sown on the surface of the branch immediately after they have ripened, for they rapidly lose their powers of germination.

*Tillandsia imperialis*

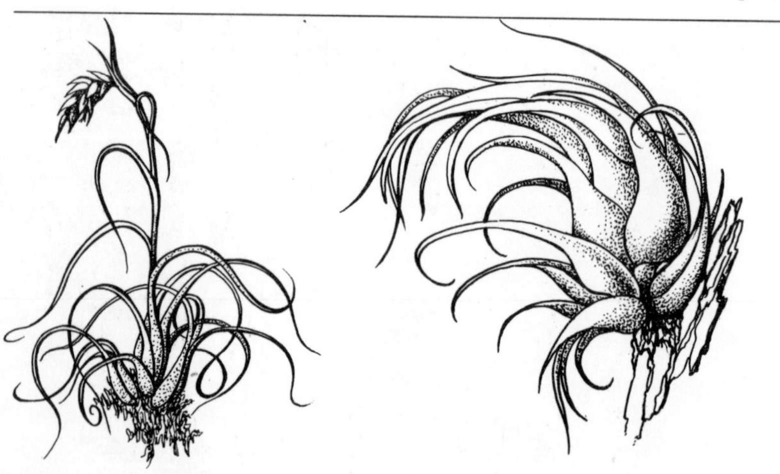

*Tillandsia butzii* from Mexico and Central America is also a very undemanding species

*Tillandsia seleriana* is a beautiful epiphyte that tolerates the dry atmosphere of modern homes extremely well

   15–25°C

# ORCHIDS

# *Arundina graminifolia*

Imagine that you are in Vietnam, in the mountains not far from the village of Tam Dao. It is autumn, in other words the season when *Arundina graminifolia* flowers. Beside the road along which you are driving there rises a steep bank covered with tall grasses and ferns above which the magnificent, relatively large flowers of this orchid appear to hover like butterflies. The specimens growing here are fairly small, less than a metre (yard) high, probably because this is the northern boundary of the orchid's range and definitely a cool locality. *Arundina graminifolia* has a relatively large area of distribution, extending from India to Vietnam and Malaysia, and therefore it is not surprising that it is quite variable in the size and coloration of the flowers. Botanical collections include specimens up to 2 m (6 ft) high with leaves up to 30 cm (1 ft) long.

All, however, are plants that resemble reeds or some bamboos and that grow in the ground. Their appearance and requirements are very much like those of the South American genus *Sobralia.* From the fleshy roots, which are extremely fragile (take care when transplanting for broken roots rot readily), rises a slender, firm, flexible stem bearing alternate, lanceolate to linear leaves. The approximately 5-cm-(2-in-) long flowers bear a striking resemblance to those of cattleyas; the sepals are lanceolate, the petals elliptical, the lip relatively large and beautifully coloured. The shape and size of the ovary are evident from the illustration.

Arundina should be grown in a light mixture composed of peat, fern roots, bits of polystyrene or bits of charcoal and sand, plus loam for nourishment. The roots must be quite close to the surface of the soil. The temperature should not be unduly high, particularly in winter, at which time water should also be limited. Not until spring, when the buds form, should the supply of water be increased and before flowering the plant should be syringed frequently, for there is danger of it drying out in a dry atmosphere. Still, it is a species that thrives in a warm home without any great care.

*Masdevallia veitchiana* with red flowers is a native of Machu Picchu, Peru

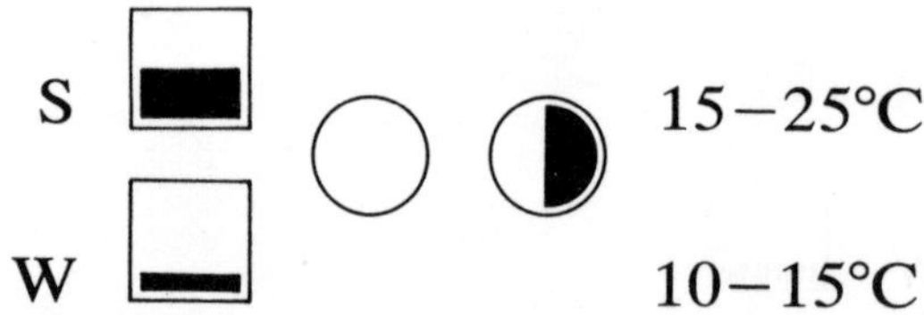

# Bifrenaria harrisoniae

Growing orchids in Europe a hundred years ago, when new species were being discovered and introduced into cultivation, was restricted only to those who owned a greenhouse. Nowadays, however, they are gradually being commonly grown as house plants. In fact, growing orchids and other epiphytes has become the fashion in western Europe since the beginning of the seventies, and many people now specialize in this branch of horticulture. A contributing factor, apart from the purely aesthetic aspect, has undoubtedly been the changes in housing and in the development of equipment, particularly indoor glasshouses and glass plant-cases that make it possible to grow even the most demanding species. Nevertheless, interest will continue to be focused on those plants that thrive and produce flowers under ordinary conditions, without any special equipment.

*Bifrenaria harrisoniae* is just such a house plant. Though it has a relatively pronounced period of rest it will be quite satisfied with just limited watering and a cooler spot during this time and is otherwise quite undemanding. In spring and summer it should be given as much light and heat as possible, plenty of air and water – conditions that practically every grower can provide.

The illustrated species is native to Brazil, like most of the 30 or so known species of this genus. It grows as an epiphyte in the wild, but in cultivation it also does very well in various containers in a light epiphyte mixture. Bifrenaria is a fairly robust plant with quadrangular pseudo-bulbs about 8 cm (3 in) high from which rise firm leaves approximately 30 cm (1 ft) long and 12 cm (4¾ in) wide. Short scapes, usually two, each about 5 cm (2 in) long and bearing 1 to 3 fragrant flowers circa 8 cm (3 in) across, emerge from the base of the youngest pseudo-bulb in spring.

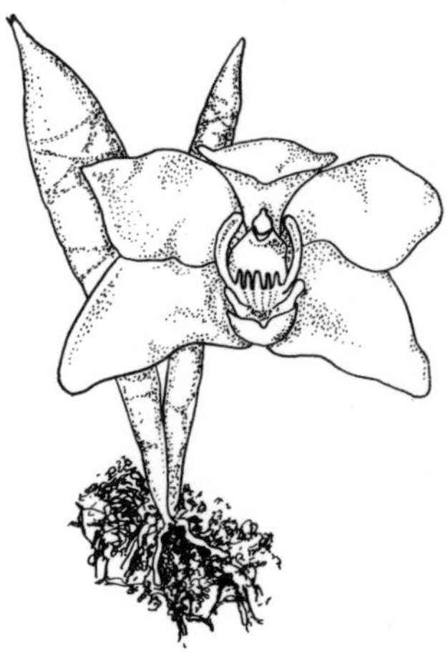

*Chysis bractescens* is an epiphytic orchid from Mexico and Guatemala

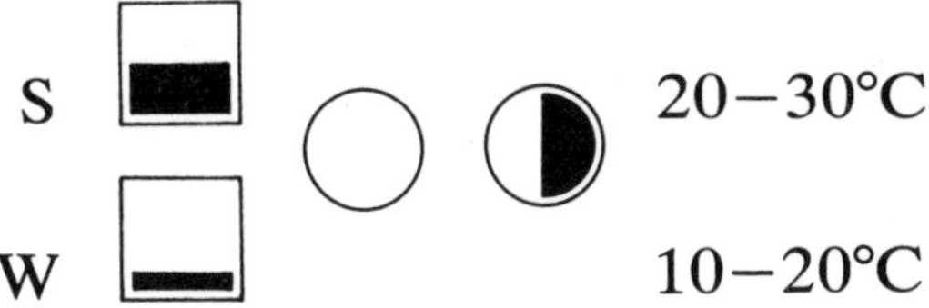


20–30°C

10–20°C

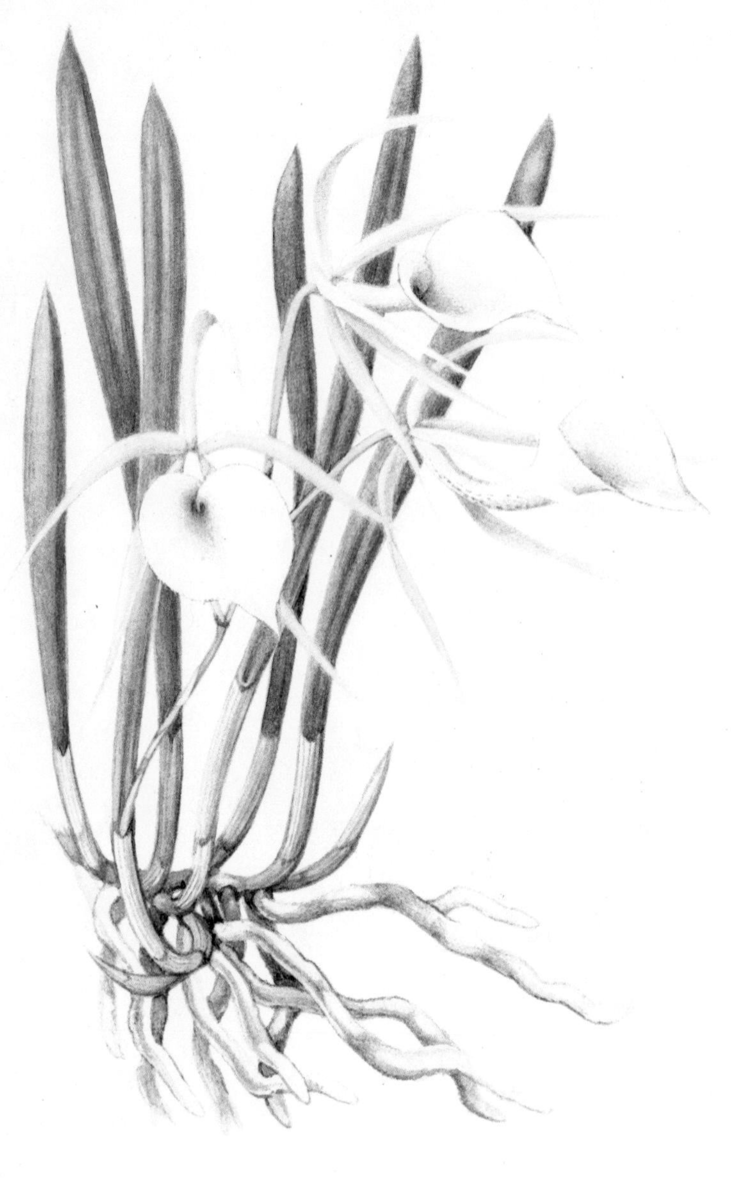

# *Brassavola nodosa*

## Lady of the Night

The genus *Brassavola* comprises only about 15 species alltold. Their range of distribution extends from the Antilles through Central America to southern Brazil, Paraguay and Bolivia. The pseudo-bulbs are generally not thickened and resemble stems. The leaves, usually one to a bulb, are long, very narrow, thick and leathery. Only in *Brassavola digbyana* and *B. glauca* are they wide – reminiscent of the leaves of the genus *Laelia*.

The flowers are very attractive and large with a striking widened lip, which is sometimes a fantastic shape, for example in *B. digbyana* it has a long delicate fringe on the margin. The other segments are narrower and either white, the same as the lip or, more frequently, with a yellow or green tinge.

Few orchids are so suitable for indoor cultivation as brassavolas. They find the conditions of modern centrally-heated homes fully to their liking, besides which they also tolerate a dry atmosphere. The illustrated species and many others do not have a marked period of winter rest and so all that is necessary is to slightly limit watering in the autumn when temperatures usually tend to be lower for a few weeks before the heating system is put into operation.

*Brassavola nodosa* has a vast range of distribution, extending from Mexico through Venezuela to Peru. It mainly inhabits epiphytic situations, growing on the trunks and branches of trees, on large columnar cacti, on the roots of mangroves, as well as on cliffs. It is usually found at elevations of more than 600 m (1,920 ft). The leaves are up to 9 cm ($3^1/_2$ in) across and very fragrant.

Brassavolas may be grown indoors either freely in a room or in a plant case, but they must always be provided with abundant light (they may even be exposed to direct sunlight). The compost may be quite simple – a ball of moss attached to a branch is sufficient.

This genus may be successfully crossed with other members of the subtribe Laeliinae, for example with *Cattleya, Laelia* or *Epidendrum;* most such hybrids are likewise excellent for indoor cultivation.

*Encyclia citrina* (formerly *Cattleya citrina*) is a cold-loving orchid from the high mountains of Central America; characteristic is its trailing habit

  15–25°C

# Coelogyne cristata

Anyone who becomes interested in orchids and would like to try his hand at growing them will find the illustrated species an excellent one to start with. *C. cristata* is native to the Himalayas where it grows at elevations between 1,600 and 2,300 m (5,220 and 7,560 ft) as an epiphyte on the bark of trees as well as on rocks and the stone walls marking the boundaries of the local fields. They are typically found growing on rocks beside waterfalls.

This description indicates the orchid's requirements in cultivation. The first and absolute must is overwintering in cool conditions, for without this the plant generally does not flower at all. The winter temperature should be between 5 and 7°C (41 and 45°F), but may also be lower, in which case the plant must be kept dry. In summer it may be moved to the balcony or to the garden, where it will thrive in partial shade under trees.

The magnificent flowers, produced in spring at the base of the pseudo-bulbs, are unfortunately short-lived, even though this orchid was at one time also used for cutting. One grower aptly compared the blooms to a soft-boiled egg – both in coloration and firmness!

The pseudo-bulbs are an important organ, for this is where food is stored, as with the bulb of bulbous plants. Old pseudo-bulbs, which as a rule are already leafless, may be used to propagate the plants by severing the creeping rhizome and putting a group of about three pseudo-bulbs to root in a plastic bag partly filled with sphagnum or in compost composed of one part cut sphagnum, one part orchid chips and one part a mixture of crushed oak bark, fern roots and a little sand.

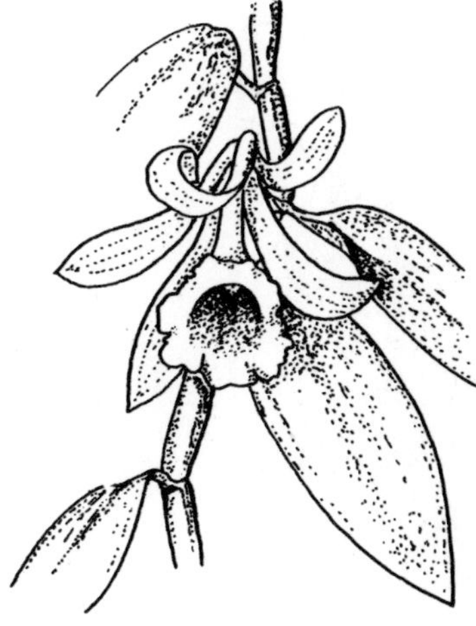

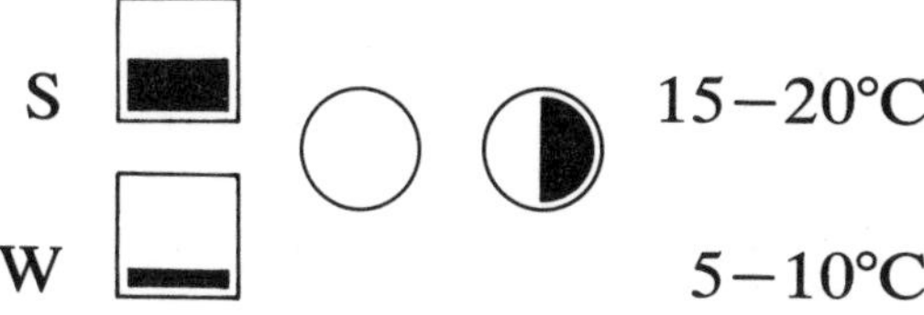


15–20°C

5–10°C

*Vanilla planifolia* yields the well-known vanilla flavouring (obtained from the seed pods)

# *Cycnoches ventricosum chlorochilum*

## Swan Orchid

The illustrated orchid is the veritable embodiment of the exotic atmosphere of the tropics. An interesting characteristic of orchids of the genera *Cycnoches* and *Catasetum* is that the flowers are unisexual, which is quite unusual among orchids. Often there is such a marked difference between the male and female flowers that the respective plants were described as separate species. This, however, does not apply to the illustrated species for the male and female flowers in this case are very much alike.

*Cycnoches ventricosum* (from which the illustrated variety differs only by the coloration and shape of the lip) grows in Central America, its range extending from Mexico to Panama. The variety *chlorochilum* is distributed from Panama to Venezuela.

The pseudo-bulbs are longish spindle-shaped, often as much as 30 cm (1 ft) high. The leaves, which are generally shed entirely during the flowering period, are up to 40 cm (16 in) long and about 6 cm (2¼ in) wide. The huge flowers, 15 to 18 cm (6 to 7 in) in diameter, appear in late spring and early summer.

The habitat of these plants is of particular interest. They are often found on the dry trunks of dead trees or on the trunks of palm trees, to which they are pressed close without any compost. The roots grow upwards and form a kind of 'brush' that catches falling leaves and bits of soil carried up to the top of the tree by ants and termites. The structure of the leaves, which are very delicate and weak, appears to be at odds with this way of life, but during the dormant period, that is during the period of drought, they are shed and only the very succulent pseudo-bulbs remain exposed to the scorching heat of the sun.

This orchid, though suitable for home cultivation, is nevertheless rather large (pseudo-bulbs with leaves reach a height of approximately 70 cm [28 in]). If plenty of space is available in a sunny window and it is grown (without a compost) on cork oak bark, with water being withheld entirely during the winter, then it will reward the grower with lovely blooms.

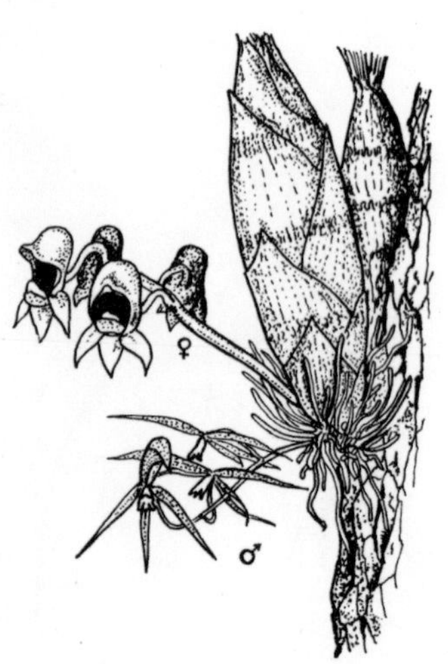


*Catasetum bicolor* from Central America has female flowers coloured green and male flowers mostly brown

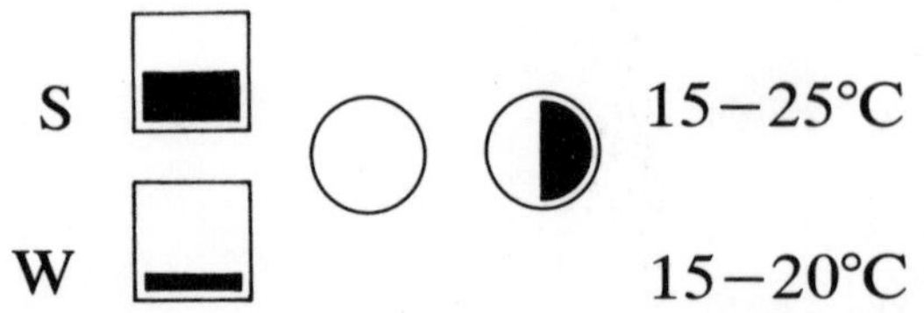

# Dendrobium nobile

*Dendrobium nobile,* like *Coelogyne cristata,* is an orchid for the beginner. It is very easy to grow and the flowers, besides being extremely attractive, are produced in profusion if the plant's basic needs are satisfied.

*D. nobile* is found over a large area from Nepal to south-east Asia, China and Formosa. It, too, is an epiphyte that grows in the mountains, mostly only up to elevations of about 1,600 m (5,220 ft). Nevertheless, it has a definite resting period of several months, during which time the temperature should be lowered and water practically withheld. When the flower buds appear the temperature should be raised and watering resumed.

It does relatively well indoors if provided with at least a slightly lower temperature during the dormant period. The rest period is not as pronounced in the case of hybrids raised in the past few decades in Japan. These plants far outshone the type species by the profusion, size and coloration of the blooms and became a great hit as soon as they were put on the market.

*Dendrobium nobile* has thick pseudo-bulbs about 30 cm (1 ft) high, which may be up to twice as large in older, robust plants. The leaves are leathery, lanceolate, and generally remain on the plant for two years – they fall during the rest period (leafless pseudo-bulbs are not a sign of ill-health; this is a common phenomenon in orchids). The flowers, usually three to a scape, are massed in the upper half to upper third of the pseudo-bulb. They measure about 9 cm ($3^1/_2$ in) in diameter and are very variable in coloration.

The illustrated species is generally grown as an epiphyte on a ball of light soil (the same mixture as for *Coelogyne cristata*). In the home it may be propagated by vegetative means – either by dividing large, older clumps or by detaching the young plants growing on the pseudo-bulbs after they have formed sufficiently large roots.

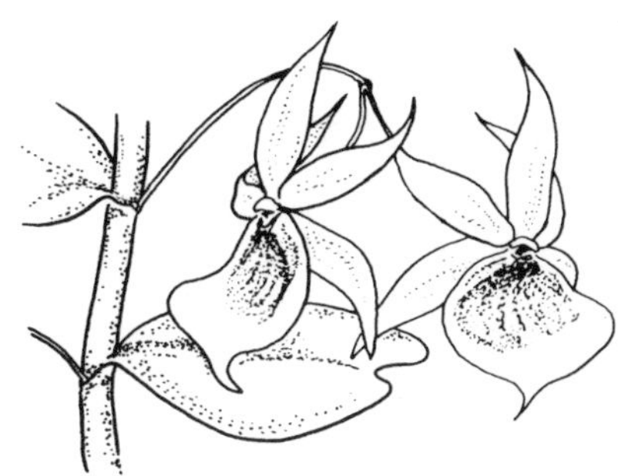

*Angraecum eichlerianum* from West Africa has yellow-green flowers

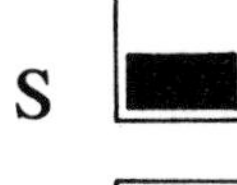

S 15–25°C

W 10–15°C

# *Dendrobium phalaenopsis*

Whereas the preceding dendrobium is a cool-loving species the one in this illustration is quite the opposite. The cut flowers are often seen at the florist's, though they may differ in colour from the illustration, for the type species is extremely variable, ranging from white to dark velvety violet-purple.

*Dendrobium phalaenopsis* is indigenous to New Guinea, Timor and Queensland, in other words to regions that are definitely tropical. Its principal requirements in cultivation are ample heat and moisture, particularly atmospheric moisture, and so it can be grown successfully in the home in a large aquarium or above a paludarium, where it is also exposed to sunlight. Syringing will also provide the atmospheric moisture. In winter it must have a brief period of rest when the temperature need not be lowered but watering should be greatly limited.

The pseudo-bulbs of *D. phalaenopsis* are erect, firm, and topped by several non-deciduous or only partly deciduous leaves. The first flower clusters (panicles) grow from the top of the pseudo-bulb, later flowering is one level lower, from the axils of the leaves. Flowers are produced even by old, leafless pseudo-bulbs that have flowered in preceding years. In the wild this species grows as an epiphyte or on the ground. The compost and method of propagation are more or less the same as for the previous species.

As one can see from these two examples, species of the same genus may have entirely different requirements as regards environment. This is not at all surprising, for the genus *Dendrobium* includes some 1,500 species and is one of the largest groups of orchids (two others are *Pleurothallis* and *Bulbophyllum*). That is why when growing these plants it is always important to refer to specialized literature which not only gives the basic requirements for the successful cultivation of individual species, but also various 'special hints'.

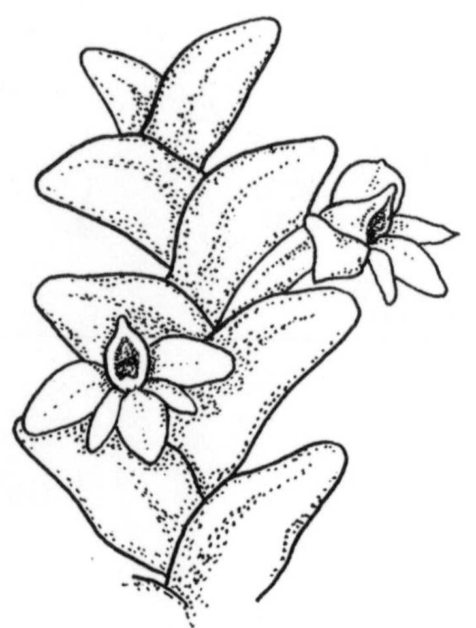

*Angraecum (Mystacidium) distichum* – a white-flowered species from West Africa

20–30°C

# Epidendrum falcatum

*Epidendrum,* which includes some 800 species distributed from Florida to southern South America, is another large genus of orchids very well suited to room decoration.

*Epidendrum falcatum* is one of the numerous species found in Central America from Mexico to Panama, where it grows either as an epiphyte or on the ground in mountains up to elevations of 2,000 m (6,600 ft). It has a pendulous habit, the leaves trailing freely downwards over the branches and trunks of trees. The pseudo-bulbs are greatly modified, only about 3 cm (1¼ in) long and single-leaved. The leaves are leathery, dark green, linear, and about 30 cm (1 ft) long. The flowers, 8 to 12 cm (3 to 4¾ in) across, are borne in summer on short scapes that are also pendent.

Since this species is a plant of higher elevations, it requires a moderate temperature rather than too much heat and in winter a more pronounced period of rest with a slightly lower temperature and greatly limited watering. There is no need to have any fears about growing it indoors – all it needs is to be put in the coolest room of the home for the winter. It can be relied on to produce good growth and flowers.

Cultivation is the same for other lovely epidendrums. Recommended for the beginner, for example, are *E. ciliare,* one of the most elegant members of the entire genus with a white-fringed lip; *E. nemorale* with pink, fragrant flowers up to 10 cm (4 in) in diameter, and *E. mariae* with 8-cm-(3-in-) long flowers coloured white and greenish yellow. Species that do well in homes which are always warm are *E. cochleatum,* with upward-facing flowers (turned through 180°); and *E. atropurpureum.* The beautiful and popular *E. vitellinum,* with orange-red flowers, requires permanently cool and moist conditions, for in its native habitat (southern Mexico and Guatemala) it grows high up in the mountains at elevations of 2,000 to 2,700 m (6,600 to 8,840 ft).

All epidendrums may be grown readily as epiphytes attached to a branch together with a handful of light compost. They are propagated either by detaching the young plants that many species produce at the base of the pseudo-bulb, or by dividing older clumps.

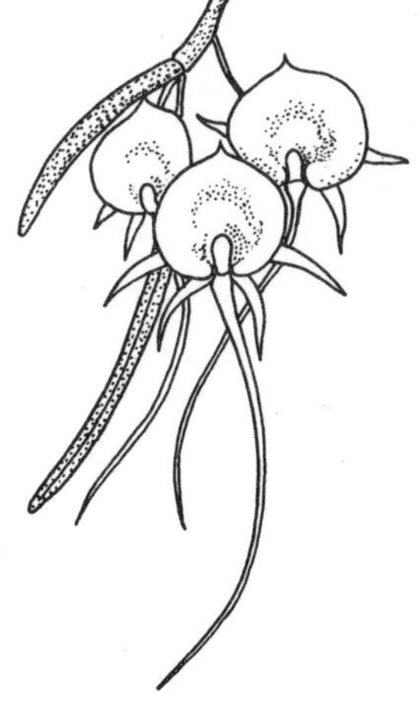

*Angraecum scottianum*

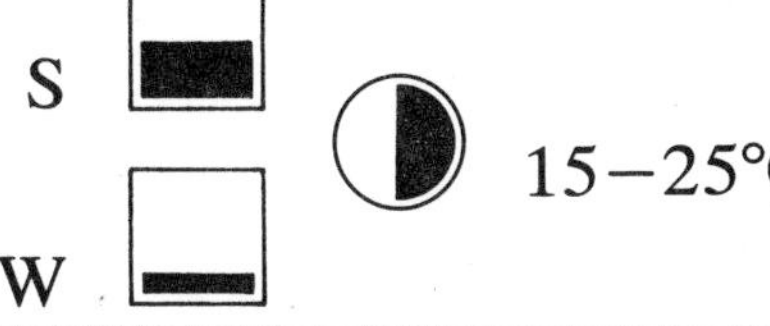

# *Gongora armeniaca*

'Like gems wrought from precious metal' is how one might describe the flowers of these magnificent plants. They are both elegant and absurd, mysterious and bizarre, as if they reflected the whole wealth of colour and shape of the world of orchids.

*Gongora* is a relatively small genus comprising only about 30 species, of which only two are generally found in cultivation, namely *Gongora galeata* (Punch and Judy orchid) and the illustrated species. *G. galeata* from Mexico has flowers up to 5 cm (2 in) across, coloured a mixture of purple, brown and yellow or yellow tinged with copper. It is extremely elegant and is often photographed as one of the most beautiful of orchids. The illustrated *G. armeniaca* is native to Nicaragua. The pseudo-bulbs are ovate, approximately 6 cm (2¼ in) high, with two leaves. The leaves are firm and dark green with pronounced longitudinal veins, narrowly elliptical, and a little over 20 cm (8 in) in length. The flowers, slightly more than 4 cm (1½ in) in diameter, are arranged in dense, pendulous trusses the same as in *G. galeata* and are generally produced in July or August. They are relatively long-lived, even though they seem very fragile, but they do not like to be sprayed with water; for this reason the plants should not be syringed while they are in flower, and water should be supplied only to the roots during this time.

Gongoras do not have a pronounced period of rest; only after flowering is finished should water be limited for about 6 to 8 weeks. Otherwise these plants should be grown the whole year long in a warm, moist spot (they tolerate the dry atmosphere of a room but in this case the leaves must be misted more frequently) in full sun or at least ample light. This is definitely the most suitable orchid for a warm home where it can be grown without much difficulty (the period of rest even coincides with the summer holiday period!). It should be grown as an epiphyte, tied to a branch together with a ball of sphagnum moss. It is readily propagated by detaching older pseudo-bulbs.

Feeding is simple, the same as for most epiphytic orchids – just add a small amount of fertilizer (a fraction of the concentration given in the manufacturer's instructions) to the water when spraying the leaves.

*Pleurothallis pectinata*

   15–30°C

# *Laelia pumila*

Who has not at one time or another longed to have a house plant with flowers as spectacular as the cattleya? *Laelia pumila* will serve the purpose well, for besides matching it in beauty it is also a miniature plant which can be added to one's collection without in any way limiting the space in one's home. It does very well in modern centrally-heated homes that have plenty of light without having to be put in a plant-case or window glasshouse.

From each of the fairly small, cylindrical pseudo-bulbs, which are about 5 to 10 cm (2 to 4 in) high, grows a single leaf, which is thick, leathery and about the same length as the bulbs. In September or October the plant bears flowers which are huge in relation to its size (they measure about 10 cm [4 in] across), very fragrant, and very long-lasting. There is usually only one flower to a pseudo-bulb, very occasionally there may be two. *L. pumila* is native to southern Brazil where it grows as an epiphyte or on the ground at elevations of 500 to 800 m (1,600 to 2,560 ft).

Also very beautiful, though not as small, are the other members of this genus, some 75 species altogether. Recommended for warm and sunny conditions are: *Laelia xanthina* from Brazil, a gorgeous golden yellow with narrow sepals; *L. anceps* from Mexico and Honduras, with scapes up to 50 cm (20 in) long, each bearing 5 flowers up to 12 cm across, similar in colour to the illustrated species; and the popular *L. gouldiana* (syn. *L. autumnalis gouldiana*) with large, deep violet flowers that have a lovely fragrance.

All laelias may be grown either as epiphytes, with a ball of light compost attached, or in the traditional manner as potted plants in a light compost (for example, sphagnum moss, peat, fern roots, bits of polystyrene and charcoal, crushed pine or oak bark, chopped beech leaves). In winter they require a brief period of rest with limited watering. The flowers are just as beautiful as those of cattleyas but are more suitable for cultivation in the home.

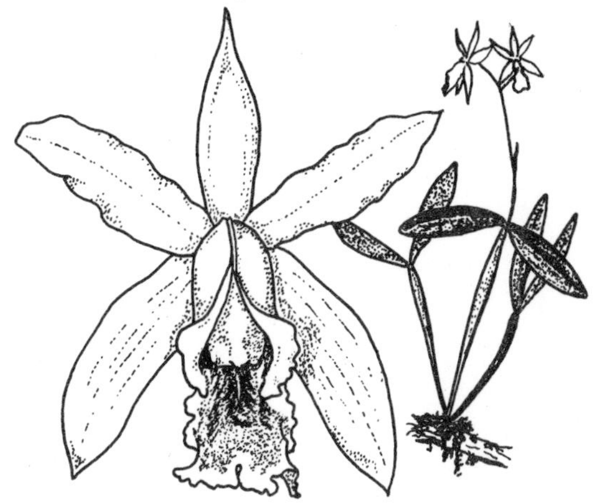

*Cattleya intermedia* is the parent of a vast number of popular hybrids

  15–30°C

# *Macodes petola*

## Gold-net Orchid

The word 'orchid' evokes the image of large, mostly brilliantly-coloured flowers resembling exotic butterflies. However, there are also several hundred species that rank among the loveliest of foliage plants, including some whose leaves rival the beauty of their relatives' blooms.

The foliage orchid that is most widely grown is *Haemaria discolor* with its several varieties and cultivars. The leaves are greenish red with delicate red veins. This is a very undemanding plant that does well in a light peaty compost and a lightly shaded spot in a warm home. It bears small, white, very fragrant flowers at Christmas-time, and can be easily managed even by the beginner.

The illustrated species, on the other hand, is one of the most difficult to grow and often even the very experienced have failed. Nevertheless, its beauty is so spectacular that it is worth trying to grow it over and over again.

*Macodes petola* is native to the mountain forests of Java and the Moluccas, where it grows on the ground in a thick layer of decaying humus formed by fallen leaves and on the fallen trunks of tree ferns. Typical characteristics of its habitat are diffused light, a permanently high temperature, and very high atmospheric moisture. From this it is evident that it will not survive as a free-standing specimen in a room. To be grown in the home it must be put in a glass plant-case provided with a constant high temperature and kept adequately moist by syringing. The compost should be a light one, composed of chopped sphagnum moss, fern roots, bits of charcoal, peat, chopped beech leaves and sand; the top should be covered with a thin layer of green sphagnum moss. If it is possible to provide the necessary conditions for these delicate plants they will grow rapidly and can be multiplied readily by division of the clumps.

*M. sanderiana,* which is perhaps even more beautiful, has the same requirements but needs more shade. The silver-veined *M. dendrophila* is epiphytic.

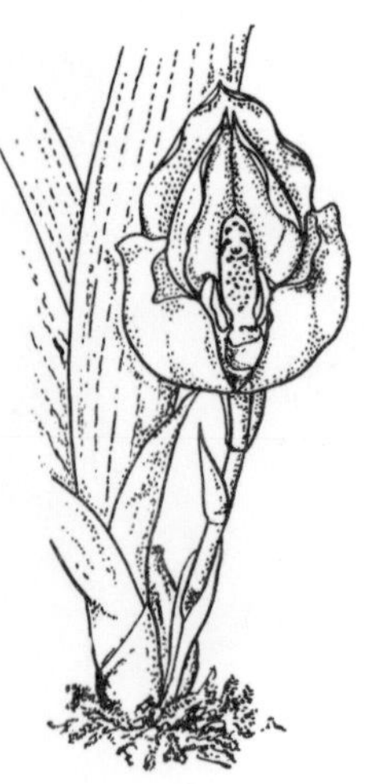

*Anguloa ruckeri* from Colombia has olive flowers spotted with black

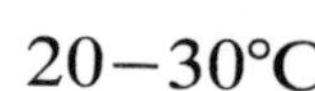

20–30°C

# *Odontoglossum grande*

## Tiger Orchid

The illustrated species is definitely one of the loveliest and showiest of orchids and one that is much in demand with beginners. It should be noted, however, that if it cannot be kept in a cold room, or one that is aired frequently the whole winter, then all efforts are doomed to disappointment, for it will grow but will not flower.

*Odontoglossum grande* is a plant of the mountains. It is native to Mexico and Guatemala, where it grows high up in the mountains at elevations of approximately 2,000 m (6,600 ft), and marked differences between daytime and night-time temperatures as well as the dry and cold conditions of winter are a prerequisite for flowering.

If you have a conservatory at home, however, there is no reason why you should not try growing it, either as an epiphyte with a ball of light compost or in a pot, the same as laelia. In summer it may be moved outdoors (like many other orchids), to the garden or a balcony where it should be hung in partial shade. During this period of growth it should be watered regularly and thoroughly. In the autumn or early winter, when it has been moved back inside or into a cool greenhouse, it will produce flowers about 15 cm (6 in) across. There are 4 to 8 of these on a 30-cm-(1-ft-) long scape and their colour is very variable, ranging from vivid red to chestnut brown.

The genus *Odontoglossum* is truly a large one, for it embraces some 300 species, among which are some that can be grown in modern, centrally-heated homes, even though these will always need lots of sun, air and conditions that are not too warm. Examples are: *Odontoglossum pendulum* (syn. *O. citrosmum*), which has showy, pendulous, white flowers with a rose-tinged lip and the scent of lemon; *O. krameri*, which has pale pink flowers with a yellow-brown base to the lip; and *O. reichenheimii* (often classed in the genus *Miltonia*), coloured mostly chestnut red.

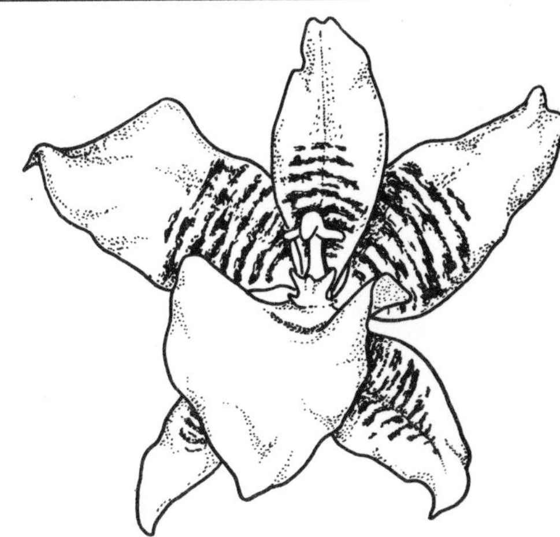

*Odontoglossum cervantesii* is a cold-loving species from the mountains of Mexico

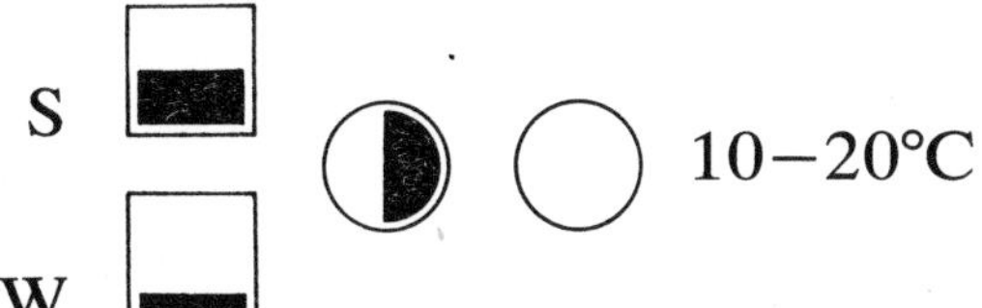

# *Oncidium papilio*

## Butterfly Orchid

In travel books and old orchid-hunters' diaries one often comes across various comparisons used to try and describe the unusual shapes of flowers. Orchids were compared to crouching tigers, helmets, skulls, and objects of wrought metal, but most of all to butterflies, and it is not surprising that Lindley, the discoverer of this species, was enchanted by its handsome flowers and gave it the name *papilio,* meaning swallow-tail.

*Oncidium papilio* is a native of South America where it is found over an area extending from Trinidad and Venezuela through Colombia to Peru. It is an epiphyte that usually grows on old trees in the forks of branches or in deep fissures in the bark. Only very occasionally does it grow on rocks in a shallow compost composed of selaginellas and small ferns.

The pseudo-bulbs are flat, oval, about 8 cm (3 in) high, and single-leaved. The leaves, which reach a length of about 20 cm (8 in), are stiff and leathery with reddish blotches, which makes these plants an attractive decoration even when not in flower. The scape is firm, wiry, and grows to a length of about 60 cm (2 ft). This must be taken into account and the plants given plenty of room when they are grown in a plant-case. The individual flowers, approximately 8 cm (3 in) in diameter, appear in succession, on the same scape often even after several years. For this reason they are not used for cutting, even though they are quite firm, for thereby we would deprive ourselves of the beauty of further blooms in the ensuing months.

*Oncidium papilio* does not have a pronounced period of rest and should therefore be kept in a warm (not hot) room and watered regularly throughout the year. Only when new growth starts should watering be somewhat more liberal. Ideal conditions for growing this orchid successfully are provided by the indoor plant-case where the plant should be attached to a branch or piece of bark, together with a small ball of light epiphyte compost. If it is grown in a container, only a very light mixture, composed mostly of fern roots, should be used.

The similar species *Oncidium krameranum,* with somewhat more brightly coloured and more wavy flowers, has more or less the same requirements in cultivation.

*Lycaste skinneri* from Central America is now generally known as *L. virginalis.* The flowers are various shades of pink

  15–25°C

# *Paphiopedilum callosum*

Some orchids may be bought as potted plants at practically every florist's and garden centre and we have come to regard them as quite common and not at all precious plants. Included among their number is one of the best-known and most popular of orchids – *Paphiopedilum callosum.*

Vietnam, Cambodia and Thailand are the home of this terrestrial species. There it grows on the damp mountain slopes in a thick layer of humus, in moss-covered valleys as well as in low grassy areas. The leaves, which are arranged in two rows in a low rosette, are pale green chequered dark green and measure about 20 to 25 cm (8 to 10 in) in length. This, in itself, indicates that the plant is a species that likes warmth and shade. Species that like full sun (for example *P. spicerianum*) have the leaves coloured a uniform green.

The flowers, about 10 cm (4 in) across, are produced on an upright scape, about 30 cm (1 ft) high, in winter or early spring. As a rule there is only one scape, but large, older plants may have as many as five flowers.

Young paphiopedilums should be grown in a mixture of chopped sphagnum moss with bits of polystyrene or charcoal added; older, established plants require a richer mixture with an addition of beech leaves and peat.

The main preconditions for success in growing these orchids is constant heat (usually the temperature of a modern home will suffice) and moisture, which may be ensured by using a humidifer and by covering the surface of the compost with green sphagnum moss. Like all orchids, paphiopedilum does not tolerate moisture that lingers permanently on the roots and therefore the plants should be watered in the morning so they can dry out a little overnight.

Naturally, the most suitable conditions for growing these, and other, orchids are provided by indoor plant-cases and glasshouses, the bottoms of which also generally meet the requirement of deeper shade. Several species are suitable for growing as house plants, for example *P. glaucophyllum* and most hybrids.

   18–25°C

*Paphiopedilum fairrieanum*

# *Phalaenopsis lueddemanniana*

Like the preceding genus of orchids, the members of *Phalaenopsis* do not form pseudo-bulbs. Many species grow as epiphytes in the permanently warm and damp tropical regions of south-east Asia, neighbouring islands and Australia. Those that grow on the ground are found on steep rock faces in thick layers of moss or on the base of ferns. A look at the roots of these plants reveals that they are relatively few in number, thick and covered with a whitish coating called velamen, which is a corky layer that absorbs water and the nutrients contained therein. The fleshy leaves have a thick epidermis that keeps evaporation to the minimum.

The illustrated species from the Philippines is extremely variable. The elliptical leaves are about 25 cm (10 in) long and 7 to 8 cm (2¾ to 3 in) wide. The scape is relatively short, barely equalling the length of the leaves; the flowers are only 4 to 5 cm (1 ½ to 2 in) wide and are coloured white with red horizontal stripes that are variable in form and intensity of colour. In cultivation they usually appear in early spring or in May.

As in many species of this genus, older plants often produce a stolon that gives rise to new, young plants which form roots (in this genus stolons are often also formed on the scapes after flowering has finished). Young, established plants that have not been severed from the parent plant produce flowers quite readily, more readily than adult specimens.

Of the approximately 70 species, the one chiefly used for hybridization was *P. amabilis,* found from Indonesia through New Guinea to Australia, which has large, white flowers (about 10 cm [4 in] across) with yellow-red markings on the lip. From the lovely *P. schilleriana,* hybrids have inherited pink flowers and often they also have attractive leaves marked crosswise with silvery bands. Hybrids have been obtained from crossings between many species of this genus as well as other related genera such as *Doritis*.

Phalaenopsis require constant heat and moisture without any definite period of rest. They should be grown in a light compost, the same as the orchids of the preceding genus, and the leaves should be misted frequently. Though they do best in a plant-case they will also do well in a room that is only occasionally aired. Ample shade is also a precondition of success.

*Phalaenopsis schilleriana* is one of the species used in breeding the modern pink-flowered hybrids

   20–30°C

# *Stanhopea tigrina*

## Horned Orchid

Comparison of the structure of the flower of the illustrated species with that of *Gongora armeniaca* will reveal marked similarities and the two orchids are duly assigned to the same subtribe – Gongorinae. The structure of the flower, particularly the lip, is very complex. The lip is fleshy and composed, as a rule, of a spindle or pouch-like hypochil, a mesochil with two horn-like outgrowths, and an epichil that is generally shortly-elliptical and often three-toothed at the tip.

The lip is also the principal identifying character of about fifty relatively quite similar species, even though of widely diverse and variable coloration. It is extremely difficult to tell them apart when they are not in flower. All species have ovate pseudo-bulbs from which grows a single leathery leaf with pronounced veins.

Stanhopeas are epiphytes with flowers that grow through the compost and hang down below the plant. For this reason they cannot be grown in pots but only in epiphytic arrangements or hanging baskets with a bottom of wide-spaced slats or large-mesh wire netting.

The illustrated species is the best-known in Europe and also the most widely cultivated, generally under the wrong name of *S. hernandezi.* Because it is a cold-loving plant it should be overwintered in a well-ventilated but rather cool room; in summer it does well in the garden, for example hung in the shade of a tree. It is definitely worth the trouble for the flowers – up to 18 cm (7 in) in diameter, are not only beautifully coloured but also extremely fragrant (a scent described as a mixture of melons and vanilla). This species is native to Mexico; the genus is distributed from Central America to Peru.

*Pterostylis curta* is a rare terrestrial orchid from New Zealand

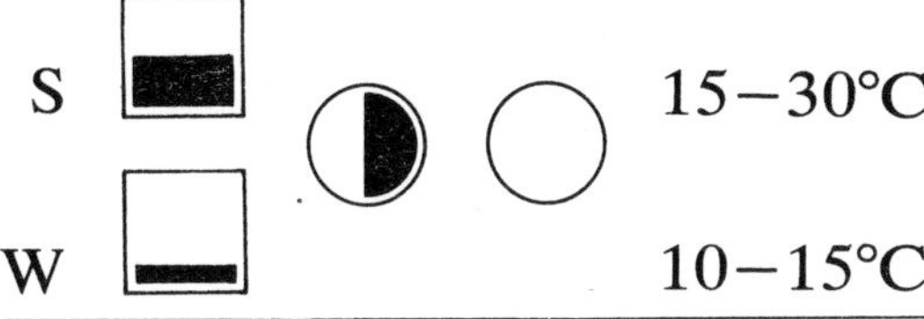

# *Vanda × Herziana* 'Blaue Donau'

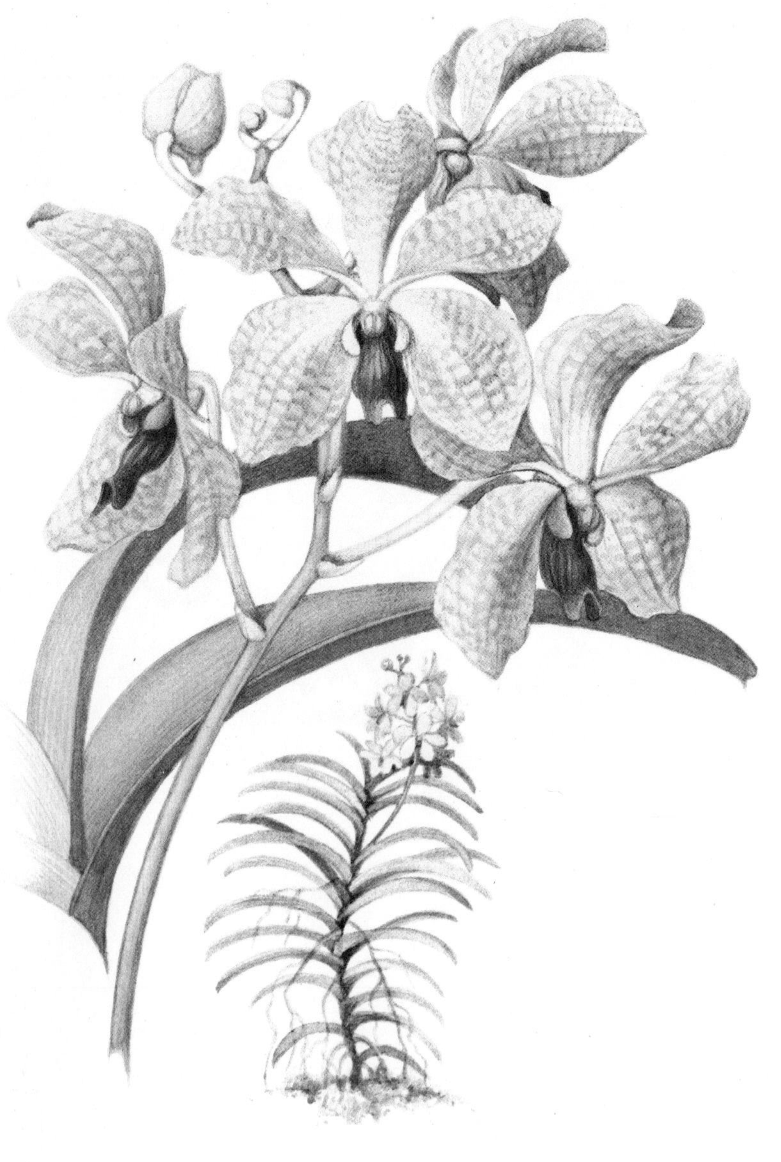

The illustrated hybrid is one of the older 'classics'. It was derived from two species that are probably the most widely grown members of the genus in Europe and ones found in every large collection and botanical garden.

The first is *Vanda coerulea,* a cold-loving species found in mountains at elevations of 700 to 1,700 m (2,350 to 5,650 ft), in the Himalayas, Burma and Thailand. This epiphytic orchid is a large plant up to 1.5 m (5 ft) high; its stem is covered with horizontal leaves about 25 cm (10 in) long and 2.5 cm (1 in) wide inbetween which grow numerous aerial roots. The flowers are blue – a very unusual and valuable colour amongst orchids – and measure up to 10 cm (4 in) across. The second parent is *Vanda tricolor* from Java and Bali. It is equally large, with longer leaves but shorter flowers which, however, are beautifully coloured – the lip is violet purple, the remaining segments mostly yellow with striking reddish-brown markings.

Vandas and their hybrids are nowadays cultivated chiefly in Hawaii, Thailand and the United States of America for the cut-flower trade. The famous hybrids were raised at the Mandai Gardens in Singapore, where other genera of the subtribe Sarcanthinae, such as *Rhynchostylis, Renanthera* and *Aerides,* were also used in subsequent crossings, yielding hybrids with magnificent flowers in the characteristic muted pastel shades. Though originally epiphytic species, they are often grown in pots and in the tropics even freely in the ground, where they do very well.

Vanda hybrids are not particularly difficult to grow, even in the home. They require ample light (only very light shading against direct sunlight) and find the temperature of most modern homes congenial. During the growth period they should be watered liberally and given ample doses of feed. During the winter rest period the soil should be kept only slightly moist so it does not dry out. They will be satisfied with a standard light compost for epiphytes (see the section on laelias).

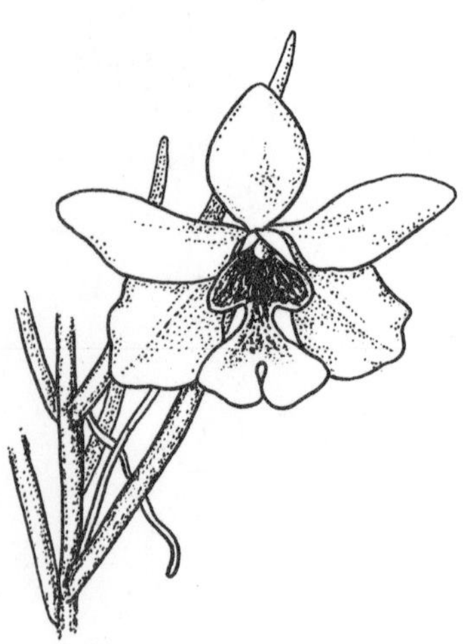

*Vanda teres* is indigenous to north-eastern India and Burma

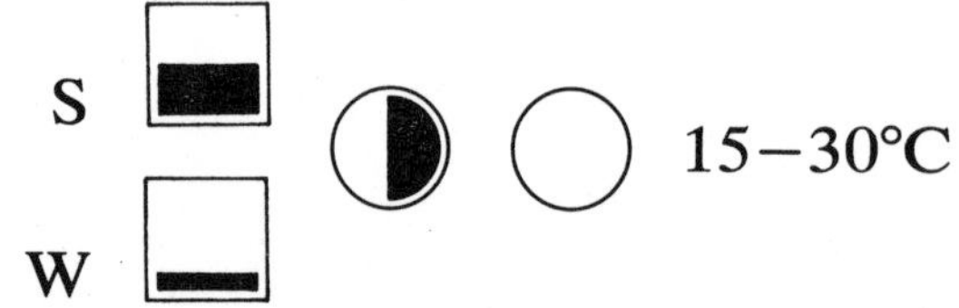

# BULBS AND TUBERS

# *Agapanthus × orientalis*

## African Lily

This section, entitled 'Bulbs and Tubers', begins with a genus that, though included in this group, is not really a bulbous plant, having instead a greatly shortened underground rhizome with fleshy roots. The genus embraces some 10 species native to South Africa, where they generally grow on bare mountain slopes or ones only sparsely covered with shrubs.

The leaves of the illustrated species are basal, strap-shaped, narrowing towards the end and terminating in a rounded tip. They are decorative in themselves for they are a vivid deep green. The flowers are borne on tall stems in umbels subtended by two bracts. They are large, bell-shaped, a lovely blue colour and very long-lived.

It is not easy to say exactly which species the cultivated plants, generally sold under the name *A. africanus,* belong to. At least three species are found in culture, namely the true *A. africanus* with leaves only about 15 cm (6 in) long and 1 cm (½ in) wide and dark blue-violet flowers; *A. orientalis* with large blue flowers and leaves up to 70 cm (28 in) long and 3.5 cm (1¼ in) wide (the leaves of both species are persistent, evergreen) and *A. campanulatus,* with leaves smaller than those of the preceding species, which dies down for the winter. Naturally all three species, which readily interbreed, have given rise to a large number of widely grown cultivars. Because the flowers of even the type species are very similar it is difficult to tell which parent figures in the ancestry of a given cultivar. Nevertheless, most plants grown in Europe answer more closely to the description of *A. orientalis.*

Hardy cultivars, introduced in the United States of America, which die back for the winter and readily survive even harsh conditions without protection, are probably descended from *A. campanulatus.*

Agapanthus should be grown in good compost, such as John Innes potting compost No. 2, in a sunny spot; it may be put outdoors in summer. During the winter rest period it should be kept at the lowest possible temperature and watering should be reduced to the minimum. Propagation is by division and readily also by seed.

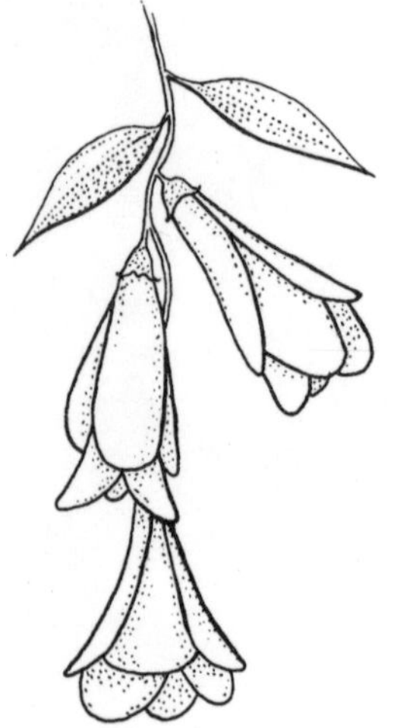

*Lapageria rosea*

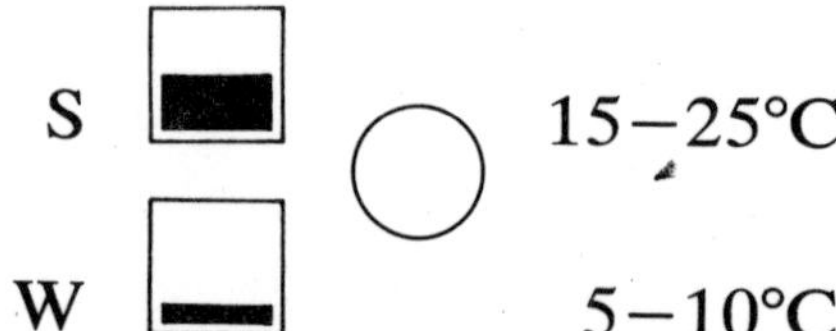

# *Alstroemeria* × *aurantiaca*

## Peruvian Lily

This lily has surely appeared as a table decoration in the home of many readers for its cut flowers can be bought at the florist's all the year round. *Alstroemeria* is a genus embracing some 60 species native mostly to the Andes. The persistent storage organs are the fleshy, tuberous, keel-shaped roots which are very fragile and prone to break readily when the lily is transplanted. The stems are covered with leaves that are turned a full 180°C so that the undersides face upward, a characteristic typical of this group which also includes the genera *Leontochir, Schickendantzia* and the beautiful *Bomarea*. The flowers, generally in loose umbels, are large, with petals arranged in two distinct rings; largest is the inner bottom petal, which, like all those in the inner ring, is spotted a different colour.

The illustrated hybrid differs only slightly from the type species *A. aurantiaca* from Chile, which grows to a height of 90 cm (3 ft) and has greyish-green leaves up to 10 cm (4 in) long. The umbels may contain as many as 30 flowers, but such a number is only to be found in older specimens that have not been moved for years.

Chile is also the home of the best known species *A. ligtu,* which in the wild grows to a height of about 60 cm (2 ft). The flowers are likewise arranged in an umbel, but the flower stalks branch so that the total number is about 20 to 25. They are mostly pale violet marked with pink and yellow. Selection and crossings gave rise to the so-called Ligtu-Hybrids, robust, profusely-flowering cultivars, particularly good for cutting.

Most species of the genus *Alstroemeria* are hardy or almost hardy and will survive the winter in sheltered areas without a protective cover. They are best grown in a cool greenhouse in good humusy compost, such as John Innes potting compost No. 2, and are readily propagated by division of the clumps. Plants attain their full beauty, however, only after being left undisturbed for several years. Propagation by seeds is also easy; these may be sown directly in the bed where they are to grow, or in pots.

*Bomarea edulis*

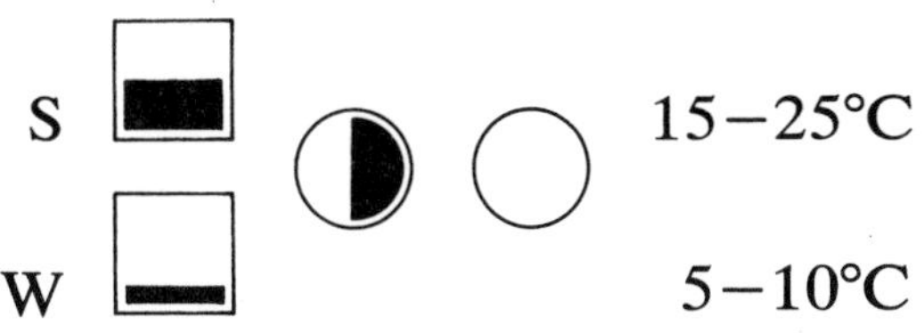

# *Amaryllis belladonna*

## Belladonna Lily

This genus, which gave its name to the whole family, is a very small one, consisting of only a single species that is relatively rare in home cultivation. Often mistaken for this plant is the widely-grown hippeastrum. It is not difficult, however, to distinguish between these two very similar plants. Amaryllis is native to South Africa, it flowers in the autumn, generally has more than 6 flowers to a stem, and round, green seeds. Hippeastrum, on the other hand, is native to South America, flowers in the late winter and early spring, has a maximum of 6 flowers to a stem, and its seeds are flattened and black.

The bulb of the belladonna lily is large and long-necked and covered with numerous dark skins. The leaves are strap-shaped, about 50 cm (20 in) long and about 2 cm (3/4 in) wide. They appear in late winter, usually turning yellow and drying up in autumn when the plant flowers. The growth period is thus in spring and summer. The flower stalk is about 60 to 70 cm (24 to 28 in) high and bears 6 to 12 large flowers, either facing outward or slightly drooping. They have a pleasant fragrance.

Cultivation is not difficult and the plants may be grown outdoors in the garden as well as indoors. They are generally put in pots, which should not be too large (only about 4 cm [1 1/2 in] more in diameter than the bulb), in nourishing but well-drained compost such as John Innes potting compost No. 2.

In spring, when the leaves appear, the plants should be watered liberally and placed in a sunny window. In summer they may be moved to a balcony or patio. As autumn approaches the leaves die back and the flowers appear; when these have finished water should be withheld. The bulb should be left in the pot for the winter (it does not like being moved too often) and kept almost dry (moisten the surface of the compost occasionally) in semi-warm conditions until spring. In exceptionally warm areas it may also be planted freely in the ground, but then the bulb must be covered with a thick layer of leaves and perhaps also a sheet of plastic as protection against winter cold and damp. Propagation is by offsets produced by older bulbs. The plants may also be multiplied from seed, but such plants take many years to flower.

*Pamianthe peruviana*

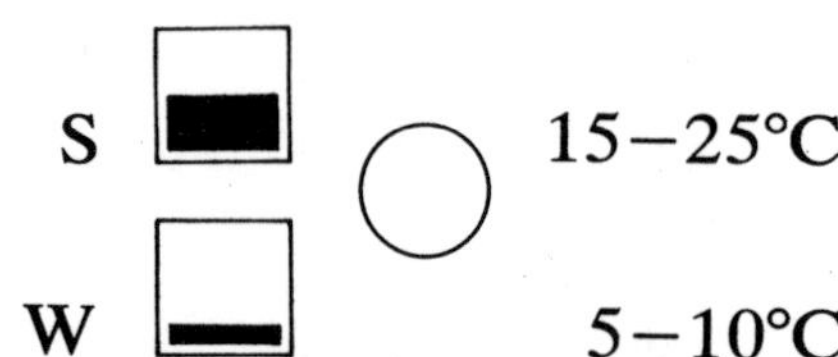

# *Amorphophallus rivieri*

This species has an interesting inflorescence as well as leaves and is suitable chiefly for those who like something unusual.

Only the illustrated species is found in general cultivation, and in botanical gardens and specialized collections only a few of the other approximately 80 species may be found. The genus is distributed chiefly in the tropical regions of the Old World, its range extending across the islands to Australia. It is a pity that it is not grown in wider assortment for it includes species that are quite small, barely 20 to 30 cm (8 to 12 in) high, as well as one that is a veritable giant (*A. titanum* from Sumatra grows to a height of 5 m [16 ft] and the inflorescence measures up to 1 m [3 ft] in diameter).

*A. rivieri* (syn. *Hydrosme rivieri*) is a native of Vietnam, where it grows in the mountains at elevations of approximately 1,000 m (3,300 ft) at the edge of dense misty forests. The tuber is located at a shallow depth, for example a specimen about 1.5 m (5 ft) high growing in the soft, thick layer of humus at the forest edge may have a tuber the size of a small child's head, located at a depth of only 10 to 15 cm (4 to 6 in).

In south-east Asia, however, some species are grown in fields. The tubers of *A. conjaku,* for example, are a popular food, chiefly in Japan. The tuber, which must be cooked thoroughly (otherwise it is poisonous), contains a gelatinous greyish-white substance that Europeans do not find particularly tasty.

After the winter rest period the tuber sends up a single leaf stalk up to 1.5 m (5 ft) high with white markings. The leaf blade, placed at right angles to the stalk, is trifoliate, and the separate sections are divided still further. Larger tubers produce 'flowers' in late winter, often before they are put in the ground. The spathe is about 30 cm (1 ft) long and coloured dark purple, the spadix is about the same length and coloured blackish violet. The inflorescence have a strong fetid odour, like that of tainted meat.

The tubers, which are lifted for the winter, should be kept dry and in a warm place during the dormant period. The compost should be a nourishing one; a mixture of peat, loam and sand is suitable, or John Innes potting compost. Sometimes cultivation outdoors in open ground is recommended, but this generally leads to weakening of the plant.

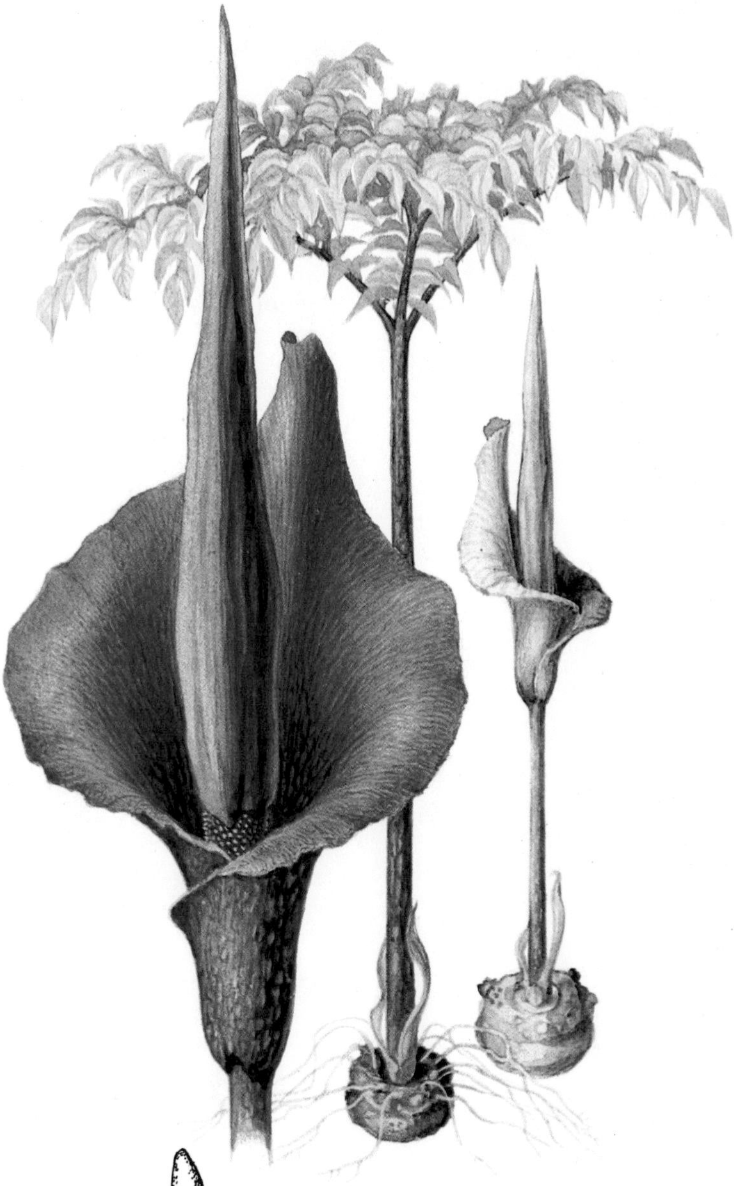

S   15–25°C

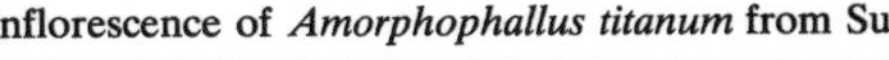

Inflorescence of *Amorphophallus titanum* from Sumatra

# *Crinum* × *powellii*

## Powell's Swamp Lily

The illustrated hybrid is becoming increasingly popular. Every year these magnificent bulbs are more and more common in parks, where they are planted in large masses that always attract attention in late summer when their lovely blooms appear.

*Crinum* x *powellii* is derived from *C. bulbispermum* and *C. moorei.* The first, a species native to South Africa, has a large, long-necked bulb from which rise strap-like leaves up to 90 cm (3 ft) long. The flowers are large, bell-like, about 15 cm (6 in) long, white tinted purple on the outside, and borne in clusters measuring about 40 cm (16 in) in length. In collections this plant is generally found under the name *C. longifolium;* it is also grown as a 'pure' species. It is almost fully hardy and can be readily grown outdoors under a thin layer of leaves or peat. The second parent – *C. moorei* – is native to Cape Province and Natal in South Africa. It is much larger than the preceding species; the bulb is about 20 cm (8 in) in diameter with a neck up to 50 cm (20 in) long. The leaves are approximately 90 cm (3 ft) long and almost 10 cm (4 in) wide. The flower clusters are about 60 cm (2 ft) long and composed of up to 10 flowers only slightly smaller than those of the other parent. They are coloured pink.

*Crinum* x *powellii* is about midway between the two parents in size. It is a plant for the cool conservatory, where it must be put in direct sun; it may also be grown outdoors in the garden. The bulbs should be planted with a small part of the long neck showing. The site should be one that is sheltered, warm and sunny, and the soil a rich, nourishing mixture. For better drainage sand should be added and the bulb placed on a thick layer of stones. During the summer the plants should be watered and fed liberally and in the autumn covered with a thick layer of leaves as protection against frost; this should not be removed until spring. Propagation is by offsets of the bulb which flower after about 3 years.

Recommended for warm, centrally-heated homes are some of the other 100 or so species, such as *C. erubescens* from South America, with large flowers coloured white inside and red outside. If you have a large paludarium you can also grow *C. purpurascens* from Africa (with narrow, red petals) in water or in a permanently wet substrate; and on 'dry land' the large *C. asiaticum* with white flowers.

*Crinum giganteum* is a robust plant, particularly suitable for the paludarium

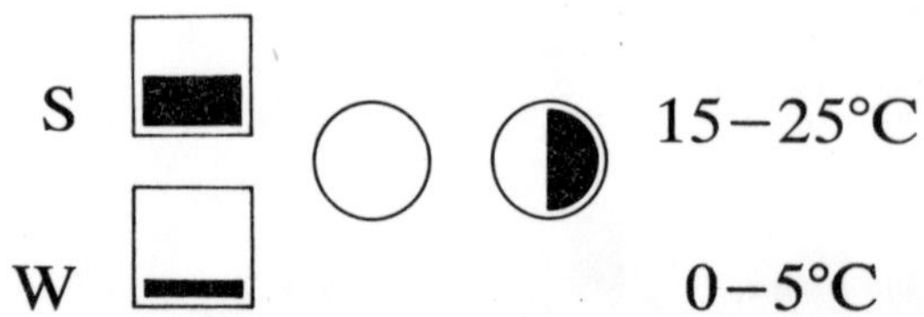

# *Eucharis grandiflora*

## Amazon Lily

The cut flowers of the illustrated species are often displayed in the florist's window. Unfortunately, few people know that this plant is very easy to grow in warm and semi-warm homes and that it produces its magnificent, snow-white, delicately scented blossoms sometimes even twice in one year.

It is often encountered in collections under the name *E. amazonica,* which is incorrect both botanically and geographically, for this species is native to the Colombian Andes, where it is said to grow at the edges of mountain peat moors. Recently this species has been assigned to the genus *Urceolina.*

Eucharis is lovely even when not in flower, for its large leaves are very decorative. The blades are deep green, broadly oval tapering to a point, and about 30 cm (1 ft) long, with a firm leaf stalk of the same length. The bulb is small, globular and covered with a brown skin.

The flowers, usually six to a stem, appear in succession at the top of the firm stem. They are slightly reminiscent of narcissus with their central cup surrounded by broad spreading lobes measuring up to 12 cm (4³/₄ in) in diameter. They remain on the plant for about a month and are very good for cutting.

Eucharis is definitely an undemanding plant. The ideal growing temperature is about 20°C (68°F), but it is very tolerant of temperature fluctuations and can be grown without difficulty in most homes. What is important is plenty of diffused light, and that is something that is generally readily available. The compost should be porous; best is a mixture of good loam, sand and peat, but eucharis will grow well in any potting compost, including pure peat. It generally flowers in spring and if provided with a rest period of about a month in summer (mainly by limiting the water supply) it may have a second flowering in the autumn.

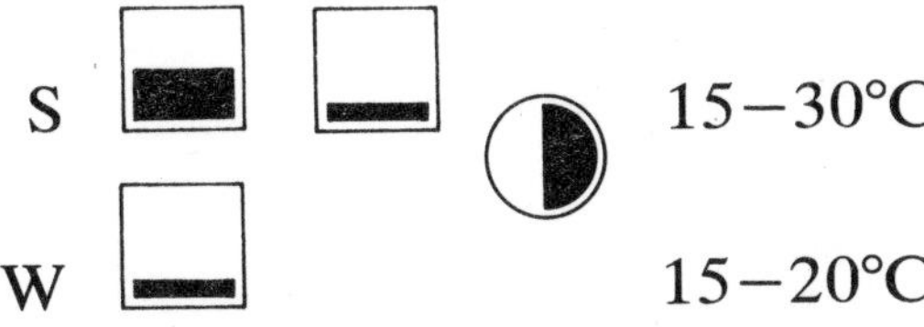


15–30°C

15–20°C

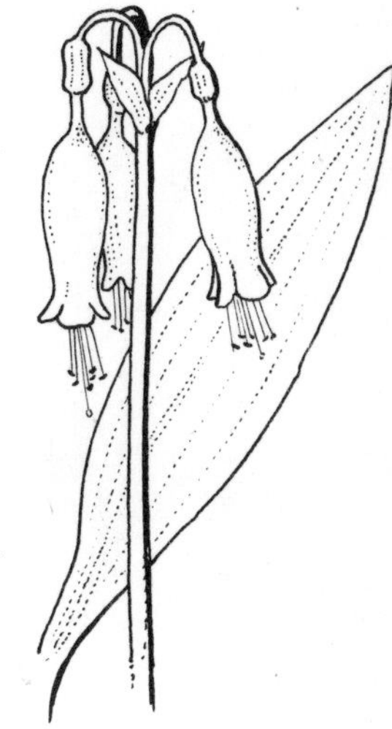

*Urceolina urceolata*

# Eucomis punctata

The illustrated plant is known chiefly to growers of South African succulents who often use it to add variety to their collections. The 10 or so species that make up the genus are found in Cape Province, Natal and partly also in the Orange Free State.

They are bulbs from which rise elongate basal leaves that are often spotted or wavy on the margin. The flowers are arranged in spikes on strong upright stems topped by a small tuft of leaves. The bulbs are usually globular.

Three species are generally found in cultivation. The first is the one shown in the illustration, which has leaves up to 60 cm (2 ft) long with a brown-spotted underside and flower stem about 30 cm (1 ft) tall. The second is *E. bicolor,* which has strap-shaped leaves about 50 cm (20 in) long and 10 cm (4 in) wide with beautiful wavy margins and greenish-yellow flowers edged violet or reddish violet with a small rosette of red-edged leaves topping the spike. The third is *E. undulata* with leaves also almost 50 cm (20 in) long, marked with brown dash-lines on the underside and wavy on the margin. The spikes are relatively insignificant, only about 15 cm (6 in) tall, composed of greenish flowers. The leaves forming the tuft at the top are also wavy.

These plants are not hard to grow but need a definite period of rest in winter. They may be grown either in open ground in the garden, where they should be provided with a thick layer of dry leaves for the winter, or in a warm home. In this case the bulbs should be lifted in the autumn and stored in a cool, dry spot. They may also be left in the pot and stored dry in a cellar or frost-proof shed.

Eucomis is readily propagated by offsets of the bulb and also by means of seeds, but the latter is a lengthier procedure. The compost should be humusy, with sand. One of the peat and sand soilless potting composts would be ideal.

*Eucomis undulata*

S  10–20°C

# *Haemanthus katharinae*

## Blood Lily

Bulbs include among their number some of the loveliest flowering plants for room decoration and they are practically no trouble to grow. Blood lily is one of the favouries, and rightly so.

Some 60 species of *Haemanthus* are found in tropical Africa, many of them is South Africa. Most are large bulbs which send up several thin leathery leaves. The flowers, though fairly small, are arranged in a head that is quite large (15 to 20 cm [6 to 8 in] in diameter).

The most widely cultivated species, *H. albiflos,* has less decorative flowers. The leaves, only 2 or 4, are fleshy, about 20 cm (8 in) long and evergreen. This is the commonest succulent grown in households; it tolerates practically any kind of treatment. The inflorescence is rather insignificant, the flowers white. Much prettier is the variety *pubescens* with leaves that are hairy on the upper surface and with pink flowers.

Most admired, however, are the species with vivid red flowers, such as the one shown in the illustration. *H. katharinae* is native to Natal. The bulb is about 7 cm (2¾ in) across and the stalked leaves up to 30 cm (1 ft) long. The flower stem is thickly spotted brown at the base and terminated by a cluster of flowers arranged in a seeming umbel nearly 25 cm (10 in) across. These are generally produced in full summer.

Crossing with *H. puniceus* in 1900 yielded the spectacular hybrid 'König Albert', which has slightly bigger and more vividly coloured flowers and is very large – it is usually sold in shops already in bloom.

Of the species with leathery leaves and red flowers the ones most often found in cultivation are *H. cinnabarinus, H. lindenii, H. magnificus, H. multiflorus, H. natalensis,* and the aforementioned *H. puniceus.* Very similar also is the related genus *Buphane* from the edge of the Kalahari desert plateau which provides the bushmen with the poison (obtained from the bulb) which they use to tip their arrows.

The illustrated species is never entirely leafless and that is why it should be wintered at only a slightly lower temperature and with limited watering. It should be placed in a well-lit window but not in full sun. It is rarely repotted, and if so then into a nourishing compost such as John Innes potting compost No. 1. It is readily propagated by seed as well as by offsets of the bulb.

*Haemanthus albiflos* is the best known member of the genus; it is a practically indestructible plant

  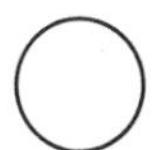 15–25°C

# *Hippeastrum* × *hortorum*

The genus *Hippeastrum* is found only in tropical America where it grows in mountains, savannas and periodically dry forests. According to various authorities the number of species ranges from 40 to 70. The total number must be far greater, however, for the genus is widely distributed in the Andes where many localities are inaccessible. Professor Vargas of Cuzco, Peru, has a specialized herbarium of this genus which includes species only recently discovered. For example, the species described as *H. machupicchense* with huge, white, bell-like flowers marked with deep pink stripes on each petal was discovered unexpectedly in the seventies, even though it is indigenous to Machu Picchu, a locality visited by tens of thousands of tourists. It was found growing beside the railway track. What discoveries await us in the future cannot even be guessed at.

The only type species found commonly in cultivation is *H. reticulatum striatifolium* from southern Brazil. The leaves are up to 50 cm (20 in) long, with a longitudinal white stripe along the midrib. The flowers, which appear in late summer, are large, pink and very fragrant.

Modern hybrids, which often have very large, conspicuous flowers up to 30 cm (1 ft) across, are derived chiefly from crossings between *H. leopoldii* and *H. vittatum,* though other species doubtless also figured in the hybridization.

Two important factors in the cultivation of these plants are good, generous feeding during the growing season, and a period of complete rest in late summer and early autumn. In general, they need cool conditions, particularly during the flowering period, for otherwise the flowers fade quickly. In summer the plants should be put in a sunny window, in small pots of rich compost such as John Innes potting compost No. 2, watered adequately and supplied with liquid feed once a week. In late summer water should be withheld and the bulbs allowed to 'bake' in the autumn sun. In winter they should be put, together with the pot, in a cool place; they may also be left in darkness.

*Hippeastrum reticulatum* ''Striatifolium''

S   15–25°C

# *Hymenocallis calathina*

## Basket Flower, Lily Basket, Spider Lily

The southern states of America, Antilles and Central and South America are the home of a genus of plants that only few others can rival in elegance of flower. In the wild they are found growing in the sand of the seashore like the European genus *Pancratium,* which they greatly resemble.

The fantastic shape of the flowers has given them the name of spider lily – the outer segments are narrow or ribbon-like, the inner ones form a low, funnel-shaped cup.

Some 40 species have been described to date, practically all of them white-flowered (a few have yellow flowers). The yellow *H. amancaes* is from Peru and the flowers measure about 15 cm (6 in) across. It is very beautiful but not common in cultivation. More widely grown is the illustrated *H. calathina* (syn. *Ismene calathina*) from Peru and Bolivia with a bulb about 8 cm (3 in) across and strap-shaped leaves up to 50 cm (20 in) long. The flowers, more than 20 cm (8 in) across, are borne in an umbel of six flowers on an approximately 60-cm- (2-ft-) high stem in June and July. Because this species was often crossed with the other similar species one sometimes comes across practically identical plants listed in catalogues as *H.* x *hybrida,* or *H.* x *stofforthiae.* Similar are *H. caribaea* from the Antilles; *H. littoralis* from all of tropical America; *H. speciosa* from the West Indies; and the lovely *H. undulata* from Venezuela.

Requirements in cultivation are not excessively demanding, only *H. caribaea, H. macrostephana* and *H. undulata* do better in very warm rooms. The other species, including the one shown in the illustration, have more or less the same requirements as eucharis. In winter they should be left in the pot in a warm place, but water should be withheld. The plants are readily propagated by offsets of the bulb as well as by seeds, which, however, only develop into flower-bearing specimens after about four years.

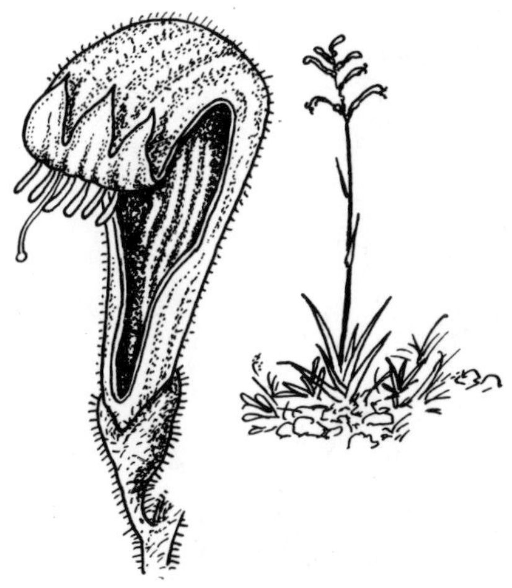

*Anigozanthos manglesii,* kangaroo paw, with red stem and emerald green blossoms is the state flower of Western Australia

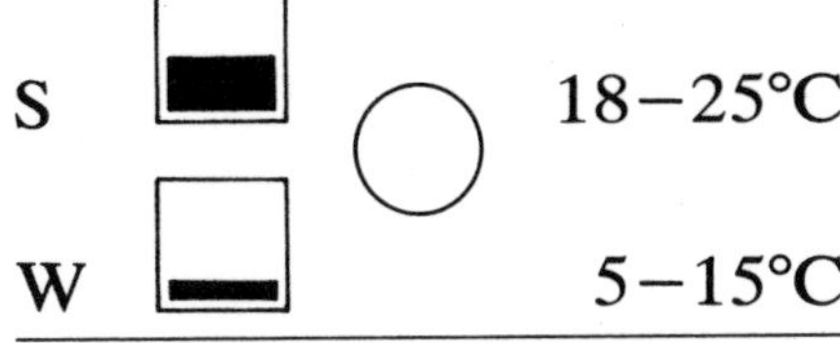


18–25°C

5–15°C

# *Lachenalia* (Aloides-Hybrids) 'Nelsonii'

## Cape Cowslip

The drawback of some bulbous plants is their size, which is often too large for the modern home. Even though we can frequently provide them with the cool overwintering they require, lack of space makes their cultivation unfeasible. This is where the small genera come into their own.

*Lachenalia,* comprising mostly smaller forms, is one such genus. It embraces about 50 species native to Cape Province. Some flower in late summer and autumn (for example *Lachenalia rubida* and *L. unicolor*), most, however, are spring-flowering. The majority have only two or less leaves, about 15 to 20 cm (6 to 8 in) long, sometimes spotted brown or reddish brown. The flowers are tubular and borne in spike- or raceme-like clusters on upright stems. The segments are often arranged in two layers, the ones on the inside often longer and extending beyond the outer segments.

Most widely cultivated is the group of hybrids derived from *L. aloides* (syn. *L. tricolor*), which are classified under the name *L.* (Aloides-Hybrids). The illustrated 'Nelsonii' is one of the loveliest and most popular. Very similar, with slightly paler flowers, is 'Luteola'. 'Quadricolor' is magnificent, with flowers which are red at the base, yellow green in the middle and purplish green at the tip of the petals. Also not to be bypassed, particularly by those who collect botanical species, is *L. glaucina,* with simple green leaves and loose racemes of pale blue, pendant flowers that are very fragrant.

Spring-flowering species should be allowed to die down after flowering and the bulbs left to ripen in the sun. In autumn they should be repotted in a fresh mixture of pine leaf mould, peat and sand and watering should be resumed. If these ingredients cannot be obtained, use John Innes potting compost No. 1. In winter they should be kept in a cool, well-lit spot and watered regularly but not much. Propagation is by the offsets of the bulb which are very plentiful.

Autumn-flowering species have a dormant period in winter.

*Lachenalia pendula*

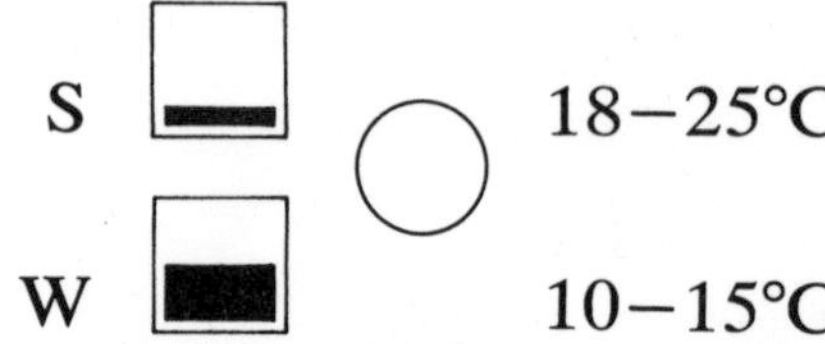

# *Neomarica gracilis*

## Apostle Plant

Amongst plant-lovers one will find quite a number who are willing to grow a specimen even if its blooms last for only one day, for example the garden tigridia or genera such as *Cypella* or *Herbertia.*

Neomarica also has flowers that last for only a single day, but these are produced in such profusion that the flowering period is lengthier. And they are so exquisite, that it is definitely worthwhile growing this plant.

The narrow leaves of *Neomarica gracilis* (syn. *Marica gracilis*), indigenous to the area extending from Mexico to Brazil, form a fan about 30 to 40 cm (12 to 16 in) high. The plants have a slender, creeping underground rhizome by means of which they spread very rapidly. This should be kept in mind when putting neomarica in, say, a dish arrangement together with other plants.

The inflorescence is generally no higher than the leaves. The flowers, approximately 5 cm (2 in) accross, open in succession, always only about 2 or 3 every day. Usually they are self-pollinated and are followed by tricapsular capsules containing a great number of seeds.

Neomaricas may be divided when they are repotted, but they may also be multiplied by seeds, sown on a mixture of peat and sand and covered with a layer of sand about 0.5 cm (1/4 in) thick. These germinate and grow rapidly into plants that bear flowers the following year. They should be potted in John Innes potting compost No 1. Sometimes young plantlets are formed also at the tips of the flower stems; these may be detached and grown in the usual way.

Neomaricas do very well in modern homes, even in windows exposed to full sun; however, a lightly shaded spot is better.

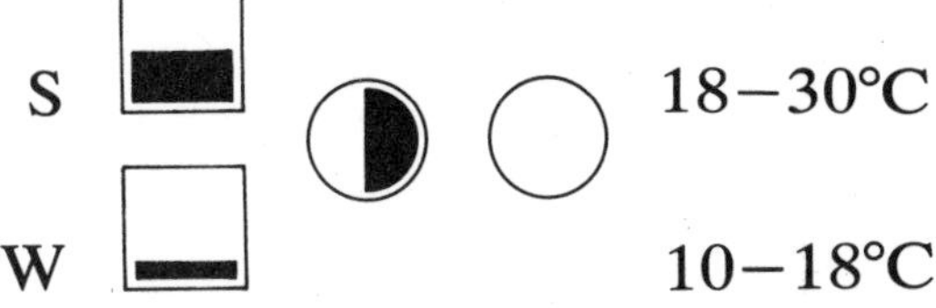


18–30°C

10–18°C

*Moraea pavonia villosa* is an easily-grown plant from South Africa

# *Nerine bowdenii*

Only a few plants can be recommended as heartily as nerines for not only are they beautiful flowers but also very easily grown. A suitable spot can surely be found in most homes for providing the cooler conditions and light they need in winter, otherwise there are no special requirements.

The genus embraces some 15 species distributed in South Africa. All are more or less alike. The leaves are generally narrowly strap-shaped to linear, about 30 cm (1 ft) long, smooth and glossy. The stems are about 30 cm (1 ft) high and carry clusters of large, pink or scarlet flowers with recurved segments and long stamens terminated by coloured anthers. The style is likewise very long and ends in a small trifid stigma.

Naturally this description does not fit all the species. *N. flexuosa,* for example, has a greatly twisted flower stem up to 80 cm (32 in) high; *N. filifolia* is a very small species with linear leaves less than 20 cm (8 in) long and small dainty flowers. Type species, however, are becoming ever fewer in cultivation, the only ones commonly encountered being the illustrated species and *N. sarniensis* – the Guernsey lily (it grows wild on the island of Guernsey where it apparently became established after a ship carrying the bulbs was wrecked on its shores; otherwise it is a native of Cape Province).

Nowadays the genus *Nerine* is the subject of intensive breeding in Europe, the United States of America, and above all Japan, where a great many attractive hybrids have been raised. This plant is very valuable not only for flower-lovers but also for the cut-flower trade, for the blooms retain their beauty for as long as 14 days in a vase.

Cultivation is not at all difficult. The bulbs should be planted in John Innes potting compost No. 1, best of all in small troughs. In winter they should be kept in a cool but well-lit spot and watered to promote the growth of leaves, for otherwise the plants will not flower. In spring, when the leaves die down, water should be withheld and the bulbs left to dry out and be baked thoroughly in the sun during the summer. Growth is resumed in autumn, which is when the plants also bear flowers, and so watering should be resumed. The plants are readily propagated by offsets of the bulb.

*Lycoris radiata*

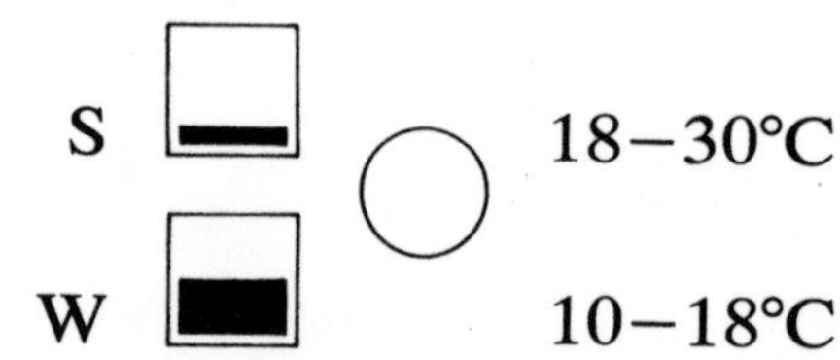

# Scilla violacea

## Silver Squill

If sansevieria was described as an 'indestructible' plant, then the same can be said of the illustrated species, for it is just as hardy, to say the least. It can be grown in well-drained potting compost, in a nutrient solution (hydroponics), as well as in pure peat; it does not matter if it is watered too much or too little; it may be overwintered at a temperature just below 10°C (50°F) as well as at a temperature of at least 20°C (68°F); it may be put beside a north-western window and even on a south-eastern window without any fear of it being harmed – in short, it will generally do quite well in any conditions. Loveliest, however, are specimens grown in rich, well-drained compost such as John Innes potting compost No. 2 in full sun, with fairly liberal watering in summer and overwintering in a cool, well-ventilated spot, though this is not a must. It even does very well if put in a window-box for the summer, in addition to which it looks very attractive there. In short, it is a plant suitable for any and every home.

*Scilla violacea,* native to South Africa, is one of the few species of the genus that is not fully hardy. Its bulbs, covered with brownish-purple scales that turn dry, grow above the ground. The underside of the leaves is also purple, but the upper surface is silvery grey with dark muted green horizontal streaks. The entire plant is 20 cm (8 in) high at the most. In spring it produces umbels of about 20 tiny flowers with reddish-violet filaments, which serve to distinguish it from the similar *S. pauciflora*. The latter has leaves that are almost sessile, green with grey spots above and not as brightly coloured on the underside. Propagation is easy, by means of offsets of the bulb.

  10–30°C

*Smilax ornata*

# *Sprekelia formosissima*

## Jacobean Lily

In 1593 the Spanish conquistadors brought to Europe a magnificent bulbous plant from the semi-deserts of Mexico and Guatemala. However, it was not described till 1764, when J. H. Sprekelsen, Hamburg's town councillor, sent the bulb to Carl Linné, well-known Swedish botanist, who was the first to do so, though he assigned it wrongly to the genus *Amaryllis.*

This plant grows wild in semi-deserts, often on a gypsum substrate. In winter, which is relatively warm, there is practically no rain for several months and the bulbs dry up entirely. The plants flower with the arrival of the first rains in spring and during the period of relative dampness they also keep their leaves (usually four), which are linear and up to 40 cm (16 in) long. In the wild the bulbs are to be found in soil that compacts, becomes baked, and is seemingly without nutrients. This is the only thing that must not be copied in cultivation, otherwise its requirements are the same as in its native land.

In spring, in March or early April, the dry bulbs begin growth, even if they were stored in the dark. At this time they should be put in rich, well-drained loamy compost such as John Innes potting compost No 2. The bulb should be given extra drainage by adding stone rubble to the compost or by making a deep bed of stone or sand under the bulb and then topping it with compost.

Apart from growing sprekelias in pots indoors, they may also be put in flowerbeds in the garden. From the beginning of flowering until the end of August the plants should be watered adequately and also given frequent applications of feed. In autumn the bulbs should be lifted, cleaned, and stored in a warm spot until growth starts again in spring.

Propagation is by means of offsets of the bulb, though the plants may also be multiplied from seeds. These, however, rapidly lose their power of germination. It takes four years for the seedlings to grow into flower-bearing plants.

*Ipheion uniflorum*

S   15–25°C

# *Zantedeschia elliottiana*

## Calla Lily

The calla lily was a traditional part of bridal bouquets in our grandmother's day and at one time it was also a very popular house plant. Times change, however, and with the increasing number of centrally-heated homes the originally cultivated species *Zantedeschia aethiopica* has been relegated to the sidelines. Offered in its stead are other, far lovelier thermophilous species with a spathe that is not white but brigthly coloured. It is almost impossible to understand why they are so slow to be adopted in cultivation when they are such extraordinarily attractive plants. As a rule they are not even to be found in large botanical gardens and are apparently waiting to be brought by interested persons from their native habitats in tropical and South Africa.

A common species, encountered in collections belonging to experienced amateurs and grown for the cut flower trade, is the illustrated *Zantedeschia elliottiana* (syn. *Calla elliottiana*) from the highlands of south-east Africa. It grows from a large tuber, or rather a shortened tuberous rhizome. The leaves are long-stalked, shortly oval, heart-shaped, with numerous white, transparent 'windows'. The spathe is about 15 cm (6 in) long and coloured deep yellow; it is not brown at the base.

Several beautiful cultivars have been raised in the United States of America, derived chiefly from this species with large brightly-coloured flowers. Also found in culture are bright pink cultivars, derived apparently from *T. rehmannii,* which has a violet-purple spathe.

Unlike the traditionally grown cool-loving species, *Z. elliottiana* as well as other variously-coloured cultivars and thermophilous species are suitable for modern centrally-heated homes. Their tubers require absolutely dry conditions in winter and temperatures of up to 30°C (86°F); the pots may be put on top of a radiator. This, seemingly drastic, procedure is necessary if the plants are to flower. In spring the tubers should be transferred to a fresh potting mixture composed of peat, sand and loam, and watering should be resumed; water as well as feed should be applied liberally throughout the growing season. The greatest enemies are mites and white flies, which are readily 'attracted' to the plants, and so it is necessary to spray them with an insecticide now and then.

   25–30°C

*Zantedeschia* x *rehmannii*

# *Zephyranthes grandiflora*

## Zephyr Lily

If it is truly a pity that some species of plants are not more widely cultivated, then this applies first and foremost to the members of this genus. They are interesting, undemanding, nicely flowering, small plants that find the conditions of modern homes ideal for their growth.

The illustrated *Zephyranthes grandiflora* (syn. *Z. carinata*) is from Mexico and Jamaica. The flowers, which appear in spring, are about 6 cm (2¼ in) across and a lovely glowing colour that makes them the focal point of any room. In collections the plant is often found under the synonym *Z. carinata* as well as under the wrong name *Z. rosea.* The latter, however, is a smaller species from Cuba, which flowers in autumn. Most rewarding as a house plant is *Z. atamasco* from the southern states of America which produces white flowers from early spring until mid-summer given the right conditions (liberal watering and additional feed). Similar are *Z. candida* from La Plata and *Z. tubispatha* from the Antilles, Venezuela and Colombia, which, however, are very rarely found in cultivation. A beautiful species, namely the yellow *Z. aurea,* grows in fallow land in Peru, on the very outskirts of the capital Lima; it is used by the local Indians to decorate graves and chapels. It flowers in autumn, the same as *Z. rosea,* and both can be used in mixed plantings outdoors in the open. Other spring-flowering species are *Z. andersonii* from Argentina (yellow and red); *Z. verecunda* from Mexico (green, white and red); and *Z. versicolor* from Brazil (red and white).

Cultivation is the same for all zephyranthes. The bulbs should be planted at a shallow depth, those that have a neck should be planted with part of the neck above the surface of the compost. The growing medium should be a rich mixture such as John Innes potting compost No. 2. An important requirement is plenty of light (there can never be too much). Most species (spring-flowerers) have a dormant period in summer at which time watering, which is otherwise liberal, should be reduced to the minimum. Propagation is very easy, for older bulbs produce large numbers of offsets which will generally bear flowers within a year.

*Habranthus robustus*

S   15–30°C

# CLIMBERS

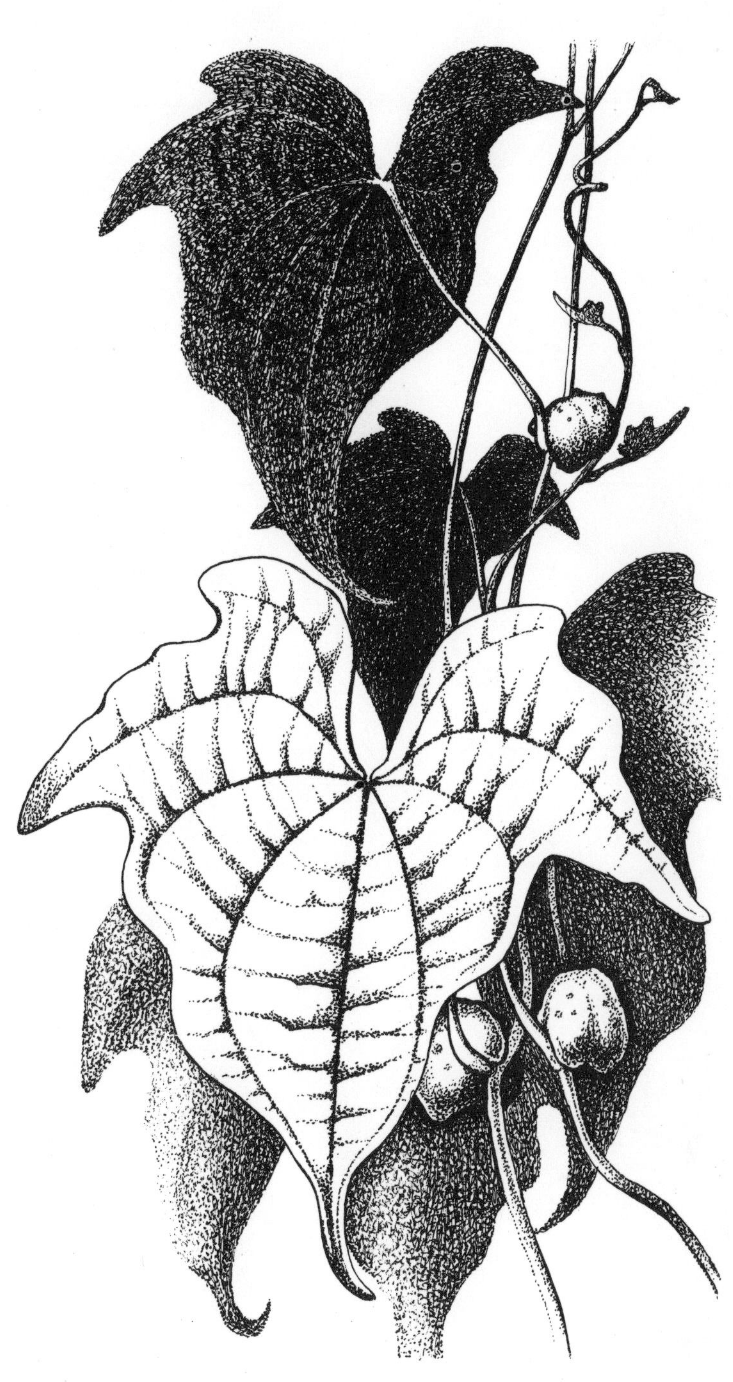

# *Allamanda cathartica*

## Golden Trumpet

It is only recently that this lovely plant began to be sold at the florist's and at garden centres. The reason for its inclusion in the assortment offered by many nurseries is the growing number of centrally-heated homes as well as the changed emphasis on interior decoration and the demand for unusual flower arrangements.

The illustrated allamanda is a woody climber from Brazil, the home of 11 further species of the same genus, just one having 'strayed' to Central America. They are very good for covering a lattice-work room divider, for framing a window with greenery, as well as for large window glasshouses and indoor glass plant-cases. Whereas in the wild they grow to a height of about 6 m (20 ft) in cultivation they rarely reach a height of more than 2 m (6 ft). The leaves, which are firm and leathery, are arranged in whorls of 3 or 4. The flowers are broadly funnel-shaped, the individual petals opening wide at the mouth. Those of the illustrated species, which is the most widely grown, measure up to 12 cm (4¾ in) in diameter.

In cultivation, *A. cathartica* flowers from mid-summer until autumn; in the tropics year-round flowering is not uncommon – this may also be achieved by growing the plants in a glass case. They benefit, however, by a brief rest period in winter – about 2 or 3 months at a lower temperature and with limited watering.

The most important requirement in cultivation is plenty of direct sun or at least a position that is very little shaded. Airing is also beneficial, but must be restricted to the warm summer months; a sudden change in temperature may cause the plant to drop some of its leaves.

The growing medium should be a mixture of leaf mould, rotted turves, peat and sand, with leaf mould predominating. Alternatively, use John Innes potting compost No. 2. The plants should be watered liberally, except during the resting period, and given an application of feed every two weeks.

Other species are also lovely, but they are not commonly found in cultivation. Only in specialized collections may one come across *A. neriifolia,* yellow striped with brown inside, or the less robust *A. violacea* with purplish-violet flowers.

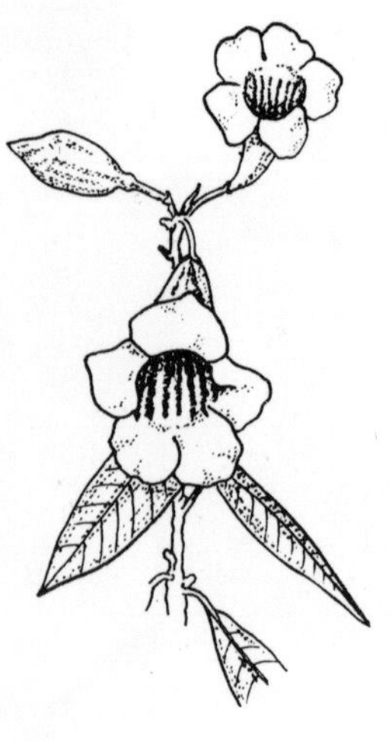

*Allamanda neriifolia*

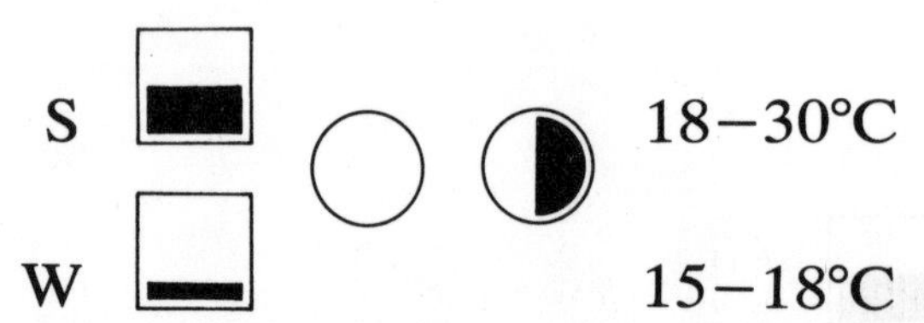

# *Aristolochia elegans*

## Calico Plant

Climbers include many plants with attractive flowers, but few with such striking ones as those of the calico plant. These are curious to say the least, with their bent tubes expanding to a cup shape, often fringed on the margin. In many species, the flowers are borne on drooping branches. They are pollinated by insects, which are often captured in the bent corolla tube and 'released' only after pollination.

The genus is so large that it offers a truly wide selection. According to some authorities it embraces 300 species, according to others 500, mostly native to the tropics. *Aristolochia clematitis* and *A. durior,* with huge leaves, often used to cover fences and arbours in the garden, are two well-known examples showing the many uses to which these plants can be put.

Those who have a warm and sunny flat, however, will probably choose one of the tropical species. The illustrated *A. elegans* from Brazil is the most suitable. It has dense foliage and flowers reliably even as a young specimen, be it raised from cuttings or from seed. The flowers are up to 12 cm (4¾ in ) long and 10 cm (4 in) across. It stands up very well to spring pruning so that it can easily be kept within reasonable bounds. Those who have plenty of space can also grow other species, for example *A. grandiflora* from the Antilles and Guatemala with flowers 30 × 35 cm (12 × 14 in) and a thread-like appendage up to 60 cm (2 ft) long. The flowers are coloured lilac with brownish-red markings. This plant, however, is much too large for the ordinary home, even though it does quite well. More suitable as a house plant is the small *A. odoratissima* from Mexico with flowers only about 7 cm (2¾ in) long and coloured mostly yellow, with a reddish brown cup.

The last-mentioned species as well as the one in the illustration should be grown in full sun, those with huge flowers in a lightly shaded position. The growing medium should be a peat and sand mixture plus loam. John Innes potting compost No. 2 is ideal. Water liberally and feed the plants often, for they need a rich diet. They are readily propagated by means of cuttings or seeds in a warm propagator.

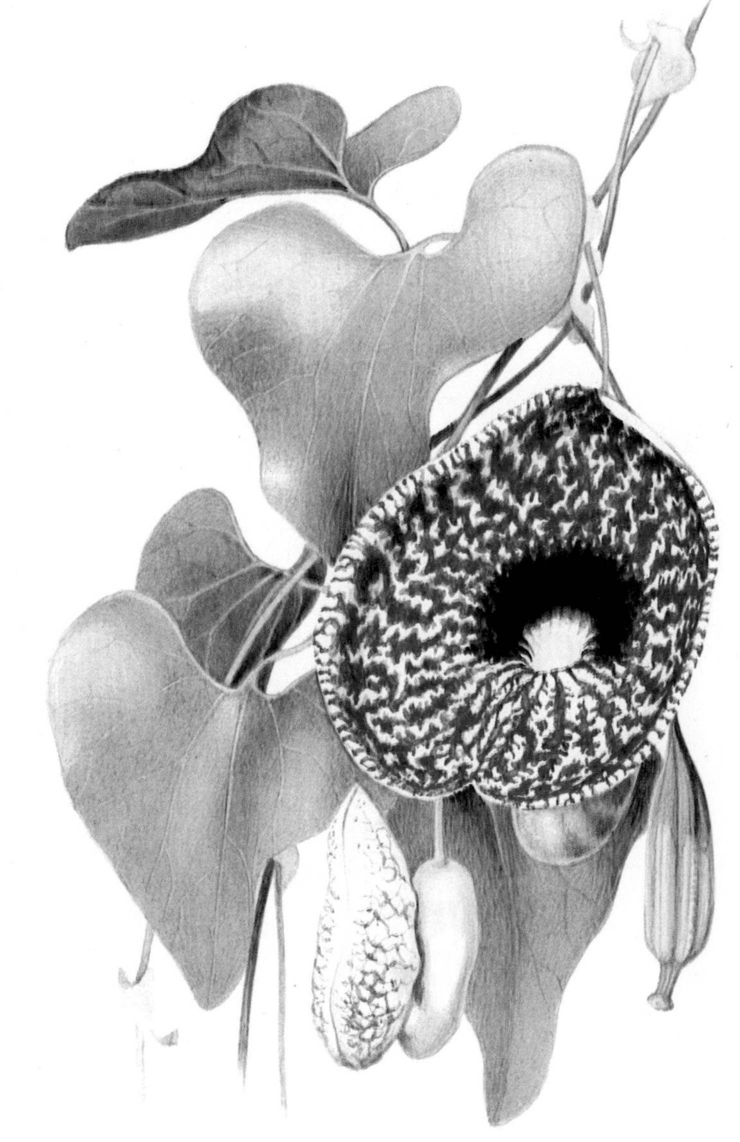

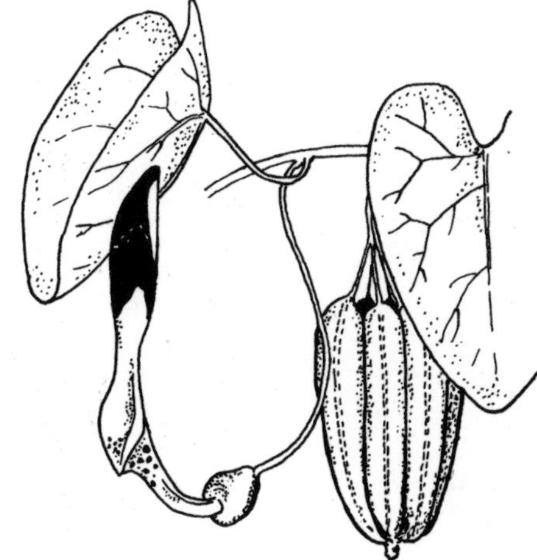

*Aristolochia odoratissima;* the ripe seeds when dried have a pleasant, spicy fragrance

  18–30°C

# *Asarina erubescens*

The illustrated species is indigenous to Mexico, where it grows at elevations of approximately 1,000 m (3,300 ft). It belongs to a relatively small genus comprising only about 10 species distributed in Mexico and the southern states of America.

In 1956 Pennel, De Wolf and other specialists revised this and related genera and gave the genus *Maurandia* the new name *Asarina* (in older literature one may find many species of snapdragon under this name).

*Asarina erubescens* (syn. *Maurandia erubescens*) is a relatively robust, 2- to 3-m-(6- to 10-ft-) high, persistent shrub that becomes woody at the base. It twines over shrubs and trees to which it clings with the leaf rachises and curved stems. It has beautiful foliage, for the leaves are unusually soft and tomentose to felted. The flowers, produced from mid-summer until autumn, are up to 7,5 cm (3 in) long. The fruit is a large spherical capsule containing a large number of tiny, flat, winged seeds.

*Asarina barclaiana,* likewise from Mexico, is also often cultivated. It has three-sided leaves and long, trumpet-like flowers covered on the outside with glandular hairs as in the illustrated species. The flowers of the type species are purple but white or lilac forms are known too; these, however, are not as pretty.

The most important condition in culture is a rich, rather heavy compost, such as John Innes potting compost No. 2, a warm, sunny and sheltered site in summer and if possible cool conditions in winter. In spring the plants should be cut back hard to the woody parts, transplanted, and watered more liberally (they should be watered lightly in winter). They are readily propagated by means of cuttings as well as seeds, which, if sown early enough in spring, will produce flowering plants the same year.

*Asarina antirrhiniflora*

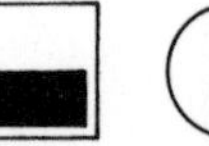  15–25°C

# *Cissus antarctica*

## Kangaroo Vine

The species shown in the illustration has been grown for room decoration since the mid-19th century. Though not a suitable plant for modern, centrally-heated homes, it has given so much pleasure that it would be inconsiderate not to include it in this book. It is an extremely undemanding plant tolerating temperatures just above freezing point as well as deep shade and dust. In a warm flat it quickly grows too big, thus losing its lovely characteristic shape. The best place for it, therefore, is a conservatory or a cool hallway.

The other 350 species of the genus, however, provide a wide choice for growing in any conditions. Those who are fond of succulents will appreciate, for example, the beauty of the climbing *C. quadrangularis,* found over an area extending from Madagascar through Africa to India; *C. cactiformis,* practically indistinguishable from a cactus from Somalia, Kenya and Tanzania, and *C. juttae* from south-west Africa. In the case of all three, cultivation is the same as for stapelias.

Best suited for today's centrally-heated homes and interior décor is *C. discolor* from Java, India and Burma. It is a magnificent climber with large, ovate, pointed leaves, coloured bright violet red on the underside and green with silvery marbling above. The stalks are also purple.

In winter, however, free-growing specimens generally do not have enough light nor enough atmospheric moisture and so they often drop their leaves; it is thus best grown in a large plant-case, to which it lends a special magic. Also better grown in a glass plant-case is *C. amazonica* with small, narrow leaves, similar in colour to *C. discolor.* Recommended for large rooms, for example trained up a trunk, are *C. gongylodes, C. njegerre* and *C. adenophora.*

All these heat- and light-loving cissuses require a fairly moist atmosphere which can be achieved by frequent syringing of the foliage and liberal watering throughout the year. The compost should be peaty with sand and some leaf mould. One of the soilless, peat-based composts would be ideal. Propagation is easy, by means of cuttings inserted in a warm propagator.

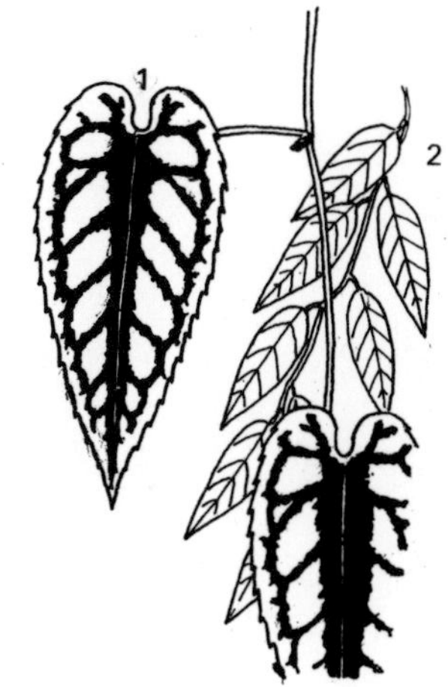


*Cissus discolor* (1) is a lovely climber for the larger plant-case. *Cissus amazonica* (2), though smaller, is also very pretty

   5–25°C

# *Dioscorea* × *discolor*

## Yam

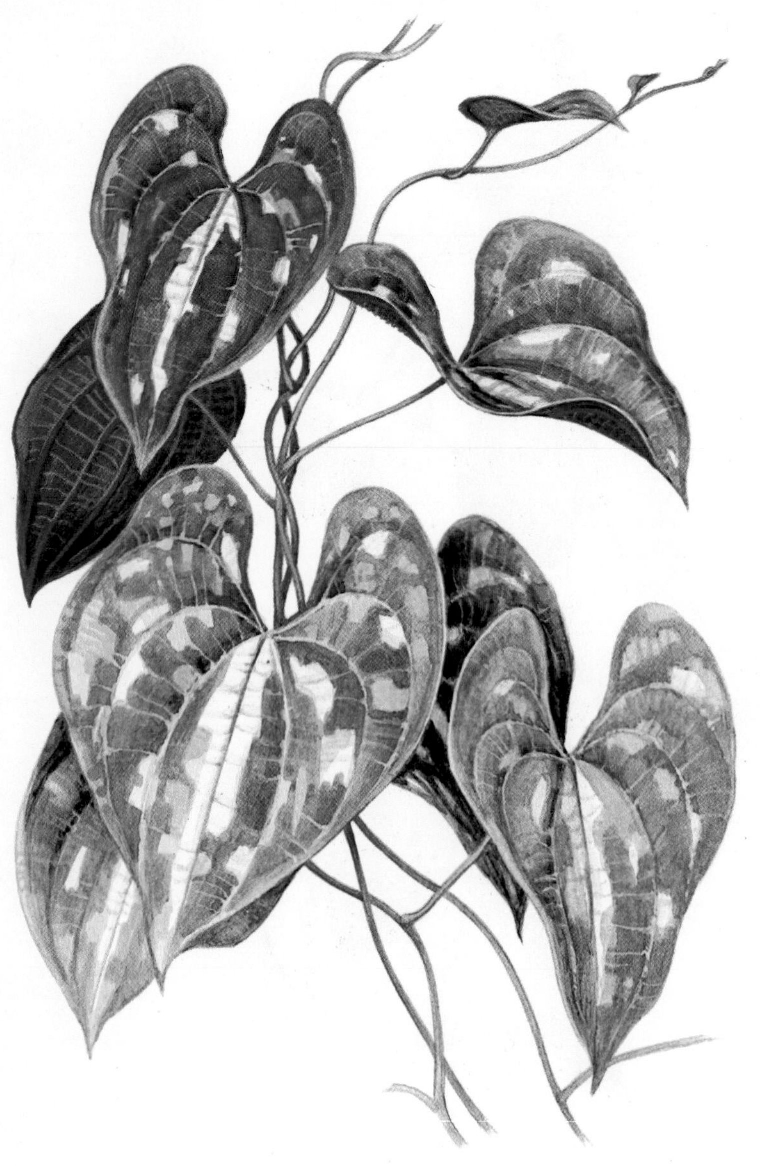

If you have a large room with plenty of sun you might like the idea of covering the windows in summer with the green foliage of an undemanding plant that sheds its leaves and dies back in the autumn, thus letting more light in again. Ideal for this purpose is dioscorea, a tuberous plant with a growing season from spring until autumn, during which time it attains a good size.

The illustrated hybrid is derived from several species that are not definitely known, but in all probability included among their number are *D. multicolor chrysophylla, D. amarantoides* and *D. vittata* from Brazil. All three are relatively small climbers, growing to a length of 2 m (6 ft) in indoor cultivation. The leaves are about 10 to 15 cm (4 to 6 in) long, variegated, often with golden glints and patches and a pale area round the midrib, but almost always reddish violet on the underside.

Of the larger climbers, *D. sansibarensis* is recommended. This is often grown in greenhouses in botanical gardens under the wrong name of *D. macroura*. The leaves are truly large, in robust specimens up to 30 cm (1 ft) across, broadly heart-shaped with auricles and tapering to a long point which serves as run-off for excess water from the leaves. The conspicuous venation is particularly attractive and the aerial tubers formed in the leaf axils by means of which the plant spreads and multiplies are of botanical interest. This characteristic is common to a number of species and has given its name to one – *D. bulbifera,* a well-known edible plant of the tropics (both the small aerial tubers and the large underground tuber are edible).

The best known edible yam is *D. batatas,* native to south-east Asia. Not only is it a good house plant but it will also grow outdoors in the garden, without protection, climbing over shrubs and the trunks of trees in summer.

Yams should be grown in rich, rather heavy soil, such as John Innes potting compost No. 3. They are undemanding, rapidly growing plants; even the green-leaved species have no special light requirements, needing only a rich diet. Propagation is by means of the small aerial tubers and by cuttings. The tubers should be lifted for the winter and stored in a warm, dry place until time for potting up or planting out again in spring.

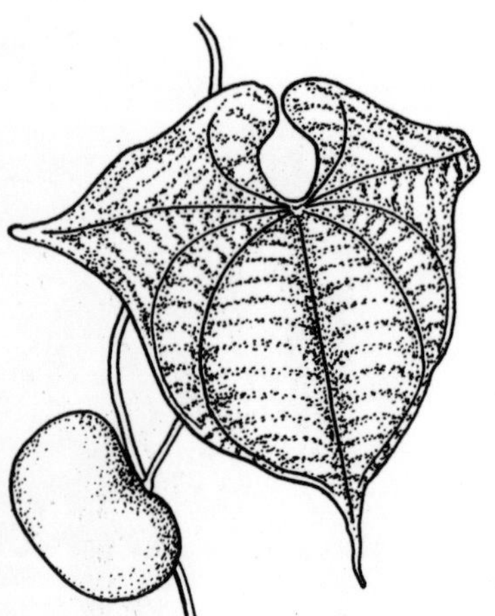

*Dioscorea sansibarensis* with an aerial tuber. This often-cultivated species is very poisonous!

S 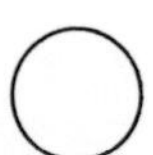  20–30°C

# *Dipladenia × sanderi* 'Rosea'

Anyone who comes across one of the botanical species of this genus growing in the wild (there are 40 of them distributed in tropical America) will find it hard to believe that it is not a cultivated plant when he sees its magnificent large flowers.

Dipladenias are not newcomers to cultivation but they were relegated to the ranks of forgotten plants until 1955 when they were 'rediscovered' by Danish nurserymen and introduced to the market. They evoke such great interest that nowadays this climber appears on the list of many horticultural establishments.

Pure species are not found in cultivation, however, only hybrids derived chiefly from the crossing of several Brazilian species, primarily *D. sanderi, D. atropurpurea, D. eximia* and *D. splendens.* They are robust, woody climbers with firm, glossy, dark green leaves and large, funnel-shaped flowers joined to form a tube at the base. The fruit is a large, heavy, double follicle that exudes a thick poisonous milk when bruised and later dries up. The seeds are small, flat, dark brown and furnished with long hairs that aid in their dispersal by wind.

Dipladenia is a rewarding house plant that flowers regularly and profusely. Its requirements and cultivation are much the same as those of allamanda. The substrate, however, should be lighter and more porous, for the roots do not tolerate lengthy contact with water. John Innes potting compost No. 2 with extra peat added would be suitable.

Propagation is also the same as for allamanda. When the plants are hard pruned in spring use the prunings as cuttings. These should be rinsed in warm water (to release the milk) and inserted in a mixture of peat and sand in a warm propagator. They root more easily than allamanda – within 3 to 4 weeks.

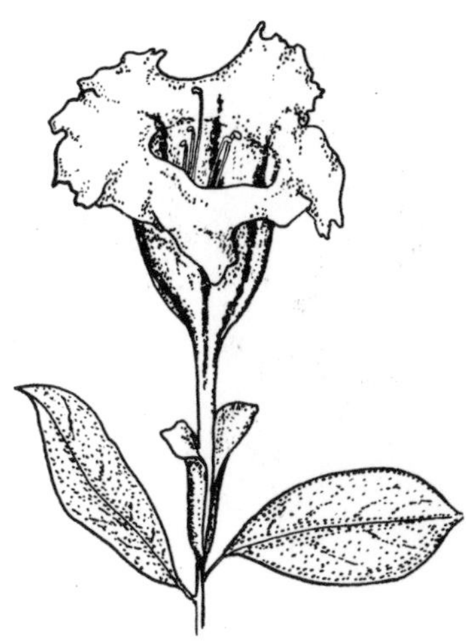

*Solandra nitida* is a robust climber of the nightshade family

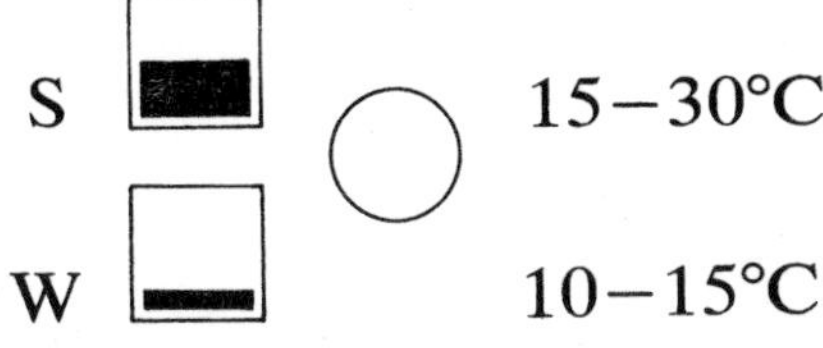


15–30°C

10–15°C

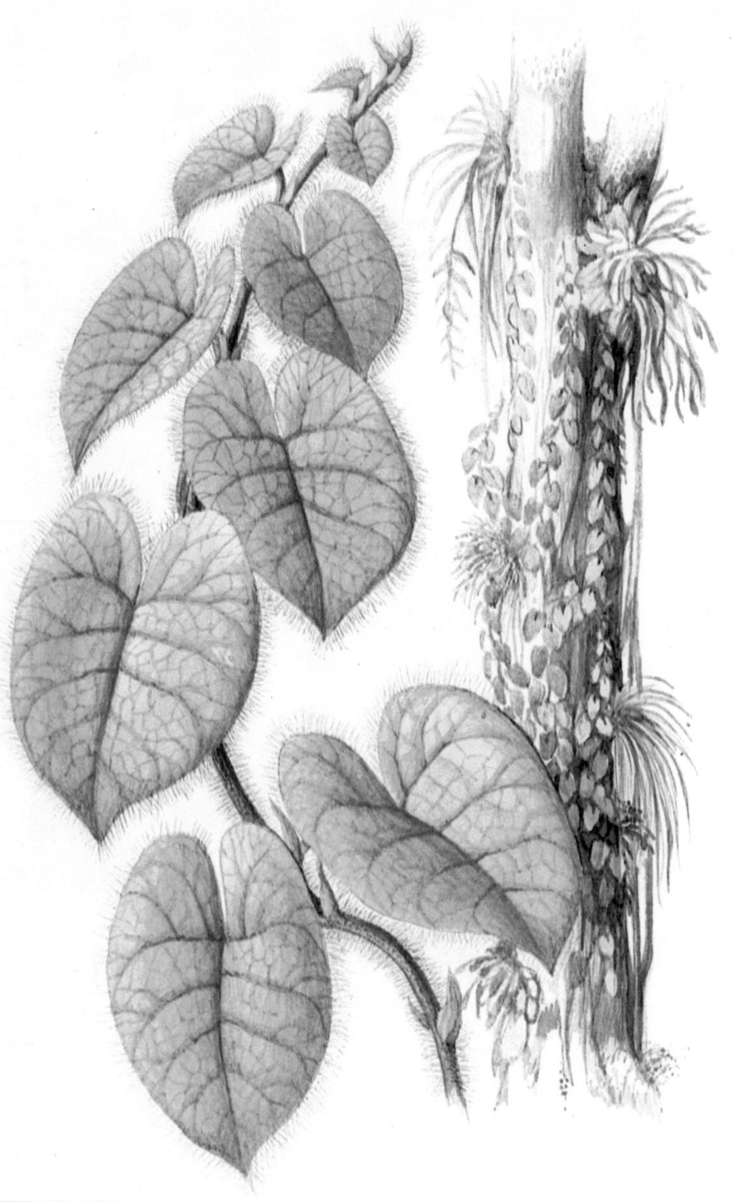

# *Ficus villosa*

If we wish to know what the natural habitat of the illustrated species is like then we must go to south-east Asia, say to the Cuc Phuong National Park in Vietnam, where it grows in relative abundance. Arising from the thick layer of humus in the undergrowth are the towering trunks of giant trees. Very little light filters down to the forest floor through these and the only plants that manage to grow here are huge ferns, such as *Tectaria decurrens,* reaching heights of several metres (yards) and often climbing to the tree tops to get to the light, and the huge lianas *Rhaphidophora* and *Piper,* the commonest climbers here. However, in the darkest part of the forest, where one would expect to find only selaginellas and shade-loving ferns, we suddenly come across *Ficus villosa* climbing up the trunk of a tree, its leaves firmly pressed to the bark. Shade, apparently, does not bother it, quite the contrary – it seems to shy away from spots touched by sunlight, even occasionally.

*Ficus villosa* (syn. *F. barbata*) is probably the most shade-loving climbing ficus. This is shown by the surface of the dark green leaves, which have a sheen typical of many shade-loving plants – an unusual velvety-blue glint when viewed from a certain angle.

Because of this peculiarity and the fact that it remains unchanged when grown in warm, centrally-heated homes, *F. villosa* is very good, for instance, in a dish arrangement that includes a trunk for epiphytes up which it can climb on the shaded side. However, it is also attractive if it is allowed to climb up the wall of a room.

Another commonly-known self-clinging fig, *F. pumila,* on the other hand, requires ample diffused light at the very least, and is thus the recommended choice for a room with plenty of light.

*Ficus villosa* is quite readily propagated by means of cuttings, which bleed 'milk', however, and should be soaked in lukewarm water for some time before insertion in the rooting medium in a warm and, what is most important, moist propagator. The rooting medium should be a mixture of peat and sand (this may also be used as a permanent growing medium). The cuttings will form roots within 5 to 6 weeks, but not until they have formed 2 to 3 leaves should they be potted up.

*Ficus parcellii,* a beautiful shrub with soft foliage, is particularly good for the glasshouse

*Ficus diversifolia* is a small shrub that also does well when grown as an epiphyte

   15–30°C

# *Gloriosa rothschildiana*

## Glory Lily

*Gloriosa rothschildiana* serves as decoration only in summer but its flowers are among the most beautiful in the plant realm. It is truly amazing that such a conspicuous and beautiful flower was not introduced into cultivation until the beginning of the 20th century. This may be explained by the fact it is native to Africa, which at that time was a continent little investigated by botanists and which, even today, still has unexplored reserves.

During the past few decades it was the Dutch who led the field in its cultivation which they fully mastered, discovering that, despite its exotic appearance, it is a plant that is not particularly demanding and can be grown by anyone who has at least a basic knowledge of horticulture.

Six species have been described to date, all native to tropical Africa and Asia. They are very much alike in the shape of the flowers, which in some species are coloured yellow or green, changing to red during flowering. The plants have cylindrical underground tubers from the top of which in spring grows a tall stem about 1.5 m (5 ft) high with long, glossy leaves terminated by tendrils with which the plant clings to the surrounding vegetation (in cultivation to a piece of twine or stick provided for the purpose). The number of flowers produced depends on the size of the tuber, the general rule being one flower to each centimetre (half inch) of the tuber's length. The flowers in the illustrated species are up to 15 cm (6 in) across and remain on the plant unchanged for up to 3 weeks. They are good for cutting and will last at least 10 days in a vase.

Cultivation is not difficult. The tubers, stored in dry sand in a warm spot for the winter, are planted in spring in John Innes potting compost No. 2 and watered. When they have started into growth they should be put in a warm spot in full sun and fed and watered liberally. Propagation is either by cutting up the tubers or by means of seeds, which develop into flower-bearing plants within 3 years.

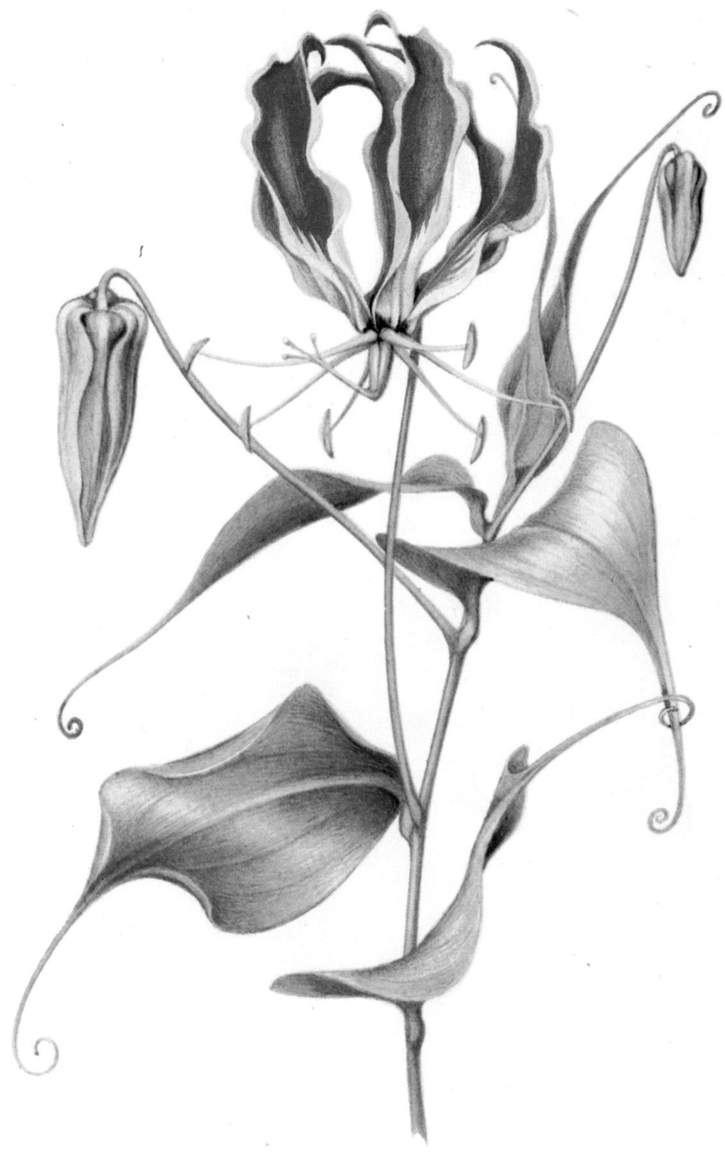

S  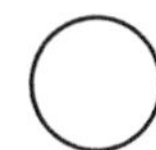  15–25°C

*Gloriosa superba* from southern Asia has markedly wavy perianth segments

# *Gynura aurantiaca*

## Velvet Plant

The extraordinarily large Compositae family has provided horticulture with the widest selection of plants – not only ones grown in Europe as annuals and perennials but also plants of the tropics and subtropics. For example gerberas, for decades popular flowers for cutting; and for more experienced growers pachystegia, mutisia and othonna. Gynura, with its beautifully coloured leaves adds a new aspect of interest to this large assortment of plants with lovely flowers, interesting habit or attractive foliage.

The genus is not a particularly large one, comprising only about 20 species native to Asia and Africa and all very much alike. The illustrated species, however, is definitely the loveliest and furthermore commonly available at nurseries.

*Gynura aurantiaca* is found in the mountain forests of Java, where it reaches a height of only about 1 m (3 ft). It is a twining sub-shrub which turns slightly woody at the base. In the juvenile form the dark green colour of the leaves, which are shallowly lobed, is masked by a thick cover of deep violet hairs. The flowers are not particularly attractive, resembling the less decorative ones of the European hawkweed.

To attain its best coloration gynura requires full sun or at most only a lightly shaded position. It finds the conditions of modern homes congenial; it tolerates both a dry and dusty atmosphere and does not even mind smoke. In winter, watering, which is otherwise liberal, should be slightly limited to bring on a partial rest period. The compost should be a peaty one with an addition of leaf mould and sand. One of the soilless composts would be ideal. The young shoots are the most attractively coloured and therefore the plant should be hard-pruned in spring. Tip cuttings form roots readily, even in water.

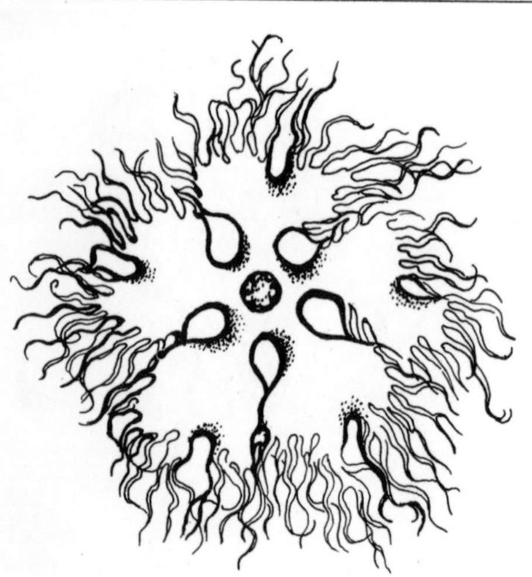

*Trichosanthes japonicum* of the gourd family is an attractive climber easily grown indoors or on the patio

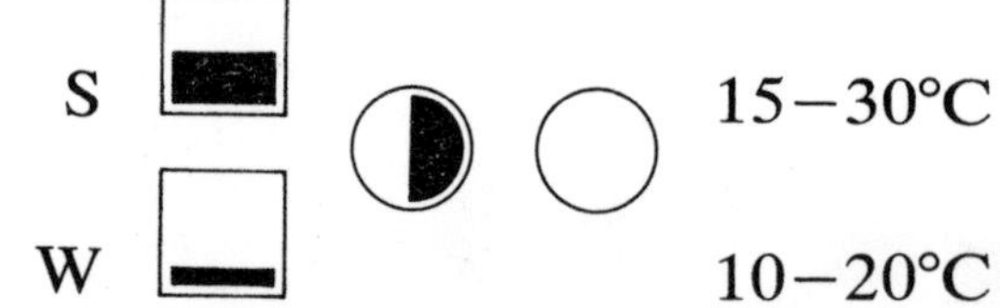

# *Hoya carnosa*

## Wax Flower, Porcelain Flower

The wax flower is one of the commonest climbers grown for room decoration, be it the typical green-leaved form or the variegated cultivar 'Variegata'. It is a member of a genus embracing some 100 species, found over an area extending from southern and south-east Asia through Malaysia and the Philippine region to Australia.

*Hoya carnosa* (syn. *Asclepias carnosa*) is native to China and Queensland. The beautiful flowers (particularly lovely when viewed close-up) are produced from May until late autumn. Plants grown indoors flower much better in a soilless medium (hydroponics).

The small species, such as *H. bella* from Burma, are much in demand. This, however, is not a twining plant; it forms an upright, much-branched shrub with pendant twigs at the tips. The leaves are barely 2.5 cm (1 in) long. The flowers are quite large in relation to the size of the plant for they measure up to 1.5 cm (over ½ in) across; they are likewise borne in clusters at the tips of the branches.

Some species have proved to be very good in terrariums where the firm leathery leaves are not damaged by small animals. These include first and foremost the narrow-leaved *H. longifolia* from the Himalayan foothills, a small twining plant with attractive flowers, which, as in the illustrated species, are produced more readily in soilless cultivation.

*H. imperialis* from Malakka is a beautiful but rare species with leaves up to 20 cm (8 in) long and drooping clusters of flowers up to 7 cm (2¾ in) across and coloured dark purple with a white centre. Quite common, on the other hand, is *Hoya* (syn. *Centradenia*) *multiflora* with beatiful clusters of yellow flowers resembling those of the wild rose.

Although many wax flowers have been grown in cultivation for a long time, centrally-heated homes now make it possible to grow the more tender species. The compost should be a mixture of peat and sand with a little leaf mould added or one of the peat-based potting composts and in summer the plants should be watered liberally. Propagation is easy; simply insert a cutting with one pair of leaves or just a leaf by itself into an ordinary rooting medium in a warm propagator where it will form roots in a few weeks.

*Hoya obovata* (syn. *H. kerrii*) is native to Thailand and Indochina. It is a rather large species with leaves up to 12 cm (5 in) long

*Hoya longifolia* (right)

 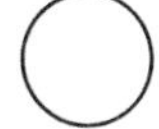  15–25°C

# *Ipomoea tricolor*

## Morning Glory

Most species belonging to the family Convolvulaceae are grown as annuals (for example, the one in the illustration which is often planted in window boxes), but many are perennial, including members of the genus *Ipomoea.* When one considers that it includes some 400 species distributed chiefly in tropical America, then it is evident that it offers countless opportunities for growers.

*Ipomoea tricolor* (syn. *Pharbitis rubro-coerulea*) does best if grown in a window-box in rich, well-drained compost, such as John Innes potting compost No. 2 and full sun. Similarly cultivated are other beautiful species, for instance *Ipomoea hederacea* with pale blue flowers; *I. nil* with flowers varying in colour from pale blue to deep purple; and *I. purpurea,* which besides the purple form occurs in many lovely colour deviations.

Perennial species are readily grown in warm, centrally-heated homes in rather heavy, rich compost, such as that already mentioned, in full sun or in a lightly shaded spot by a window. *Ipomoea horsfalliae* has a profusion of beautiful pink flowers (particularly 'Lady Briggs') and palmate leaves; *I. learii* has many-flowered clusters of rose-purple blooms edged with pale blue and measuring about 10 cm (4 in) across. *I. purga* with its large, deep pink to red flowers is also beautiful, and excellent for a sandy spot beside water in the paludarium is *I. pes-caprae* with leaves cut out at the tip and large deep pink flowers. All the species can be readily propagated by cuttings.

A special group is formed by the xerophilous species, for example *Ipomoea arborescens* from Mexico – a tree reaching a height of up to 4 m (13 ft) in the wild (but much smaller in cultivation) with large white flowers; and *I. stans,* likewise from Mexico, which is of shrub-like habit with a short stem, but with a large underground woody rhizome and pink flowers. These species should be grown in full sun in poor, stony soil and kept in a cool spot without water during the winter rest period.

*Ipomoea horsfalliae*

 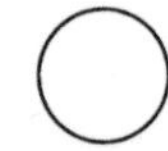  10–30°C

# Monstera acuminata

Monsteras are generally known as large, handsome climbing plants but there are also small species suitable for growing as epiphytes on a branch or in a small plant-case.

The illustrated species is from Guatemala. The stem is slightly flattened, with short internodes (only about 6 to 10 cm [2¼ to 4 in] long). The leaf stalks are up to 15 cm (6 in) long at the most, but usually only half that, the leaf blades between 10 and 25 cm (4 and 10 in).

In the illustration a juvenile plant is shown with margin still entire, only irregularly perforated. Adult plants have leaves resembling those of *M. deliciosa* (in cultivation, however, they do not reach this stage even after many years).

Cultivation of the illustrated species is not difficult. In the wild similar species of small monsteras almost always grow as epiphytes and this should be kept in mind when growing it at home. As a compost use a blend of peat, cut sphagnum moss, sand and charcoal, but a ball of sphagnum moss in which the roots are spread out will serve the purpose too. In the latter case, however, growth will be much slower, particularly at the start. The ball should be tied to a trunk or branch.

For good growth *Monstera acuminata* requires a constant high temperature (normal room temperature that does not permanently drop below 18°C [65°F] is sufficient), frequent syringing of the leaves and an occasional light application of feed.

Propagation is easy; simply cut the stem at the points where aerial roots are formed in the internodes; the cuttings will readily form roots even in water.

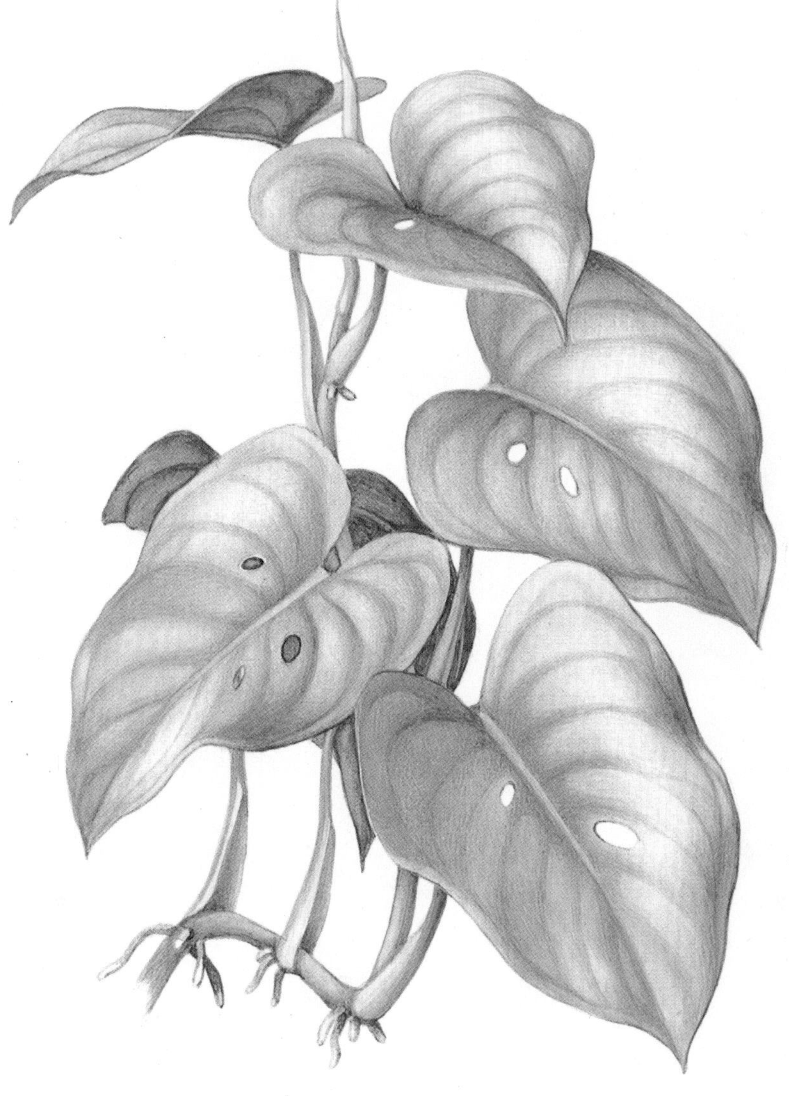

*Monstera spruceana*

  18–30°C

# *Passiflora caerulea*

## Passion Flower

The showy blossoms of passion flowers have inspired and excited growers since time immemorial for they are a fantastic shape and colour. The odd name (*passio* – suffering) dates from the 16th century when J. Ferrari, a Jesuit, saw a remarkable likeness between the instruments of Christ's suffering and the various parts of the plant. The trifid stigma he likened to the nails with which he was fixed to the cross, the stalked ovary to the cup of sorrows, the fringed corona to the crown of thorns, the tendrils to the cat-o-nine-tails, and the lance-shaped stipules to the spear thrust into Christ's side.

More than 400 species, distributed throughout the tropics and subtropics of the whole world, have been described to date. *Passiflora caerulea,* at one time the favourite and also most widely-grown species, is native to Brazil, Paraguay and Argentina. It requires relatively cool overwintering and thus is not suitable for the modern flat. Nevertheless, it continues to be grown for its popularity is well-established. Selection has yielded several attractive deviations and hybridization has resulted in many beautiful hybrids listed as a group under the name *P.* Caerulea-Hybrids. One that continues to be primarily grown is 'Kaiserin Eugenie' with deep pink sepals and corona filaments a deeper hue.

Those who can provide the necessary conditions for overwintering (a temperature of about 10°C [50°F] should certainly not miss the opportunity of growing this plant. Those who cannot are advised to consider such species that do not have a pronounced period of winter rest and thus do not need a lower temperature at this time.

It is often stated that heat is better tolerated by species with pink flowers, but this, of course, is not true. For example, *P. mollissima* from Peru, which grows in the Andes at elevations above 2,000 m (6,600 ft) and requires cool conditions the whole year (it even survives a light frost without any damage) has large, magnificent pink flowers. When choosing a suitable species for cultivation it is necessary to determine its origin and the conditions of its native habitat and base the choice on that.

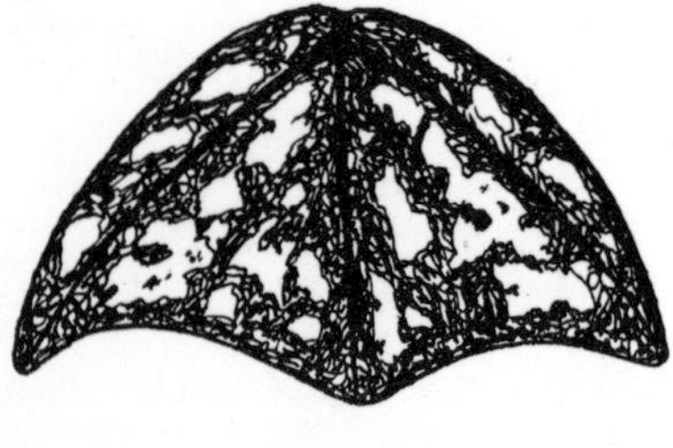

*Passiflora maculifolia* (left) and *P. trifasciata* (right) are grown mainly for their attractively coloured foliage

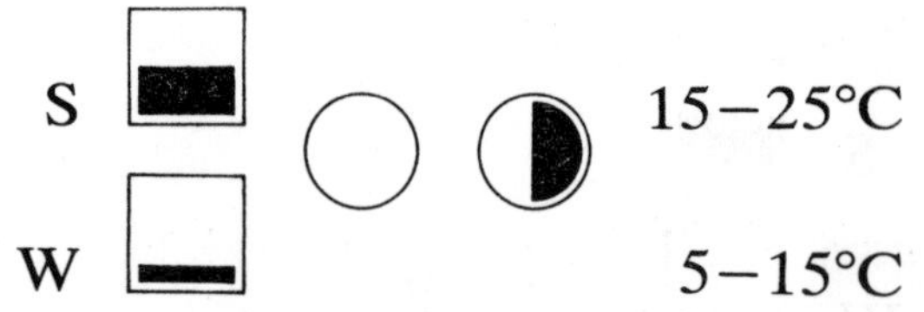

# *Passiflora racemosa*

## Passion Flower

The illustrated species is native to Brazil, growing in places where temperatures are lower in winter, but not as low as in the preceding species. Furthermore, it is not as tall as this species, and thus very suitable for the modern centrally-heated home. The flowers, about 10 to 12 cm (4 to 4¾ in) across, are beautifully coloured. The principal requirement in cultivation is porous, well-drained compost such as John Innes potting compost No. 1, and in winter practically no water.

This is not the only species suitable for use as a house plant. If there is enough space in the room, a good choice is *P. alata* with flowers about 10 cm (4 in) across, the perianth segments coloured red and the long corona filaments striped horizontally a darker colour. The similar *P. quadrangularis* has flowers about 12 cm (4¾ in) across, but the sepals are white and the white and purple corona filaments are arranged in five rows. Both species are widely grown in the tropics for their fruit, the seeds of which are enclosed in a gelatinous pulp that tastes somewhat like gooseberry.

Where space is limited the very small, annual *P. gracilis* is recommended. The leaves are 3-lobed, dark green, the flowers small, 2.5 cm (1 in) across and coloured white and green, the fruits are deep red when ripe and very decorative.

Passion flowers also include amongst their number some that have decorative foliage, for example *P. maculifolia* and *P. trifasciata* with predominantly rose-red foliage. Both species are particularly good for growing in a case for epiphytes for they do not tolerate a dry atmosphere.

Passion flowers should be put in a sunny spot. Large-flowered species require abundant heat but all species have a rest period in winter at which time the heat should be lowered and water limited. Feed should be provided only about once a month. Propagation is relatively easy – either by means of seeds, which germinate in succession but reliably even after a long dormant period, or by means of cuttings with two pairs of leaves inserted in a warm propagator in a compost that is preferably sandy rather than peaty. The popular *P. racemosa* (syn. *P. princeps*), however, takes a long time to form roots, sometimes even several months.

*Passiflora coriacea*

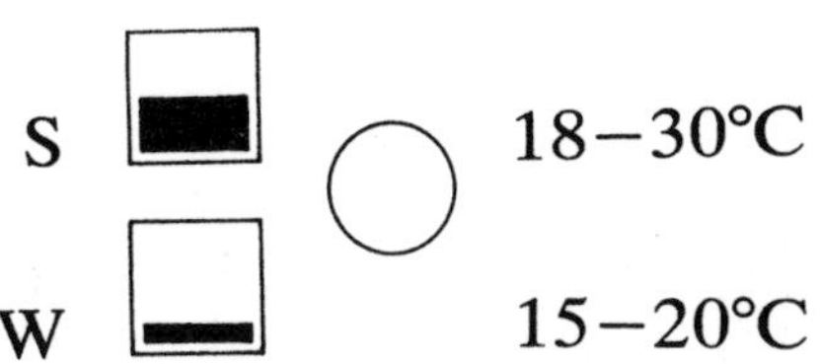


18–30°C

15–20°C

# Philodendron elegans

Some climbing species of philodendron were already mentioned in the section on foliage plants, namely *P. scandens,* good for room decoration, and *P. surinamense,* used chiefly in terrariums.

*P. elegans* belongs to the group of plants which are climbers and have lobed or incised leaves. The illustrated species is from South America, where it is widely distributed in many tropical parts of the continent. It is a robust liana climbing high up to the tree tops with leaves that in adult plants are up to 70 cm (28 in) long, 50 cm (20 in) wide and deeply incised almost to the midrib. It has far smaller dimensions if cultivated in the home, the leaves being only a third to half the natural length. Unlike other species, the leaves are also incised in the juvenile stage so that the plant can be kept within bounds by pruning, without loosing the effect of the incisions.

An ideal house plant is *Philodendron laciniatum* (also known in cultivation under the synonyms *P. laciniosum, P. amazonicum* or *P. pedatum*) from Brazil. The internodes are short, barely 5 cm (2 in) long, the leaves very variable in shape, being three-lobed, with the lobes further lobed themselves. In the home the leaf blade does not generally grow to a length of more than 20 cm (8 in). It is a fairly rapid grower but can be readily shaped by pruning.

It may also be trained over a support, a single plant thus covering a whole wall. Similar species, but less widely known, are *P. tripartitum, P. squamiferum* and *P. lacerum.*

All the philodendrons referred to should be grown in peaty compost with an addition of sand and loam or leaf mould. The compost must never be allowed to dry out at any time, for the plants do not have a pronounced period of rest. They are readily propagated by cuttings which will form roots even in water.

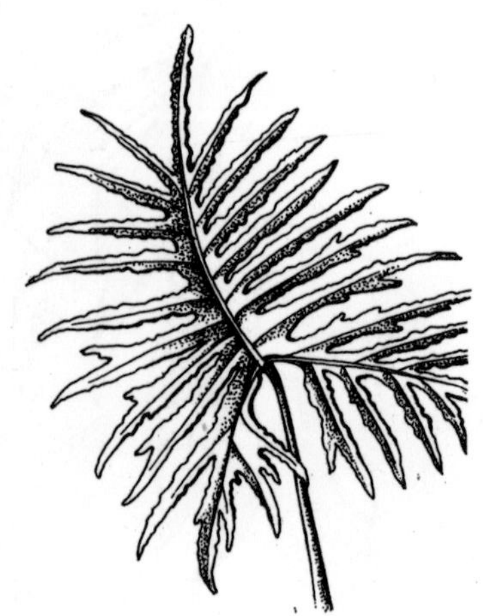

*Philodendron crenulatum* is native to Brazil

15–30°C

# Pothos scandens

The name pothos is often encountered in the greenhouses of botanical gardens but rarely does the plant in question truly belong to the genus *Pothos.* For instance, the most widely grown 'representative of the genus' – *Pothos celatocaulis* – belongs in fact to the genus *Rhaphidophora,* and this is only one example. The genus includes only climbing plants with leaves distinctly composed of a blade and leaf stalk, the latter being wing-like. The inflorescence is relatively small, a spadix enclosed by a spathe; the flowers are hermaphroditic.

Some 50 species growing in tropical Asia, mostly Malaysia, have been described to date. They are generally found climbing over the trunks of trees and stones, often in relatively deep shade. They require a very moist environment and so are found mainly beside streams and waterfalls where they are continually sprayed with water.

The base of the plant often rots, leaving only the stem which grows as an epiphyte attached to the growing compost by short clinging roots; this seems to be the rule rather than the exception, supported by the experience of gardeners in botanical gardens.

The illustrated species, native to India, Pakistan and Malaysia, is often found in botanical gardens. The entire leaf is about 12 cm (4¾ in) long and its division into a winged stalk and flat blade is clearly evident in the picture.

Pothos should be grown as an epiphyte, primarily in a plant-case on a trunk on bare bark. Each section of the stem with at least two pairs of leaves will readily give rise to a new plant if detached and grown separately.

*Epipremnopsis media*

  15–30°C

# *Rhaphidophora aurea*

## Scindapsus, Ivy Arum

The illustrated plant is one of the most widely-grown climbers, the yellow-mottled or white-mottled forms being the ones generally used for room decoration.

The history of this species reads almost like a detective story (as is the case with many other plants). It is better known to the public under the name scindapsus. It was Engler who assigned, or rather reassigned it to this genus, for the plant had already been described as *Pothos aureus*. It was not until a few years ago in Florida, when a specimen grown there produced flowers, that the botanist Birdsey found it to have the same characteristics as those of the genus *Rhaphidophora*. However, this plant can still be bought at the florist's or at garden centres under the old name of scindapsus.

Specimens grown in the tropics differ markedly from those grown in modern homes. Their leaves are often up to 40 cm (16 in) long and the blade is incised much the same as a monstera. Specimens climbing to the tops of trees that are several tens of metres (more than seventy feet) high are quite common.

Other species of this genus are also very beautiful, particularly the widely-grown *R. decursiva,* whose range of distribution extends from India through northern Burma to northern Vietnam. There it is often encountered in mountain forests at elevations of approximately 1,200 m (3,940 ft) rising from the thick, dark undergrowth and climbing the trunks of trees. Most specimens growing there in their native habitat are smaller than those found in botanical gardens, perhaps because conditions are cooler and thus growth is not as vigorous. The leaves of this species are regularly and deeply incised almost to the midrib; the blade is about 70 cm (28 in) long and 40 cm (16 in) wide.

Both the species mentioned are readily grown in warm homes, where they should be put in a spot that is well-lit but slightly shaded against the sun. They are easily propagated by stem cuttings which will readily form roots even in water. Cultivation is the same as for the genus *Monstera.*

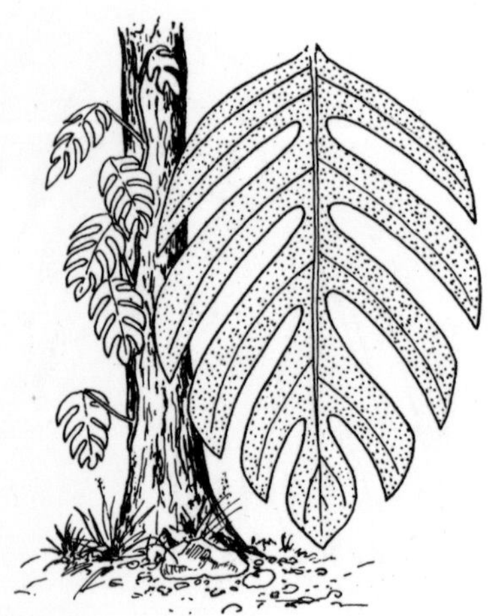

***Rhaphidophora decursiva*** **is a rewarding house plant that is excellent for growing on larger epiphyte trunks**

   15–30°C

# Scindapsus pictus

The approximately 20 species that make up this genus are distributed in India, the Malay archipelago and New Guinea; one – *Scindapsus occidentalis* – is also found in the Amazon region. To date, however, only the illustrated species has been introduced into cultivation.

*Scindapsus pictus* is native to the Malay region where it grows in lowland forests. The stem climbs high up to the tree tops, clinging to the trunks by means of aerial roots that penetrate the crevices in the bark. The leaves have short stalks (2 to 4 cm [3/4 to 1 in] long), the blades are roughly heart-shaped and measure up to 15 cm (6 in) in length. They are coloured deep green to blackish green with blue-white markings when they first appear; these mottlings later merge.

More frequently found in cultivation is the variety *argyraeus*, differing only in that the leaves are more pronouncedly heart-shaped at the base and have conspicuous silver mottlings on the underside that do not merge to form patches. It is quite possible, of course, and even probable that this is not a variety but merely the juvenile form of the given species; such mistaken identification is quite common amongst aroids.

Cultivation is very easy, and practically the same as for other aroid climbers. Propagation is by means of cuttings, which may be put to root in water, though it is recommended to put them in a closed plastic bag together with green sphagnum moss where they will reliably form roots within about 14 days. The growing medium should be a light, porous, acid mixture composed chiefly of peat; the plants may also be grown in pure fibrous peat. They should be given only light applications of feed, taking care not to give them too much nitrogen which results in less conspicuous mottlings.

Scindapsus and all other such climbers may be used to good effect on a trunk together with epiphytes. They may also be grown as solitary specimens, and look attractive in a flat, ceramic dish.

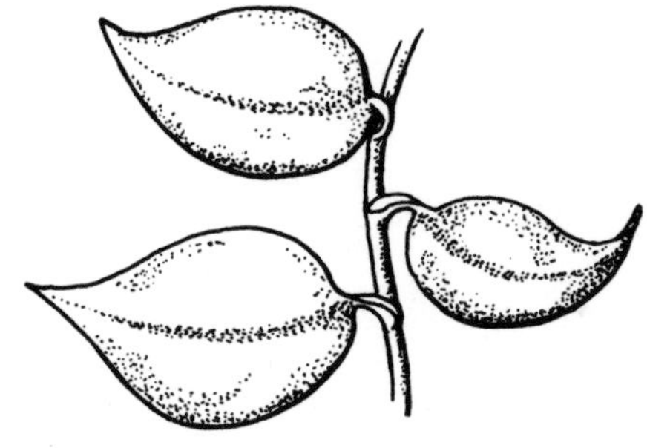

   18–30°C

*Scindapsus treubii* is a hardy plant from south-east Asia that is only recently beginning to be cultivated

# *Stephanotis floribunda*

## Wax Flower

*Stephanotis floribunda* is grown primarily for its attractive and pleasantly scented flowers. Indigenous to Madagascar, it is one of the approximately 16 species that make up the genus. It is a twining, evergreen shrub that in its native habitat reaches a height of 5 m (16 ft). It can, of course, be kept within reasonable bounds either by pruning or by training it over a framework. The dark green, leathery leaves, about 8 to 10 cm long, are very lovely, but the plant's chief attraction are the blossoms which were always included in bridal bouquets because of their heady fragrance.

Following a decline in popularity, this shrub is making a big comeback, and no wonder, for it does very well in centrally-heated homes. The average night-time temperature should be between 16 and 18°C (61 and 65°F); during the day it may be much higher. Only in winter should the plant be put, if possible, in a cooler, well-lit spot. Watering, which is otherwise liberal, should be limited accordingly.

The growing medium may be any packaged peaty mixture or else this can be prepared by mixing peat, leaf mould and sand. Not even in summer, when the plants are watered daily, should the compost be permanently wet or water-logged. The roots need a constant supply of oxygen so water the plants carefully, and they will greatly benefit from regular syringing. They should be placed in full sun or at least in a spot with plenty of light. Propagation is easy – from cuttings inserted in a warm propagator, or by means of the tiny, flat seeds.

*Asclepias curassavica*

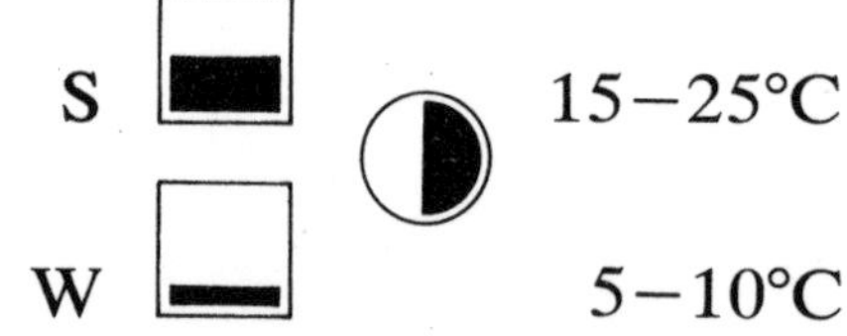

# *Syngonium podophyllum* 'Albolineatum'

## Goose Foot

Imagine you come across this species in the wild, say outside the town of Atoyac on Mexico's Pacific coast. At an altitude of about 1,000 m (3,300 ft) above sea level, its bare stem climbs up a trunk terminating some 3 m (10 ft) above the ground in a large tuft of leaves. In the wild, however, *Syngonium podophyllum* has an entirely different habit of growth to plants grown in cultivation, for in the first instance the plant has very little light at ground level and the leaves can carry on photosynthesis only when they are above the surrounding vegetation. In this region syngoniums may be seen on practically every tree, generally at elevations of 1,300 to 1,400 m (4,260 to 4,580 ft). It also grows in other Central American states, for example Honduras, Guatemala and San Salvador. The leaves are sagittate only in seedling and juvenile forms; later they are divided by deep incisions into 5 to 11 parts.

Though the type species may be encountered in cultivation, cultivars are generally grown. Besides the one shown in the illustration these include, for example, 'Green Gold', with silver and yellow markings on the leaves,; and 'Imperial White', with silver leaves narrowly edged with green.

Other species are also often grown, in particular *Syngonium auritum* (syn. *Philodendron trifoliatum*) from Mexico, Haiti and Jamaica, and *S. hastifolium* from Brazil.

Syngonium is most effective when trained over a framework such as a room divider, or up a trunk with epiphytes. One way or the other, it should be kept in mind that the plant will need plenty of space for it grows quite rapidly and in time, given congenial conditions, attains quite sizeable dimensions. Cultivation is the same as for rhaphidophora.

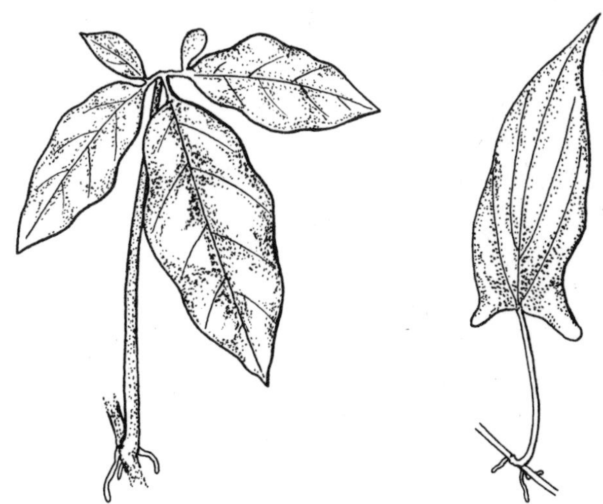

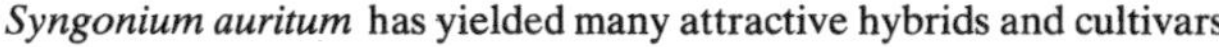

*Syngonium auritum* has yielded many attractive hybrids and cultivars

*Syngonium erythrophyllum* is a rarely cultivated species

15–30°C

# *Thunbergia alata*

## Black-eyed Susan

Thunbergias may be said to be still waiting to be 'discovered'. The illustrated species is one of the few that are found in cultivation even though it cannot be said to be the prettiest of the 100 or so known species that make up the genus. Nevertheless, it is a nice plant and suitable for growing as a house plant.

Black-eyed Susan is generally grown as an annual sown in March. In a sunny, sheltered spot in the garden it will flower from June until autumn, but it does better indoors where it should be put in full sun. The growing medium should be fairly heavy, such as John Innes potting compost No. 2. Water should not be supplied too copiously even in summer and should be practically withheld in winter, when the plants are moved to an unheated room. They quickly make new growth after spring pruning when provided with warm conditions, and soon bear flowers – after about 1½ months.

The type species has flowers about 2.5 cm (1 in) across, but in some cultivars they are twice as large. It is interesting to note that the species primarily grown in cultivation are from Africa, be it the one shown in the illustration or *T. natalensis, T. erecta* or *T. gibsonii.*

Much prettier thunbergias, however, may be found in the tropical regions of Asia, even though most are quite large climbers. Nevertheless, their blooms, which often measure up to 10 cm (4 in) across and are borne in pendant, many-flowered clusters, fully make up for the space they occupy. *T. grandiflora* from northern India has lovely pale blue flowers almost 8 cm (3 in) across, in long, thick clusters; *T. laurifolia* from northern India and Malaysia has lavender-blue flowers with a creamy throat; *T. coccinea* (syn. *Hexacentris coccinea*) from India and Burma, with 50-cm-(20-in-) long clusters of scarlet flowers only about 1.5 cm (¾ in) across, is one of the loveliest members of the genus; and *T. fragrans,* from the same area, is the recommended choice for those who like white flowers. Cultivation is the same as for the illustrated species, but the winter rest period is not as pronounced.

*Thunbergia grandiflora* is a stout climber with large, pale blue flowers

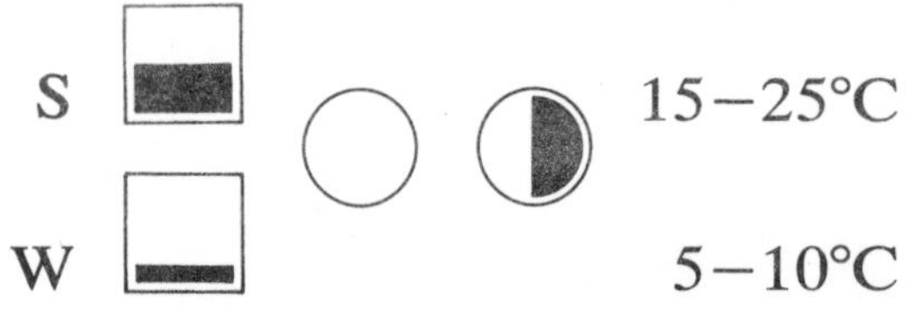

# EPIPHYTES

# *Aeschynanthus marmoratus*

## Zebra Basket Vine

In popular books, such as this, plants may be arranged in alphabetical order, which makes for quick reference, but only if the reader knows the correct and valid Latin name (and is able to remember it at the given moment), or else the way they are arranged in this book – in groups. This, however, results in many inaccuracies and unfortunately the section on epiphytes is the most striking example, for it should, by rights, include pratically all the orchids and bromeliads. Schefflera, for example, often grows as an epiphyte in the seedling stage. On the other hand, it is of a woody nature, and so could be placed in that group but, in fact, it is grown as a foliage plant, and that is the group under which it will be found in this book. The index of Latin names, however, will prove a handy aid to those who are in difficulties.

The genus *Aeschynanthus,* the first in this section on epiphytes, embraces some 200 species found in south-east and southern Asia. Most grow on trees in the forks of branches and on trunks, or in a thin layer of humus on rocks, their branches trailing downward to form long, thick veils.

In cultivation, species are grown for their beautiful foliage, for example the illustrated *A. marmoratus* (syn. *Trichosporum marmoratum*) from Thailand and Burma, or for their lovely flowers. One that has become very popular in recent years is *A. speciosus* from the mountains of Java, Borneo and Malaysia. The stems are pendant, about 60 to 80 cm (24 to 32 in) long, the leaves opposite (sometimes in groups of three), green, firm and up to 10 cm (4 in) long, the flowers bright orange red and borne in terminal clusters up to 10 cm (4 in) long. Much alike are *A. lobbianus* and *A. pulcher,* both more or less green leaved with red flowers; the first, however, has the calyx and corolla a single colour and covered with hairs.

Aeschynanthus are excellent, hardy plants that do well in modern centrally-heated homes. In summer they should be sprayed frequently. Otherwise cultivation is the same as for columneas.

*Aeschynanthus speciosus*

  15–25°C

# *Columnea* × *schiedeana*

Columneas may be said to be the aeschynanthas of South America, for not only do they have the same requirements but they are also very similar in appearance. However, they may be readily distinguished by the fruit which in the genus *Aeschynanthus* is an elongated capsule and in *Columnea* a berry, usually coloured white. Also, the flowers of columneas are not arranged in terminal clusters but are produced along the entire length of the stem.

The illustrated species is from Mexico. Specimens exposed to the sun have leaves coloured such a bright red that they look like flowers from afar. In the wild the separate stems may be up to a metre (yard) long (in cultivation about 60 cm [2 ft]), the leaves are approximately 10 cm (4 in) long and the flowers about 7 cm (2¾ in) long.

Of the many cultivated species and hybrids of this large genus (comprising some 120 species), *Columnea microphylla* from Costa Rica is a fine example. It has small orbicular leaves with a heart-shaped base measuring less than 1 cm (½ in) and covered with a relatively thick coat of white, red-tipped hairs. The flowers are about 5 cm (2 in) long and coloured a glowing orange red. *C.* x *kewensis* is a cross between *C. magnifica* and *C. schiedeana*. Its stems are thickly covered with appressed hairs, the leaves are about 3.5 cm (1¼ in) long and very narrowly ovate, the flowers a glowing scarlet and up to 7 cm (2¾ in) long. The last-named hybrid is the hardiest for indoor cultivation; it will flourish even if placed freely in a room, where it bears a profusion of flowers and fruits.

Members of the genus *Columnea* are somewhat more sensitive to low atmospheric moisture than *Aeschynanthus* and so, with the exception of *C.* x *kewensis,* it is better to grow them in a glass plant-case. Though the plants may be grown directly on bark together with small ball of sphagnum moss growth is slow and thus it is better to put them in a very porous mixture composed of pine leaf mould, sphagnum moss, cut-up beech leaves and perhaps, also, cut up fern roots and crushed charcoal. A bit of dried cow manure added to the mix is recommended as a supply of nutrients. If these ingredients are unobtainable, one of the proprietary soilless composts would suffice. Plants are readily propagated by means of cuttings, which should be about 5 cm (2 in) long, inserted in a peat and sand mixture in a warm propagator, where they quickly form roots.

*Columnea lepidocaula* from Costa Rica has leaves about 8 cm (3 in) long. The flowers are orange

  15–25°C

# *Dischidia rafflesiana*

## Malayan Urn Vine

We have already seen many ways in which plants adapt themselves to their enviroment. Some adaptations, however, are so amazing that they cause us to marvel at nature's ingenuity and to wonder as to how they came about. One of the most frequent causes for adaptation is the lack (or excess) of water – and it is against drying out that the illustrated species is adapted.

*Dischidia rafflesiana* is found over a large area extending from India to Australia. It grows in monsoon forests that are periodically dry as well as in semi-deciduous forests at higher elevations and during the course of the year it goes through a period when water is in short supply. Striking, at first glance, are the two different types of leaves on the twining stem: the 'normal' leaves are fairly small, flat and broadly ovate, the others are sac-like and much larger and on closer inspection are found to be hollow with an opening at the junction with the stem, through which several aerial roots, growing in the axils of the leaves in all members of the genus, penetrate inside the leaf. A cross-section of such a leaf reveals that there is a supply of water stored for the said roots. Whether it is rain water or whether the plant exudes it into the hollow is open to dispute, but the latter seems the more probable.

Similar 'rooting into itself' may also be found in the cultivated species *D. merillii,* which differs only in the shape of the sac-like leaves and in the plant being of more robust habit. There exist, however, other species with flat 'normal' leaves protected against drying out only by a thicker cuticle, for example *D. nummularia* with small, orbicular leaves, and *D. benghalensis* with lanceolate leaves, likewise only about 2.5 cm (1 in) long.

All dischidias are grown without any compost, or at the most only on a moss-covered branch. They do best in cases for growing epiphytes and in indoor glasshouses, where they have both ample atmospheric moisture and light. They can also be grown freely in a room, but development, though reliable, is somewhat slower. Propagation is easy – either by seeds or, the more common method, by detaching individual 'branches' from the clump or cutting up the stems.

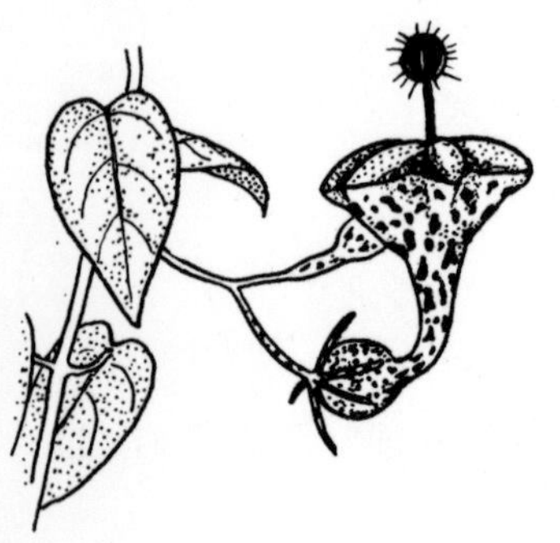

*Ceropegia haygarthii* is a very rewarding house plant

18–30°C

# *Hypocyrta* × *glabra*

Let us go back for a while to Central and South America, home of the genus *Hypocyrta,* which is very similar to the already described genera *Columnea* and *Aeschynanthus.* Some 9 species have been described to date, 8 of them found in Brazil and only one – *H. nummularia* – in southern Mexico, the remainder of Central America and possibly also the Antilles. All grow chiefly in the forks of branches, often also on rotting, fallen trunks.

All species have creeping or trailing stems and thick, fleshy or leathery leaves of moderate size. Both stems and leaves are often thickly covered with hairs (trichomes). From the leaf axils grow fairly large and beautifully-coloured orange or red flowers of a remarkable shape – the petals are joined to form an inflated, irregularly shaped flask with a narrow mouth. The tips of the petals are short and rounded. The reason behind this is that these plants generally flower in summer, a period of increased rainfall in their native land, and as the pollen is intolerant of direct contact with water it is excellently protected by the practically-closed corolla.

Besides the species from which the illustrated hybrid is derived, also cultivated is *H. nummularia* which has stems covered with red hairs, orbicular or obovate leaves about 3 cm ($1^1/_4$ in) long, and corolla about 2 cm ($^3/_4$ in) long, coloured bright red with a yellow mouth. Similar but slightly more robust is *H. strigillosa,* with flowers about 2.5 cm (1 in) long and coloured dark scarlet with a yellow mouth. Several cultivars have been developed in the United States but these are not much different from the type species.

Hypocyrtas may be grown in the traditional manner in a light, well-drained peaty compost, where they make rapid growth and soon flower, as well as in the more natural manner as epiphytes. In this case, they should be grown on coarse cork oak bark in cracks filled with just a little sphagnum moss, where they will make reliable growth and be of compact habit. Unlike columneas, they can tolerate full sun as well as a dry atmosphere. They are readily propagated by cuttings.

*Hypocyrta strigillosa*

  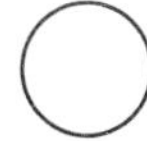 18–25°C

# *Myrmecodia echinata*

The intimate living together of plants and animals, where such an association is of mutual advantage, is called symbiosis. This is a general term that applies to many kinds of organisms but we shall confine ourselves to a single example, to the living together of plants and insects, more specifically ants.

This phenomenon is frequently encountered in the wild and plants 'aid and abet' the ants in various ways. Some species of *Acacia,* for example, have thick hollow spines that are partly open, forming a sort of 'entrance' for the ants that live in these spines. In some species of *Tillandsia* the hollow base of the sheaths is also inhabited by ants. To facilitate access the leaves are covered with thin 'windows' which the ants readily bite through, thus gaining entry themselves. What is the reason for this? The ants are protected against enemies without having to build a complex structure themselves and in return they provide the host plants with protection against pests on which they generally feed as well as with food remnants (which in the case of the given epiphytic bromeliad are a welcome fertilizer).

Some plants, such as the illustrated myrmecodia, have developed 'artificial ant nests' in their body tissues. Myrmecodia grows from a large tuber interlaced with several 'stories' of tunnels inhabited by ants. Rising from the tuber is a short stem with large flat leaves. The entire plant is rarely more than 25 cm (10 in) high. Very similar is *M. platytrea* from Australia (the illustrated species is from Malaysia), which is equally common in botanical gardens. Other species, which number approximately 20, are very rarely grown.

The biologically very similar genus *Hydnophytum* is occasionally represented in botanical gardens by the species *H. formicarum,* which has smooth tubers with several stems.

*Myrmecodia echinata* (syn. *M. tuberosa, M. inermis*) has no special requirements and thrives even in warm centrally-heated homes. It is grown either simply on bark or in a light epiphyte mixture composed of sphagnum moss and fern roots plus some crushed bark and charcoal. It is readily propagated by sowing the seeds, as soon as the berries are ripe, into the same compost.

*Hydnophytum formicarum* is an epiphytic plant inhabited by ants

  18–30°C

# CACTI

# *Astrophytum myriostigma*

## Bishop's Cap, Star Cactus

The highland plateaux of central and northern Mexico are the home of this plant, which is one of the first that beginners should start with. Like most cacti, astrophytums have succulent stems without foliage, the function of the leaves (photosynthesis) having been taken over by the outer surface of the thickened stem.

The thick outer skin is coloured greenish grey to whitish grey and thickly covered with white-felted spots, hence the name *myriostigma,* meaning with thousands of spots. There are usually 5 pronounced ribs (rarely 3 or 4) with sharp edges on which are spaced round or elliptic areoles with brown wool, which later disappears. The flowers, which appear on the crown, are pale yellow and measure about 5 cm (2 in) in diameter; they are produced at irregular intervals throughout the growth period.

The body of the young plant is almost globose, becoming columnar in age. The variety *columnaris* has exceptionally tall forms. In cultivation one may also occasionally come across the variety *glabrum,* with sharper edges and pale green skin.

The illustrated species has no spines. In *Astrophytum capricorne,* however, lovely twisted brown spines, up to 7 cm (2¾ in) long, grow from the areoles in varying numbers. In the young plants they are flexible, but in older specimens they readily fall.

What is the best compost for cacti? In their native habitat cacti often grow in heavy, compacted ground but the substrate is usually very porous. In cultivation, therefore, they should be provided with a well-drained compost, such as John Innes potting compost No. 1 with additional fine gravel thoroughly mixed in.

A thick layer of stones should be spread over the bottom of the pot or container before filling it with the compost. Also becoming widespread nowadays is hydroponic cultivation in sterile granular matter (for example crushed brick) with water, to which nutrients are added from time to time. Cacti grown in this way do very well. In general the soil for cacti should be neutral or only slightly acid (pH 6.0 to 7.0), the only exception being astrophytums, which require an alkaline substrate containing lime.

*Astrophytum asterias* – one of the most popular cacti

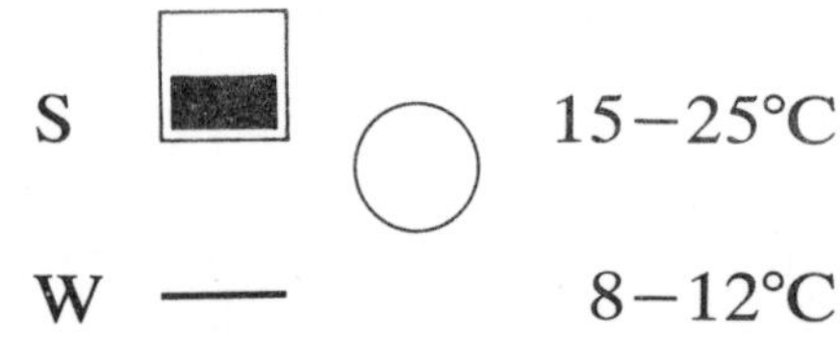

# *Cephalocereus senilis*

## Old Man Cactus

The popular 'old man' introduces us to the vast realm of columnar cacti. Naturally the cactus purchased at the florist's is only a small specimen but if it could be grown in congenial conditions for several decades (this being the time necessary for it to reach its true proportions) then it would measure up to 15 m (50 ft) in height!

Young plants (the ones usually available) are covered with long, soft white hairs, which practically hide the body from view. The stem under the hair is greatly furrowed, the number of ribs being 20 to 30. The edges of these are thickly set with areoles.

Adult plants, when they are about 6 m (20 ft) high, develop a cephalium at the top of the column – the ribs change into spirally arranged tubercles covered with areoles which produce a thick cover of spines. Such a cactus looks like a member of the 'royal guard' with his shaggy headgear. The flowers are produced from the cephalium. These are almost 10 cm (4 in) long and 7.5 cm (3 in) across and coloured white and pale yellow. After pollination they are followed by the fruit, which is a lovely red colour and contains a large number of seeds in the dark red pulp.

The substrate for this cactus must be free-draining and should contain some lime, therefore limestone rubble should be added to the compost. Grown in ordinary pots, columnar cacti are not as attractive as if put in a dish arrangement where the bizarre stems of the succulents make a more striking effect. The dish should be simple in design – ideally buff-coloured ceramic ware. Also very attractive is a group of large porous rocks planted with small species of cacti or other succulents. Since most cacti have more or less the same requirements there is no need for the grower to fear failure.

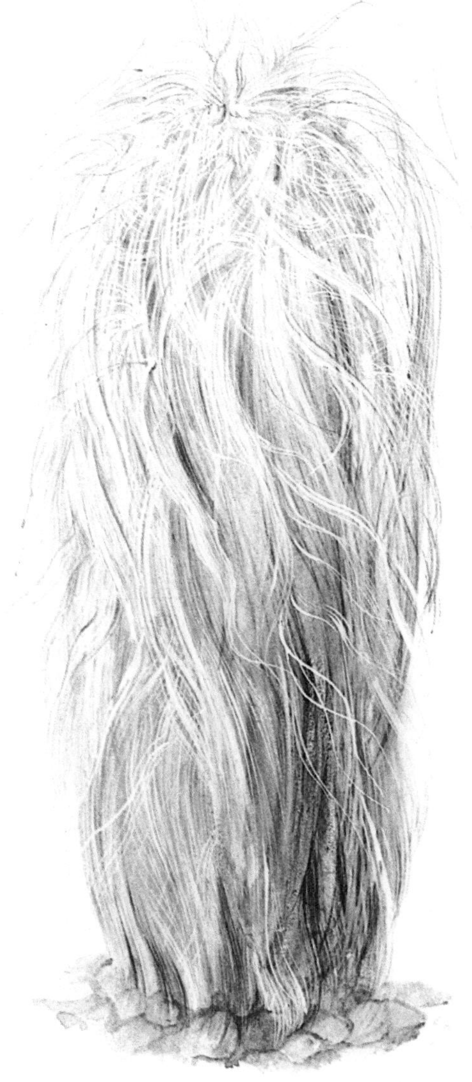

 10–25°C

*Espostoa lanata,* one of the so-called 'old men'. The long hairs are modified spines

# *Chamaecereus silvestrii*

## Peanut Cactus

The growing of cacti, like the growing of other plants and as a matter of fact like any other human activity, is subject to the dictates of fashion – the momentary vogue may be *Gymnocalycium mihanovichii* colour mutations or miniatures – and more is the pity, for cacti number many species that should be included in every collection of succulents and perhaps even grown in every household. They are undemanding plants that reliably produce flowers and because they are small it is no problem to find room for them.

*Chamaecereus silvestrii* (syn. *Lobivia silvestrii*) is one such undemanding plant, and for good measure, it is practically indestructible. It is a small, branching cactus reaching a height of 10 cm (4 in) at the most. The 'branches' are prostrate and attractively ribbed. The ribs, 6 to 9, are dotted with areoles from which emerge short spines, generally coloured white. Loveliest, however, are the bright red flowers, which are surprisingly large for such a small plant – up to 4 cm (1½ in) long. There are always several on a branch at one time so that the plant is truly smothered in blooms.

This cactus is native to the mountains of Tucuman province in north-western Argentina and is almost entirely hardy. A must, however, in cultivation is that the soil be kept absolutely dry if the temperature drops to freezing point or below.

Many cacti are hardy, and not just *Opuntia phaeacantha camanchica,* which is frequently grown in the rock garden. If their need for absolutely dry conditions is satisfied, many species can be grown outdoors in a window box. It is recommended, however, that this be provided with a heating cable and a thermostat to provide warmth if the temperature drops below −5°C (23°F). Otherwise ventilation should be resumed in early spring and watering in April. As a rule, the plants will then flower very well.

Some cacti, of course, tolerate the environment in central Europe without any damage and will readily flower in the rock garden, often when there is still some snow on the ground. These include: *Echinocereus viridiflorus, E. baileyi, E. melanocentrus, E. coccineus, E. purpureus, Coryphantha vivipara, Neobesseya missouriensis* and *Maihuenia poeppigii.*

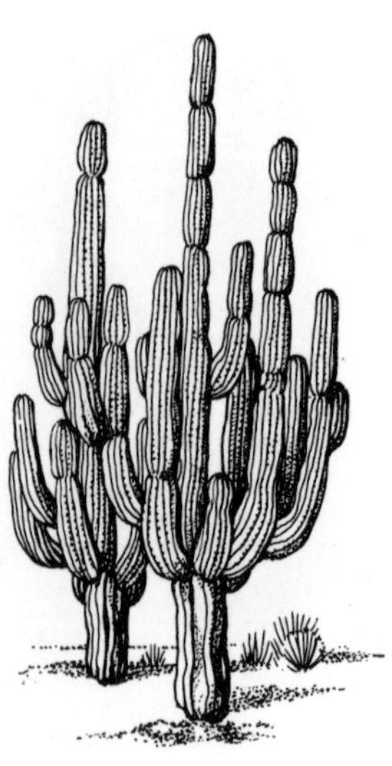

*Pachycereus pringlei* grows to a height of 11 m (36 ft) in the wild

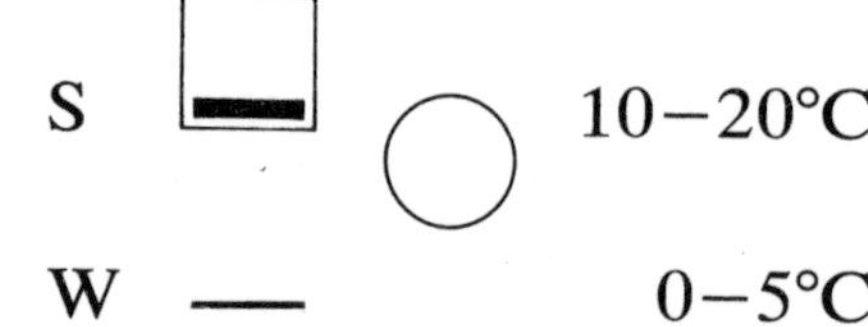

# Dolichothele longimamma

*Dolichothele longimamma* may be found growing wild in Hidalgo, Mexico. The spherical body of this cactus is covered with large cylindrical tubercles (mamillae) up to 7 cm (2¾ in) long tipped with areoles bearing 9 to 10 radial spines, about 2 cm (¾ in) long and coloured white or pale yellowish brown, and 1 to 3 central spines that are stronger, more rigid and darker. The flowers grow from the axils of the tubercles; usually 2 or 3 appear at one time round the periphery near the crown. They are pale yellow and measure up to 6 cm (2¼ in) across. The yellow-green fruit is club-shaped and contains a large number of black seeds.

Besides vegetative propagation by means of offshoots or cuttings (in the case of the illustrated species the separate mamillae will reliably form roots), most cacti are generally multiplied from seed.

The seeds require several conditions for germination, namely lots of light (that is why they should be sown on the surface of the compost), moisture and heat (preferably 25 to 30°C [77 to 86°F]). If it is impossible to provide bottom heat and artificial light then it is better to wait until late spring to sow the seeds.

The sowing medium should be free-draining, such as a mixture of 1 part peat to 3 parts sand. The dish containing the seeds should be covered with glass. If glass preserving jars are used as containers, the compost can be sterilized with heat before sowing takes place. After the seeds are sown the jars should be closed tightly to prevent mould from forming in the moist atmosphere and placed in a warm, well-lit spot. When they are sufficiently large the seedlings should be removed from the dish or jar with a wooden peg, taking care to damage the roots as little as possible, and potted up, using the compost recommended for astrophytums. They should be shaded slightly and kept dry for a short while after being moved.

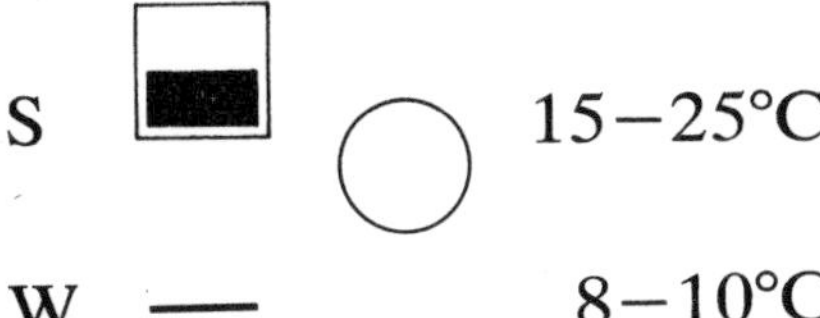


*Machaerocereus eruca*

# *Epiphyllum* × *hybridum*

## Orchid Cactus

Some cacti have become very popular, even with those who do not cultivate them otherwise, because of their showy flowers. Heading the list, next to the widely-grown Christmas cactus, is the illustrated orchid cactus, a complex hybrid derived from crossings between the species themselves and usually also with related genera. In Europe they are generally known by the name phyllocactus. True *Epiphyllum* species are cacti that generally flower at night and that is why they are often hybridized with the genera *Selenicereus* and *Nopalxochia;* the resulting hybrids have flowers that often remain open for 2 days.

Epiphyllums, as their name indicates, are of epiphytic nature, generally rooting in the forks of branches, their long thin stems twining over the bark to which they hold fast by means of clinging rootlets; the leaf-like expanded shoots either hang downwards or stand away from the trunk. Seedlings often root in the humus collected in the fork of a branch by another plant and so, for example, one often comes across orchids (such as laelias) covered with these cacti or leafy cacti sharing a small bit of life-giving humus with anthuriums.

A great many hybrids in colours ranging from pure white to violet purple are cultivated nowadays. The flowers are truly huge, sometimes up to 30 cm (1 ft) in diameter. Leafy cacti may be grown as epiphytes, but then (because of the other plants) it is difficult to provide them with the necessary dry and cool conditions in winter, without which they flower poorly. It is better to grow them in the traditional way in a porous, humusy compost where they make very rapid growth.

Two of the loveliest varieties, which have become classics, are the crimson 'Ackermannii' and the many-flowered, soft pink 'Deutsche Kaiserin'.

*Cryptocereus anthonyanus* is a magnificent species for larger epiphytic arrangements. The similar species *Marniera chrysocardium* has even more deeply cut leaves

 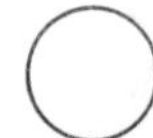  10(W)–25(S)°C

# *Gymnocalycium quehlianum*

South America is the home of the large genus *Gymnocalycium,* which includes more than 80 species. Many are often found in cultivation and some, or rather their colour forms, have even become 'fashionable' plants. Mention has already been made of *G. mihanovichii,* which comes in red, orange, pink and yellow. This is caused by lack of chlorophyll and the plants would not be able to survive under normal conditions, for they are incapable of carrying out photosynthesis. That is why they must be grafted in the seedling stage on to stock which provides them with food. These colour aberrations have become very popular, chiefly in Japan, where they are raised and multiplied by special nurseries.

The illustrated species is a flattened spherical shape, about 7 cm (2¾ in) across, later becoming cylindrical and attaining a height of 15 cm (6 in). There are usually 11 ribs broken into tubercles separated by sharp cross grooves. Each areole produces 5 radial spines about 0.5 cm (¼ in) long. The skin is grey green, appearing reddish in the sun. The flowers are relatively large, about 6 cm (6¼ in) long, white with a red centre.

*Gymnocalycium quehlianum* is native to the mountains of Cordoba in central Argentina. Because it grows at high altitudes it does not tolerate excessive sunlight and heat combined with a dry atmosphere, which other cacti find congenial. In its native habitat it grows in grassy places and thus it is best to provide it with light shade in summer. Watering, which generally alkalizes the soil, causes the plant to lose its roots for they are intolerant of an alkaline environment. It is therefore recommended that gymnocalycium be grown in fine crushed brick, the required nutrients being supplied by being added to the water. Cultivation will thus pose no problems and the plant need not be moved for years.

*Gymnocalycium kurtzianum* tolerates even partial shade; it is one of the least demanding cacti

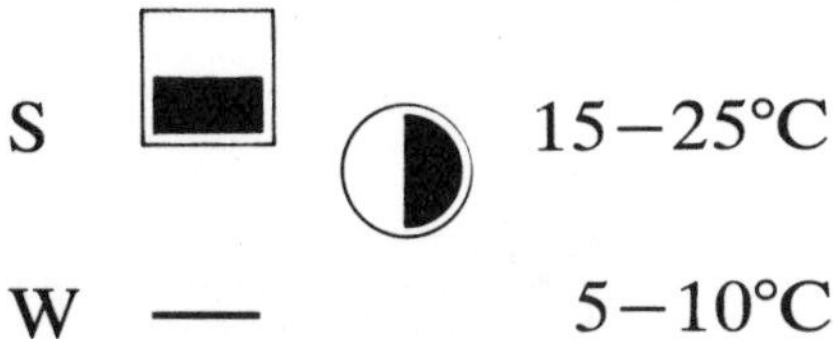

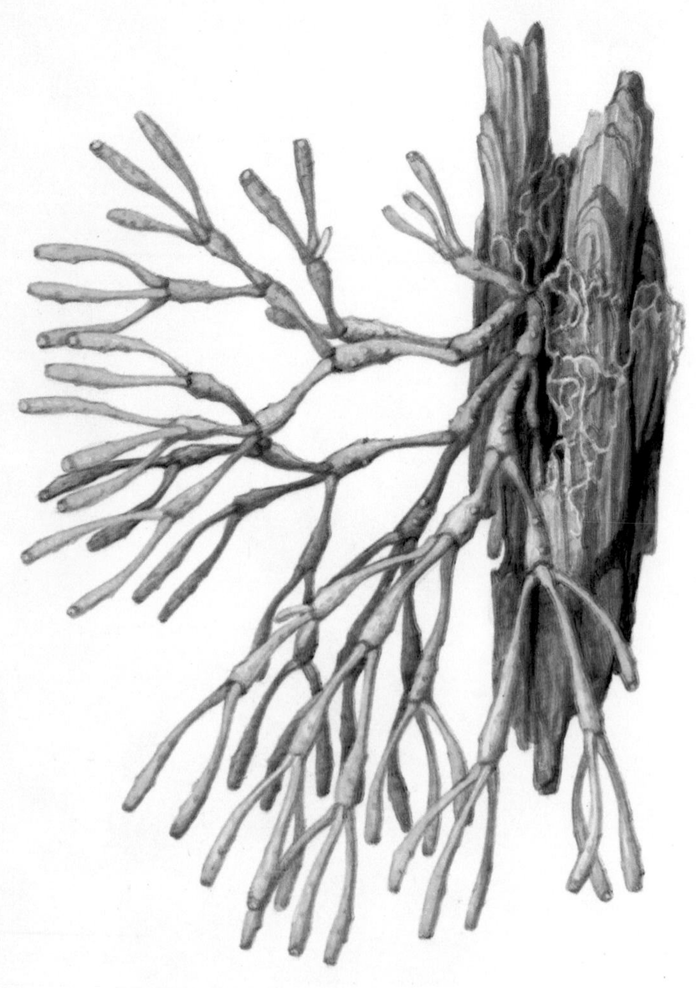

# *Hatiora salicornioides*

## Drunkard's Dream

The genus *Hatiora* comprises only 4 known species of cacti, all native to Brazil. They are either epiphytes or petrophytes (growing on stones or rocks) with a jointed body that is greatly branched, like a shrub. The areoles are spaced irregularly; those at the ends of the joints produce bell-like flowers of moderate size coloured yellow, orange or pink.

Though these are truly lovely and at the same time undemanding plants that would add beauty to any epiphyte branch, only rarely are they encountered other than in botanical gardens.

There is no need for a growing compost. Simply insert a 'branch' of the plant in a crack in the bark; it may be secured in place by packing it with a bit of sphagnum moss, which will fully suffice for rooting. If the plant is syringed frequently and put in a spot with full sun, then it will develop into a beautifully branched specimen by the end of the year and will produce flowers at Christmas-time. The fruits, which are rounded, white or pinkish, and partially translucent, are also lovely. The black seeds may be sown directly on bark, the same as with the related genus, *Rhipsalis*. The plants also appreciate a more nourishing compost and can be grown together with orchids in an epiphyte mixture or in a log filled with such a mix. Such plants will naturally grow more rapidly and will attain larger dimensions.

The illustrated species is from Brazil, from the states of Rio de Janeiro and Minas Gerais. It has, however, been found far south in the state of Paraná. The flowers are only about 1 cm (½ in) across, bell-shaped and yellow; the fruits are white tinged with pink at the end. The fact that it flowers at Christmas makes this beautiful cactus even more appealing.

*Ariocarpus fissuratus* blends perfectly with the stony terrain in the wild

  15–25°C

# Lobivia famatimensis

The body of this tiny cactus (about 3.5 cm [1¼ in] high and slightly less across) is shortly cylindrical when grown in the wild; in cultivation, where the plants are frequently misted, it is longish cylindrical. The skin is coloured vivid green or greyish green. There are 24 shallow ribs covered fairly thickly with areoles from which grow short, soft, white spines. The flowers are surprisingly large, the same length as the body of the cactus – in other words about 3 cm (1 in) and coloured pale yellow.

The species has been the subject of debate among cacti authorities, and there is some confusion over the correct nomenclature. The problem will not be discussed here – suffice it to say that *Lobivia famatimensis* may also be found under the name *Lobivia pectinifera* as well as *Hymenorebutia.*

*L. famatimensis* is a hardy mountain type of cactus, for in the wild it grows in the Famatima range, which is part of the Argentine Andes, at elevations of 2,000 to 3,000 m (6,600 to 9,900 ft). It is at mountain heights, in clear air and direct sun that it attains its full beauty. However, there is no need to be wary of growing it in a city in the lowlands for it can be relied on to do well even there.

It can be grown in a standard cactus mix of humusy loam, sand and stone rubble. In summer it should be watered copiously and syringed frequently; in winter, however, it requires a cool and dry atmosphere and completely dry compost.

The approximately 105 other species of this genus grow equally well as house plants.

*Lobivia pentlandii* is native to Peru and Bolivia. It is often listed under the synonym *L. corbula*

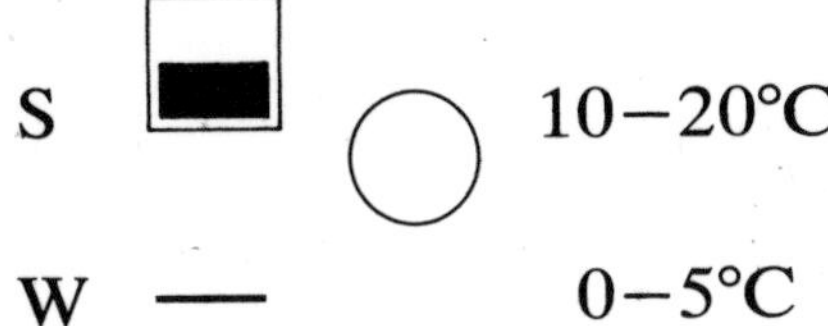

# *Lophophora williamsii*

## Peyote, Sacred Mushroom

The body of this cactus is grey green with a bluish tinge. It measures about 8 cm (3 in) across and has 8 to 10 shallow ribs. In young plants tufts of stiff hairs grow from the areoles. The turnip-like root is approximately 15 cm (6 in) long. The flowers are not large, only about 1 to 1.5 cm (1/2 to 3/4 in) in diameter, and coloured pale pink. Sometimes one may come across specimens with violet-pink flowers, found at the florist's under the name *Lophophora jourdaniana,* but in both instances it is one and the same species.

In the wild it grows in heavy, compacting soils from the southern states of America (by the Rio Grande) to the city of San Luis Potosí in Mexico.

In cultivation this soft-bodied cactus is considered to be one of the hardiest, practically indestructible plants for room decoration. If it is to bear flowers it must have a period of winter rest at a temperature of about 10°C (50°F).

Few plants are as well-known as *Lophophora williamsii.* The very name peyote (which is what it is called by the Indians) calls up visions of the ancient and widespread cult of the peyote. The cactus contains some 20 alkaloids, best known being mescaline which causes colour and auditory hallucinations. Its narcotic and hallucinogenic effects were well known to the Indians, who worshipped the cactus as a god, long before the Spanish conquest. There is no need to point out that its ingestion was always accompanied by religious ceremonies and that its use was and still is prohibited. Some groups of Indians, however, continue to disregard this prohibition, for example the Huitchols inhabiting the Sierra Madre Occidental north of Guadalajara, who make an annual pilgrimage of up to 300 kilometres (180 miles) to the locality where this cactus grows to collect specimens which they bring back, dried, to their villages.

*Ferocactus latispinus*

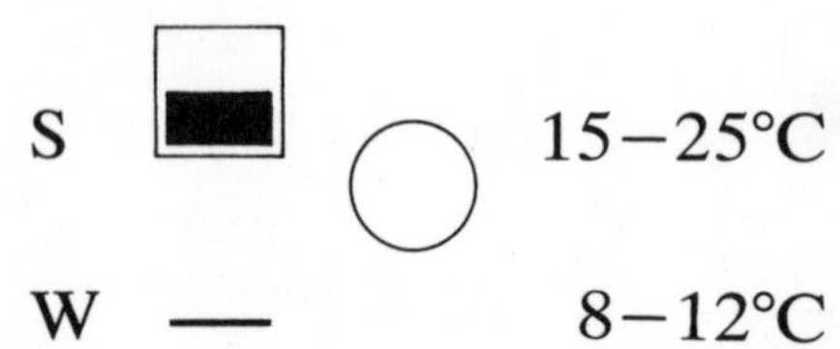

# *Mammillaria bombycina*

Few cacti are as popular as mammillarias. For one thing they include a vast number of species and secondly they can be relied on to flower. The flowers, furthermore, form a delightful wreath on the crown and are followed by carmine red or bright red club-shaped fruits.

The name of the genus is derived from the word mammilla, meaning nipple. This may be encountered in literature spelled in two ways: *Mammillaria* or *Mamillaria*. The first is the correct spelling (not in Latin, but botanically) for that is the officially recognized name by which it was first described.

The approximately 300 species described to date are distributed over an area extending from the southern states of America through Central America, including the West Indies, to Colombia.

The body of *Mammillaria bombycina* is about 20 cm (8 in) high and 6 cm (2¼ in) across. It is covered with conical areoles from which grow two types of spines: radial spines and central spines. The first number 30 to 40, are white, about 0.2 to 1 cm (⅛ to ½ in) long and radiate outwards; the central spines, usually 2 to 4, are darker, attain a length of 2 cm (1 in) or more and terminate in a hook. The flowers, forming a wreath near the crown, are about 1.5 cm (¾ in) across and coloured pale carmine, often with a darker centre. The plant's attractiveness is enhanced by the thick white wool growing from the axils of the areoles. *Mammillaria bombycina* is native to Mexico.

Many mammillarias tolerate very low temperatures in winter if kept dry and so can be successfully grown in a window glasshouse placed outside the window. The most suitable species for this purpose are *M. centricirrha* and *M. hidalgensis*.

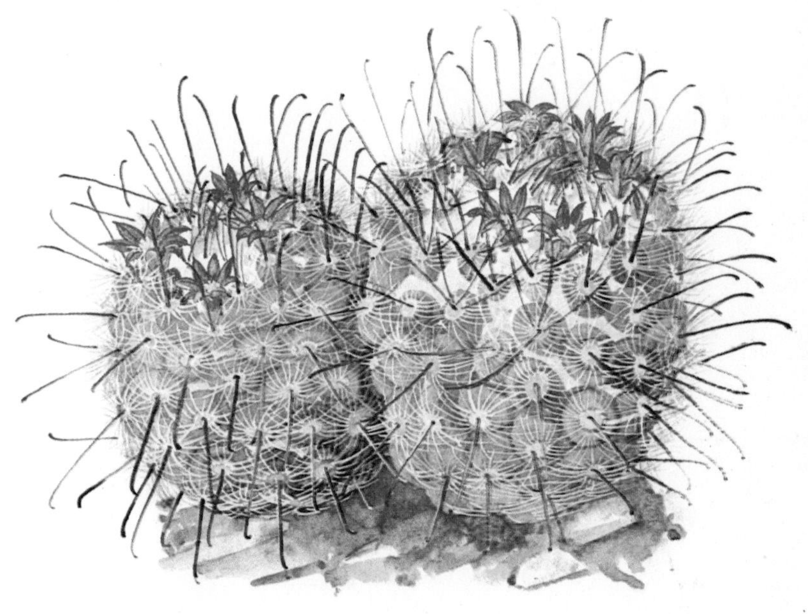

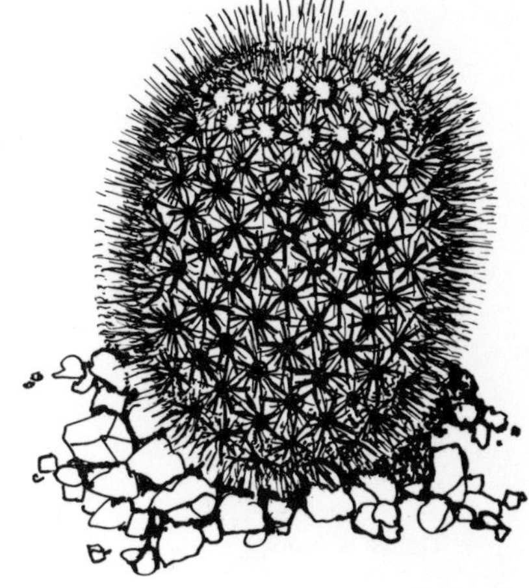

*Mammillaria columbiana*

S 15–25°C

W — 5–10°C

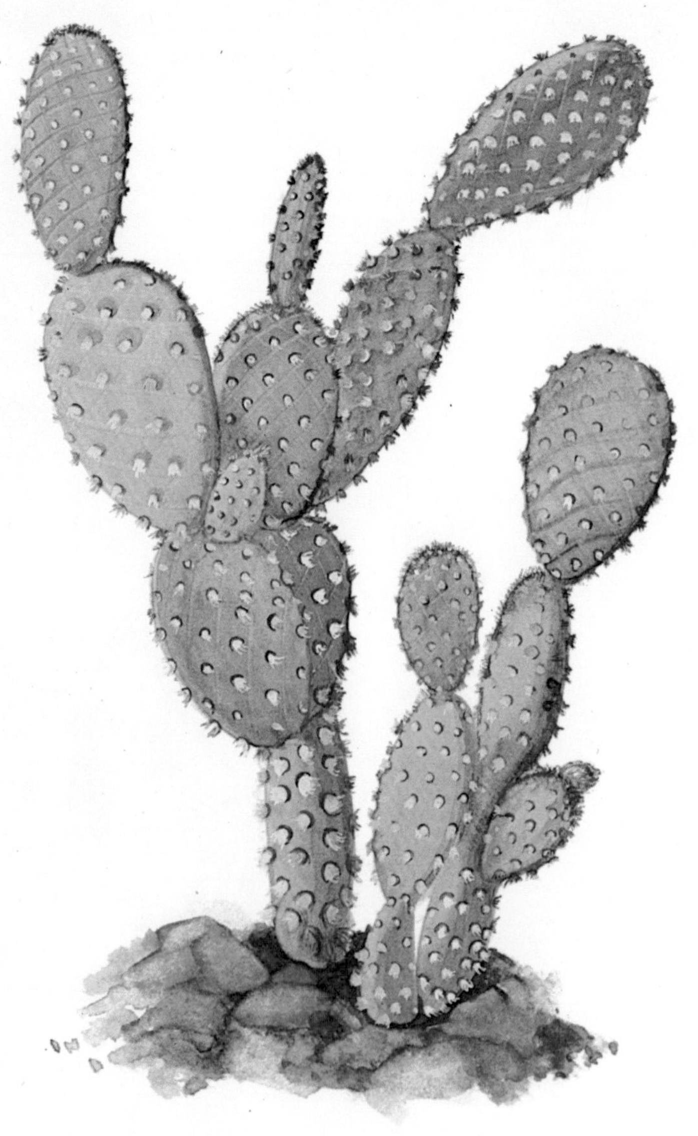

# *Opuntia microdasys*

## Bunny Ears

Northern Mexico is the original home of the illustrated cactus, a characteristic member of this large genus numbering some 250 species.

It is a jointed, rather tall, shrub-like cactus that grows to a height of 60 to 100 cm (24 to 40 in) in cultivation. The individual joints are about 15 cm (6 in) long and 10 cm (4 in) wide, covered with regularly spaced areoles from which grow tufts of short barbed bristles (glochids). The flowers are numerous, 4 to 5 cm (1 ½ to 2 in) long, and vivid yellow turning to red as they fade. The elliptic fruits, about 4.5 cm (1¾ in) long, are coloured violet red and contain a large number of seeds.

*Opuntia microdasys,* the type species, has golden-yellow glochids and is accordingly known as the golden opuntia; the widely cultivated variety *O. microdasys albispina* has white glochids. This variety also includes a miniature form (*minima*) which is a paler green and is less than half as large.

Opuntias are veritable symbols of the regions where they grow. In some parts of Mexico they comprise more than half the existing vegetation, mostly due to the fact that they multiply readily, both by means of seeds and detached joints. This proved to be a catastrophe in Australia where they were introduced and where they had no natural enemies to curb their rapid spread. The problem was solved by bringing in pests that would keep their number within reasonable bounds.

Opuntias, of course, also have their good points. Their fruits are edible and very popular in Central America. In some species even the whole joints are edible. It is not only the poorest Indians who eat them, as sometimes stated in reference books; recipes for making tasty dishes from opuntias may be found in some of the best cookery books.

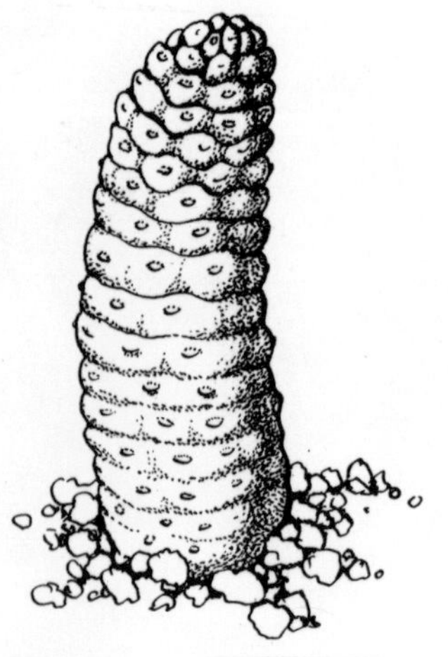

*Opuntia strobiliformis* is now classed in the genus *Tephrocactus.* It forms dense cushions

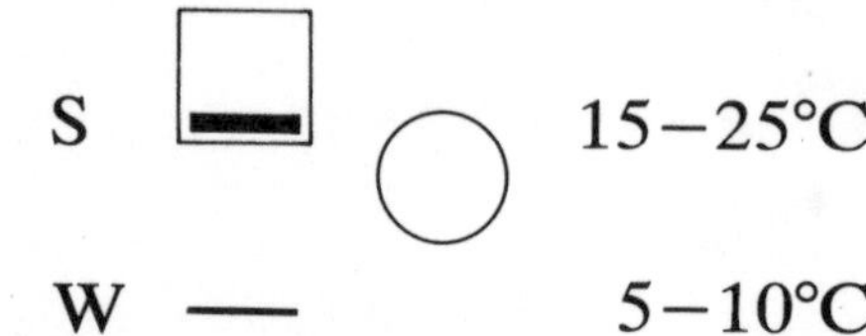

# Rebutia senilis

The Province of Salta in Argentina is the home of the illustrated *Rebutia senilis*. All the approximately 20 known species of the genus are native to northern Argentina and Bolivia.

*Rebutia senilis* is barely 8 cm (3 in) high and only a little less broad. The spines are many, numbering some 25, about 3 cm ($1^{1}/_{8}$ in) long and pure white. The flowers, usually several at one time, are carmine red and measure about 3.5 cm ($1^{1}/_{4}$ in) across. A noteworthy characteristic is that they are self-pollinating.

Various differently coloured forms of this species are often encountered in cultivation, chiefly: *Rebutia senilis lilacino-rosea* – with pale lilac-rose flowers; *R. s. kesselringiana* – with pure yellow flowers; *R. s. iseliniana* – with orange flowers, and *R. s. aurescens* – with pure red flowers.

In the wild rebutias grow on stony slopes together with grasses and low shrubs and their natural environment may be simulated in cultivation. Start with a relatively large dish and in this put low species of sedges, such as New Zealand sedges which require dry and cool conditions in winter, separating their underground roots by large flat stones. A suitable shrub to include in the arrangement is one of the lower species of *Baccharis* of the Compositae family. This natural-looking arrangement may be supplemented with a plant that is decorative for only a short period such as zephyranthes of the Amaryllidaceae family, which is often found together with cacti in semi-deserts and which flowers when the cacti are just beginning to 'awaken'.

*Rhipsalis houlletiana*

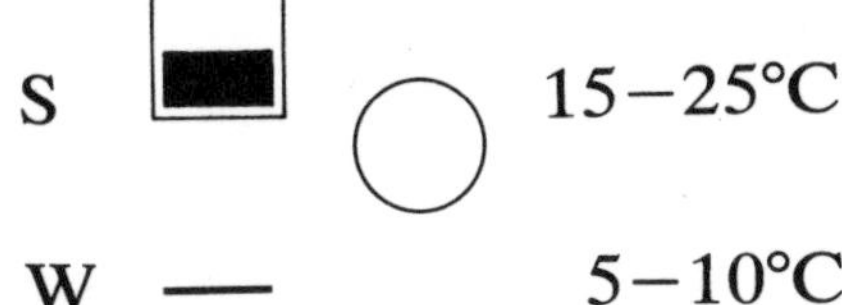

S 15–25°C

W — 5–10°C

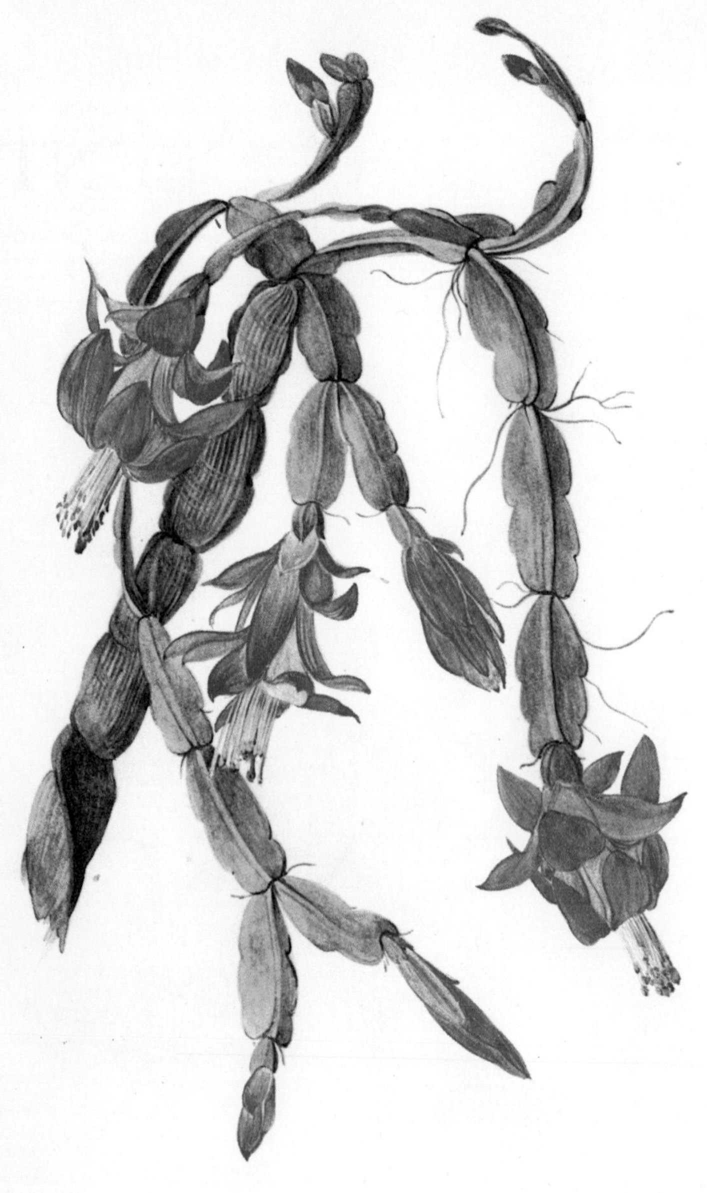

# *Zygocactus truncatus*

## Christmas Cactus

The Christmas cactus needs no introduction for it is one of the most widely cultivated of plants. It is native to the mountains of the State of Rio de Janeiro in Brazil, where it grows as an epiphyte on trees and shrubs or as a petrophyte on stones, but always in the partial shade of tall trees. For this reason even in cultivation, unlike other cacti, it does not tolerate full sun.

Rising from the short woody stem are richly branched shoots composed of flat, leaf-like joints. These are of widely diverse shape – in the type species there are 2 to 4 teeth on the narrower edge of each joint. Nowadays, forms with very sharp, pronounced, large teeth as well as ones with smooth-edged joints are cultivated. The flowers are zygomorphic, 6 to 8 cm (2¼ to 3 in) long, and pinkish red in the type species; in cultivars the colour ranges from white through salmon to violet red.

Though it may be grown as an epiphyte, Christmas cactus cultivars do better in a soil that is sandy and light but at the same time rich. John Innes potting compost No. 1 with extra sharp sand added would be suitable.

Growers often complain that the plants do not flower. Usually the reason is that they do not provide them with the two rest periods that zygocacti require. One is approximately a three-month period from August till October (or November) and the second is after flowering has finished, in February to March. At both these times the temperature should be lowered (in the autumn by placing the plant in the window) and watering reduced to the minimum. The joints produced during the current year will thus 'ripen'; then in late November, when the buds are visible, the plant should be moved to a warmer spot and watering resumed, also syringing. After flowering the temperature should again be reduced and water withheld altogether.

Christmas cactus may be propagated readily by detaching the joints, which will quickly form roots in moist sand.

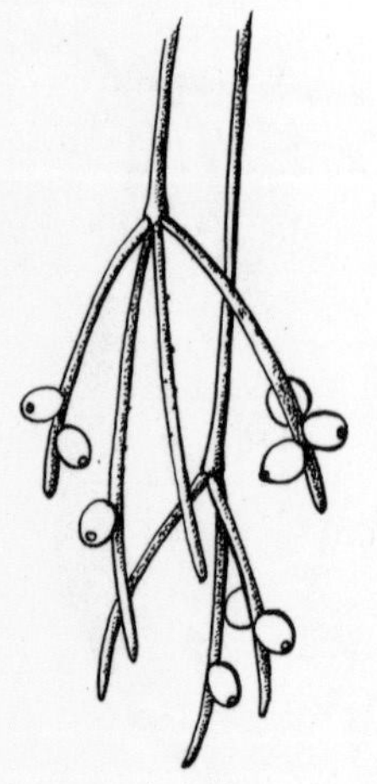

*Rhipsalis cassutha* is the only cactus to be found in other places as well as the American continent; it is widespread from Africa to Ceylon

**See text**

# SUCCULENTS

# *Adromischus cristatus*

## Crinkleleaf Plant

This section deals with plants similar to cacti in that they are also succulent but which belong to various other families. Here, too, succulence enables the plants to survive when there is a shortage of water. Other similar forms of adaptation on the part of some succulents is the absence of leaves and a globose body, which makes them practically indistinguishable from cacti (for example *Euphorbia obesa* and *E. horrida*). In other plants the leaves are thickened and covered with a thick cuticle, sometimes also with waxy layers or thick hairs – all adaptations limiting the evaporation of water.

Cacti are a typical family of the American continent. Other succulents may be found throughout the world; most, however, are distributed in the Cape Province region, Madagascar and the Canary Islands.

The genus *Adromischus* embraces 52 species found chiefly in southern and south-west Africa. Many are shrub-like, but very small, often only several centimetres (a few inches) high.

*Adromischus cristatus* is one of the hardiest members of the genus. It is a small plant, about 8 cm(3 in) across, with a short woody stem and a rosette of stiff, succulent leaves that are wavy at the tip. The colour is grey green. The stem often bears numerous aerial roots. Several small flowers coloured greenish white, sometimes pinkish, are produced on a stalk about 20 cm (8 in) long from July to September.

For successful growth the plant should be put in a warm and sunny spot. Reference books often state that it needs cool conditions in winter, but this is not a must – it will survive even in a warm room. The compost should be very free-draining, best of all a mixture of loam, sand and stone rubble; feed should be applied regularly in summer.

Related species are also lovely, in particular *Adromischus maculatus* with long reddish-brown markings on the leaves; *A. marianae* with leaves spotted the same colour; *A. poellnitzianus* and *A. trigynus*. They are, however, slightly more tender than the illustrated species and should be provided with cool conditions in winter.

*Adromischus cooperi* from South Africa is only about 5 cm (2 in) high

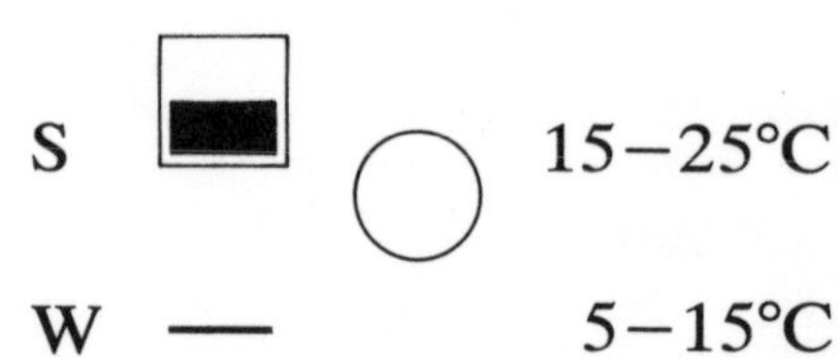

# *Agave victoriae-reginae*

## Queen Agave

Anyone who has travelled in Mexico will never forget the stony semi-deserts dotted with *Yucca, Nolina, Beaucarnea* and *Agave*. Some 200 species of the latter genus are to be found there, ranging from 'dwarfs' several tens of centimetres (a few feet) high to veritable 'giants' measuring about 2.5 m (8 ft). Agaves, of course, are also of economic value, use being made of the fibres from the leaves, called sisal, and of the sap, which is fermented to give pulque and after distillation the well-known intoxicating beverage tequila. They may be encountered in every suitable place, growing in whole plantations or at least in belts marking the boundaries between separate tracts of land; such a 2-m- (6-ft-) high barbed fence is a formidable barrier. Flowering plants are a spectacular sight with their huge branched spikes of yellow, green or white blossoms, often towering several metres (yards) into the air. When they fade the whole plant dies, but not before making several offshoots.

The illustrated species is one of the most beautiful. It is relatively small, mature plants measuring 50 to 70 cm (20 to 28 in) in diameter at the most. The leaves are arranged in a dense rosette. They are green with white stripes, smooth-edged and furnished with one long plus two short spines at the end. *A. victoriae-reginae* is native to the Nuevo León region in northern Mexico.

Cultivation is not difficult. Like most succulents it requires plenty of space for the underground parts and should thus be put in a large container filled with a good, nourishing compost – a mixture of loam, sand and stone rubble. A thick layer of gravel on the bottom of the container will ensure good drainage. Feed should be supplied in sufficient quantity during the growth period, best of all once a week when watering.

Like most plants of this genus, *Agave victoriae-reginae* is generally grown indoors throughout the year and not moved outdoors in summer. It must be provided with a rest period in winter when the temperature should be reduced.

Though it is not a large plant, the flower stem, which develops only under optimum conditions and after many years, measures up to 4 m (13 ft) in height.

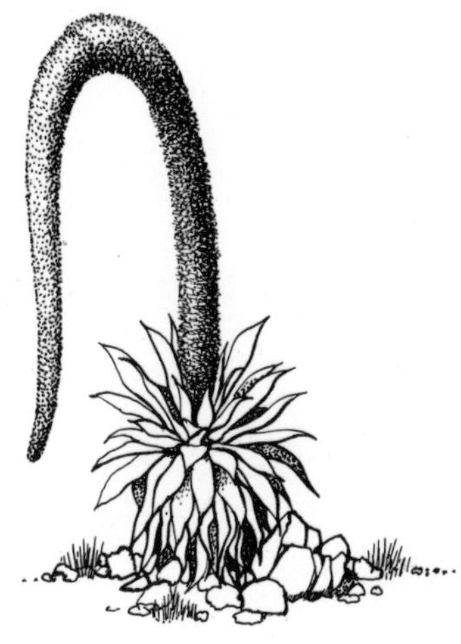

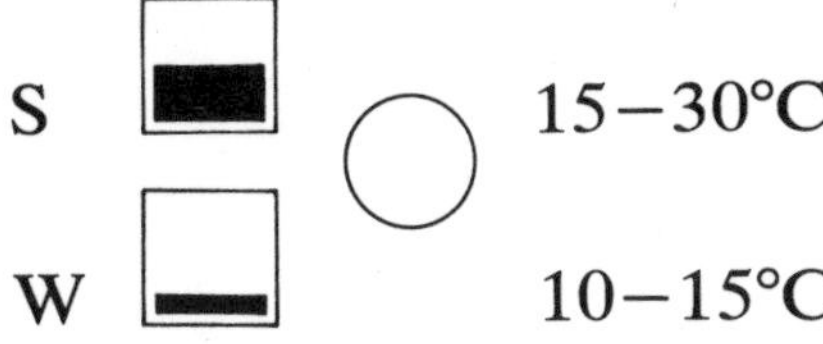


15–30°C

10–15°C

*Agave attenuata* from Mexico is noted for its thick, up to 3 m (10 ft) long flower spikes

# *Aloe variegata*

## Tiger Aloe

Just as agaves determine the look of the landscape in certain arid sections of Central America, so aloes are the characteristic plants of South Africa's arid country. Externally the two plants are very similar and the one is often mistaken for the other by the layman. How can they be distinguished?

Aloe belongs to the Liliaceae family, agave is a member of the Agavaceae family. Agave has leaf rosettes that are generally stemless, those of aloe are usually carried on a short stem. The leaves of agave are stiff and contain numerous fibres, those of aloe tend to break readily. Aloe may produce flowers every year; these are yellow, orange or red, rarely white. The inflorescence is never more than 1 m (3 ft) high, the flowers are arranged in a spiral, and when are spent, hang mouth downard. Agave flowers only once during its life-cycle, the inflorescence is much taller, and the flowers, arranged in clusters at the tips of the branches, face upward.

The similarity between these two different genera from two different families is not accidental – they are both found in the same type of environment and both have developed the same adaptations. Cultivation is thus the same for both.

The illustrated species is one of the best known and is native to Cape Province. The leaves, unlike those of most members of the genus, form sessile rosettes and are spirally arranged on a short stem. The whole plant attains a height of about 30 cm (1 ft). If it can be put in a cool, well-lit spot in winter, it will regularly produce flowers in February and March. It tolerates warm conditions in winter but in this case it rarely flowers.

Other species are also frequently encountered in cultivation, for example *Aloe aristata, A. eru, A. striata* and *A. arborescens.* All have similar requirements and cultivation is thus the same for all.

Succulents, of course, may also be planted together to create attractive and striking arrangements. Such arrangements may include members of different genera found growing together in the wild, for example *Aloe aristata* with *Stapelia ambiqua* and *Mesembryanthemum nobile.* You can choose any number of combinations according to your taste and fancy.

*Aloe mitriformis* from Cape Province has leaves about 15 cm (6 in) long

*Aloe suprafoliata* is a beautiful plant in the juvenile stage. It is native to Swaziland

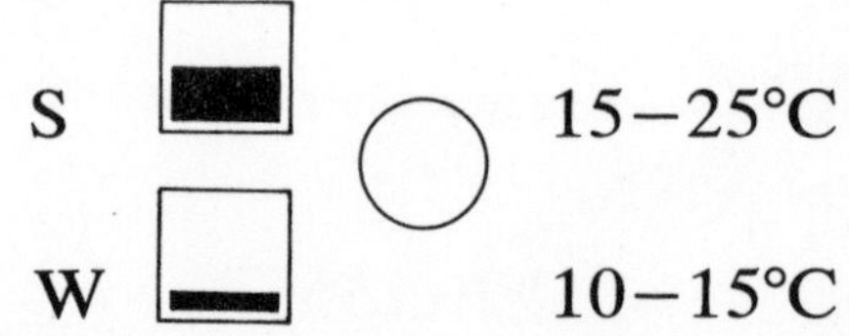

# *Caralluma europaea*

This plant takes us back to the stem succulents. The approximately 130 species of the genus *Caralluma* inhabit dry localities from South Africa through north Africa and the Island of Socotra to India. The illustrated species is found on the Island of Lampedusa in the Mediterranean, its range extending to the northern coast of Africa and the variety *Caralluma europaea confusa* marking the northern limits of the genus on the southern coast of Spain.

The square stems, which are very succulent, form a small shrub about 10 to 15 cm (4 to 6 in) high. The small flowers, only about 1 cm (1/2 in) across, and coloured brown, streaked with red, brown and yellow, are produced in summer. They are not particularly attractive and have an unpleasant scent, but there is no denying that they are interesting. Besides, a plant need not have bright, showy flowers to be attractive, which caralluma definitely is.

Carallumas are very undemanding plants. In southern India they may be encountered on sun-baked stone rubble where one will find nothing else but a few practically dry acacias, several clumps of dry grass and the tree-like spurge, *Euphorbia trigona.* Dry heat and full sun in a window are thus manna to this modest plant and certainly not an environment in which it is merely capable of surviving. If it can be provided with cool conditions in winter then these are strongly recommended; however, it also tolerates warm overwintering, but in this case it should be placed as close to the source of light as possible.

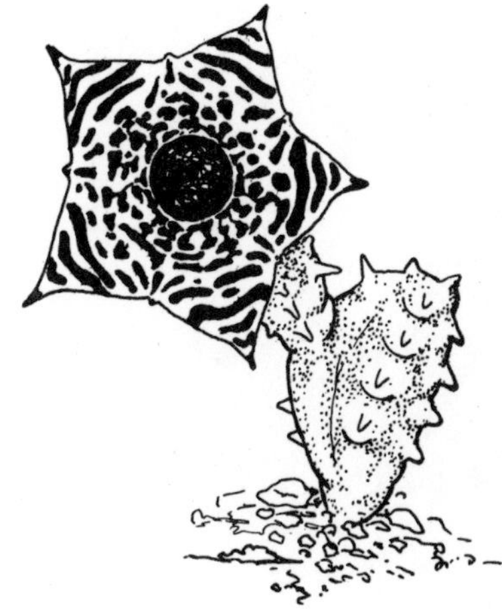

10–25°C

*Huernia zebrina* has the same requirements as stapelia

# *Cotyledon undulata*

## Silver Crown, Silver Ruffles

Succulents also include amongst their number plants for the more experienced grower. The genus *Cotyledon* is definitely not one for the beginner for it includes rarities, that, though beautiful, are very sensitive.

The approximately 45 species that make up the genus are distributed chiefly in South Africa. They are divided into two basic groups. The first has a thickened stem and small deciduous leaves and includes, for example, *Cotyledon bucholziana, C. reticulata, C. pearsonii* and *C. ventricosa* (the last two are extremely poisonous). The second group, which includes the illustrated species, has larger leaves with a thick chalky bloom.

In the wild *C. undulata* forms branching shrublets, in cultivation usually a single stem about 50 cm (20 in) high. The leaves are up to 12 cm (4¾ in) long and very wavy on the margin. The bloom is particularly evident on the margin, which is snow white. The flowers, only about 2.5 cm (1 in) long and coloured golden orange, are carried on a stem that is about 35 cm (14 in) long.

Though in the wild (in Cape Province) *Cotyledon undulata* grows on laterite soils, in cultivation it is better to provide a lighter but nourishing mix such as John Innes potting compost No. 1 with extra sharp sand added. It also does well in crushed brick, with nutrients being provided with the water (hydroponic cultivation). This has the added advantage that the plant need not be transplanted and there is far less danger of rubbing off the beautiful but delicate chalky bloom. This could also be damaged by water and so the plants should always be watered from the base and never syringed.

In winter the temperature must be reduced but at the same time the plant should be provided with as much light as possible. If one is successful with this plant, then it is worth trying to propagate it, either by cuttings or simply by inserting whole leaves in a sand and peat compost. This is easier and not as lengthy as propagation from seeds.

*C. undulata mucronata* is a pretty variety which has smaller leaves with a reddish-brown margin.

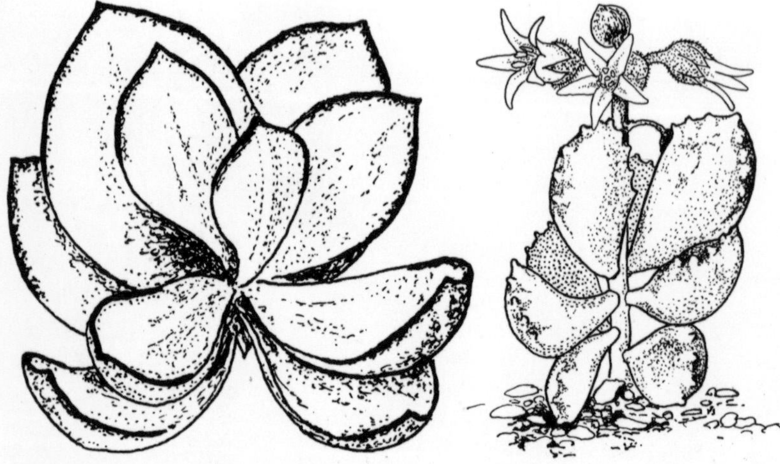

*Cotyledon orbiculata:* the silvery-white colour of the leaves and the narrow red margin make a striking contrast

*Cotyledon tomentosa* has leaves of about 2.5 cm (1 in) in length

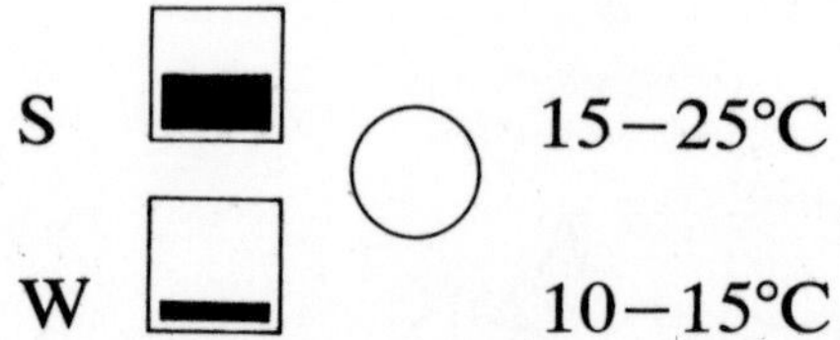

# *Euphorbia horrida*

Everyone has seen spurges, both at the florist's and in the wild. More than two thousand species are to be found throughout the world on all the continents. Most are 'normal' herbs or shrubs but quite a few, more exactly about 440 species, have developed into succulents as an adaptation to their environment.

Some are very common in households, for example *Euphorbia milii,* the Crown of Thorns, with striking scarlet 'flowers' (these, however, are not petals but scarlet bracts surrounding the actual, inconspicuous flowers). Other succulent spurges, however, are still waiting to be 'discovered' for room decoration; to date they are more likely to be found in botanical gardens than at the florist's. One such plant is the very undemanding species from Cape Province shown in the illustration. It looks like a cactus, because the body is divided into approximately 12 ribs with toothed edges from which grow long, hard thorns. The plant is a slow grower so there is no need to fear that it will soon reach the dimensions it does with age in the wild or as do the decades-old specimens. In botanical gardens it may reach a height of 1 m (3 ft), but these plants are several decades old. In Cape Province it grows at elevations of approximately 1,100 m (3,620 ft) in rock crevices, between stones and on steep slopes amidst low bushes, generally in groups.

In cultivation *Euphorbia horrida* is a very rewarding plant that tolerates the dry and warm atmosphere of the home. In winter it has a rest period, at which time the temperature should be reduced, but this can be done without if the plant is provided with plenty of light. Propagation can be by cuttings, but the better method is by means of seeds.

If you would like to enlarge your collection of 'cactus-like' spurges by adding small, spineless specimens, two similar species – *Euphorbia obesa* and *E. meloformis* are ideal. Both grow to a height of about 10 to 15 cm (4 to 6 in) and are native to the same region as the illustrated plant, which means that they have the same requirements in cultivation, in other words they are equally undemanding.

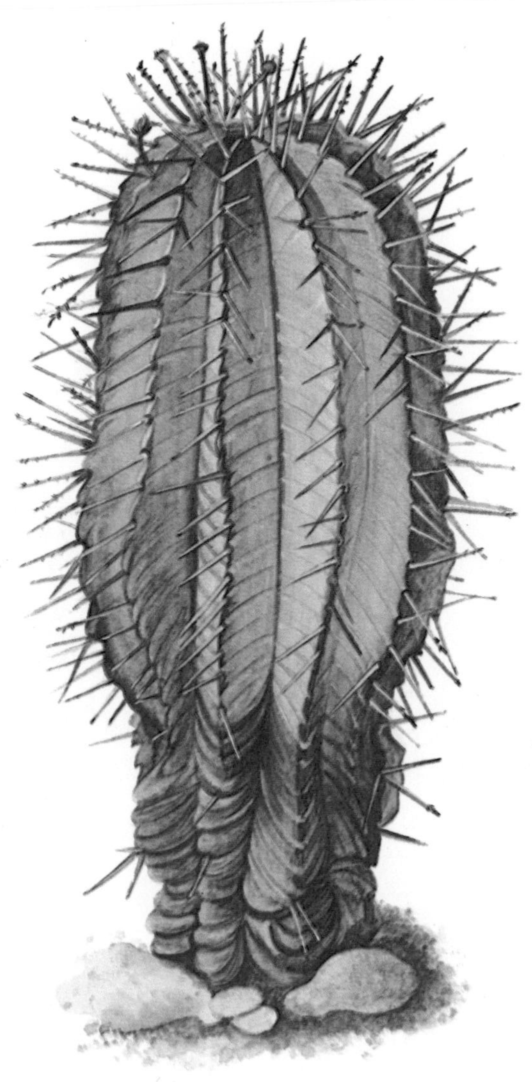

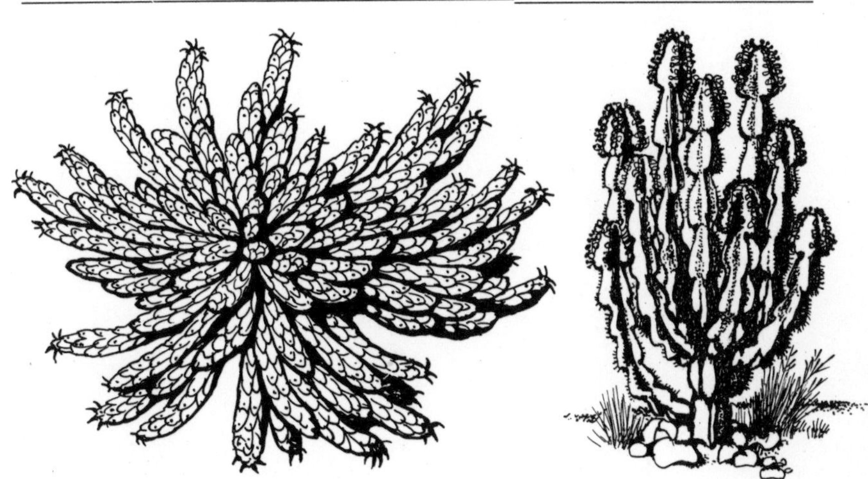

*Euphorbia bergeri* grows to a height of about 15 cm (6 in); it is native to Cape Province

*Euphorbia cooperi* grows to a height of 5 m (16 ft) in the wild in South Africa

10–25°C

# Faucaria lupina

If you have a warm, dry, sunny flat and room on the window-sill, then the plant shown in the illustration will prove a welcome addition to your household.

The genus *Faucaria* embraces 33 species indigenous to the deserts and semi-deserts of South Africa. They are relatively small plants with succulent leaves which have fine teeth on the edges curved towards the centre of the plant, making them look like the open jaws of a beast of prey (hence the names by which it is known such as tiger's chaps and cat's chaps).

The illustrated species has a short firm stem which sends up deep green leaves to a height of about 15 cm (6 in). In time it forms a clump of plants so that it nicely fills the dish in which it is grown. The golden-yellow flowers which grow from the centre of the rosette are surprisingly large, up to 3.5 cm (1¼ in) in diameter.

All species of *Faucaria* are undemanding plants requiring only nourishing well-drained compost, such as John Innes potting compost No. 1 with additional sand, and a spot with plenty of sun. The growth period is relatively short; water should be provided from late May and when flowering is finished (in August or September) limited to the minimum, only to keep the compost from drying out completely. Ample ventilation is very important.

Propagation is not difficult – usually by division, though plants may also be multiplied from seed, which has good powers of germination. In the latter instance, however, the grower must have a great deal of patience, for the plants will not produce flowers until after about three years.

Dish arrangements containing *Faucaria* and other members of the same family from the genera *Pleiospilos, Lampranthus* and *Lithops,* which have the same requirements in cultivation, make a striking display. A word of warning, however; water must be definitely limited to the bare minimum for several months, otherwise the plants may be completely destroyed, even though the grower means well.

*Faucaria tuberculosa*

S 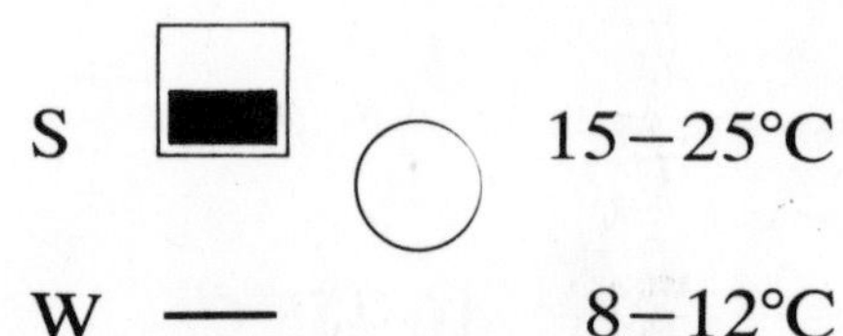 15–25°C

W — 8–12°C

# *Fenestraria rhopalophylla*

## Baby Toes

The adaptations developed by certain plants are sometimes truly fantastic. Perhaps the most remarkable method of adapting to excessive sun is by remaining underground and having the light affect the leaves not from outside but from the inside. How is this achieved? The plant's leaf tips, the only parts emerging above the surface, are blunt and furnished with translucent panes or 'windows' through which the light penetrates to the colourless tissues inside and is dispersed onto the layer of cells containing chlorophyll that line the walls of the 'light shaft'.

This phenomenon may be found in many species, growing chiefly in South Africa but belonging to different families. Window plants, as they are called, include even the South American peperomias (only a few species) that have several slit- or dot-like translucent 'windows' in the thick skin covering the leaves. The method of light dispersal is the same.

Window plants are inhabitants of sun-baked, stony plains. As has already been said they grow underground and several 'windows' are all that can be seen on the surface.

In cultivation, where it is impossible to provide them with even a fraction of the light intensity to which they are exposed in the wild, they grow normally above ground.

*Fenestraria rhopalophylla* is a window plant and is even named thus in Latin (*fenestra* = window). It grows together with another species of the same genus in South Africa. It forms a ground rosette of 5-cm-(2-in-) long leaves and the flowers, which appear in September or October, are amazingly large – about 5 cm (2 in) in diameter. The other species, *F. aurantiaca,* has even larger flowers, about 7 cm (2¾ in) across and coloured golden orange.

Fenestraria should be grown in a very porous soil but one that contains ample nutrients, such as John Innes potting compost No. 1 with extra sand added. It is readily propagated from seed, developing into flower-bearing plants in about two or three years.

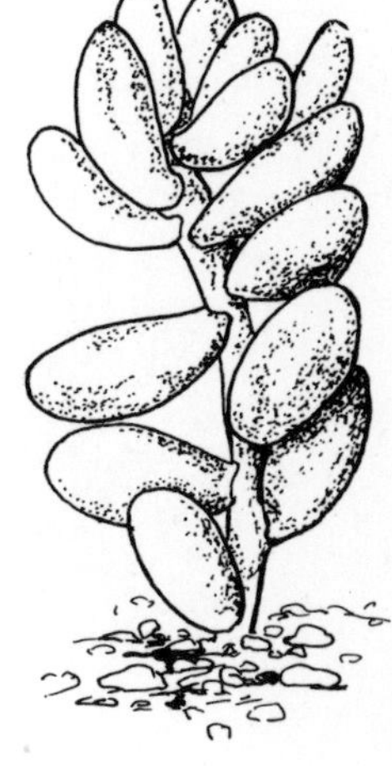

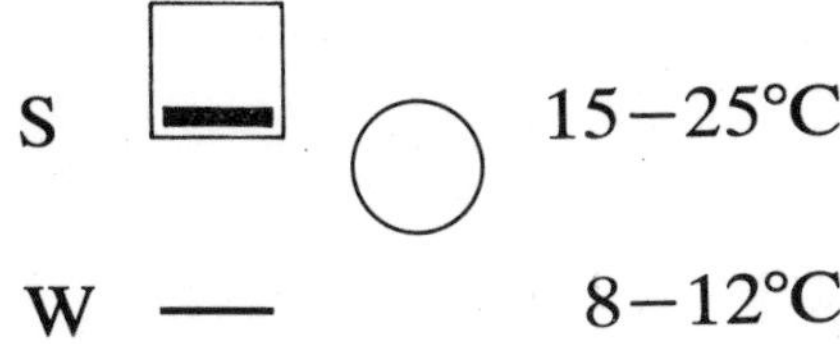


*Sedum craigii* is a white-flowering succulent from the Chihuahua desert

# *Gasteria maculata*

Gasterias are plants commonly found in many homes, for they are easy to grow and their leaves serve as decoration throughout the year.

The approximately 70 species of this genus are indigenous to Africa, found mostly in Cape Province. They are very similar and readily cross-breed so that in cultivation one generally encounters hybrids whose parentage would be difficult to determine even for a botanist, let alone the amateur.

The leaves of *Gasteria maculata* are about 20 cm (8 in) long and arranged in two rows, sometimes spirally. The surface is flat or slightly convex, smooth, dark green with pale spots that are pinkish in the sun. Mature, robust specimens reach a height of about 40 cm (16 in). The flowers, which generally appear in spring but may be produced at any time of the year, are borne on about 30-cm-(1-ft-) long stem. They are relatively large and their shape and coloration is evident from the illustration.

As has already been said, gasterias have no special requirements and are easy to grow. The soil should be a fairly heavy, nourishing mix, for example a blend of compost soil and loam with leaf mould plus some sand, though any packaged compost for house plants available at the florist's will do. Unlike other succulents in this section they do not like direct sunlight; though they tolerate it, they do better in partial shade. However, one may come across lovely plants that have been grown in a south-east window and equally good ones that have been grown in full shade. A lower temperature in winter is desirable but not a must for successful cultivation.

Propagation is easy – either by leaf cuttings or by seeds, though in the latter case the resulting offspring may not be uniform for cultivated plants are mostly hybrids.

*Gasteria obtusifolia*

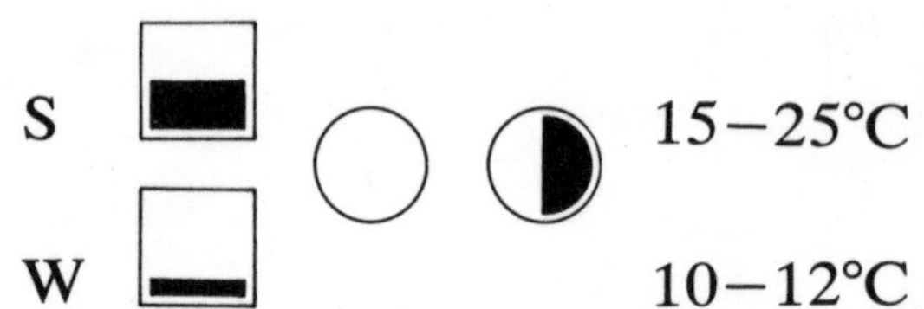

# *Haworthia fasciata*

## Zebra Haworthia

Like the preceding species, *Haworthia fasciata* is one of the basic plants of every collection of succulents, a plant that can be grown even by children and, in fact, a good one to start with and awaken their interest in this fascinating hobby.

Once again, this is a succulent from South Africa, chiefly from Cape Province. The genus embraces some 155 lovely species, many of which (including the illustrated species) grow on dry, stony banks in the partial shade of low xerophilous shrubs and clumps of grass, while others are found in desert or semi-desert localities amidst stones. The members of this second group have developed the same adaptation to their environment as the Mesembryanthemaceae family – the leaf tips are blunt and furnished with translucent 'windows'. A typical example is *H. truncata,* which in cultivation likewise grows with the entire leaves above the surface.

Cultivation of *Haworthia fasciata* and other striped or 'pearl'-bedecked plants is not at all difficult. One thing that must be kept in mind, however, is that they have two rest periods – one in winter, when the temperature should be reduced if possible (but this is not a must), the other in summer, from May till August, when the plant should be put in a warm, well-lit spot and watered only occasionally. The two growth periods are accordingly from March to May and from late August to mid-November, when the plants should be watered amply and regularly. If possible this species should be grown in diffused light – too much sun is damaging and so is a dry atmosphere.

Propagation is easy – by detaching the side rosettes produced at the base of adult plants which are about 8 to 10 cm (3 to 4 in) high.

**See text**

*Haworthia retusa* from Cape Province barely reaches 5 cm (2 in) in height

# Lithops volkii

Other inhabitants of the stony wastes of South Africa are the 'stone plants' or 'living pebbles' – members of the genera *Lithops, Conophytum* and *Pleiospilos*. All are 'window plants'. Their leaves are extremely succulent, round or cylindrical, with blunt tips furnished with windows in the form of irregular marbling or small translucent dots. In general they are not coloured green but tinted red, brown, bronze or grey as protection against the sun. The cells containing chlorophyll and carrying on the process of photosynthesis are located inside the body behind a layer of cell tissue that disperses the light.

Because these are very small, often even miniature plants, a great many can be grown in a small space and thus are ideal for the collector. However, they are very sensitive, requiring not only full sun and cool but well-lit conditions in winter but, first and foremost, tolerating no mistake in watering.

Most of the 70 species of the genus *Lithops* have their growth period in early spring, from February to April. The groove in the body opens and from this grows a small new plant which takes its food and water from the old one. At this point most beginners start watering the plant, thereby destroying it completely. In fact, it should be watered only lightly, just so the compost is moistened and dries out again right away, from late May until early September, or at most October – in other words during the period of relative rest. After that, water should again be withheld for about 7 months. Only thus will the grower be rewarded with a thriving plant that will produce attractive large flowers. These appear between June and October, depending on the species.

The compost should be very free-draining, sandy and stony, with an addition of leaf mould.

*Lithops deborei*

**See text**

# Rochea coccinea

The several preceding species were of interest from the ecological and biological viewpoint but not much can be said for them in the way of room decoration. However, the following plants make up for this.

*Rochea coccinea* is one of the 3 species that constitute this genus native to South Africa, where it grows high up in the mountains in sandy, well-drained localities in the partial shade of taller shrubs.

This small shrub with succulent leaves bears dense, cymose clusters of red flowers in April. After flowering has finished the plant should be moved outdoors to the garden, or else placed in an open sunny window. The tips should be pinched out in late June to promote branching as well as growth. Feed should be supplied regularly but watering must not be too copious. In winter, the plant should be put either in a cool room or in an unheated corridor. In modern houses it is generally impossible to provide ideal winter temperatures, that is 3 to 5°C (38 to 41°F). In early spring, from about March onward, the plants may be propagated by taking 5- to 7-cm- (2- to 2¾-in-) long cuttings from the tips and inserting them in a peat and sand mixture in a warm room, where they will quickly form roots.

Other popular genera of this family may be grown in the same way, requiring only slightly warmer conditions in winter, for example *Crassula portulacea* and *Kalanchoe blossfeldiana.*

Rochea and the other mentioned genera should be grown in a light mixture such as a blend of peat, leaf mould and sand, or one of the soilless composts. Feed should be supplied only in summer.

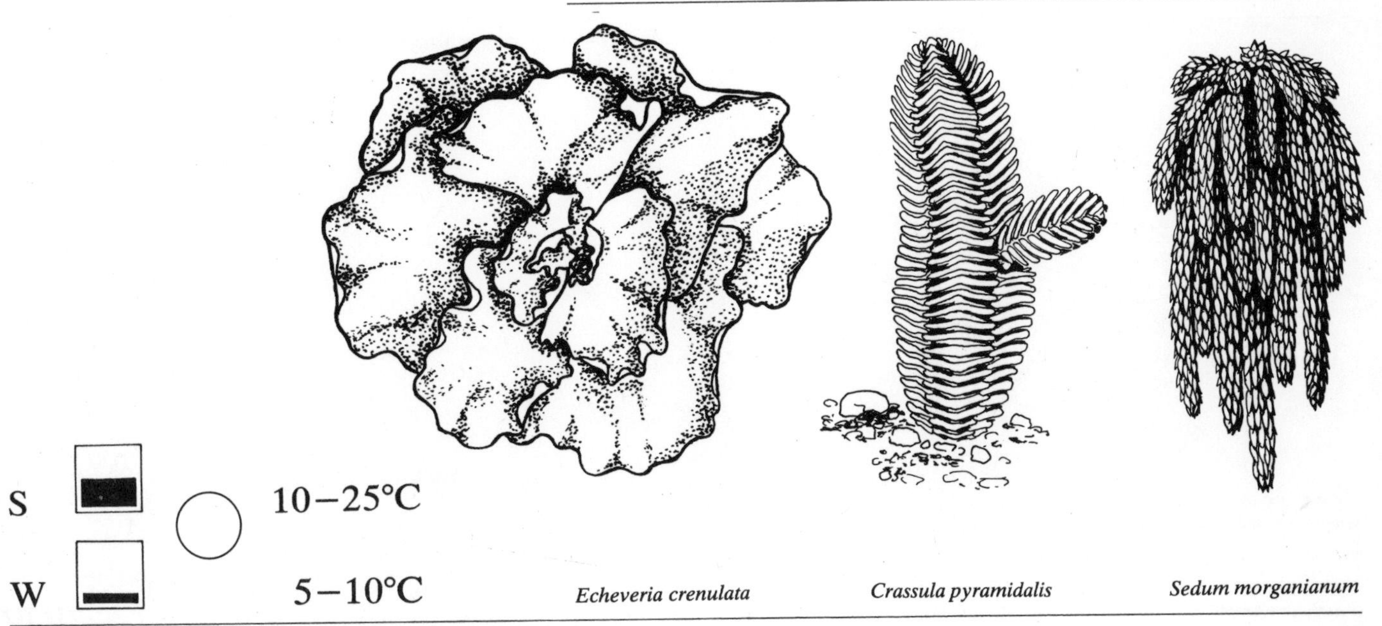


*Echeveria crenulata* *Crassula pyramidalis* *Sedum morganianum*

# *Stapelia variegata*

## Carrion Flower

The last plant in this section belongs to the popular and widely-grown genus *Stapelia.* The more than 100 species are mostly native to South Africa. They form clumps of stems either entirely without leaves or only with rudimentary leaves.

The illustrated species is one of the commonest. The clumps of stems are barely 10 cm (4 in) high and coloured pale green or grey green. The buds, which grow on short stalks from the base of the plant, are large and pale green and develop into flowers up to 8 cm (3 in) across, coloured greenish yellow with brownish-red spots.

More attractive is the larger *Stapelia grandiflora,* which has quadrangular stems up to 30 cm (1 ft) high with rudimentary leaves on the edges. The flowers are brownish red, up to 20 cm (8 in) across, and covered with long hairs over the entire surface. Equally long hairs cover the flowers of *S. hirsuta,* a smaller species, which are coloured an undefinable blend of red, brown and violet.

In the wild, stapelias are often found growing in sandy areas at the edge of alluvial deposits and on landslides as well as on stony banks and rock fractures, where they form large cushions.

Propagation is very simple. In the home the plants are usually multiplied by vegetative means – by breaking or cutting off one of the stems. The cut should be left to dry in the sun for several days and may be dusted with crushed charcoal to prevent it from rotting. The cutting should then be inserted in dry sandy compost where it will form roots. Water should be applied carefully but not until one month later.

Stapelias may be also be readily propagated from seeds, which are produced in great numbers in follicles. They are flat and furnished with a long pappus. Germination takes place within several days, but a high temperature and moist atmosphere are necessary.

Stapelias should be grown in a sandy compost with humus and stone rubble.

*Kalanchoe tomentosa (K. pilosa)* is from Madagascar. The white tomentum on the leaves has earned it the nickname of panda plant

*Stapelia gigantea*

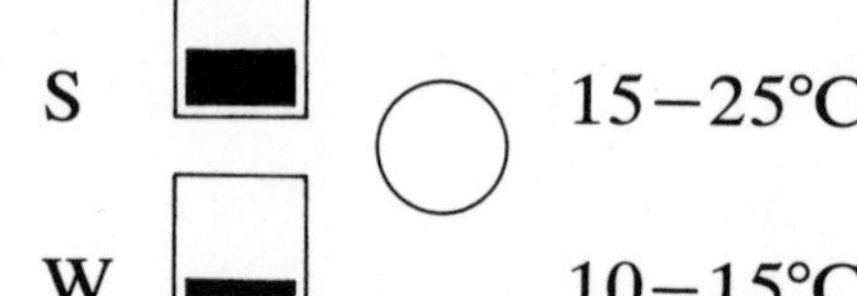

# PALUDARIUM PLANTS

# *Acorus gramineus* 'Aureovariegatus'

## Sweet Flag

South-east Asia is the home of this small species, or rather form, often found in reference books under the name *Acorus pusillus* or *A. gramineus pusillus*. It grows in the mountains at elevations of about 1,000 m (3,300 ft) on stones in mountain streams as well as on rocks sprayed by waterfalls, but definitely not in mud as is generally stated, though it can, in fact, be grown in mud.

Two cultivars are generally encountered in cultivation – the one shown in the illustration with green and yellow striped foliage and 'Argenteostriatus' which is longitudinally striped white instead of yellow. The plants are 20 to 40 cm (8 to 16 in) high. The leaves, growing from a short rhizome, are not divided into a stalk and blade but are sword-shaped.

The flowers are not particularly striking – the spadix is yellow green and grows up and outward from the stem, the spathe is green, reminiscent of a leaf, and likewise grows upward. The fruit is a red, many-seeded berry. As a rule, neither flowers nor fruits are produced in cultivation.

The entire genus contains only two species, the one described and *Acorus calamus,* the common sweet flag found growing on the margins of European ponds. It, too, is native to tropical Asia but has become naturalized in Europe, where it was first introduced by Clusius in 1574 – at the Vienna botanical gardens.

These small plants should be grown in a paludarium located in a conservatory, porch or glassed-in terrace, for they appreciate cooler conditions in winter. They may also be grown outdoors by a pool but then they should be covered with a thick layer of leaves and evergreen twigs in winter to protect them from frost. If the paludarium is located in a warm room and fitted with fluorescent light then this species may also pass the winter in warm conditions.

Propagation is by division of the clumps, and the plants should be grown in a mixture of loam and peat.

Flowering *Acorus gramineus*

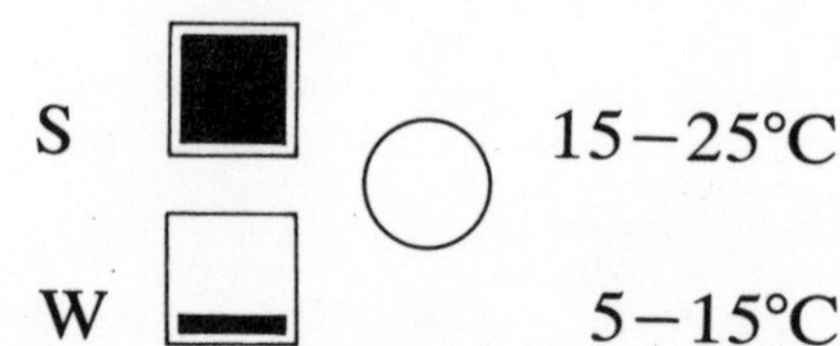

# *Cyperus alternifolius*

## Umbrella Plant

Plants of the Cyperaceae family are well known to everyone and not only to those who grow house plants. Take, for instance, the common sedges. In most cases these are wrongly mistaken for grasses with which they have little in common, apart from appearance. They are more closely related to the rushes (Juncaceae) and are an offshoot of the lily family.

The genus *Cyperus* is a very large one, comprising some 400 species distributed mostly in the tropical and subtropical regions. They are practically always found close to water, though some are xerophilous.

The illustrated *Cyperus alternifolius* is from Madagascar, where it forms almost impenetrable growths on the shores of lakes and water courses. In cultivation it generally reaches a height of 50 to 100 cm (20 to 40 ft) and will form dense clumps if its needs are satisfied.

In the home it may be grown beside or in the shallow water in a paludarium placed in a warm room. The compost must be sufficiently nourishing, composed, for example, of loam mixed with rotted turves, sand and some peat. Alternatively, use John Innes potting compost No. 1. The surface should be covered with a thick layer of sand. The temperature need not be reduced in winter.

Better suited for small pools are *Cyperus haspan,* which is relatively small (50 cm [20 in] at the most) with stems terminated by a thick 'ball' of narrow leaves; or *C. natalensis.* For a large pool use can be made of the classic *Cyperus papyrus,* the famous plant of ancient Egypt, which grows to a height of 2 to 5 m (6 to 16 ft).

Propagation is not difficult. The plants may be divided when they are moved (but they should be moved as little as possible as they will form nice clumps only if left undisturbed) or by cutting off the terminal rosette of leaves together with a piece of stem about 1 cm (1/2 in) long and placing it either on the surface of water or in a muddy compost in a warm propagator, where it will soon form roots.

*Cyperus haspan*

 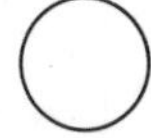  10–30°C

# *Eichhornia crassipes*

## Water Hyacinth

The water hyacinth is thought to be native to tropical America but is nowadays found in all lakes and rivers in the tropics. Though it is a very beautiful plant, it has caused more problems than delight in tropical countries for it spreads very rapidly, thus making water courses unnavigable.

In some places, however, the attitude towards this plant is quite favourable. Round Hanoi, for example, the Vietnamese grow it in ponds enclosed by a floating frame of bamboo to keep the clumps from being scattered by the wind. In these parts eichhornia is important as fodder and practically the only source of food for small Chinese pigs and water buffaloes.

For the European, of course, *Eichhornia crassipes* will remain a lovely plant for room decoration, floating on the surface of water. Its large root system is spread out underwater, and the spongy leaf stalks are arranged in a rosette on the water's surface. The leaf blades are orbicular. The flowers, about 8 cm (3 in) across, are produced throughout the year, but chiefly in late summer and autumn.

The water hyacinth may be grown in a paludarium or aquarium and outdoors in a pool in summer. If cool conditions can be provided in winter (temperature of about 5 to 7°C [41 to 45°F]) the plant should be laid loosely on mud. It tolerates warm overwintering too, but in that case the pool must be provided with artificial illumination. Water hyacinths multiply very rapidly by means of side rosettes.

*Eichhornia azurea*

 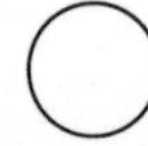

10–25°C (S)
5–7°C (W)

# *Nymphaea* × *daubenyana*

## Water Lily

If you wish to establish a paludarium or own a large pool and are looking for suitable plants to put there you will generally not be satisfied with mere foliage plants but will look for species with attractive flowers, ending up with those whose flowers are the loveliest of all – the tropical water lilies.

The illustrated hybrid, derived from the crossing of *Nymphaea micrantha* (syn. *N. vivipara*) and *N. coerulea,* is perhaps the most suitable for small pools. If it is provided with little nourishment and kept in shallow water then its leaves will remain small, only about 10 cm (4 in) in diameter, and the flowers, barely 3 to 5 cm (1¼ to 2 in) across, will give great pleasure.

Water lilies are very demanding plants as regards food and need many nutrients for full development. The compost should be composed of good loam, compost and sand and to this should be added both organic and inorganic fertilizers. Some well-rotted cow manure may also be put on the bottom of the container in which the rhizome is put after being overwintered in a cool spot in mud or in a plastic bag filled with deep damp moss. The container should not be too small – big enough for a sufficient supply of nutrients for the entire growing season.

This applies chiefly to the larger species, which can be used if you have a large heated pool indoors or in a greenhouse. The available choice is a wide one, two of the best being *Nymphaea capensis zanzibarensis* 'Bagdad' with numerous blue-violet flowers about 15 cm (6 in) across; and *N. colorata* from Dar-es-Salaam in Tanzania, which bears a profusion of pale blue flowers, or its cultivars and hybrids.

The water for all the species and cultivars should be at a temperature of about 25°C (77°F), which in small paludariums may be provided with a standard heating element used in aquariums.

Water lilies may be propagated from seed, which must be fresh, or (in the case of cultivars where the seeds would not come true) by cutting up the strong rhizome. The illustrated hybrid is viviparous, in other words, young plantlets grow from adventitious buds on mature leaves.

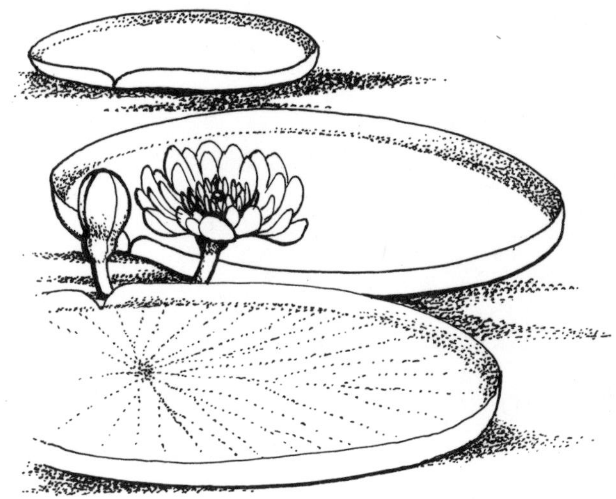

*Victoria regia*

 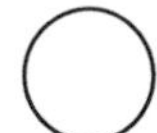

18–30°C (S)
10–15°C (W)

# *Pistia stratiotes*

## Water Lettuce

An attractive paludarium must include plants that float on the water's surface. Mention has already been made of *Eichhornia crassipes,* but the selection is much larger, as you will find by going to a specialist supplier.

If you are setting up a small paludarium in a warm, well-lit to sunny spot, then you should not fail to include the small floating aquatic *Pistia stratiotes,* whose lovely pale green foliage will be a permanent decorative element in the pool. The only member of the genus, it is found throughout the tropical regions of the world, though its native land is tropical America, where it grows chiefly in lowland country (even in slightly brackish water where rivers flow into the sea and form quiet, peaceful lagoons); very occasionally it is found farther south as high up as 1,000 m (3,300 ft) above sea level.

To give one an idea of a natural grouping of plants for a paludarium, listed here are plants that grow together in the wild in the El Farallón Lagoon near Nautla in the state of Veracruz, Mexico: *Cyperus articularis, C. ligularis, Ludwigia* sp., *Nymphaea ampla, Typha dominguensis* and *Pistia stratiotes.*

Naturally other species of the various genera may be used in their stead. Such pools, containing a grouping copied from the wild, are very pretty and natural-looking and furthermore they soon establish a symphathetic balance.

Pistia forms floating rosettes of soft, pale green leaves about 10 to 15 cm (4 to 6 in) wide. The inflorescence is greatly reduced: a whitish hairy spathe encloses a single male and a single female flower, the whole measuring less than 1 cm (½ in).

*Rhektophyllum mirabile*

 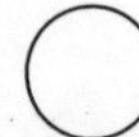 18–30°C

# *Typhonium giganteum*

This plant is not a common species and if you want to grow it you will perhaps have to look about a bit before you track it down. *Typhonium giganteum* is native to China, where it grows in muddy ponds in the vicinity of Peking. The leaves are up to 60 cm (2 ft) high, the blade up to 30 cm (1 ft) long and 15 cm (6 in) wide. The flowers are a striking shape, the spathe being up to 20 cm (8 in) long, and are produced several times from late spring throughout the summer.

In cultivation one may occasionally also come across the slightly larger *Typhonium giganteum giraldii* with flowers coloured almost black.

The genus embraces some 20 species found from India through eastern Asia to Australia and the Pacific islands. Most are rewarding plants in cultivation but those thus grown are usually smaller forms with green or yellow-green flowers.

The only drawback of the illustrated species is that it dies down in autumn, the tuberous rhizome overwintering underground. This characteristic is also to be found amongst a number of other plants that grow in bogs, for example caladium and alocasia, which are cultivated despite this drawback. The rhizome may either be left in the mud or lifted and put in a bag filled with peat and sand and stored dry for the winter, the same as the tubers of caladium. In this way the plant will last a good many years.

The chief requirements of this species are heat and moisture. In a dry atmosphere, for example when it is grown in a pot, it is not likely to survive for long.

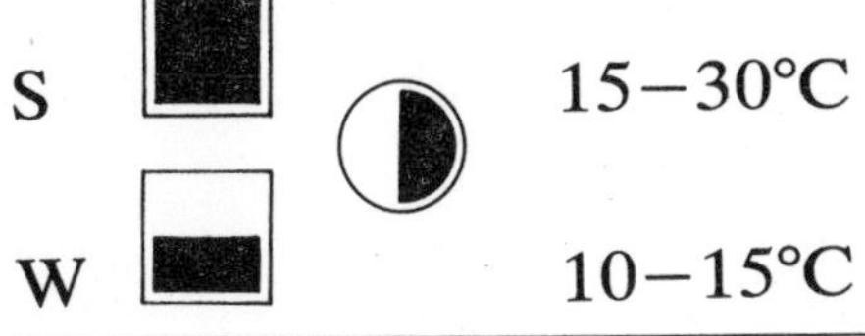


15–30°C

10–15°C

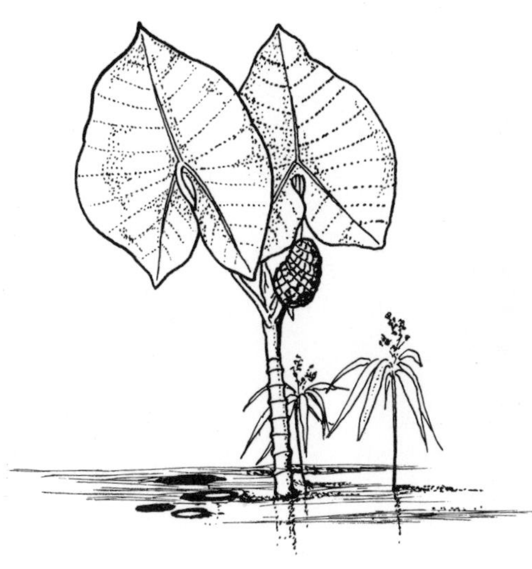

*Montrichardia arborescens*

# Xanthosoma nigrum

Picture the South American tropics: A small forest stream flows through the Ecuador lowlands near the town of San Domingo de los Colorados. The forest giants and lianas form a tunnel that arches above its shimmering surface. Its banks are covered with a dense growth of philodendrons, anthuriums and tree-ferns, with here and there the crowns of palms rising majestically above the surrounding vegetation. From the very first, however, our gaze is attracted to a spectacular plant growing by the riverside – *Xanthosoma mafaffa.* It is almost 2 m (6 ft) high and its large, heart-shaped ovate leaf blades, more than 75 cm (30 in) long, are a beautiful emerald green.

The genus *Xanthosoma,* numbering some 40 species, is to be found not only in South America, but also in Central America and neighbouring islands. The illustrated species is native to Guadeloupe, Jamaica, and Puerto Rico. It, too, is a large plant, the leaf blades often 50 cm (20 in) long. It is frequently grown in the tropics for its leaves, which are eaten as a vegetable. In Mexico, in the state of Veracruz, the large species *X. robustum,* which reaches a height of about 1.50 m (4 ft), is often encountered. Its huge leaf blades are up to 2 m (6 ft) long and nearly 1.50 m (4 ft) wide; they are used by the Indians like umbrellas to keep them from getting wet in the torrential downpours. The most beautiful of the lot, however, is *X. lindenii* of Colombia, which grows to a height of 75 cm (30 in) (tolerable, even if grown for room decoration); the leaf blades are about 40 cm (16 in) long, shield-shaped, and coloured deep green with a white midrib and principal veins.

Xanthosomas are tuberous plants that can be grown successfully only in a warm and sunny room. They are grown chiefly in a paludarium or indoor glass-case where it is possible to provide the necessary high atmospheric moisture. The compost should be light but nourishing – a mixture of peat, loam and sand. *X. lindenii* has the greatest heat requirements – a temperature of no less than 20°C (68°F) even in winter. The others do better if provided with slightly cooler conditions in winter. Propagation is by seed and by division of the clumps.

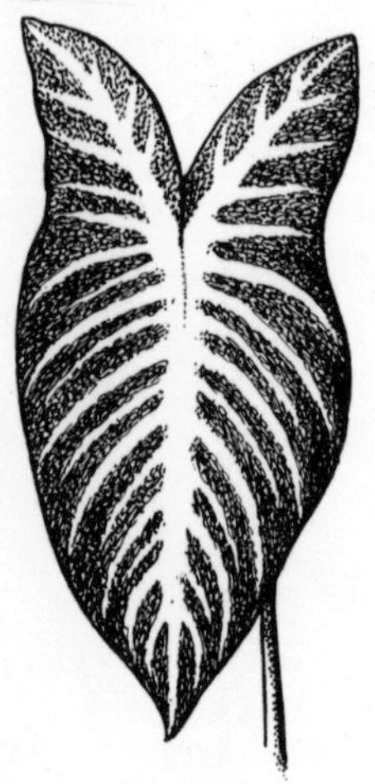

*Xanthosoma lindenii*

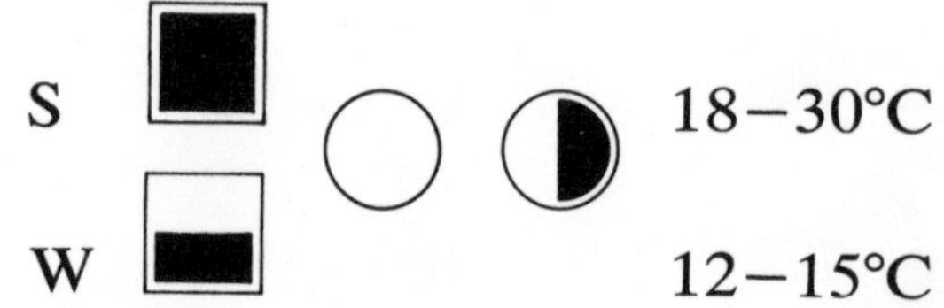

# CARNIVOROUS PLANTS

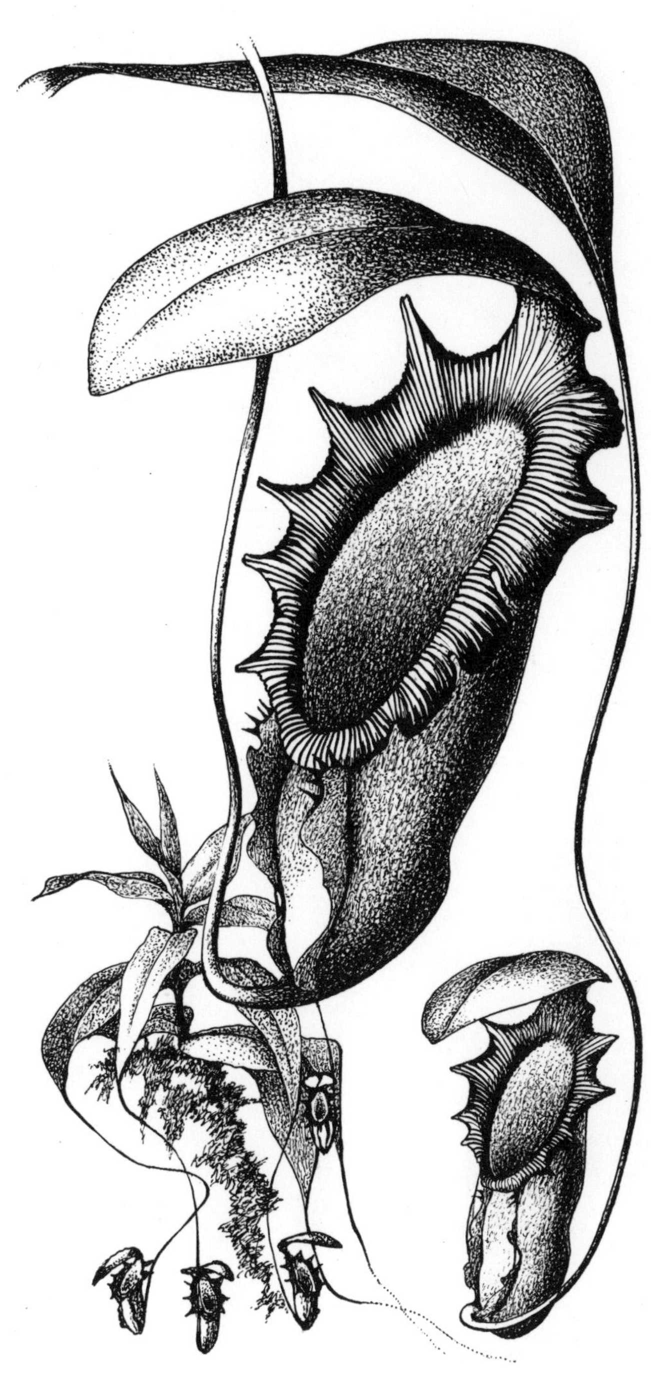

# *Dionaea muscipula*

## Venus's Fly-trap

Those who like the odd and unusual will surely add this carnivorous plant to their collection, and will not regret having done so.

Though in older books dionaea is generally described as a very sensitive plant, this is not true. It can be grown in a room for many years if its basic requirements are met.

Dionaea is indigenous to North America, more precisely to the swamplands of Carolina and Florida. Its only special requirement is constant high humidity throughout the whole year. For this reason it should be grown either in a demijohn or aquaterrarium, or by the waterside in a paludarium. The compost must be acidic, not too rich, best of all a mixture of cut up green sphagnum moss, some beech litter, including leaves that have not yet decayed, charcoal and sand. The surface should be covered with green sphagnum moss. Though it is recommended to reduce the temperature in winter, if the plant is put in a well-lit spot (such as a southern window) in an enclosed, moist environment, then it may be overwintered even in warm conditions.

Dionaea is loveliest in late spring and early summer when it flowers and the leaves begin to turn a deep red. The greenish-white flowers are attractive and, in relation to the plant's size, large. In gardening catalogues they are often described as pink, but unfortunately this is only a promotional trick, and quite an unnecessary one at that, for the plant is very decorative as it is.

The leaf blade serves as a trap to catch insects which provide the necessary nutrients that the plant is unable to obtain in the nitrogen-poor peat bogs where it grows. The fly that alights on the red surface of the leaf irritates one of the four sensitive hairs on either half of the trap, thus causing it to snap shut (within 2 to 3 seconds). The imprisoned insect is then digested by the enzymes secreted by the leaf. If you grow this plant you need not capture flies to feed it; it will get hold of them by itself, and if not it will do well even without this supplementary diet.

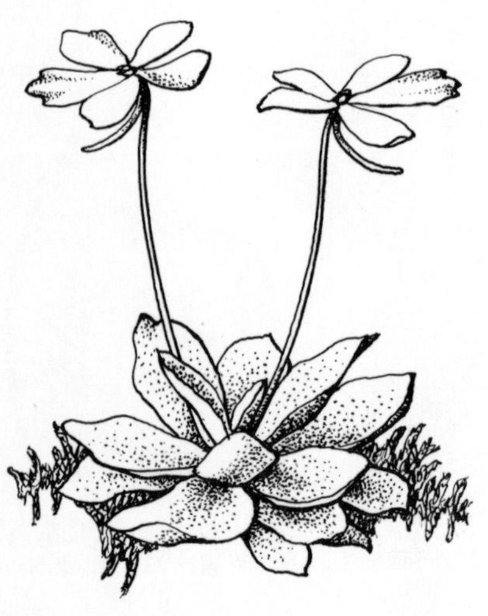

*Pinguicula caudata* from Mexico has lovely blue flowers

 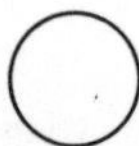 

15–25°C(S)
5–15°C(W)

# *Drosera binata*

## Sundew

Dionaea, shown in the preceding illustration, is not the only insectivorous plant that can be grown at home. Best known, and just as attractive, is the genus *Drosera,* which includes some 85 species, three of them being native to Europe's peat bogs. Their distribution, however, is chiefly centered in Australia and New Zealand, home to more than 50 species.

The one shown in the illustration is from southeastern Australia and New Zealand where it grows in peat bogs and permanently damp meadows together with mosses, from sea level to elevations of 600 m (1,920 ft). The leaves are thickly covered with glandular trichomes, which secrete drops of viscous fluid. This serves to attract small insects and hold them fast; it also contains proteolytic enzymes and thus the plant obtains necessary nitrogen that cannot be supplied by its environment. There is little information about whether the glittering drops of sticky fluid are just a kind of 'dew' serving as an optical attraction, or whether they also emit a scent which is imperceptible to humans but attractive to insects.

*Drosera binata,* often found in collections under the synonym *D. dichotoma,* is a relatively large plant, reaching a height of more than 40 cm (16 in), given perfect conditions. The main root soon perishes and is replaced by numerous strong adventitious roots. In summer it produces moderately large white flowers, about 30 in the case of robust specimens. Do not be taken aback when the leaves start to wilt in autumn for the plant begins dying down at this time prior to overwintering, when the temperature should be reduced and water limited. Species that have long and thick adventitious roots – of those found in cultivation this includes *Drosera capensis* – are propagated in early spring by means of 2- to 3-cm- (3/4 to 1-in-) long root cuttings laid on wet peat and covered with a light sprinkling of sand.

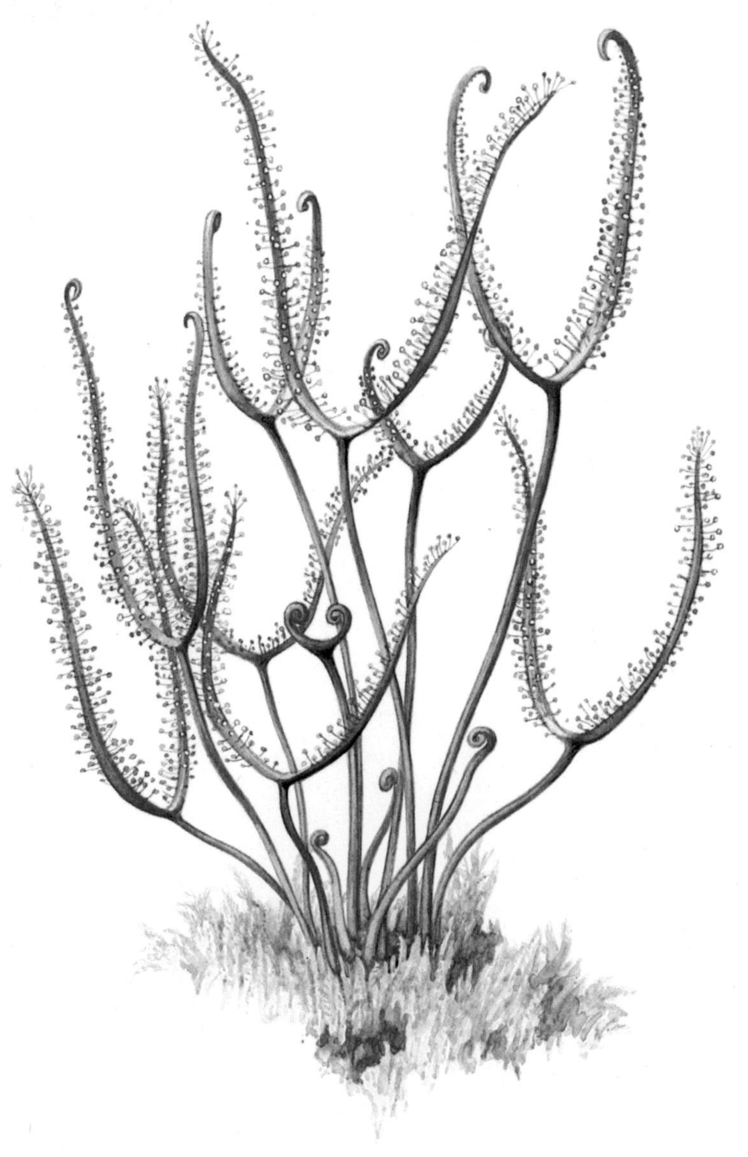

*Darlingtonia californica*

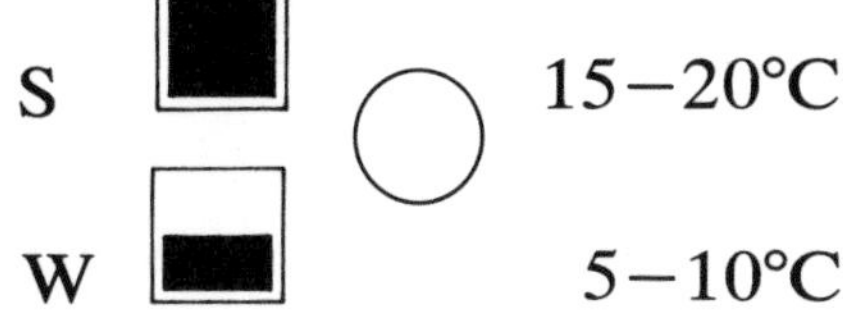

# *Drosera spathulata*

The illustrated drosera is one of the commonest species. It is native to the same regions as the preceding one but its range also extends into tropical south-east Asia. The reddish leaves, arranged in a dense rosette, are covered with red trichomes; the flowers are white. This plant, the same as many other species of the genus, generally lasts only two seasons (if overwintered in the proper, cool conditions) and so all are preferably grown anew from seed each year.

More frequently encountered in collections is *D. capensis,* which makes a large rosette often more than 20 cm (8 in) in diameter and in summer produces purple flowers. Grown just as widely is the species *D. pygmaea,* whose name indicates that it is a miniature. It greatly resembles the common European species *D. rotundifolia,* but is barely half as large. Lovely flowers are produced by *D. cistiflora,* from Cape Province, which has an upright stem covered with leaves about 3 cm (1 1/8 in) long and less than 0.5 cm (1/4 in) wide pointing up and outward from the stem. The flowers, borne at the tip of the stem, are up to 4 cm (1 1/2 in) wide and range in colour from deep pink to bright purple.

All droseras are readily propagated by sowing fresh seeds. Best for this purpose is a flat dish filled with peat covered with a thin layer of sand, or peat mixed with sand. The seeds are merely pressed in, for they only germinate in light. The dish should be put in a larger container with water and covered with glass to ensure constant high atmospheric moisture. The seeds germinate in about three weeks, and after two months the seedlings should be pricked out into their permanent place – a dish, demijohn, aquaterrarium or paludarium. The compost should be the same as the sowing medium. In winter, reducing the temperature at least slightly is an absolute must, but at the same time the plants must always be provided with ample light. Feeding poses no problem; at the most the plants may be transferred in spring into a fresh peaty mixture.

Very similar to drosera is the genus *Drosophyllum* consisting only of the single species *D. lusitanicum* which grows in the area from south-eastern Spain through Portugal to northern Morocco. Unlike droseras it needs dry conditions and a sandy soil with compost, but the need for direct sunlight is the same.

*Drosera spathulata* is one of the most commonly grown species

 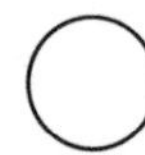 15–25°C

# *Nepenthes* × *mixta*

## Pitcher Plant

The two preceding specimens were examples of the various ways in which plants are adapted for capturing insects. They are far from being the only ones. A truly exquisite example of such adaptation is the pitcher plant, in which the midrib is extended to form a fly-catching pitcher at the end of the leaf, one that is even closed by a lid. The edge and sides are smooth and waxy so that the insect readily slides down to the bottom where it drowns and is decomposed in the liquid secreted by the plant.

Pitcher plants are native to the tropical regions of the Old World, where almost 80 species are distributed over the area extending from Madagascar to Oceania. The greatest number is to be found in Borneo, where they grow from lowland elevations to the height of the Kinabalu volcano. Most are epiphytes; some, however, root in the undergrowth of the rain forests and climb up trees, others even grow in the ground with their pitchers laid on the surface so that the insects can scramble inside.

Pitcher plants found in cultivation are generally hybrids, breeders having attempted to grow plants with pitchers as large and as brightly coloured as possible. The illustrated hybrid is a classic cross between a species from the vast area reaching from Borneo to New Guinea *(Nepenthes maxima)* and another from Borneo *(N. northiana)*. It has inherited the beauty of its parents, but unfortunately also their tenderness, requiring a permanent high humidity of 80 to 90 per cent; otherwise it will grow but will not form pitchers. Because it is relatively robust, the only place to grow it is in a glass-case for tropical epiphytes. If you have such a glass-case you can also grow the magnificent *N. rajah* with deep red pitchers measuring up to 50 cm (20 in) and edged with black 'teeth'. An excellent small pitcher plant is the greenish-yellow *N. ampullaria,* which is ideal where space is restricted.

Nepenthes should be grown in an epiphytic mixture composed of peat, beech-leaf litter, fern roots, crushed pine bark and bits of charcoal, also sand. The plants should be moved every spring and cut back hard at that time.

*Nepenthes gracilis* is a small species which is excellent for plant-cases

  18–30°C

# *Sarracenia purpurea*

## Northern Pitcher Plant

This section on carnivorous plants is concluded by a North American genus of nine species usually growing on the wet shores of forest lakes, in bogs and in swamps. This indicates that they are plants requiring a very moist compost (as well as high atmospheric moisture) and at the same time relatively cool conditions, which makes them suitable for growing in a conservatory as well as a home without central heating. Some of the hardier species may be overwintered outdoors, either plunged in a frame or in some cases merely provided with a light cover of evergreen twigs. These hardy species may be put by the water in an outdoor paludarium.

Sarracenia has pitcher-like leaves with glands inside which secrete proteolytic enzymes that aid in the digestion of insects and small arthropods. These plants have lovely flowers but they are very attractive even when not in flower, what with their interesting shape and the conspicuous colouring (usually deep red) of the veins.

Nowadays, hybrids are generally found in cultivation. These are more colourful than the species (the venation is more striking) and they often have larger flowers. Species found in cultivation include the illustrated *S. purpurea,* which in the wild grows over the area extending from Newfoundland to Manitoba and south to Alabama and Florida, and *S. flava* from the southern states of America.

The compost must be light, acidic and permanently moist – a mixture of peat, chopped green sphagnum moss, pine leaf mould, sand, and some charcoal. Feed requirements are minimal – all that need be done is to move the plants to fresh compost each year, and in the case of older specimens to remove only part of the soil and replace it with new.

The seeds of sarracenia remain viable for only a short time and should therefore be sown as soon as they are ripe. Sow them on the surface of green, wet sphagnum moss and cover the dish with glass. As soon as the seedlings are about 2 cm (3/4 in) high, prick them out into the growing medium.

*Cephalotus follicularis* from the swamps of West Australia is a rare plant that requires much light and moisture but at the same time cool conditions and good ventilation

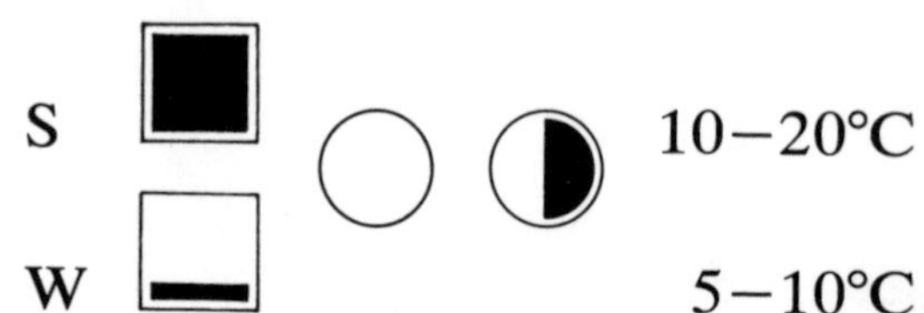

# PLANTS FOR THE BALCONY AND WINDOW-BOX

# *Anemone × coronaria*

## Poppy Anemone

Up to now this book has dealt with house plants, in other words ones that are grown for interior decoration. But what is an interior? Many people live in houses where the living area is directly linked with a patio by sliding glass doors. City dwellers often have a balcony or terrace adjoining their flat, and, of course, practically everyone has a window-sill. These are all spaces that belong to the home and furthermore they are areas that are exposed to the view of passersby. For this reason we have decided to conclude this book with at least a sampling of plants, both annuals and perennials, for 'exterior' decoration that will add beauty to your living quarters from outside. This survey is truly brief, designed to serve only as a mere reminder of the many possibilities and ways of decorating such spaces. Readers who want further and more detailed information will find it in special books on the subject.

*Anemone coronaria* is a tuberous plant native to the Mediterranean region, the Near East and Asia Minor. The large flowers are white, pink, pale violet, deep blue, or scarlet and that is why this variable species soon became a subject of interest for nurserymen. The first crossings with related species, chiefly with *Anemone pavonina,* were carried out as early as the 16th century and so nowadays a wide range of lovely cultivars in various colours and forms (single, semi-double or double) is available.

The poppy anemone is a plant that flowers in spring and early summer. The tubers may be planted either in autumn (the plants will then flower in early May) or in spring. Before planting they should be immersed in lukewarm water for 24 hours. The growing medium should be a sandy, humusy mixture with some peat added. The window-box should be placed in a slightly shaded window for the flowers wilt fairly rapidly in full sun. In a shaded spot they will remain unchanged for about 10 days and cut flowers will last for about a week in water. The tubers should be lifted and put in a dry, frost-free spot for the winter; in warmer regions they may be left in place but then the box should at least be provided with a cover of evergreen twigs.

*Begonia* of the 'Pendula' group

## 1 *Chrysanthemum × carinatum*

Painted Lady

## 2 *Rudbeckia × hirta*

Black-eyed Susan

## 3 *Phlox × drummondii*

If you have a sunny balcony or similar spot a combination of annual plants arranged in a large earthenware urn would make an attractive display. If you do not have much time to care for the plants in the way of watering and feeding, then make sure that you select your plants from those that are the least demanding.

All the illustrated flowers will be content with poor, well-drained soil that may even be stony. The principal requirement is ample sunlight and good drainage, for they readily rot in permanently soggy soil.

*Chrysanthemum carinatum* is native to the American continent. Black-eyed Susan grows in North America at the edge of rather dry thickets and on dry banks, phlox occurs farther south and is a typical meadow plant of New Mexico, where it grows together with castilleja, lupinus and oenothera – it can therefore also be combined with these plants to good effect.

*Phlox* x *drummondii* is the shortest of the three plants selected for our arrangement, reaching only 5 to 25 cm (2 to 10 in) in height. Recommended is one of the low variegated cultivars, such as 'Cuspidata' with star-like flowers, that will cover the surface of the container with a brightly coloured carpet from as early as mid-June. In the centre you may put several chrysanthemums, preferably single-coloured forms or cultivars without a conspicuous dark centre such as 'Dunnettii Aureum' – yellow, or 'Pole Star' – white. The tallest flowers should be planted at the back, farthest from the viewer, and that is where to plant black-eyed Susan. The choice of cultivars is again a wide one, best for the purpose, however, being flowers coloured red and brown or a uniform bronze.

All the illustrated plants should be sown in spring, rudbeckia and phlox in mid-March, chrysanthemum about a month later, in a seedbox indoors. They should be pricked out into the urn in early May, where they will flower until late autumn.

*Tagetes* 'Rusty Red' *Zinnia* 'Wind Witch'

# *Dianthus × caryophyllus*

## Carnation

Carnations are definitely among the most popular of flowers, both for garden use and as cut flowers.

The genus *Dianthus* embraces some 300 species distributed in Europe, Asia and very occasionally also in Africa. Many of the type species can be grown in window-boxes arranged as miniature rock gardens. They look best if combined with small, lime-loving alpines found growing together with them in the wild such as acantholimon, biscutella, draba, helianthemum and silene, or the grasses festuca and sesleria.

The most important species from the horticultural viewpoint were *Dianthus caryophyllus* and *D. barbatus* from the Mediterranean region and *D. chinensis* from east Asia. Crossings between these (as well as many other species) yielded whole groups of hybrids containing numerous cultivars, annual as well as perennial. There is no point discussing the importance of the various groups on these pages for a good selection together with tips on cultivation may be found in every gardening catalogue. Best for growing in the window box, however, is the cultivar 'Feuerkönig' of the Tyrol carnation group which has deep green, slightly drooping leaves and long, down-curved stems with fairly large, uniformly red flowers. Carnations of this group are simply ideal for the purpose because they flower profusely and the window 'glows' with colour the whole summer long. They do not combine well with other plants, however, and should thus be grown by themselves or only with asparagus fern.

Tyrol carnations are plants that will grow for several years, but it is recommended to renew them each year by cuttings taken either in autumn or in spring. Plants from autumn cuttings are stronger and flower sooner.

The soil should be well-drained, sufficiently rich and with some lime. The plants do not tolerate permanently water-logged soil. They do best in full sun or light shade and appreciate protection against rain.

*Dianthus* 'Merry-go-round' should be grown on as many window-sills and balconies as possible: particularly good are the trailing 'Tyrolean Carnations'

## 1 *Dorotheanthus bellidiformis*
Livingstone Daisy

## 2 *Portulaca × grandiflora*
Sun Plant, Rose Moss

## 3 *Venidium fastuosum*
Monarch of the Veldt, Namaqualand Daisy

## 4 *Verbena × rigida*

The illustrated plants, each from a different family, appear to have little in common. They also come from different continents: dorotheanthus and portulaca from South Africa, the other two from the temperate and tropical regions of America. The one thing that is the same for all, however, is their requirements in cultivation – heat, dry conditions and full sun – which makes them valuable companions for city dwellers. None will be damaged if you occasionally forget to water them; the first two may even rot if watered too frequently.

Dorotheanthus and portulaca are ideal for the window-box. Both are low herbaceous plants only about 10 cm (4 in) high with large, brightly coloured flowers nearly 5 cm (2 in) across. They will grow in practically any well-drained soil. As a rule they are not grown together with other annuals so that the beauty of their blooms can be fully appreciated.

The other two plants, venidium and verbena, are taller, reaching a height of about 30 cm (1 ft) and more suitable for planting in large earthenware urns. Like the first two they do not tolerate permanent damp and must be put in full sun; the soil, however, should be slightly richer. Verbena affords a wide selection of cultivars listed as *Verbena hybrida* 'Grandiflora' plus the name of the variety; 'Mammoth' Hybrids (up to 40 cm [16 in] high) or *V. hybrida* 'Compacta Nana' (forms only about 20 cm [8 in] high). These groups of hybrids are multiple crossings between approximately six or seven South American species.

All the illustrated species should be sown in boxes in March, the seedlings pricked out once, and then put in their permanent places in mid-May.

*Celosia* 'Tango' *Salvia patens*

# *Erica × hybrida*

## Heath

Most annuals and perennials suitable for growing in a window-box or earthenware urn flower in summer. In spring, however, window-boxes are generally empty and bleak. That is why plants that flower in early spring, albeit only briefly, are so popular.

The illustrated hybrid, raised in France, is derived from crossings about which little is known. The parents were probably hybrids of unkown origin – *Erica* x *cylindrica* and *E.* x *willmorei.* Their progeny are relatively robust plants, up to 50 cm (20 in) high, bearing long trumpet-shaped flowers, coloured whitish pink, pale pink to bright red, in spring. In many cultivars they are set almost at right angles to the stem.

The type species, which yielded also the group of cultivars designated *E.* x *hybrida,* are from the mountains of South Africa, so that even plants grown in cultivation are not frost-resistant. However, they are naturally tolerant of cold conditions and even require them, likewise plenty of fresh air. They should be overwintered at a temperature of 5 to 8°C, (41 to 47°F), in other words the same as azaleas and camellias. They are fairly demanding as regards soil, which should be acidic with a pH of 4 to 4.5, and will thus appreciate a mixture of peat, well-rotted pine-leaf litter and coarse river sand. They should be fed with care, only with organic fertilizers that have ample nitrogen. Heaths need a sunny situation and regular, moderate watering.

The plants are put outdoors in a window-box, earthenware urn or stone trough on the patio in spring. They are particularly attractive in a setting with conifers and grasses.

Heaths are propagated by cuttings taken either in winter (between January and March) or summer (in June or July). In warm and moist conditions they will form roots in about a month and a month after that the growing tips should be pinched to promote branching; they will flower the following year.

*Lobelia* 'Rosamund'

*Aquilegia hybrida.*

*Viola* 'Picotee'

# *Eschscholzia × californica*

## Californian Poppy

For those who like bright vivid colours this is definitely an annual that should not be overlooked. Though its flowers are not long-lasting, they are produced continuously so that the window-box makes a colourful display the whole summer long.

The approximately 130 species of the genus *Eschscholzia* grow wild in both North and South America. The most important of all is *E. californica,* which has bright yellow flowers with a reddish orange blotch. Selection and crossing with other similar but generally smaller species yielded the present-day varieties that are usually grown in a mixture of colours. Their flowers are white, pale or dark yellow, orange or bright to purplish red, often with a darker blotch. They are relatively large, 5 to 8 cm (2 to 3 in) across, and have an unusual silky sheen that underlines the purity of the colour. The leaves are very decorative, finely divided and coloured grey green. The plants make an attractive display even when not in flower, especially if spaced close together. They are about 30 to 40 cm (12 to 16 in) high.

Eschscholzia requires ample sun to develop fully. It does not tolerate soggy soil, thus being a very good plant for the sunny windows and balconies of modern blocks of flats. The compost should be free-draining – a mixture of leaf mould, compost and sand. Californian poppy has no special food requirements. Seeds should be sown directly in the window-box in early spring, for the plants, which have a tap-root, do not tolerate transplanting. The seeds should be sown fairly thickly and the seedlings thinned to a spacing of about 15 cm (6 in).

For those who like the unusual and also appreciate smaller flowers, other species from the same genus are recommended, for example *Eschscholzia tenuifolia,* only about 15 cm (6 in) high with pale yellow flowers only about 2 to 3 cm (¾ to 1 in) across. These smaller species are very good for small earthenware bowls where they make a lovely bright carpet. Whereas *E. californica* is generally grown by itself, the small species make attractive arrangements grown together with other plants, such as *Lobelia fulgens.*

*Moluccella laevis*

*Antirrhinum* 'Bright Butterfly'

1 *Gaillardia* (Grandiflora-Hybrids)
Blanket Flower

2 *Coreopsis* × *grandiflora*
Tickweed

3 *Helenium* × *autumnale*
Sneezeweed

4 *Rudbeckia nitida*
Coneflower

The illustrated flowers are allied not only in that they all belong to the same family but also in that they all (or at least the parent species) are native to Florida, where they grow as perennials. In Europe, however, they are often killed by frost (except for helenium) and so it is advisable to sow them anew every year.

Gaillardia hybrids are derived from the type species *Gaillardia aristata, G. pulchella,* and perhaps several more. The choice of cultivars is large, ranging from small forms about 20 cm (8 in) high ('Kobold' – red yellow) to ones reaching 80 cm (32 in) in height ('Sonne' – golden yellow tinted orange). The seeds should be sown in boxes in March and the seedlings put out in their permanent site in May. It is recommended to provide them with a good protective cover of evergreen twigs for the winter.

Coreopsis is even more tender; usually it lasts only two or three seasons. It grows to a height of about 50 cm (20 in) and some forms have flowers up to 9 cm (3 ½ in) across ('Badengold'). It has the same site requirements as the preceding species, but whereas gaillardia is grown in rich humusy soil, coreopsis does better in rather poor, light, sandy soil.

Helenium is a well-known and very popular plant that is found in practically every garden. Like the other illustrated flowers it can be grown not only in an open bed but also in a large earthenware urn. Helenium likes deeper, rich, moist soil in full sun. It flowers from late June until the frost.

The last plant, rudbeckia, grows in similar places but ones that are slightly shaded. It reaches a height of about 120 cm (4 ft), the lovely cultivar 'Herbstsonne' even as much as 2 m (6 ft). A light protective cover in winter is likewise recommended for this plant. Older specimens that have survived the winter in good condition may be readily propagated by division of the clumps.

*Gaillardia* 'Goblin'

*Gazania krebsiana*

# *Godetia × grandiflora*

Nowadays it is no longer possible to determine the parentage of the various cultivated forms of this genus. Perhaps the Californian species *Godetia amoena (Oenothera amoena)* figured in their breeding at the start but it was far from being the only one, for America is the home of some 20 members of the genus *Godetia,* most of them very pretty plants.

Present-day cultivars are divided into three basic groups: semi-tall single forms about 40 cm (16 in) high (probably the prettiest), such as the scarlet 'Duke of York'; semi-tall double forms, similar in height, the same as the foregoing, but with double flowers resembling azaleas; and finally forms only about 20 cm (8 in) high that are pretty but tender and can be used only in the warmest regions of Europe.

There is no denying that godetias are very tender plants. They do not tolerate heavy, wet soil and should thus be provided with a light, warm and nourishing mixture of leaf mould, compost and sand, or one of the peat-based composts. A warm, sunny spot is a precondition of success, but the plants should not be exposed to too much direct sunlight. Plenty of air should be provided as well, but at the same time the spot should be sheltered from winds for the plants are quite fragile. Water should be supplied in sufficient quantities but only in the early morning, for godetias do not like to be watered when exposed to sun.

The seeds should be sown in early April directly into the box where the plants are to grow. If all the conditions are met the plants will bear lovely flowers in late June which are good for cutting. There is sometimes a second flowering if the plants are cut back immediately after flowering.

*Impatiens* 'Huckabuc'

# *Lathyrus × odoratus*

## Sweet Pea

Sweet peas are favourite climbing plants in gardens as well as for the balcony and window-boxes.

Some 160 species have been described to date. The one selected for cultivation for its fragrance as well as the lovely shape and colour of the flowers is native to southern Italy and Sicily. Because it has been grown for as long as 250 years, its hybrids are many, divided into several groups according to habit of growth, number of flowers on the separate stems, and height.

Tall forms are either cultivars belonging to the Spencer group (such as 'Flagship' – dark violet) or the large-flowered and multiflowered Cuthbertson cultivars (such as 'Jimmy' – dark scarlet). More important for our purpose (even though robust plants may be suitable for terrace decoration) are the low-growing sweet peas, suitable for window-boxes. Though the flowers are smaller and not as good for cutting as those of the tall forms, these plants are only 20 to 30 cm (8 to 12 in) high. There is no point in naming the various cultivars for quite a few have been developed in Britain and the USA. They are generally offered in a mixture that includes all shades and colours except yellow.

Window-boxes in which sweet peas are to be grown should be filled with a heavier, rich and at the same time freely-draining mixture such as John Innes potting compost No. 2. Though the seeds may be sown and the plants grown-on indoors, it is better and easier to sow them directly in the window-box in late March. It is recommended to sow them at 14-day intervals so as to prolong the flowering period. The flowers, which appear from June onward, should be removed as soon as they have faded to prevent the formation of seeds, otherwise flowering soon ceases. Feed should be supplied the whole summer long.

*Cobaea scandens*

Hybrid gourd of the 'Piriformis' group

*Clematis* 'Nelly Moser'

# *Petunia × hybrida*

The early 18th century saw the introduction of two of the fourteen South American species of *Petunia* into European gardens. Both were from Argentina, almost 1 m (3 ft) high, with glandular, sticky leaves and large fragrant flowers. The first, *Petunia axillaris* (syn. *P. nyctaginiflora*), was white, the second, *P. violacea,* had flowers coloured scarlet, carmine or pinkish violet. Their crossing gave rise to a vast number of hybrids of diverse size and colour. Of the many groups, three are of primary interest here, namely bedding petunias (also good for growing in earthenware urns), trailing forms for the balcony and window-box, and the 'Grandiflora Nana' petunias that are of small, round, bushy habit, about 25 to 30 cm (10 to 12 in) high, and simply ideal for the window-box.

Bedding petunias are taller, greatly branched and include such cultivars as: 'Brillantrosa' – pink, 45 cm (18 in) high; 'Schneeball' – white, only about 20 cm (8 in) high; 'Senator' – dark blue with a white mouth, also smaller; 'Topaskönigin' – carmine pink, almost 30 cm (1 ft) high.

Trailing forms are the loveliest for the window-box and are very attractive when combined with other annuals. Recommended are: 'Alba' – white; 'Marktkönigin' – pale carmine; 'Purpurea' – vivid red; and 'Violacea' – violet.

The 'Grandiflora Nana' group is the most popular. Recommended are: 'Weisse Wolke' – white; and 'Karmesinrot' – carmine red. The list could include many more lovely forms if space permitted. Extraordinarily attractive are the cultivars raised in recent years in the United States and Japan. Besides the aforesaid groups there are also others that include double and frilled forms.

Though petunias may be grown from seed sown in February, nurseries offer a wide choice of plants already in bloom so that you can be sure of getting the shape and colour you want. The window-box should be filled with a fairly heavy rich soil such as John Innes potting compost No. 2 and the plants put out in May, spaced about 25 cm (10 in) apart. It is necessary to supply fertilizer during the growing season because petunias have relatively high food requirements.

*Petunia* 'Picotee'

# *Reseda × odorata*

## Mignonette

Another plant selected for this brief survey is the well-known but often neglected reseda.

Reaching the peak of its populariy some 100 years ago when catalogues listed more than 30 sorts, it has since fallen into oblivion. This plant was always grown mainly for its fragrance, and that is something cities lack more now than a century ago. Furthermore, limiting of the assortment almost always has one advantage – namely that only the loveliest cultivars are retained.

*Reseda odorata,* the type species used in breeding, is a native of North Africa. It is a branching plant 15 to 50 cm (6 to 20 in) high with elongate leaves that are smooth or only slightly toothed on the margin. The tiny flowers are inconspicuous, greenish yellow with prominent yellow or red anthers.

Of the several available cultivars, recommended are 'Machet' – about 25 cm (10 in) high with dark foliage and pale red flowers; and 'Goliath' – reaching a height of more than 30 cm (1 ft) with red anthers.

The minute seeds should be sown directly in the box, urn or pot in early spring; they will germinate in about 10 to 14 days. It is best to sow them in pinches about 25 cm (10 in) apart, later thinning them and leaving only the strongest seedlings. After about a month the tops should be pinched out strongly to promote branching. The flowers appear in July and are produced until late autumn. The growing medium should be rather heavy, rich soil, such as John Innes potting compost No. 2.

Reseda is generally grown as a companion to other annuals for fragrance. Though it is inconspicuous, it can be used to good effect, for example, in large earthenware urns containing plants of a woody nature.

*Dimorphotheca ecklonis*

# *Tropaeolum* × *majus*

## Nasturtium

Creeping, climbing and trailing plants are generally popular but though annuals include such forms amongst their number they are by no means plentiful and besides, they are usually rather tender species. Nasturtium combines desirability of habit and hardiness, which is particularly welcomed by the working man and woman of today.

The approximately 80 species of the genus *Tropaeolum* are indigenous chiefly to the Andes, being found over an area extending from Central America down the entire length of South America. In their native habitat they are often perennial. Many species there are grown not only for decoration but as food. *Tropaeolum tuberosum* has edible tubers and the young leaves are used to make a tasty salad.

The varieties grown nowadays are the product of selection and breeding, the type species used for hybridization being *Tropaeolum majus* and *T. minus,* sometimes also *T. peltophorum,* which differs from the other two by having scarlet flowers and being softly felted all over. Now and then one may encounter other species in cultivation, for example *T. azureum, T. brachyceros, T. pentaphyllum* and *T. tricolor*. However, the large-flowered cultivars are of greater value as decoration. Recommended are the following: 'Scarlet Gleam', 'Golden Gleam', 'Salmon Baby' and 'Cherry Rose'.

Best for a window-box are the low or trailing cultivars because tall climbing forms need a strong pole or framework as a support (a wire or piece of twine such as used for beans is not enough).

Though they may be sown elsewhere and then pricked out, the large seeds are generally sown in early May directly where they are to grow, spaced 30 to 60 cm (1 to 2 ft) apart depending on the species. Flowering begins in June and the flowers are produced continuously until the frost.

If plants are provided with a free-draining, sandy loam they will flower profusely. Too much nitrogen encourages only a mass of foliage and it is then necessary to supply a phosphate fertilizer.

*Tropaeolum polyphyllum*

# BIBLIOGRAPHY AND RECOMMENDED LITERATURE


Auger, H. A., Chapman, P. R. & Martin, M. J.: *Cacti and their Cultivation.* Faber and Faber.

Bailey, L. H. & Bailey, E. Z.: *Hortus Second.* MacMillan Company, New York.

Davidson, W.: *Women's Own Book of Houseplants.* Hamlyn.

Graf, A. B.: *Exotica 3, Exotic Plant Manual.* Roehrs Company, New Jersey.

Hay, R. & Synge, P.: *The Dictionary of Garden Plants.* Michael Joseph.

Hunt, P. F. & Grieson, M.: *The Country Life Book of Orchids.* Country Life.

Reader's Digest: *Encyclopedia of Garden Plants and Flowers.* Hodder and Stoughton.

Rochford, T. C. & Davidson, W.: *Guide to House Plants, Cacti and Succulents.* Hamlyn.

Rochford, T. & Gorer, R.: *The Rochford Book of House Plants.* Faber and Faber.

The Royal Horticultural Society: *Dictionary of Gardening,* 4 Vols. and Supplement. Oxford University Press.


# JOURNALS

| | |
|---|---|
| *American Orchid Society Bulletin* | USA |
| *Begonian* | USA |
| *Bloembollencultur* | The Netherlands |
| *Bloemenvriend* | Belgium |
| *Blumen und Garten* | Germany |
| *Cactus and Succulent Journal of Great Britain* | Great Britain |
| *California Garden* | USA |
| *Garden, The: Journal of The Royal Horticultural Society* | Great Britain |
| *Garden Journal* | USA |
| *Gardeners' Chronicle* | Great Britain |
| *Horticulture* | USA |
| *Jardins de France* | France |
| *Kew Bulletin* | Great Britain |
| *Mon Jardin et Ma Maison* | France |
| *Orchideen* | The Netherlands |
| *Ornamental Horticulture* | Great Britain |
| *Plants Alive* | USA |
| *Succulenta* | The Netherlands |

# COMMON NAME INDEX

# INDEX OF BOTANICAL NAMES